PENGUIN BOOKS
## THE SINGAPORE STRAIN

Raju Chellam is author of *Organ Gold*, published in 2018, about the illegal sale of human organs on the Dark Web. He's a former editor of *Dataquest*, India's first dedicated publication on the information technology industry, and former BizIT Editor of *The Business Times*, Singapore. He is a regular contributor to *The Straits Times*, Singapore, *The Edge*, Malaysia, and *Dataquest*, India. He has been on the inaugural panel of advisers for the *Singapore Writers Festival* from 2021 to 2023. Raju is a Fellow of the National University of Singapore's Advanced Computing for Executives, a Fellow of the Singapore Computer Society, Chair of Cloud and Data Standards at Singapore's IT Standards Committee, and on the Executive Committee of SCS Cloud and AI & Robotics Chapters.

His list of articles and blogs are at https://rajuchellam.com

ADVANCE PRAISE FOR *THE SINGAPORE STRAIN*

'*The Singapore Strain* reimagines a world in the alternate history genre that is not entirely impossible. Raju Chellam's insights into the juxtaposition of tech and medical science, biodiversity and sustainability, and the future of humanity makes compelling reading.'

—Dr Chong Yoke Sin, Member of the Board,
Mount Alvernia Hospital

'Raju Chellam has a remarkable gift for crafting gripping narratives. *The Singapore Strain* is an absolute masterpiece, propelling readers into uncharted territories of the mind. It is an eloquent and evocative narrative that feels both exhilarating and hauntingly plausible.'

—Prof. Ashok Kumar Seetharaman,
Director, Digital Government, School of
Computer Science, Carnegie Mellon University

'Raju has cleverly married his knowledge of medical science and information technology to create an ingenious tale about an undiscovered strain of the Covid-19 virus that modifies a person's DNA to create an interesting, albeit intriguing, human. You cannot put it down until you have read all the way to the chilling ending.'

—Prof. Alex Siow, Chair, Singapore National High
Performance Computing Roadmap Committee

'After his eye-opening exploration of the trade in human organs in *Organ Gold*, Raju's newest medical thriller features an apparently benign variant of Covid-19 and a spellbinding detective story with twists and turns that will keep you spellbound until the shocking ending.'

—Vikram Khanna, Associate Editor, *The Straits Times*

'Written in the alternate history genre, Raju Chellam's style adds a shocking layer of authenticity. The detailed descriptions, well-developed characters, and insightful observations contribute to the immersive nature of the storytelling. I highly recommend this book.'

—Sam Liew, President, Singapore Computer Society

# The Singapore Strain

Raju Chellam

PENGUIN BOOKS

An imprint of Penguin Random House

PENGUIN BOOKS

USA | Canada | UK | Ireland | Australia
New Zealand | India | South Africa | China | Southeast Asia

Penguin Books is part of the Penguin Random House group of companies
whose addresses can be found at global.penguinrandomhouse.com

Published by Penguin Random House SEA Pte Ltd
9, Changi South Street 3, Level 08-01,
Singapore 486361

First published in Penguin Books by Penguin Random House SEA 2024

ISBN 9789815144529

Typeset in Garamond by MAP Systems, Bengaluru, India

www.penguin.sg

*To active environmentalists worldwide*

# Prologue

## Monday, 7 September 2015

It was the day the sky exploded. A fiery intruder from outer space, a blazing bolide, tore through the atmosphere and detonated with a deafening boom over the tranquil Thai waters.

The shockwave rattled windows and hearts across Phuket, Kanchanaburi, and Bangkok, where drivers caught the apocalyptic sight on their dash-cams. It was nine in the morning on 7 September 2015, when the bolide blew itself up, in an orange glow, about 100 kilometres high.

Except for this black swan event, life went on as normal in Phuket, the tropical paradise with a coastline of soft, white sands and turquoise waves on the edge of the Andaman Sea. However, 'normal' signifies different strokes for different folk.

For visitors from other cities, especially congested ones like Singapore, Jakarta, Bangkok, and Kuala Lumpur, the sight of breathtaking beaches with pristine white sand, beautiful palm trees, clear turquoise water, and mountains on three sides is anything but usual.

That's what two dozen executives from Malaysia, Singapore, Thailand, and Indonesia wanted to enjoy in Phuket as they congregated at a beach-facing hotel to indulge in an offsite retreat, fully paid for by Singapore-headquartered Scenz Software Pte Ltd.

This morning, they gathered at the picturesque Anona Beachfront Resort for breakfast. The hotel had laid out a buffet in its open-air restaurant when the bolide lit up the morning sky by bursting into a billion pieces that scattered across the horizon.

Some shards of burnt and burning rock hurtled towards the chalet and tore into the canvas awnings but miraculously didn't injure anyone seriously. The red-hot chunks seared the rubber and palm plantations strung across the mountainside but didn't cause a conflagration. However, it forced most Scenz employees to scurry indoors for safety. A few brave ones stayed put to witness and film the extraordinary event.

'What, in the name of God, is that?' Carmine Chan—or Cory as she was called by her friends and colleagues—exclaimed staring at the sky. She was left-handed and proud of it but, at that moment, she wished she had a free hand to grab her phone and shoot a video. She held a plate in one hand and a fork in the other.

A dazzling array of red, orange, yellow, and black colours filled the air like a giant kaleidoscope. She dumped the plate and fork on a table and fished around in her laptop bag with her left hand, but only made a mess. Tissues, a sanitary pad, and a half-eaten granola bar fell to the floor.

'Where's my damn phone?' She snapped, feeling a surge of frustration.

'*Nee khuh pathihan,*' the Thai delegate exulted. 'This is a miracle.'

Prem Pujari, who was standing beside them, dropped his cup of coffee. 'Oh wow! We were discussing a black swan event last night and now this. Coincidence or miracle?'

'It's a spectacle, bro,' Wong Wai Mun dashed out from inside the hall. 'Comet bursting above your head,' he laughed, 'and coffee cup bursting below your feet. That is a miracle!'

Prem ignored his Malaysian buddy. He moved closer to Cory, who had her phone and was filming the fiery debris of the meteor. 'How come—'

'Shh,' Cory silenced him.

Prem stooped to pick up the tissues and pad. 'You dropped this . . .'

'Shut—' she blinked but didn't glance at Prem as he put stuff back into her bag.

A small lump of burning rock hit Cory's face, searing her cheek and lips. She screamed and swatted it away, but some bits of the charred stuff flew into her open mouth. It tasted like burnt cheese, salt, oil, and ash. She shoved Prem away as she coughed and spat it out.

'Did the freaky meteor just hit you?' Prem grabbed a jug of water and emptied it over her. 'How terrible. Did you get burned, Cory?'

'Damn it, Prem,' she gasped, 'you've soaked me!'

'Sorry, sorry,' he wiped the water from her shirt, annoying her even more. 'I was worried.'

'Good thinking, bro,' Wong clapped. 'Cory is the first human to have tasted a meteor.'

Hotel staff and Scenz executives who had witnessed the incident from the hall ran out to help Cory. She pushed them away when she realized she was dripping wet.

She saw Prem's hurt look. 'Dunno whether to thank Prem or curse Prem,' she joked. 'Better go to my room and change.' She grabbed her laptop bag and ran out awkwardly, dropping tissues along the way. Prem didn't pick them up this time.

Soon the meteor was spent, its dying embers scattered in the wind across the sea. Some of the debris had damaged the tiny fleet of fishing vessels that bobbed up and down on the shimmering waters, which had suddenly turned choppy. A gust of wind blew black soot over the pristine beach, forcing the few who were still standing outside to brush the ash off and seek shelter inside. The lush green mountainside had withstood the onslaught well with no forest fires.

It took them half an hour to calm down and gather in Anona's conference room.

Scenz's CEO, Walter Lang, a short, balding man on the wrong side of fifty with a noticeable paunch, urged the staff to settle down, called the session to order, and flashed the first slide. Despite that, they spent the first hour discussing the strange spectacle that the world would not take seriously until almost four years later.

Only in 2019 did the Thai government reveal that the energy impact of the bolide was the largest in all of 2015, at four kilotons, the equivalent of four simultaneous nuclear blasts.

\* \* \*

That night, the hotel set up three wooden tables in the sand with piles of food and drinks—beer, wine, and whiskey. Walter sat at the first table, occupied mostly by ladies and senior managers from the company. The middle table had the engineering team, including Prem and Cory.

And the last table had sales and marketing staff, including Jon Tan, Scenz's marketing head, who was pontificating about the unique event they had witnessed that morning.

'God is sending us a message,' Jon held up a half-empty bottle of locally brewed Singha beer, his fifth. 'He already scalded Carmine. He wants us sinners to repent before—'

'Why us?' A guy brandished a half-consumed lobster leg at him. 'What have *we* done?'

'Because we're boozers,' Wong retorted. 'But God wants *you*, Jon, to repent first.'

'It's people like *you* who will lead us all to hell,' Jon pointed a chicken drumstick menacingly at the taller, stouter Wong. 'Stop joking about the power of God.'

'I think God, in creating man, somewhat overestimated His ability,' Wong gesticulated with his middle finger. 'That quote from Oscar Wilde applies to you, bro.'

Jon's face turned red. 'I seriously want to curse *you*, you stupid son of a . . . canine person.'

'The word is bitch, bro,' Wong burst out laughing. 'Say it! Say it and repent in hell.'

The balmy sea breeze added to the intoxication. Prem picked up pieces of the conversation and ambled over to their table to join in the banter. Carmine excused herself to go use the restroom.

'Chill, guys,' Prem interrupted them. 'We witnessed a black swan event. So did half of Thailand. It's just a meteor crashing through Earth's atmosphere and burning up. Just chill.'

'Are you a *bodoh*[1] Indian godman *mamak*[2] or what?' Jon threw the drumstick bone at him.

Prem ducked. 'What has my being an Indian got to do with this, you drunken idiot?'

'Who are you calling an idiot?' Jon stood up menacingly. 'I'm not drunk. You are!'

---

[1]  In Malay, stupid

[2]  In Malay, uncle

A couple of other engineers joined in—to mock Jon. A few others stood ready for a fight.

Some guys from the middle table took their beer bottles and crowded on to the third table.

By the time Cory got back from the bathroom, chicken drumsticks, lobster claws, and bamboo chopsticks were flying through the air and glasses were being knocked over. Cory darted to the first table, ducking under it as pieces of food flew past her.

Prem, Wong, and the other guys were yelling at each other. One of them grabbed a fistful of beach sand and flung it at another guy, who fell over, swearing. Cory and some of her colleagues scooted under the big table to avoid the flying objects.

CEO Walter Lang, who had celebrated his fifty-first birthday on 1 September, wasn't used to physical fights. He made a mistake by joining the ruckus—and got hit by a ketchup bottle that burst on his face. A blob of tomato sauce, mixed with blood, stained his forehead, shocking everyone but ending the fight.

'You're going to pay for this!' Walter licked the blood-red paste dripping down his face.

Years later, this unexpected event would become part of Scenz's corporate legend that every new hire would hear in whispers. That two black swan events had occurred on a single significant day at their Phuket offsite on 7 September 2015.

# PART I.

# Chapter 1

## Saturday, 7 September 2019

Dozens of schoolgirls clad in uniforms trampled the verdant grass, its once pristine surface now splotched with bloodstains. In the midst of this mayhem, in the thunderstorm, Cory stood in the muddy terrain, bewildered by the mindless slaughter. Her voice, frozen with fear, stayed in her throat as a dark figure emerged from the shed. He held a shining sword. With one quick, silver slash, the glistening blade cut through the air, slicing off her classmate's head.

And Clarise was dead.

Clarise's crown hit the ground. It landed with a resounding thud that reverberated through Cory's being, causing her to tremble in pain. She awoke abruptly, with an intense headache. She clutched her throbbing temples and shut her eyes tightly, seeking solace in the darkness as raindrops lashed against the windowpane.

Cory kept her eyes closed and stretched her left hand to grab her mobile phone from the desk beside the bed. She squinted to check the time: 5.30 a.m.

*Should I get up and drink water?*
*Or complete the slides due last week?*
*Or go back to sleep?*

She stared at the gap in the curtains and searched for any sign of movement in the pitch-black night. The only sound was the drumming of rain on the windowpane, like a thousand needles pricking her skin.

*Should I get up to pee?*
*Or check if the windows are closed?*
*Or go back to sleep?*

Cory pushed off the blanket and shivered as the chilly draft from the air conditioner penetrated her flimsy nightgown. She wondered whether the aircon was the reason for her recent migraines, especially at night. Or was she coming down with the flu? Again?

She plodded towards the bathroom, paused before the switch, and decided not to turn on the light. The faint illumination filtering through the window cast a calming glow upon the space. She felt a wave of relief as she sat on the cold toilet seat and relieved herself.

With her head nestled in her hands, she drifted into a drowsy state. Time stretched and blurred, an indeterminate period of restful tranquility enveloping her. Yet, just as her fatigue began to consume her, her head sank forward, jolting her abruptly awake, as if some dark force had yanked her from the depths of sleep.

*Alamak[3], I went to sleep on the darn toilet bowl? Crap!*

She laughed aloud as she pushed the flush lever and then dragged herself back to the bedroom.

*Must crank up the thermostat.*

*Must not sleep on the toilet seat.*

*Must drink some water.*

She waddled to the kitchen and picked up the steel water bottle; a stray beam of light streaming in through the window glinted off the bottle cap and made it look like a spacecraft with pilots ready to lift off. Just as she was about to take a swig, she heard a scurrying sound that made her freeze in fright.

Hesitantly, Cory switched on the kitchen light.

*Is that a rat?*

*A roach?*

*A lizard?*

*A ghost?*

She scanned the room but couldn't spot whatever was causing the noise. The storm outside had intensified, the pitter-patter of pins was

---

[3]  In Malay, oh no or oh my God

now like the cacophony of pots and pans being banged by batons. She felt a surge of fear as the wind howled and the lightning flashed.

*Must call pest control tomorrow.*

*Must fumigate the kitchen first.*

*Must not think about exorcisms.*

She picked up the water bottle and trudged back to her bed and curled up tight, then checked her phone. There were a dozen messages on WhatsApp. She ignored all of them except one—from her ex-colleague, Prem Pujari: CALL ME WHEN UR FREE. HV SOMETHING INTERESTING 4U.

Cory had joined Scenz six years ago as a software engineer and had risen rapidly to head the company's business analytics software line. Prem had joined the sales team a year later after he had completed an MBA at the Singapore Management University. Prem had interned under Cory; Scenz's competitor, Tolledo Tech, headhunted him a year ago.

WHATSUP? Cory typed with both thumbs. IZZIT URGENT?

She yawned and disabled the Wi-Fi on her phone. After ten minutes of trying to get back to sleep, she gave up—and enabled the Wi-Fi. Prem had seen her blue tick on WhatsApp.

U'RE AN EARLY BIRD. Prem had messaged her. HOW COME UR UP SO EARLY?

COULDN'T SLEEP. HDACHE. Y?

I CALL YOU? QUICK 1. He didn't wait for her response and called immediately.

She grabbed her earpiece from the desk.

'Good morning,' Prem was cheerful.

'Stop it. I'm cranky. Got a headache.'

'Means you have a head ha, ha. Old joke.'

'Shut up.'

She picked up the remote and switched off the aircon.

'Relax, *lah*. Tell you two things. AI software launch at Jackal on Monday. Can come?'

'You woke me up to ask me to attend a stupid conference?'

'No, *lah*. Listen. Joe, the *angmoh*[4] we met last year. Remember him? Environmentalist?'

'Joseph Daniel? With Rick. Yeah, what about him?'

'He's dead. Shot in New York.'

'What?'

'Murdered. Mafia-style. Two bullets.'

She sat up. 'Mob?'

'Dunno. NYPD might be on it.'

'Why you tell me?'

'Well, we're meeting on Monday, right?'

'Wrong. What's this to do with me? Why go to Jackal?'

'We talk more on Monday. Something else too. See you at MBFC at 9.'

He hung up.

'What the—?'

Cory was now wide awake—and agitated. She placed her mobile phone on the desk.

*Whoosh.*

It was the swishing-scurrying sound from the kitchen. Again. A bead of sweat appeared on her brow while her body shivered. Her mind raced through the options: pest control could eliminate rats, lizards, and roaches. Living creatures and pests could be exterminated.

*What about a ghost?*

*A poltergeist in the flat?*

*Who will exorcise that?*

As a young girl, Cory had read *The Exorcist*—and could not sleep in her own bed for fear that it would levitate, like it did in William Peter Blatty's scary novel. For a week after that, she had slept on the floor with the lights on. She had watched *The Exorcist*, *Poltergeist*, and *The Entity* with her primary school friends; that had scarred her mind forever.

It was to exorcise herself physically and mentally—to face her fear of ghosts—that she had moved out from her parents' house in Dover Road and rented an apartment at the Central Green Condo opposite Tiong Bahru MRT station in Singapore. That was also the period during

---

4   In Singlish, a white person

which she was going steady with Prem; she didn't want her parents to know whenever he visited or stayed over. He had since moved out, but something maleficent had moved in.

*Whoosh.*

The sound rattled her. Despite the aircon having stopped, the room felt like a refrigerator.

*I should get a cat.*

*A mean cat.*

*A hungry cat that will eat the rats.*

Cory clenched her trembling hand, mustering every ounce of strength to steady it. Her fingers fumbled anxiously, struggling to locate the flashlight function on her mobile phone. She crept forward, her footsteps muted, as if treading upon a forbidden path. The kitchen lay before her, bathed in the ethereal glow seeping through the windowpane, casting an otherworldly pallor upon the familiar surroundings.

Pausing at the threshold, her heart pounding, she brandished the flashlight. Its beam cut through the darkness like a blade. The light danced across the pristine expanse of the white-tiled floor, revealing no secrets, no signs of an intruder, either corporeal or ethereal, lurking in the shadows. The silence pressed upon her, heavy and suffocating, broken only by the sound of her own shallow breaths.

She waited, uncertain whether to even continue to breathe. But there was nothing. No sound. No movement. The emptiness clung to the air, pregnant with anticipation. Still, she stood, an interminable vigil in the face of an enigmatic void that refused to yield its secrets.

She tiptoed to switch on the main kitchen light. There was a sudden swishing sound, followed by the sound of steel utensils and spoons crashing to the ground.

Cory's scream ripped through the silence, a primal cry born from the depths of her terror and the horrors that lurked in the dark recesses of her imagination. Her body convulsed, quivering with a mixture of fear and revulsion, as her mind grappled with the unfathomable truth that something beyond comprehension had invaded her sanctuary.

# Chapter 2

## Monday, 9 September 2019

The Marina Bay Financial Centre (MBFC) comprises three office towers and two residential buildings that occupy four hectares of space in downtown Singapore. MBFC clinched the top award in the office category at the FIABCI Prix d'Excellence awards in 2012, which recognizes the world's outstanding real-estate developments.

Cory was familiar with MBFC. Scenz Software collaborated with JQL. And JQL—popularly called Jackal—had multiple clients at MBFC, including IBM, BHP Billiton, American Express, Barclays, Macquarie Group, Murex, and Nomura Securities.

This Monday morning, Cory rode the lift to the eighteenth floor, where a robot greeted her at the reception. It snapped a photograph of her face and spat out a registration sticker. She scanned the hall. There were a dozen-odd men sipping hot beverages from paper cups and just a couple of women, one of whom was absorbed in her mobile phone.

*Where the hell is Prem? Did I get stood up?*

*None of these guys look familiar to me.*

*Should I slink out and go home?*

Cory stuck her nametag on her shirt and turned around to walk back to the lift lobby. A lift door had just opened to spew out another bunch of corporates—all men. Before Cory could navigate between them, she felt a tap on her shoulder and turned around. It was Prem.

'I thought—'

'—that I stood you up?' Prem finished the thought. 'I had gone to the loo. If I had been just a minute late, you'd have left.'

'I was looking for the restroom.'

'In the lift lobby?'

'Wanna fight with me?'

'Sorry, sorry,' he held up both arms. 'I missed you. I wanted
to discuss—'

Cory ignored him and walked to the foyer.

JQL had set up a barista with two automated coffee machines.
Six men in suits were already in the queue for coffee. Prem and Cory
joined the line. She scanned the hall; just four women.

'How's your migraine?'

'Guess it's the aircon. Need to see a doc. Dunno if there're lizards
or rats in the kitchen. Need to call a pest control company. Or get a cat.
Or something worse.'

'Worse?'

'I know this sounds silly but what if there's poltergeist activity
going on in my kitchen?'

'Poltergeist? As in ghosts? In your kitchen?' Prem laughed so hard
that his whole body shook.

The two others in the queue and the barista turned to glance at
Cory; the barista smiled.

Prem saw the discomfort on Cory's face. 'I guess they must be
hungry ghosts,' he covered his mouth. 'This is the funniest story I've
heard in a while.'

'I'm not laughing,' she said sternly. The barista had stopped smiling.
'What if it was your kitchen? Would you find that funny?'

'Let me guess . . .' said Prem. 'I think the ghost in your kitchen is
hungry for Indian food.'

'Your wit this morning is refreshing,' she grimaced. 'Glad I made
you laugh today.'

The guy ahead of them in the queue turned around to give them a
confused look before taking his cup of coffee and leaving the counter.
The elderly barista kept his composure.

'Two cappuccinos, please,' Prem told the barista, then turned to
Cory. 'You should—'

'Call for an exorcism?' Then she asked the barista, 'Does that sound funny to you?'

The barista cleared his throat to stop himself from breaking into laughter. Prem noticed it and hurried Cory along before she could see the barista stoop below the counter and guffaw.

'Maybe you should get a cat, after all,' suggested Prem. 'That'll keep you company too, right?'

They took their coffee to a round stand-up desk. Prem scanned the hall. 'The conference seems to be a big deal. The line for coffee is snaking all the way out. There's our old friend, isn't that him?'

Cory turned around to see a tall, African American man in a suit wave at her from the corner of the room. She waved back. He had a lapel microphone clipped to his collar, the white wire snaking up against his dark suit. He held a paper cup of coffee in his hand—and gingerly moved through the crowd, careful not to spill the beverage on himself or others.

'Welcome to sunny Singapore, Rick,' Cory gave him a quick hug.

'Delighted to be here,' Rick gave her a peck on the cheek. 'Howdy, Prem.'

Prem touched Rick's arm. 'Remember you introduced us to your colleague from NY . . . Joe? We had dinner together last year when you were both here. What happened to him?'

'Joseph Daniel?' Rick sipped coffee. 'Err . . . he quit Jackal. Don't know exactly—'

'I heard someone shot him in New York City.'

'He was active in Greenpeace and PETA I believe,' Rick scanned the hall; it was filling up with more delegates. 'Hey, listen, I don't wanna talk about this.'

Cory patted his hand. 'How long are you here? How about getting together for drinks?'

Rick smiled at Cory. 'Sounds cool. I'm here till Friday. Let's plan something.'

'I'll get my school friends to join us. Want to introduce you to Angela, Gina, and Simi.'

'Err, I'm still here . . .' Prem smirked. 'What about me?'

'You're invited,' said Cory with a flourish. 'Please join us, Prem. And settle the bill.'

\* \* \*

## Wednesday, 11 September 2019

Mustafa Centre is one of Singapore's busiest department stores that sells almost everything, including groceries and gold, toys and textiles, and phones and fridges. It's in the heart of the Little India district and open 24/7. It's most crowded on weekends when hordes of foreign workers and tourists descend on the massive mall, as well as on most weekday evenings.

Cory had invited three of her primary-school classmates—Angela Ang, Gina Gonzales, and Simi Sundar—to meet Rick for drinks and dinner at 7 p.m. They met at Mustafa where Rick wanted to buy a suitcase, then head to dinner somewhere in Little India. Prem dropped out because of a last-minute engagement.

'It's a working Wednesday,' Angela declared with disgust, her voice barely audible over the bustling crowd. Mustafa was teeming with people, and the crowded aisles made it difficult to navigate. Angela, tall and slim, with straight, black hair tightly tied in a bun, seemed to be a magnet for the chaos surrounding her. Men brushed past her, some deliberately bumping into her as they hurriedly manoeuvred through the throng. Angela's frustration grew as she became the target of lingering gazes from shoppers who couldn't resist stealing glances at her. The jostling in the crowd only heightened her annoyance, as she longed for some respite from the constant invasion of personal space. 'This is terrible.'

Simi, shorter and stouter, grabbed Angela's hand. 'Cover your breasts with your bag.'

Angela was getting irritated. 'Guys, can you decide what you want to buy? Maybe we should've gone shopping at Orchard or Suntec City, right? Let's get outta here ASAP.'

'I want to check out the luggage section,' protested Rick. 'Need a roller bag. Mine broke.'

Simi led them up the wide, marble stairs to the second level. To the far left was a secluded area that had dozens of suitcases, briefcases, and assorted luggage crammed into shelves and laid out on the floor. The crowds were considerably thinner here. Angela smiled for the first time.

'Quite an assortment here,' Rick went around the suitcase islands, inspecting the labels and examining specific pieces of luggage. 'Prices seem quite reasonable.'

'Must be cheaper than the US, right?' Angela asked. 'Money is honey—'

Rick picked up a brown trolley suitcase. 'This seems to be good. Hey guys, since there's less of a crowd here, how about we take a picture?'

'Picture in a shopping mall?' Simi scowled. 'Crazy or what?'

'I'll take a selfie, I mean a groupie,' Rick said. 'I have a wide-angle on my iPhone.'

'Pay for the luggage first,' Cory pointed to the cashier. 'We can take pictures after that.'

Rick wheeled the suitcase to a counter. 'This seems to be the shortest line here.'

'We have no choice but to wait,' Gina assessed the queue. The counter had six people waiting in line to pay for their purchases. Crowds were milling about, inspecting goods, speaking with each other, some talking loudly on their phone.

'It's like this every evening,' said Simi. 'I avoid coming here in the evening.'

'Finally,' sighed Rick as soon as the transaction went through. 'Boy, that was an adventure. What's next on the agenda? Pictures? Dinner?'

'I'd like to go home after a quick dinner,' said Gina. 'Have an early morn meet.'

'I'll stay with you, Rick,' Cory touched his arm. 'No hurry to go back to my apartment which I seem to be sharing with rats, or lizards, or roaches—or ghosts.'

'Ghosts?' Simi raised an eyebrow.

'Let's take a picture with all these people behind us,' Rick said. 'Girls, girls, groupie.'

Rick steadied his iPhone. But he could barely stand still with all the people milling around. Just then, a tall man who was walking with a shopping basket stopped and waved at Rick.

'I'll help you take a group picture,' offered the man. 'May I?'

Rick hesitated for a couple of seconds, gripping his expensive iPhone. He had heard stories of tourists getting robbed or scammed in foreign countries. But this was Singapore, one of the safest cities in the world. He looked around. The mall was bustling with people and security cameras. It would be impossible for the stranger to try to make off with his phone. Rick spotted at least three CCTV cameras focused on the luggage section alone.

'Sure, brother,' he said and handed his iPhone to the stranger. He joined the three girls who were holding their handbags in front of them. He wrapped his arms behind them and smiled. 'Say cheese!'

Cory was momentarily distracted by the crowd; she didn't hear Rick and smiled absentmindedly. She turned her head slightly to look at something in front of her, just as the stranger touched the app. He grinned and handed the iPhone back to Rick with a polite nod.

'Thank you,' said Rick, checking the photo. The guy had shot three snaps in quick succession. Two of them were blurry and off-centre, with Cory's face half-hidden. The third was perfect. He smiled and looked up, but the stranger was already gone, swallowed by the crowd.

# Chapter 3

**Friday, 31 December 2021**

She wasn't sure whether she was hallucinating or falling sick. The pitter-patter of raindrops hitting the windowpane had lulled her to sleep. She heard church bells in the distance signalling the end of Mass, followed by the tinkle of breaking glass. She dreamt she was climbing and falling off an ark—and woke up with a start.

Baffled, she turned over on the bed and stared at the floor. The photo frame had fallen from the nightstand, its glass cover shattered. Fortunately, her mobile phone was intact. That was a relief.

She picked up the phone. It showed 23:37.

*Did I sleep for just a minute?*

There was a message: ARE YOU HOME TONIGHT? It was from an unknown number.

*Has the rain suddenly intensified?*

*Is a storm brewing?*

*How did the photo frame fall?*

A flash of lightning struck the windowsill, making her blink, followed by a clap of thunder, a roaring gust of wind and rain that almost blew the glass pane off the window. She sprang up and stared at the fury of the raindrops striking the windowpane.

*Has the window glass cracked?*

*Will it withstand the onslaught?*

*Hope poor Bella is not scared?*

The aircon suddenly stopped humming.

*Alamak, has the fuse blown?*

*Call the condo electrician?*

*Call Prem to come fix it?*

There was a soft knock at the bedroom door. Before she could react, the door clicked open. A tall man in a black trench coat—maybe a raincoat—and a peaked cap pulled low over his brow stood in silhouette against the dim, white light from the hall, his face obscured.

She tugged the blanket closer to her chest and crouched. 'Who the hell are you?'

The stranger raised a hand in greeting. He did not step inside. 'Hi, I'm Larry.'

*Is he a ghost? Unlikely.*

*Is he a burglar? Possibly.*

*Is he a trespasser? Absolutely.*

'How the heck did you get into my flat?'

'The door to your apartment was open, my dear,' his tone was gentle, reassuring. That alarmed her even more because he seemed to be in control of the situation—in *her* bedroom.

'Anybody could have walked in, dear. Be thankful it was me.'

'Impossible! Nobody can just walk into condos in Singapore.'

'But then . . . as you can see . . . I'm already here, my dear.'

'I'm not "your dear" and I don't know any Larry,' she said nervously and picked up the phone, keeping a wary eye on him. He stood just outside the bedroom and didn't attempt to enter. 'I'll call the cops. Two bolts on my door. How the hell did you open the door from outside?'

A bolt of lightning streaked across the windowsill, making her blink. It was like a knife, slicing through the darkness and threatening to strike her aching head. This was followed by a crash of thunder that rattled the windowpanes, making her shudder and shriek. It sounded like the rumble of a train, hurtling towards her with enormous force. She felt a surge of panic in her chest, as if she were trapped on the tracks with no escape.

He held up his hands. 'Look, no gun, no knife, no weapons . . . don't cry.'

A chill shot through her spine. 'Where's Bella, my cat? Have you killed her? Is she okay?'

'Of course, dear,' Larry waved his hand. As if on cue, the feline dashed in from the hall and on to the bed to Cory and purred. She hugged and kissed the cat.

'Aww, so nice to see such love between two animal species . . .'

The cat continued to purr. Maybe he wasn't a killer. Maybe a burglar caught unawares.

'Do you want my money, bozo? Take it from my purse on the table and get out.'

'Easy, Cory. Couldn't I have burgled you while you slept?'

She gulped. 'How the hell do you know my name? I don't know any Larry or Harry.'

'You don't know me, but I know you,' he chuckled. 'Okay . . . can you pick up the photo?'

'Why?'

She wondered whether she should risk letting her guard down. He made no move to step inside the bedroom; that gave her a small sense of comfort. Was this a standoff between two animals, each waiting for the other to make the first move? She felt a mix of fear and curiosity as she stared into the blackness of his face. She kept a wary eye on him as she bent over the side of her bed and picked up the broken photo frame. She tapped the frame on the floor to dislodge any loose shards of glass. 'What about it?'

'That photo was taken on 11 September 2019 at Mustafa, remember? Lovely picture of you, Gina, Angela, Simi, and Rick. How cool that Rick was visiting.'

'You know my friends? Phew! Are you one of their friends?'

'Nope. I was shopping, passing by, caught Rick's eye. He asked me if I could take a group picture on his phone. I guess he gifted the framed photo to you as a birthday present.'

Cory held Bella closer and wrapped the blanket around her, annoying the animal. This conversation was getting out of hand. 'Are you a bloody stalker? What do you want?'

'All I want is to be your friend, Cory. And wish you a happy new year.'

Was this guy a psycho? A smooth talker or a silky stalker? Cory glared at him. She needed to take control of the situation. It was like a chess game and he had made the first move. She had to counter his strategy or else he would checkmate her. She felt a surge of adrenaline, almost as if she were ready to take a calculated risk. 'My boyfriend should be on the way,' she furtively glanced at the watch on the nightstand.

*Say I'm on my period? He'll know I'm not.*

*Say I'm HIV positive? He'll know that's absurd.*

*Can he read my mind? He'll call my bluff.*

She blurted out: 'What the hell do you want, you freak?'

Larry held up his arms. 'I haven't touched you. I haven't stepped inside your bedroom. Here's what happened. You had a headache and dozed off at 11.36 p.m. I sent you a text at 11.36. Check the time on your phone.'

'You even know what time I fell asleep?' She cautiously checked her phone. 'Were you in my flat all this while? Yes, the text came in at 11.36.'

'Good.' He straightened his cap. 'I will now tell you why I'm here, my dear.'

'Don't call me "dear"!' She thumped her fist on the nightstand. 'You don't know me.'

'You are Carmine Chan. Your dad's a businessman who trades in computer components. Your mom's a real-estate agent.' He paused. 'And you are a Dynaborg.'

A crack of lightning struck the windowsill, startling Cory. It was like a gunshot, piercing through the silence and shattering her nerves. The photo frame fell to the floor like a bomb, exploding into pieces and sending shrapnel everywhere. This made Bella jump in fear. She sprang out of Cory's arms and scurried under the blanket. She was like a mouse, hiding from a predator and hoping to survive.

'You son of a—'

'Bitch?' He laughed. 'True. I have canine genes in me. I'm a second-gen Dynaborg. Larry is my generic name. Stands for Last Appliance Running Radon Yag.'

Cory pinched herself. 'Hell, am I having a nightmare?' She blinked. 'Yag? Rag? Fag?'

'Yag is right. Yttrium Aluminium Garnet. A synthetic crystalline compound used as a host in solid-state lasers. I've been crafted with Yag with radioactive radon. I'm the last in the second-gen line of Dynaborgs.'

'Why the hell are you telling me this?'

'Because you're the first in the third-gen line of Dynaborgs, my dear.'

'Don't call me "dear"!' She thumped the nightstand in fury. 'Get out. Dynaborg? Yeah, right.'

'Dynaborgs are humans with an altered DNA. We're different from cyborgs, which are just cybernetic organisms. Cyborgs have bioelectronic body parts. We have no electronic parts, just altered DNA. Dynaborgs are 100 per cent biological, like all living beings.'

'That is the biggest bullshit I've ever heard.'

He lowered his voice. 'Another secret for you. Check the time of my text again.'

'Why?' She checked her WhatsApp. 'Same time. 23:36.'

'I sent it at 23:36 on Thursday, 30 December. Today is Friday, 31 December.'

'You think I'm an idiot, don't you? I dozed off today, which is Thursday.'

'You did. On Thursday,' he paused for effect. 'But today is Friday.'

'*Alamak!*' She glanced at her mobile phone. It showed Friday, 31 December 2021. 'Holy crap! I've been asleep for twenty-four hours?' She rubbed her eyes. Was she waking up from a coma, disoriented and confused? Bella burrowed under the blanket. Cory wished she could do the same and hide from this weird reality, hoping it would go away.

'Don't. Cry, I mean.' He took a step forward; she recoiled on the bed. 'This is not a nightmare. It's a gift given to people like you and your friends. Embrace it. Appreciate it. Use it.'

Cory was suddenly alert.

*Did my buddies go through this?*

*Did this psycho con them? Kill them?*

*Am I next to be conned? Raped? Killed?*

'What happened to my friends?' She mopped her brow with the edge of the blanket. 'Are they okay?'

'Your friends are fine. Rick is doing well at JQL in Raleigh. Angela continues her run at Pistonex Singapore. Gina is going to be promoted at Genome Germanica.'

'How come you know about my friends in such detail?'

'*Our* friends,' he held up his hands. 'Rick is a second-gen, like me.'

'Simi?'

'Angela and Gina are third-gen, like you.'

'What? My friends are aliens? That is the biggest bullshit—'

He clapped once. 'You are the chosen one, Cory. Wake up.'

'Nonsense!'

'You have the power, the responsibility, the duty to awaken others. For that to happen, you need to wake up first. That's what I'm here to do.'

'Screw you.'

'Using profanity will not change your destiny.'

'What destiny? I never signed up for this bullshit. I want to lead my life my way. Travel the world. Sample the world's cuisine. Who the hell are you to tell me what to do?'

'I'm Larry, the Last Appliance Running Radon Yag.'

'Broken record,' she held up her hand. 'What about Simi? You didn't mention her.'

Larry ignored her question. 'Second-gens like me must transition to third-gens like you. It's my job to awaken third-gen Dynaborgs like you.'

'For what?'

'To fulfil your destiny.'

'Which is what?'

He paused. 'Can I step in, please? I won't come close to you, a couple of steps inside.'

*Should I let this bozo inside by bedroom?*

*I have a sliver of glass from the broken photo frame.*

*If he tries something funny, I will slash his face.*

The onslaught of rain against the window had abated, like a slowing drumbeat pounding on her ears and nerves. The storm may have passed. Bella had slipped out from under the blanket to scurry back to her cardboard box in the hall. And the stranger didn't seem a threat—or did he? He was still an ominous puzzle, hiding his secrets and motives.

'Stay where you are,' she gestured with her hand. 'I don't believe you.'

'Don't worry.' He took two measured steps inside, making Cory shriek. She drew the pillow closer to her chest. The door gently clicked shut behind him, alarming her even more.

*Was that poltergeist activity?*

*Is this weirdo human? Is he a zombie?*

*I must not panic. I must not panic.*

'Did the damn door just close on its own?'

'Must have been a draught of air,' he waved his hand. 'Don't worry, I'm not a ghost.'

'You're a bloody burglar. A thief. A psycho.'

'I'm Larry—'

'I know, I know. Why the heck did you enter my bedroom despite my protests?'

'Let me explain, okay?' He adjusted his peaked cap a wee bit to let a little light through. 'There are three states of being. The first is consciousness or feeling you're alive. All living things feel they're alive and need food to keep going and air or water to breathe. The second is sentience or seeing, which is when you notice what is around you. Birds and animals can see their surroundings. The third is awareness or caring, not just about yourself, but also about the world around you. Understand that all living things are connected and precious.'

'A psycho philosopher?' Cory mocked him. 'Are you from Greenpeace? PETA?'

'Greenpeace has been doing a great job since 1971. Likewise, People for the Ethical Treatment of Animals. They're voluntary organizations,' he paused. 'We're different.'

'You are. I'm not. I didn't sign up to be a member of your weirdo club.'

'You didn't sign up to be born either,' he clapped once. 'But then, here you are.'

'You're mocking me?'

'Wake up, Carmine Chan.'

'From this horrible nightmare?'

'The nightmare began in 1986 when Chernobyl blew up. That represented everything that could go wrong if left to humans. Something had to be done. A new breed of human had to emerge. A genetically mutated human. Like me. Like you.'

'What? I'm genetically mutated? I had Covid-19, I was in hospital. Did that mutate me?'

'Maybe. Maybe not. Think of it as a positive side effect.'

'Of what? The Delta Strain? The Omicron Strain?'

'The Singapore Strain.'

'You're mocking me.'

'I wouldn't dare.'

'There's no Singapore Strain. Don't bullshit me.'

'There're no Alpha, Beta, Delta, Gamma, Omicron, or Omega strains. They just pick letters from the Greek alphabet to name a new virus. Just assume you have the Singapore Strain.'

'I must see a shrink. I'm screwed.'

'You're blessed. You're part of an elite breed of new humans.'

'Screw you.'

'Unnecessary. Genetic mutations can happen without copulation.'

Cory glared at him, 'Don't joke with me.'

'No joke. There're 12 million third-gens in the world.'

'Whoa, you expect me to believe this rubbish?'

'Before the second-gens die, we must awaken the third-gens, to save Earth and its biodiversity.'

Cory narrowed her eyes. 'Are you for real, you bozo?' She pushed the pillow aside and stepped down from the bed—and winced when a shard of glass pierced her sole.

'Careful, Cory,' Larry took a step forward.

Cory raised her hand. 'Stay where you are.'

'Okay, okay, don't be scared. I'm only trying to help.'

'No need.' She sat on the bed and removed the splinter from her foot. She scanned the floor in the dim light from the window. 'My slippers should be here somewhere.'

'Right under your bed.'

She peered under the bed, pulled them out and slipped them on.

'You want me to come there?' Larry asked.

'Not with your stupid raincoat and cap. Let me turn on the light.'

'You can't. The lightning blew out the fuse, remember?'

Cory flipped her mobile phone on. 'Let me turn on the flashlight app. Uh-oh, I'm running low on battery. But this should work.'

She directed the flashlight's beam on Larry's figure from the bottom up. He was wearing black shoes that reflected the light from her phone, like tiny stars dancing on his shiny shoes. His trousers were dark and obscured by the overcoat that flowed all the way to below his knees, like a cloak covering his body and concealing his identity. The overcoat was buttoned up to the collar like a shield, securing him from the outside and keeping his secrets inside.

*How come he's not wet from the rain?*

*Was he in the flat for a long time?*

*One day? Two days? Drugged me?*

'Your raincoat is not wet. How long have you been in my apartment?'

'Maybe I should come a little closer.'

'You're a weirdo, aren't you? In that thick overcoat, like you've just flown in from London.'

'Doubles as a raincoat.' He tipped his cap a bit higher. 'Your apartment is quite cold.'

'Let me look at your face,' she focused the beam of light from her phone on his face. He was clean-shaven except for a faint moustache. A wisp of dark hair had strayed from under his cap. It was like a brushstroke, painting a thin line of contrast on his pale skin. His eyes were dark and deep, like wells that could drown her in their secrets. His lips were curved in a faint smile like a bow that could shoot an arrow of charm. She felt a flutter of fear and anticipation in her heart, as if she were facing a handsome stranger who was concealing a horrible secret.

'Are you Chinese? Caucasian? You don't look Malay or Indian to me.'

'Does it matter? My race? My nationality? My sexual orientation?'

'Are all Dynaborgs like you? Turn pop psychology into gender and race neutrality?'

'Ask instead whether race, nationality, gender, sexual orientation—do these matter?'

'For what?'

'To protect Earth's biodiversity. What's the solution to save the planet from the abyss?'

'What's the solution?'

'A new breed of humans. We call them Dynaborgs. You can call them whatever you wish. The nomenclature doesn't matter. A rose—'

'I'm a software engineer, but I read *Romeo and Juliet* in high school. I too can misquote the bard. What's in a name? Shit, by any other name, would stink as much.'

'Spot on. Now, can I come a wee bit closer to you?' He didn't wait for her answer and stepped briskly forward, his coat flapping. 'I think I must. You need me to.'

'Why?'

'Because your phone battery is running low and you're going to—'

A frisson of electricity sent a shiver down Cory's legs.

*Is that smell coming from roasted sheesh kebab?*

*Or tandoori chicken?*

*Why is it tasting like burnt cheese?*

She looked up. A blanket of fog was descending from the ceiling. She flailed her arms and tried to cover her nose. Her neck craned up awkwardly. The phone slipped out of her hand, the dull glow from its flashlight app flickering out like a dying light from a wick.

She didn't know whether she was hallucinating or falling sick. The pitter-patter of raindrops hitting the windowpane had lulled her to sleep. She heard church bells in the distance signalling the end of Mass, followed by the tinkling of breaking glass. She dreamt she was climbing and falling off an ark—and woke up with a start.

Baffled, she turned on the bed and stared at the floor. The photo frame had fallen from the nightstand, its glass cover shattered. Fortunately, her mobile phone was intact. That was a relief.

She picked up the phone. It showed 23:38.

*Did I sleep for just a minute?*

There was a message: ARE YOU HOME TONIGHT? It was from an unknown number.

*Has the rain suddenly intensified?*

*Is a storm brewing?*

*How did the photo frame fall?*

A flash of lightning struck the windowsill, making her blink, followed by a clap of thunder, a roaring gust of wind, and rain that almost blew the glass pane off the window. She sprang up and stared at the fury of the raindrops striking the windowpane.

*Has the window glass cracked?*

*Will it withstand the onslaught?*

*Hope poor Bella is not scared?*

The aircon suddenly stopped humming.

*Alamak, has the fuse blown?*

*Call the condo electrician?*

*Call Prem to come fix it?*

There was a soft knock at the bedroom door. Before she could react, the door clicked open. A tall man in a black trench coat—maybe a raincoat—and a peaked cap that hid his brow stood in silhouette against the dim, white light from the hall, his face obscured.

She tugged the blanket closer to her chest and crouched. 'Who the hell are you?'

The stranger raised a hand in greeting. He did not step inside. 'Hi, I'm Harry.'

# Chapter 4

**Friday, 7 January 2022**

Strict Covid-19 regulations were still in effect in Singapore, with a maximum of five people per household permitted to meet. Cory had invited three of her closest friends from school—tall and lissom Angela, stout and buxom Gina, and petite and nerdy Simi—to her apartment for dinner. She was not sure whether they would like pizza and fries or noodles, curry, and chicken rice. Cory seemed confused and frazzled and had ordered all the options.

The girls had arrived at 7 p.m. and were getting hungry and angry. It was only by 8 p.m. that the Grab guy delivered the piping-hot food packets containing Chinese chicken rice, vegetarian and pepperoni pizzas, french fries and garlic bread. They pounced on the food like hyenas.

'Next time, make sure the food gets here before we do?' Angela belched. 'If I knew we were doing supper, I'd have eaten dinner and come, *lah*. Can't have beer on an empty stomach, right?'

'Don't blame me if the Grab guy's delayed,' Cory retorted. 'Ever since you got here, you've been complaining—and belching—like a gastric cow.'

Gina laughed. 'Just love your cribbing and carping, Cory. Sometimes I wonder why I'm still your friend. Then I tell myself you're always feeding us. Ergo, I love you.'

'Girls, girls,' Simi clapped. 'Food's hot, night's young, beer's cold. Cheers,' she opened the beer bottles and handed them around. 'Pass me the French fries, please. Did you know it was the third US President, Thomas Jefferson, who introduced fries to America?'

'We know you know all kinda crap,' Gina smirked. 'Spare us your lecture, Indian prof.'

'Stop belching like a racist cow,' Simi laughed. 'I ate before coming.'

'Stop bickering,' Cory raised her bottle of beer. 'Cheers!'

They raised their bottles of Singapore-brewed Tiger beer. Bella, Cory's female cat, was hovering around, hoping to get some tasty titbits. She purred and rubbed herself on the girls' legs, in vain. They had strict orders to not feed the cat food that was meant for humans. 'Bella, your food's in that bowl,' Cory pointed at it. 'Eat that. Not this.'

Angela picked up the purring creature and dropped her next to her food bowl. The cat ignored the cat food and ran back to the girls, nestling against Gina's leg.

Gina ran her fingers over Bella's brown-and-white fur. 'She's hungry for love, not food.'

Angela dipped a piece of chicken into the fragrant garlic-chilli sauce and polished it off with a piece of pizza. 'Cory, did the four hunks just pop up in your bedroom one by one? Were they tall, dark, and handsome?'

'I only remember Larry, he was tall and creepy,' Cory grimaced at Angela. 'He told me that you, Gina and Rick were already Dynaborgs. That freaked me out.'

'Maybe they are,' Simi said. 'What about me? I'm not?'

'He never answered. Maybe he did, I don't remember.'

'I have an idea,' Gina patted Cory's arm. 'Can we install CCTV cameras in your bedroom? We can view the footage to see if they were humans. Or ghosts.'

'Gina, you dumbo,' Angela slapped her shoulder. 'The hunks have come—and gone.'

'CCTV cams may work,' Simi said. 'Ghosts don't appear in mirrors; they do on cams.'

'Stop talking,' Cory slammed her fist on the nightstand. 'You're scaring me. D'you think I should move back to my parents' house?'

'You shift to my flat, *lah*,' Angela laughed. 'My bed's big enough for both of us. Or even three, if we cuddle.'

'Oh Angela, there you go again,' Cory said in mock disgust. 'You're a nymphomaniac.'

'You've no right to call me that, Cory. I have a healthy interest in men.'

Simi's phone buzzed. Gina dropped a bowl on the floor. Angela reached for the fries and knocked over a tiny, ceramic cup of garlic-chilli sauce. Cory heard the doorbell ring. She froze.

'I'm not expecting anyone,' Cory shushed her friends.

'Oops, sorry,' said Angela. 'What?'

'Didn't you hear the doorbell?' Cory asked.

'Nope,' said Simi.

'Me neither,' Gina gingerly replaced the bowl on the coaster.

'Could it be one of those guys?' Angela laughed. 'Shall I open the door?'

'Please do,' Cory mopped her brow and braced herself.

Angela went to the door and flung it open. The corridor was dark. 'No light here, *meh*?'

'The bulb blew two days ago,' Cory said. 'Should remind them to change it tomorrow.'

Angela stepped out and looked around. 'No one here. Sure the bell rang?'

'I heard it loud and clear,' Cory said, the colour draining from her face. 'Didn't you?'

'Sit down, Cory,' Simi helped her to a chair. 'The beer's gone to your head, or—'

'Covid-19 has screwed with your brain,' Gina rushed to her side. 'You okay? You should move back to your parents' house. We'll help you move.'

'I'm going to shut the door, okay?' Angela closed the door gently.

Simi moved closer to Cory and touched her face. 'You look tired.'

'I remember Larry or Harry telling me I had the Singapore Strain of the virus.'

Angela took a gulp of beer. 'Got a Singapore Strain of Covid, *meh*?'

Gina examined Cory's eyes. 'I'm in genetics. Never heard of this variant before.'

'Neither have I,' said Simi, 'and I'm analysing genetics data all day long. There's no such thing.'

'Never mind whichever strain,' Cory laughed. 'He was kidding, I guess. Total crap.'

'Get serious, *lah*,' said Simi. 'I too want to help save our planet. Become a Dynaborg.'

'What if we are Dynaborgs and don't know it?' asked Gina.

'Think about this, we've had many genocides,' Simi closed her eyes to focus on the thought. 'The Holocaust, Cambodia, Rwanda, Bosnia, Darfur, ISIS, Rohingya.'

'Wha . . . you a nerd on genocide, too?' Cory asked.

'History was my favourite subject in school. History is about people killing other people, usually in the name of religion. As George Carlin said, they have murdered more people in the name of religion than for any other reason. My God has a bigger dick than your God, so screw you,' she paused. 'Dynaborgism seems so refreshing.'

Gina clapped. 'My team's working on a project to get bacteria to eat plastic. The Great Pacific Garbage Patch is bigger than Mexico, you know.'

Angela held up her chopsticks. 'No amount of bacteria can digest that big a patch, *lah*.'

'The black-footed albatross eats the debris,' Simi went on. 'The albatross feeds plastic to its chicks, which die of starvation. Over 300 species are harmed. The oceans will have more plastic than fish by 2030.'

Gina thumped the table. 'We're the problem. Seven billion now. Nine billion by 2040. By 2050, we'll all be eating each other. No bacteria yet that can digest humans.'

Simi took a swig of beer. 'That's what Larry was trying to tell you. I agree with him. I want to become a Dynaborg. I like him already.'

'So do I,' Angela laughed. 'We need to find out how to meet Larry or Harry and discuss saving the world over a glass of wine or beer, right?'

Gina tapped Cory's arm. 'Were those guys different or the same with different names?'

Cory shook her head. 'Dunno. Only heard their voices. They were all tall, with raincoats and fez caps. They stayed near or outside the door. Couldn't see their faces. Does it matter?'

'It does,' Simi said. 'Someone took a pic of us at Mustafa. Larry? Somehow, he got into Cory's flat. But who were the others?'

Gina nodded. 'Good point. Let's ask Rick. It was his phone. You have his number?'

Cory sighed. 'I tried calling him. Voicemail says he's in LA. Maybe back in Raleigh.'

Gina checked her watch. '10 p.m. here; 10 a.m. there. Call him on WhatsApp. Speaker on.'

Simi called Rick on WhatsApp. No answer. 'His WhatsApp is off. I'll try direct.'

'Who's this?' a sleepy male voice snapped.

'Rick, it's Simi from Singapore.'

'Yeah. What's wrong?'

'We're at Cory's place. Need your help. Some weirdo got into her bedroom.'

'So?'

'The guy who took our pictures in Mustafa in September. He was in Cory's bedroom.'

'So? Maybe Cory knows him.'

'I don't,' Cory inched closer to the phone. 'Do you know any Larry or Harry?'

'Nope. Not in Singapore.'

'Anything weird been happening to you lately?'

'Nope,' he yawned loudly and then coughed.

'Does the word "Dynaborg" ring a bell?'

'Nope.'

'Did you even hear what I just said?'

'Nope.'

'Okay, Rick. Thanks for nothing. Bye.'

'Nice prank, girls. You woke me up. I need a drink,' he hung up.

'We need a drink, too,' said Cory. 'I have four beers left.'

'I'm driving, I'll pass on the beer,' said Angela. 'Cory, can you get that photo from your bedroom? The glass frame is still broken, right?'

'I changed the frame,' Cory went into the bedroom. 'It broke when it fell on the floor.'

'Exactly my point,' Angela said. 'If you'd had more visitors, you'd have had to change the glass twice, right? D'you remember getting it fixed multiple times?'

'I don't,' Cory replied from the bedroom. 'Let me get the photo first.'

'I'll get the beer,' Simi walked into the kitchen.

Bella followed Cory into the bedroom. Cory held up the framed picture for them to inspect; the glass was intact. 'Come here, guys. The frame is the same, on my nightstand.'

'Good job!' said Angela. 'Glad you replaced the glass frame.'

'Lemme see,' Simi placed the beer bottles on the nightstand. 'Don't see what's odd.'

'Something's surely odd . . .' Cory said softly, her voice becoming garbled. 'I mean, odder, like in, right now. Do you guys hear a guttering sound? Like a goods train or something?'

'What sound?' asked Gina, looking concerned. 'I don't hear anything.'

'Neither do I,' Angela craned her neck. 'Tiong Bahru station is nearby, but underground.'

The cat started mewing loudly and began clawing at Cory's legs.

Simi rushed to her side. 'Are you okay, Cory?'

Cory shielded her ears with her hands as the metallic roar of a heavy, diesel locomotive hurtling down the railway track pierced her eardrums, its horns blaring as the engine tore down the track, followed by the clanking coaches careening away in a crescendo. She screamed in pain and crumpled to the floor to allow the raging locomotive and the cannonade of coaches to race over her body at tremendous speed.

Angela and Gina rushed to Cory's side to stop her from keeling over and hitting her head. They caught her just in time and eased her gently on to the bed.

The photo frame slipped from Cory's fingers. Simi tried to catch it—and missed.

The photo frame crashed to the hard tile floor—and its glass cover shattered—once more.

# Chapter 5

## Sunday, 9 January 2022

Singapore's National University Hospital (NUH) is a clinical training and research centre for the medical and dental faculties of the National University of Singapore (NUS). It has more than 1,500 beds and serves 700,000 outpatients and 60,000 inpatients. In 2005, the NUS School of Medicine celebrated its Centennial Year. It also received a donation of S$100 million from the Yong Loo Lin Trust, so they renamed the school the Yong Loo Lin School of Medicine.

The hospital ran a comprehensive neurology department—with highly qualified staff and the latest equipment—to diagnose and treat neuromuscular and cerebrovascular disorders. Neurology Ward 57 had fifty beds and a high-dependency section with six beds for unstable neurological conditions.

Cory's parents—Mark and Mary Chan—had booked a private, single-bed room for Cory to recuperate in after they ran some tests to diagnose the cause for her epileptic seizure. The neurosurgeon had found an intracranial aneurysm that had burst. He performed a keyhole craniotomy to drain it. She was kept in the neurology ICU for four hours before being moved to the ward.

Post-op nursing aides had wheeled Cory back to the ward. She was sedated and her head was heavily bandaged. An intravenous line, connected to a vein in her right arm, pushed saline. A blood-pressure monitor pumped a cuff on her left arm every five minutes. An electroencephalograph (EEG) monitored the electrical activity in her brain via probes stuck to her temples. Leads snaked from her chest to an electrocardiograph (ECG) monitor on the wall. Since Cory was breathing on her own, there was no need for a ventilator.

Mary was jittery and kept pacing the ward, silently chanting a prayer for her daughter. She had not slept or eaten since the accident and her hands were trembling. She wondered if she could have done something to prevent the mishap. Her eyes perked up when a nurse entered to check on Cory's vitals. She was hoping for some good news but was afraid to ask.

Mary waited for the nurse to finish. 'Hope she wake up soon, Sister?' She cautiously asked the nurse. 'I very, very scared.'

'She will, don't worry,' said the nurse, checking her notes. 'I'm Salma. Call me if you need me or when she wakes up. I have to do some tests then.'

'Been two days,' said Mary, adjusting her mask. 'I very worried.'

'The surgery was successful,' said Salma. 'She's breathing on her own. She's just sedated. Give her some time.'

Mary squeezed Cory's hand. 'Cory, sweetie, can you hear me?'

Mark walked in, staring at his phone. He had a big deal to close today and had no time for this. 'Cory's friends want to visit at 5 p.m.,' he said to the nurse. 'Can they come in an hour?'

'Uh, you should ask the doctor,' said Salma. 'Your daughter had brain surgery. She might be confused when she wakes up.'

'Okay, I'll ask the doc,' said Mark. 'They can meet us otherwise. Only day I'm free.'

'Who are they? Angela? Gina? Simi? Rachel? Roy? Tushar? Tanaya?' asked Mary.

'The first three, *lah*,' Mark snapped. 'They called the ambulance, remember'

'Thank God for them,' Mary wiped a tear. 'Let them come, *lah*.' She turned to Cory. 'Your friends are coming. Wake up, Cory.'

Salma checked and updated the readings from the monitor into her clipboard and left the room. Mary pulled a chair closer to her daughter's bedside, patted her daughter's cheek, and continued to talk to her. She touched the bandage on Cory's forehead. 'Mark, see this? Bandage wet, *lah*. Supposed to be dry or not? Can call the nurse? Check outside. Nurse station.'

'Maybe supposed to be wet,' he glanced at Cory, then went back to checking his phone.

'I not so sure . . .' Mary glared at him. Mark closed his phone and ran his fingers gently around Cory's bandaged head.

'It's wet in this area only. Hope head's not leaking. Hope brain's not leaking. Hope—'

'Stop joking,' retorted Mary. 'Call the nurse. I ring bell.'

Mark tugged his mask over his nose and ran to the nurses' station.

Cory's fingers twitched. Her mouth contorted. Mary held her hand and pressed the buzzer. Perspiration beaded on Cory's forehead. Mary's eyes filled with tears.

Salma entered the room. 'What's happening?'

'She having a fit?' Mary cried. 'Help her, please!'

Salma checked the bandage, flashed a light into Cory's eyes, adjusted the drip, and felt her pulse.

Mark stood by the door, scared. 'What's wrong?'

'She'll be fine, calm down,' said Salma. 'These are normal signs.'

Mary pointed at the bandage. 'Supposed to be wet here?'

Salma inspected the bandage and lifted Cory's head. There was a stain on the pillow. 'I'll call Dr Lim.'

'Xie xie nǐ[5], Sister,' Mary wiped her brow. 'Hope another surgery not required.'

'If she does, let them do it,' Mark said. 'Dr Lim knows best. We want Cory to wake up.'

'Happened because of Covid, meh?' Mary asked. 'She got hit hard by Covid, you know.'

Salma didn't answer her. 'I'll be back soon,' she said and left the room.

'What do you think, Mark?' Mary asked, holding his arm.

Mark reached for his phone but stopped when he saw his wife's angry face. 'I don't know,' he said, turning away. 'We're paying them to think for us.'

'No use discussing anything with you, lah,' Mary turned her attention to Cory. 'Can hear me, baby? Your school friends coming.

---
[5] In Mandarin, thank you

Gina, Angela, Simi. Did they find you in time?' She wiped a tear. 'Or did they do this to you? Can hear me, baby? Blink if you can. Blink.'

Cory did not respond.

In ten minutes, the door opened and Salma stepped in. 'I briefed Dr Lim. He said not to worry. He's on his way here. The patient's vital stats are stable.'

'Then why she not wake up?' Asked Mary. 'Give her drugs. Wake her up. Can or not?'

'Please ask Dr Lim,' replied Salma.

They didn't have to wait long this time. A couple of young male doctors appeared first, followed by Dr Lim and two females. They all had stethoscopes and wore masks.

'These are my interns,' Dr Lim, who was in scrubs, acknowledged their presence. 'Let me check how our young lady is doing. Sister Salma told me about a pink stain.'

Mary put her palms together. 'Dr Lim, why my baby not wake up? I worried. Scared.'

Dr Lim nodded. 'Let me check. Don't worry, Mrs Chan. Give me some space.'

He bent over Cory's head and ran his gloved fingers around the bandage, which was now quite wet. He placed his stethoscope on three regions of her chest, lifted her eyelids to check whether her pupils were dilated, and scanned the continuous EEG reading on the monitor.

'Everything looks good,' said Dr Lim. 'I need to remove the bandage and drain some fluid. I'll have to ask both of you to step outside for a while, please.' He nodded to the interns to step closer and gestured to Salma, who promptly produced a pair of surgical scissors.

As soon as they were outside the ward, Mark's mobile phone buzzed. 'Cory's friends are here,' he said, 'in the lobby. We'll go meet them while Dr Lim and his team attend to Cory.'

The neurology lobby comprised a set of four large sofas and a wall-mounted TV in the corner which was running health-related videos with subtitles and no sound. An elderly man, with his mask hanging on his chin, was dozing on a sofa. A young woman, probably his daughter, was sitting beside him and texting on her mobile phone.

Gina, Angela, and Simi sat on another sofa, masked and anxious. They greeted Mary and Mark.

'Nice of you to come,' Mary hugged them. 'We just met Dr Lim. He say got some improvement in condition. But she still deep sleeping. I terribly worried.'

'Keep your spirits up, Aunty,' said Gina. 'Cory should be okay. She's in expert hands.'

'Dr Lim seems optimistic,' said Mark. 'He's changing her head bandage now. If she's back to normal, we can celebrate her birthday in the first week of Feb.'

'We were planning a get-together on Jan 16 at Gina's house,' said Simi. 'We met for lunch on Friday, Jan 7, at Star Vista. She suddenly lost consciousness and fell off the chair. Her fingers were twitching. Her face was contorted like she was having a fit.'

'Strange,' said Mark. 'Perfectly healthy one day, extremely sick the next.'

'Thanks to three of you girls,' Mary folded her hands and bowed. 'You rush her to NUH. You save my Cory's life. Guardian angels.'

'Actually, I'm glad we were with her when it happened,' said Gina. 'I'm trained in CPR, but she didn't need it. We called 995. The ambulance rushed her to NUH. She had a stroke?'

Mark looked at his watch. 'Do any of you want coffee? Chinese tea?'

'We had coffee before coming up,' said Angela. 'We were wondering whether Covid may have caused this. Cory had Covid before us, right? She fully recovered, right?'

'We asked Dr Lim also,' Mary said. 'He cannot explain one. Covid from new virus, not study fully by experts, he say. He brain doctor, not virus doctor, you know.'

Just then, a male intern who had accompanied Dr Lim opened the door to the lobby. 'Dr Lim wants to invite the parents of Carmine to her room,' he said. 'Please come with me.'

'Hope Cory is okay?' Mark asked the intern.

He didn't reply.

Nurse Salma was outside the door. 'Before you go in, Dr Lim wants me to tell you this,' she whispered. 'We removed the bandage and cleaned up the surgical site and we have applied another bandage. Your daughter has woken up. Please don't talk loudly and get her excited. Her blood pressure is high, which is not good for the brain.'

'Is Dr Lim inside?' Mark asked.

'He has just stepped out to take a call,' replied Salma. 'He'll be back in a while.'

As soon as they stepped inside the room, the astringent scent of antiseptic hit them. Dr Lim—and the interns—had disappeared. They had drawn the curtains and dimmed the room lights. Cory's head had a light bandage; her eyes were closed. The intravenous line was still connected to a vein on her right arm, but the blood pressure cuff on her left arm and the EEG probes on her temples had been removed but the ECG leads were still present. Mary ran to Cory and hugged her.

'Cory, baby, you awake?' Mary wiped a tear. 'Thank God. I so happy now.'

'Mama,' Cory muttered. 'Throat hurts. Head hurts. So thirsty.'

'Can give her water, *mah*?' Mary asked Salma, who was checking the charts.

Mark was already pouring water from the hospital jug into a glass tumbler. He unwrapped the paper and stuck in a plastic straw.

Salma touched Cory's forehead. 'You can give her sips, not too much. Your throat is hurting because it is dry, not because you're dehydrated. The glucose-saline drip is keeping you hydrated. Your BP is slightly high. You can sip a little water, okay?'

Mark held the straw for Cory to sip from the glass tumbler. 'Can we help her sit up?'

Salma shook her head. 'We can't have her sit up, too risky, but I will tilt the bed up slightly.'

Cory took a couple of sips through the straw. She squinted to focus and then gave up. 'Eyes are heavy. Dad, how did I get here?'

'You had a fall or something—and blacked out. Your school friends called an ambulance; you're in NUH. Doctor said you suffered a mild stroke and did surgery on your brain. You're okay now, get some rest first. Your friends are outside, waiting to meet you.'

'Who? Gina? Angela? Simi? Last thing I remember is having dinner with them.'

'Dinner?' Mark touched her forehead. 'You guys met for lunch or not?'

'Guess I'm confused. Can you ask my friends to come here, please?'

'Not yet,' Salma told her firmly. 'Wait for Dr Lim. He has stepped outside to take a call and he told me to only allow the parents to come in.'

'Did he do the surgery on me?' Cory asked without opening her eyes.

'Yes. He's a senior consultant neurosurgeon.'

She yawned. 'Sleepy. Lower the bed. Eyes are heavy.'

Cory slept for thirty minutes and woke up when she felt someone raise her head. 'So soon?'

'You can go back to sleep in a few minutes,' a male voice said. 'I just want to check . . .'

Cory didn't open her eyes.

Dr Lim turned to Mark. 'The stain was just serum; we drained it and relieved some pressure on the skull. That was enough to get her to wake up.' He tapped Cory's cheek. 'Hello, Miss Carmine. Glad to see you've woken up. Can you open your eyes for me?'

'Very tired,' she whispered. 'Very thirsty.'

Dr Lim checked the IV and raised Cory's arm to check her pulse. 'All is well. The BP medication may cause slight drowsiness. I will come back in a while to check on her.'

He patted her cheeks. Cory opened her eyes to glance at the surgeon who'd saved her life. The room was dimly lit, and Cory couldn't focus very well. 'Thank you, doctor . . .'

Dr Lim lifted her eyelids one by one and inspected her pupils. 'You're welcome,' he said. 'You can take small sips of water. Not too much or you will gag, okay?'

'Your voice sounds very familiar,' Cory blinked. 'Have we met before?'

'Unlikely.'

'Can you please remove your mask?'

'Not a good idea. You're in a hospital and you've just had surgery done on your brain.'

She tugged at his gown. 'Just a few seconds. Your voice is so . . .'

'You're probably suffering brain fog, which is normal,' he stepped back. 'Even though we're in a clean environment here, let's not take liberties. I'll keep my mask on.'

'Okay,' said Cory, 'but I'm allowed to talk?'

'What do you want to ask me?'

'Aren't you Larry?'

'I am not. My name is Terence. Who told you I was Larry? Have we met before?'

'I know you,' she opened her eyes and stared at him. 'You know me. You're Terry.'

Mark touched her arm. 'He's Dr Terence Lim. Stop calling him Terry and Larry.'

'Let her continue,' said Dr Lim. 'This must be an interesting side effect of surgery.'

'No side effect,' Cory tugged at his coat. 'You're Larry. Can I please see your face?'

Dr Lim gestured to her to wait. He checked the monitors, then used his stethoscope to listen to her heart. 'Vitals are good. I'm going to remove my mask for a couple of seconds.'

He pulled his mask down and stood in the light so she could see his face but kept his distance. 'I don't recollect we've met before, have we?'

'Absolutely,' Cory smiled. 'You definitely are Larry. Same height. Same voice. Same face, although I barely saw you in full. Only the fez cap is missing. You're Larry, aren't you?'

Dr Lim put his mask back on. 'This is indeed strange,' he chuckled. 'My nickname is Larry. But only my parents call me that. There's no way you'd know my parents.'

Cory was now wide awake. 'Sorry for being brash. I apologize.'

'Don't . . . apologize, I mean. My name is Terence. Does that sound familiar to you?'

'It does! You're Terry?' Cory smiled. 'But you know, it's Larry whom I liked the most.'

Dr Lim scratched his head. 'I didn't know a brain aneurysm could have this side effect.' He stepped closer and peered into her eyes. He touched her forehead. 'No fever. I'm totally puzzled by what you're saying, Carmine. You know Terry, but you like Larry?'

Salma smiled. 'Dr Lim, do you have another nickname? Your colleagues call you Terry.'

'I think he's both Larry and Terry. I know he's both. I've met both, though not together.'

Dr Lim straightened his collar. 'Larry was a nickname given by my parents because their first son died at birth. Only my mother calls me Larry. Nobody else.' He turned to the Chans. 'How does Carmine know this? Do you guys know my parents?'

Mark and Mary shook their heads, bewildered.

'You're Larry, the second-gen Dynaborg.'

'Huh? What?'

'A second-gen Dynaborg. D-Y-N-A-B-O-R-G. You told me so. How could you forget?'

'Are you awake?' He touched her forehead again. 'Salma, check her temperature.'

'You're Larry, the Last Appliance Running Radon Yag.'

The room was suddenly silent, except for the soft beeping from the ECG. Salma fished out a digital thermometer from her wide pocket and stuck it in Cory's ear. 'Slightly high. 37.2°C.'

'Now I'm really baffled,' Dr Lim looked at the ECG monitor. 'This is amazing. You look alert. You're lucid. Your BP is good. You seem normal. Yet, you appear to be in delirium.'

'Er, sorry, Dr Lim,' Mary asked with concern. 'She go mad?'

'Delirium is a state of mental confusion. I've never heard of patients in delirium being able to recognize people they haven't met before.'

'Larry, how could you forget?' Cory stared at him. 'Hang on. I believe my friends are waiting outside. Mama, are Gina, Angela, and Simi outside? Can we invite them here, Dr Lim? They are just dying to meet you, Larry. I told them everything about you over dinner.'

'This is getting weirder by the minute,' Dr Lim gulped. 'Your friends know me too? Sister Salma, can you call her friends in, please?

I want to witness this. Maybe record this and write to *Lancet*. It'll be the most controversial neurological case-study, ever.'

Salma rushed out of the room.

'Shh,' Mary patted Cory. 'Can't call Dr Lim "Larry". Show respect. He much older.'

'Don't worry, Mama,' Cory managed a laugh. 'Larry and I—we know each other well.'

'We do?' Dr Lim laughed. 'But then, nothing you've said so far rings a bell. Let's hear from your friends. Maybe they can shed some light.'

In a short while, the ICU door opened and the three ladies walked in with nurse Salma. They had their masks on, and Salma had briefed them to maintain social distancing.

Gina rushed to Cory but kept a distance. 'How are you, Cory? Thrilled to see you awake.'

'Thanks, buddies, for being here. I don't remember how I got here. Did I black out or something after our dinner?'

'We were planning a party on Jan 16 at my flat,' Gina said. 'We met for lunch on Friday at Star Vista, remember? You lost consciousness and fell off the chair, remember?'

'You're mistaken, Gina. We were having dinner in my apartment.'

'In your apartment? When was that?'

'*Aiyoh*, you forgot? Especially you, Angela? Your handsome Larry is here.'

Angela blushed. 'Sorry, what are you talking about, Cory? You're not mad, right?'

'We met in my flat a few days ago and had pizza and beer and chips. The four of us. I told you about Larry, Harry, Kerry, and Terry. What's wrong with you girls?'

'I think you need rest,' said Simi. 'What you're saying didn't happen.'

'Simi, how could you forget? You have a photographic memory. You had listed all the genocide events. Gina, you were working on a bacterium to digest plastic. And Angela, ha, well, you just wanted sex.'

'Now you're really embarrassing me, Cory,' Angela grimaced.

'Angela, you so wanted to meet Larry and Harry. Sorry I called you a nympho.'

'That's the weirdest thing I've heard,' said Angela. 'And the most scandalous.' She looked at Dr Lim, 'Doc, can you give Cory a sedative so she can go back to sleep?'

'Did she dream all this before she had the stroke?' Simi asked. 'Or after? Or just now?'

'This is getting quite intriguing,' Dr Lim laughed. 'I'm sure *Lancet* would love a case-study. Let's rewind. I told you about Dynaborgs and about my being what?'

'Yes, L-A-R-R-Y. That's short for Last Appliance Running Radon Yag. You're the last in the second-gen line. You made sense and I was so rude to you and the others. I'm so sorry.'

'Who're all of those guys?' Asked Dr Lim. 'Do their names also mean something?'

'I don't remember. I just remember you—and our long conversation in my bedroom.'

'I don't even know where you stay, Carmine. And I met you in your bedroom?'

'Can I ask you, Larry, to wake up . . . just as you told me to?'

'Shh,' Mary patted Cory. 'Don't call Dr Lim "Larry". Show some respect. He much older.'

'Never mind, Mary. As Cory says, we know each other well. I even went into her bedroom. Strange. When exactly was that? Do you remember the date or time?'

'You asked me to check the date on my phone. You told me I had slept for a straight twenty-hours hours. Don't you remember?'

'I don't. When do you think you met your friends for dinner at your apartment? Must have been quite recent, right?'

'Let me think . . .' Cory looked at her friends for support. Dr Lim gestured to them to keep quiet. 'I think we met on Friday, 7 Jan at night for dinner and drinks.'

'The ambulance brought you here that Friday afternoon,' Dr Lim said. 'I operated on you in the evening. It's now 9 p.m. on Sunday, 9 Jan. Does that make sense, Cory dear?'

'There you go, Larry,' Cory clasped his hand in delight. 'You just called me "Cory dear".'

'Er, sorry. Was I rude?'

'That's what you called me in my flat. I was so pissed with you then. I'm so sorry now.'

'You're not angry with me now?'

'Not any more. Now I have great respect for you. I love you, Larry.'

'Whoa!' Dr Lim recoiled in mock horror. 'This conversation is getting out of hand now.'

Cory smiled. 'It was only after talking to my three buddies here that I understood your message. That we must wake up and save our planet.'

'Er, and when did you talk to us?' asked Simi. 'We met on Friday for lunch at Star Vista.'

'D'you girls have amnesia or what? We met in my flat a couple of nights ago. I can remember our conversation clearly, how you could forget so quickly?'

'And what was that?' Asked Gina. 'That we're all Dynaborgs? What's that, by the way?'

'We discussed this before, Gina. Dynaborgs are humans with a modified DNA, like GM-foods. Larry and Rick are second-gens. They're on a mission to wake up third-gens like us. Simi, not yet.' She paused and looked at Dr Lim. 'How come, Larry?'

'How come what?'

'How come you missed Simi? Have you woken her up already?'

Dr Lim scratched his head. 'Er, I'm a simple, stupid neurologist. No clue about Dyna.'

'Come on, you're the one who educated me on Dynaborgs and our mission, Larry.'

'Shh,' Mary patted Cory. 'Cannot call Dr Lim "Larry". Show respect. He much older.'

Dr Lim laughed. 'I'm a neurosurgeon and I might need to get my head examined . . .'

'Can I ask a question?' Gina looked at Dr Lim. 'Could this be a side effect of Covid?'

Cory clapped. 'Good point. Larry, you told me I had the Singapore Strain of the virus. You also mentioned it was a positive side effect. D'you remember?'

'Er, Long Covid has side effects, but they're all negative. Singapore Strain?'

'You told me the Singapore Strain is new; not studied yet. That's what I guess you said.'

Dr Lim raised an arm. 'That's incorrect. The Singapore Strain was mentioned by news media as a subvariant of the Omicron strain. But it did not originate in Singapore.'

There was a moment's silence, broken by a loud sigh from Mary Chan.

Simi caught Dr Lim's eye. 'I have a biased question, sorry. I had read somewhere that left-handed people are more likely to suffer from alcoholism, dyslexia, schizophrenia.'

'No clinical relevance,' Dr Lim replied. 'In fact, left-handed people are better at divergent thinking and have better coordination skills.'

Cory yawned. 'Aww, don't be so pessimistic, guys. I think I need to wake you all up.'

'You contradict yourself,' said Dr Lim. 'You said I'm the one trying to wake you up.'

'But you refuse to believe you said so. Maybe you've gone back to your sleep state.'

'Which means you're not a Dynaborg yourself, right?' Asked Angela.

'Not yet. But you are, Angela, Gina, Larry. Simi and I are not.'

Gina crossed herself. 'Are you possessed by the Devil, Cory? Your weird behaviour and talking in tongues remind of Linda Blair in *The Exorcist.*'

'But my bed is not shaking, ha, ha,' Cory laughed. 'Ouch, my head hurts. Now, if you'll excuse me, I feel exhausted. I want to take a nap. Goodnight.'

# Chapter 6

## Tuesday, 11 January 2022

There is a joke that Singapore has three seasons—hot, hotter, hottest. Since Singapore is near the equator, it enjoys a tropical climate, with uniform temperatures, abundant rainfall, and high humidity all year. The only way residents can cool themselves is by using aircons.

Singapore's founding father, Mr Lee Kuan Yew, famously said in an interview published in the *New Perspectives Quarterly* winter 2010 issue that air conditioning was the most important invention for Singapore—and perhaps one of the most significant inventions in history. It changed the nature of civilization by making development possible in the tropics.

'Without air conditioning, you can work only in the cool early morning hours or at dusk,' they quoted Mr Lee. 'The first thing I did upon becoming prime minister was to install air conditioners in buildings where the civil service worked. This was key to public efficiency.'

It is not by chance that Singapore is called the 'air-conditioned nation' with aircons being ubiquitous in the city-state. It was only during the Covid-19 pandemic that the Singapore government urged offices, homes, and hospitals to open windows where possible to allow for fresh-air circulation to stem the spread of the virus.

Before they could discharge Cory, Dr Terence Lim arranged for a 'psychological consultation' to evaluate Cory's mental state. He wanted a top psychiatrist to assess her extraordinary symptoms. Dr Lim spoke with his buddy, Professor Wilson Tan, head of the Department of Psychiatry and Psychological Medicine at NUH. Dr Tan suggested they hold the session in the NUH garden, but Cory was unwilling to leave the air-conditioned comfort of her room.

Mary asked whether she and her husband could sit in to listen to the conversation.

'That's not recommended because Carmine will be self-conscious,' Dr Tan told the Chans. 'I will meet your daughter first and update you later. I prefer to meet her alone.'

'That's fine, Dr Tan,' Mark folded his hands. 'We hope you will cure her condition.'

NUH's Department of Psychiatry scheduled the meeting with Cory in her room at 4.30 p.m. on 11 January. Cory was not looking forward to it. However, Dr Terence Lim had insisted and had made it a precondition for her discharge. Cory had no choice but to agree to meet Dr Tan.

At 4.40 p.m., there was a knock at the door and an elderly man in a white lab coat entered.

'Ms Carmine Chan, I assume? May I come in? I'm Dr Wilson Tan.'

Cory sized him up like a lion assessing its prey. He was of medium height, had a shock of grey hair which resembled a storm cloud, and a sheaf of documents in a plastic folder under his arm. A stethoscope hung around his neck and four pens adorned his coat pocket like medals of honour. A whiff of antiseptic wafted through the door as he entered, announcing his presence as a doctor. Cory couldn't see his whole face as he was wearing a surgical mask.

'So, you're the shrink who's going to evaluate me?' Cory asked nonchalantly.

'You may call me that,' he chuckled softly, a sound that was meant to convey empathy and understanding but sounded more like a rehearsed gesture of politeness. 'But not just any shrink. Top shrink. Head of the Department at NUH.'

'To what do I owe this honour? Is it because I pissed off Larry? I mean, Dr Lim?'

'You present strange symptoms that seems inexplicable. Dr Lim gave me an overview and I'm intrigued by your experience. Could you please explain it to me? I'm here only to listen.'

He pulled a chair closer to the bed. 'I'm going to remove my mask. Is that okay with you?'

'Absolutely. I was wondering how to have a conversation with a masked ranger.'

'Ha, good one!' he laughed. Cory thought this one was genuine. 'Waiting to hear your story.'

Cory studied his features from close up, looking for a chink in his armour. Clean shaven, maybe in his sixties, professorial dignity. She had to try to puncture that façade to see how he would react to being challenged on his own ground. 'You can have a good laugh at me, and I can see your smile or smirk while you label me as being delusional or mad.'

'I'm not here to judge you. You're attaching labels against my name. Is that being fair?'

'I'm being realistic. Maybe I'm delusional, maybe I'm hallucinating, maybe I am mad.'

'I'm here to learn from you, Carmine,' he gently touched her hand. 'I know you're very sharp and observant, so here's the deal. I'll try to answer your questions about psychology and psychiatry honestly, and you'll tell me what happened, also equally honestly. Deal?'

Cory perked up. Maybe he wasn't such a bad guy after all. 'Okay.'

Dr Tan waved his hand. 'You go first.'

'Okay, what's a delusion? What's a hallucination? Are they symptoms of a deranged mind?'

'Too many questions,' he smiled. 'Let me simplify it for you. A delusion is a false belief which you can't shake off. A hallucination is something you see, hear, or feel that isn't there. They may seem real to you, but they're not. Don't worry about them.'

'Why not?'

'Well, they could be caused by an underlying medical or mental problem. But I'm not here to diagnose you, just to listen and understand, okay?'

'I didn't understand all of that,' Cory grimaced. 'Give me examples later. Your turn. You wanted to know what I experienced, right? A tall guy who looked like Dr Lim came to my room one night and wanted me to join the Dynaborgs to save the Earth. No one believes me. They say it never happened. I'm crazy, right?'

'Can we dig a little deeper? The word, Dynaborg, is that something you read about?'

'Never heard that word before. I'm a software engineer. I rarely read sci-fi. I'm a nerd.'

'Aren't we all, dear? I'm also a nerd. My life, my hobbies, my interests revolve around medicine, psychiatry, and medical literature, period. I'm an all-work, no-play kinda guy.'

'You're kidding.'

'Have you read *The Geeks Shall Inherit the Earth* by Alexandra Robbins? It's about how nerds rule the world. The things that make you weird in school make you awesome later.'

Cory raised her index finger, slighted at being accused of not reading enough, as though that were a crime. 'Correction, Dr Tan, I read books, although not much sci-fi, except I liked to read Isaac Asimov when I was young. Point noted that we're both alike. My turn. Psychosis?'

'Psychosis is when you can't tell reality from imagination. Like feeling watched, poisoned, lied to, plotted against, or loved secretly. It's a wrong way of seeing things. Psychosis can mess up your life.'

'Is that me?'

'I don't know, and I don't want to judge. I'm just curious about what you saw. Psychosis can happen once or more often. It can be caused by a brain problem, like an aneurysm, a bulge in a blood vessel that bursts and causes a stroke. Or something else. Or maybe it was true—what you saw, but I don't judge. It was real to you.'

'It felt real because I remember it so well. Like a slow movie in my head. But I agree some elements may seem impossible. Such as somebody popping up in my bedroom almost every night. Or me sleeping for twenty-four hours straight. Or Larry being an acronym for something more profound. Maybe I'm a psycho.'

Dr Tan tapped her shoulder. 'You're connecting the dots too fast. Slow down.'

Cory wiped a tear. 'I didn't make up Dynaborgs or the Singapore Strain. How could I know they woke up 12 million? How could I know

Dr Lim's nickname was Larry? How did I imagine my friends Gina, Angela, and Simi were at my flat when I was here? Explain that.'

'I can't. That's why your case is so fascinating. You experienced something amazing. Let's try and figure it out together. You want to join a cause to save the Earth's biodiversity? That's noble. The Dynaborg part? A mystery, right?'

Cory stroked her chin. 'Is there a label for my condition? Am I going mad?'

'I don't like labels because they limit us. But I'll give you one to consider: Charles Bonnet Syndrome. It makes people with eye problems see things that aren't there. Glaucoma, cataracts, macular degeneration can cause this. It may seem real, but eventually you realize it's not. Does that ring a bell?'

'Maybe. But then, how do you explain the long conversations I had with Larry? And Terry, Kerry, Perry?'

'Let's try this. Let's call them Larry. You recall the whole conversation, right? That's called vivid dreams. Vivid, because they feel real. Dreams, because they're not real. Vivid dreams occur just before you wake up. Some like to call this the twilight zone.'

'Did I briefly live in a parallel universe? Had multiple vivid dreams? Every night?'

'Maybe it was one dream where everything got mixed up in your mind. Your aneurysm could make your brain do weird things.'

Cory paused to ponder. 'What about the food and drinks with my friends? Same dream?'

'That's more basic—food and drink. You dream of food when you're hungry. Like you dream of peeing. Then you wake up and find your bladder is full and you need to go.'

'I recollect I had a kinda fight with Angela. You think I hurt her in my dream?'

'Follow me. Dr Lim said you called Angela a nymphomaniac. The men who visited you were tall, strong, handsome. Like food, sex is a primal need, a strong drive.'

Cory mulled that over, feeling a knot of confusion in her stomach. If she called Angela a nymphomaniac in her dream, why should Angela be offended? Was this psycho doctor insinuating that she was juxtaposing her sexual needs on Angela by proxy? Cory felt a wave of indignation and wondered if he was trying to manipulate her or help her.

Dr Tan stood up. 'I'm going to get some tea from that pot over there. Do you want some?'

'No. I just had some before you came.'

Dr Tan took one of the three inverted ceramic cups and poured himself Chinese Oolong tea from a tall flask. The aroma from the beverage wafted across the room. With his back to her, he asked Cory, 'A personal question. Do you have a boyfriend or a girlfriend? Was his name Larry or something close?'

*A ha, here we go again*, she sniggered. Trying to ferret out information about her sexual life. Should she lie or tell him the truth? Cory decided to come clean. 'No link. My ex was an Indian from Mumbai. His name was Prem Pujari.'

'Got it.' Dr Tan walked back, pulled the chair closer and sipped from the cup. 'Your other point—trying to save the Earth's biodiversity—that's on everyone's mind. We read so much about it; it has become part of our subconscious, which comes up when we dream.'

Cory's eyes glazed over. Dr Tan caught that.

'Bored? Impatient? Want tea to relax? Cool water should help.' He didn't wait for her response. He poured water from the jug into a glass and gave it to her. She gulped it down.

'That feels good. Thank you.' She closed her eyes. 'Am I hallucinating? Is this real?'

He patted her arm; this was real. Cory knew that gesture was meant to convey affection and validation but dismissed it as a routine response from a shrink. He would listen with an open mind and a compassionate heart, but keep a distance, like a lifeguard watching over a swimmer. He was there to help, not get involved; trained to be professional, not personal.

'Hallucinations are often a sign of other problems, like brain tumours, schizophrenia, and so on. Hallucinations depend on where in the brain the problem is. If it's in the vision area, you may see spots, shapes, and light flashes. In other areas, you may smell weird things or taste metal. If you can't smell, you can't taste. You had Covid-19 Delta variant; you know that.'

'Glad you reminded me. Now I'd like to smell and taste some tea.'

Dr Tan went to the desk. The aroma of the acerbic Oolong tea filled the room. 'By the way, your surgery was for an aneurysm, not a tumour.'

'Sorry for taking up your time,' Cory folded her hands. Dr Tan clasped them in his.

'Don't be. We're friends now. We trust each other, don't we?' His eyes bored into her. It was as though he could see straight through her body into her soul. She felt exposed and vulnerable, like a butterfly pinned to a board. She tried to look away, but his gaze was firm, drawing her in. He seemed to know everything about her—her secrets, her fears, her desires.

'We do, I guess,' Cory blinked. *Was he joking?*

'I'm not joking,' he'd read her mind. 'I'm taking your story very seriously.'

'I have a headache, it comes suddenly. It's like I'm on my period, which I'm not.'

He touched her forehead. 'Migraines and schizophrenia and auras. Ever heard of them.'

'I've had migraines before, but no auras. Schizophrenia sounds scary.'

'Don't worry, I'm just explaining. Migraines can cause visual hallucinations, like seeing halos around people's heads. Schizophrenia can cause all kinds of hallucinations, like hearing voices or smelling things. Crazy, right?'

'You're hinting I'm crazy? I'm left-handed. Does that make me crazy?'

Dr Tan held up both hands. 'No, no. You're left-handed. So are Obama, Oprah, and Einstein. Nothing wrong with that.'

'Then why do I see things that others don't?'

'That's what we shall try to figure out. Together.' He checked his phone. 'And now, I must leave. I have other patients waiting.'

Cory squeezed his hand. 'You're an honest man. I want to trust you, confide in you.'

Dr Tan stood up. 'I'll get my secretary to fix up another appointment with you. Here's a tip, maintain a diary. Write down everything about Dynaborgs, your thoughts, your feelings, whatever. Paper, laptop, phone, doesn't matter. Just write. No self-diagnosis. No judgements. No labels.'

Dr Tan shook her hand with both of his and walked over to switch off the room's light. The dull glow from the window was enough. He gently opened the door and left the room.

Cory closed her eyes and took a deep breath. The room was quiet, except for the low hum from the aircon. It had started raining. The rhythmic hum of the aircon and the pitter-patter of raindrops against the windowpane lulled her to sleep.

She didn't know whether she was hallucinating or falling sick. She heard church bells in the distance signalling the end of Mass, followed by the tinkle of breaking glass. She dreamt she was climbing and falling off an ark—and woke up with a start.

There was a soft knock at the door; somebody opened it. A tall man with a peaked cap and a long coat stood in silhouette against the dim, yellow light from the hall that obscured his face.

'Who are you?' She braced herself.

'Hi, I'm Larry.'

\* \* \*

Long before the first White man set foot in the Americas, Native Americans carved images on rocks and other materials to tell stories about their lives and culture. At the very top was the symbol for the triangle—which represented the *tepee*—or home of the family.

The large triangular tepee held many smaller triangles, which symbolized extended family members, other tribe members, or the children who would grow up and form their own tepee. Since many tribes embraced the idea that all living beings were interconnected or related to each other, depictions like these expressed the oneness of all beings under one roof.

For thousands of years, the indigenous peoples called the Creeks inhabited the area that's now called the State of Georgia in south-eastern United States. Standing Peachtree, a Creek village where the creek flows into the Chattahoochee River, was the closest Native American settlement in what is now Atlanta. Through the early nineteenth century, European settlers encroached on the Creek of northern Georgia, forcing the Native Americans out. Under the Indian Removal Law by the US Federal Government, the Creek left the area in 1821—and European American settlers occupied their land.

In 1959, the Research Triangle Park (RTP) was created to boost high-tech innovation, with three educational institutions—Duke University, North Carolina State University, and the University of North Carolina at Chapel Hill—bordering it. The RTP was in a pine forest area and spanned 7,000 acres with 22.5 million square feet of built-up space; it was home to 330 companies that employed some 60,000 workers.

One of those companies was JQL Corp. One of those workers was Ricardo 'Rick' Ramsey, a Georgia native who could trace his roots back 100 years when his grandfather was bought as a slave from Africa by Joshua John Ward of Georgetown County, South Carolina.

Dubbed 'the king of the rice planters', Mr Ward owned 1,092 slaves in 1850, making him the largest slaveholder in the US before he died in 1853. In 1860, his estate held 1,130 slaves. The estate now bordered the railway tracks where five Amtrak lines—Silver Meteor, Silver Star, Palmetto, Carolinian, and Piedmont routes—served the Research Triangle.

Rick lived in a house near the railway tracks and loved the shrill notes—steel on steel—that the trains made. He had dozed off at about midnight after partying with friends. He heard sounds of train engines roaring past, followed by the sound of breaking glass.

'Whoa?' His mobile phone had vibrated and fallen from the bed but had not cracked. Rick picked up the phone and wondered who the hell would be calling him.

'Ricardo?' Matthew McKenna, his immediate boss, was at the other end. Matt insisted on calling him Ricardo even when everyone else called him Rick.

'Yes, Matt?' Getting a call from your boss on the last day of a week-long vacation was not a good sign. Rick felt his palms go clammy. Had he screwed up? 'What's up?'

'You were supposed to be back at work yesterday. Are you ill, Ricardo?'

'Good Lord!' Rick was suddenly alert. 'I totally forgot. Today's Monday?'

'Today's Tuesday, 11 Jan,' replied Matt. 'Why didn't you show up yesterday?'

'Sorry, my bad. I forgot about my leave having ended Sunday.'

'You just forgot? What the—?'

'No, no. I needed to rest since I got back from SF. Been ill. Fever, chills, cough.'

'Get the hell outta your house and get checked for Covid! You had it once before, right?'

'Nah, don't think it's that,' Rick pretended to cough. 'Been there, had that.'

The lie was a double-edged sword—either Matt would sense it and pile on to him, or he would believe it and offer Rick a couple of more days off—to recuperate. His fib worked.

'Do you wanna take a couple of days off?' Matt asked. 'Get back to work Thursday?'

'That would be awesome, man. Thanks a ton, Matt.'

'I want you to get yourself checked for Covid-19 first. Don't come in and infect us.'

'Got that, boss.'

'Great. I got a coupla stuff that need discussing first thing when you get in.'

'Oh?' Rick felt his stomach tighten. 'Like what? You want to gimme a hint, please?'

'I want you to go see a goddamn doc first. Then get Malia to fix an appointment with me.'

He hung up.

Rick closed his eyes. He wondered whether Malia, Matt's secretary, would call him, or if he should call her first. She was business-like, pretty, petite, but always preoccupied. He wondered whether she had a boyfriend.

Rick slammed his fist on the desk. How could he have forgotten that he was supposed to join work today? He should stop boozing; it was making him forgetful. But first he needed a stiff drink. He'd also have to find a doc, get tested and produce a Covid-negative certificate.

His mobile phone buzzed. Maybe it was Malia. Rick slid his index finger impatiently on his iPhone. It was an unknown number. Rick took the call. 'Who's this?'

'This is Gina from Singapore. Is that Rick?'

'Yes. How come you're calling from an unknown number?'

'I'm calling you from my IP-phone, it won't show my number. Can we talk? Our good friend, Cory, had a stroke. She's warded in NUH. She's kinda lost her mind.'

'Carmine? She's too young to have a stroke.'

'Had brain surgery. She woke up and said we're all infected with a new DNA virus.'

'We?'

'You're a second-gen Dynamite or Dynaborg or Dynashit. Angela and I are third-gen.'

Rick let that sink in for a while. He felt a surge of anger and confusion, a mix of emotions that made him clench his fists and grind his teeth. He had no idea what the word meant, but he sensed it was something derogatory and offensive. He wanted to retaliate with a witty comeback, but he also felt insecure and ignorant. He hoped that whatever he said would hide his uncertainty and hurt, but he also wondered if it would expose his vulnerability and weakness.

'I've been called an asshole, a nigger, a Black bastard,' he told Gina calmly and clearly, 'but never anything so profound.'

# PART II

# Chapter 7

**Thursday, 13 January 2022**

Rick arrived early at East Cornwallis, where JQL Corp hosted a vast campus at the RTP. JQL, one of the pioneer companies at the RTP, had set up operations there in 1969. The RTP now housed JQL software, engineering, retail, finance, and global services. Rick specialized in selling retail and finance solutions to large enterprises like banks and hospital chains.

He tapped his ID card at the entrance of an adjoining building and rushed to the mens' room to relieve himself. He washed his hands and ran his fingers through his hair. He remembered watching a video which postulated that your hair and attire could determine how much people empathized with you. There was one other reason to look smart: Malia.

He also wore his favourite sky-blue shirt. A colour-wheeling expert on YouTube had suggested blue shirts were ideal for inspiring a sense of confidence. Rick needed to feel confident today; he wasn't sure what brick Matt wanted to throw at him. On the other hand, if Matt was going to give him good news, then blue would inspire him to trust Rick's potential.

His smartwatch showed 8.30 a.m. His meeting with Matt was thirty minutes away. Rick went to his desk to see if anyone had left anything for him—documents, snail mail, flyers. A few people were on the phone at their desks; he didn't know them. Many were 'hot-desking' and others were working from home. He powered on his laptop and cleared a dozen emails.

At 8.45 a.m., Rick slicked back his hair, puffed out his chest and stood before Malia.

'Morning.'

'Welcome back,' Malia smiled. 'Blue shirt. Blue tie. Blue jeans. In uniform today?'

'Symmetry,' he laughed. His eye caught a glint in her hair. Nestled in her small afro was a tiny rose, so small he had to squint to see it. 'Nice. Is that a flower in your hair?'

'It's a tiny, red rose.' She shuffled papers on her desk. 'What'd you do to upset the boss?'

Rick was suddenly alarmed. 'I've no clue, really. What'd I do? Am I really screwed?'

She gave him a sidelong glance. 'He's in a foul mood this morning.'

'Does he get to work so early every day?'

'Only if he has meetings or con-calls. He has both today.'

Her desk phone buzzed.

Rick marveled at her efficiency. She kept her desk uncluttered. A ceramic vase in a corner held a single stalk of a purple coneflower, a common flower found across south-east US.

Just then, the door to Matt's cabin opened.

'Ricardo, welcome back,' Matt's booming voice resonated across. 'How's your health?'

'Morning, Matt,' Rick returned the smile. 'Good to be back. I'm good. I needed the rest.'

Matt ushered him inside and closed the door. Rick liked Matt, a middle-level manager in a major MNC who was aware of his standing and importance in the organization. Matt knew he was an asset to the company, a leader who could handle multiple projects and teams with efficiency and skill. He impressed his superiors with his results and his subordinates with his guidance, but he also felt the growing pressure of delivering results, quarter after quarter.

'We need you to be in a fit condition,' said Matt. 'Take a seat. Let me shut this,' he closed his laptop. 'Did you have Covid-19 or the flu? Or did you lie to get two extra days off?'

Rick blinked and coughed. How the hell did Matt know he had been fibbing? 'I really—'

'I was kidding, you don't have to answer that.'

'Jeez, you got me there, man.'

'I have some news for you. From White Plains.'

Rick gulped. White Plains, New York, was JQL's global headquarters. White Plains only called when you screwed up big time. 'I'm not sure what I did—'

'It's not true that you get a call from HQ only when you screw up,' Matt read his mind again. 'They also call to recognize your work. So, chill. You didn't screw up, not big time, not yet.'

Rick ran his fingers through his hair. 'Phew, I thought I was getting fired.'

'You're getting a promotion. HQ wants to know if you'd like to lead product sales for a new line of solutions in retail and e-commerce, your specialty. Are you ready to step up?'

'Is this a new position? Why me?'

'Why not? Not a new position. They fired the guy running it last week. You get a 50 per cent wage hike, relocation allowance, and a three-month probation to learn the ropes.'

Rick didn't respond. He saw two women walk past the window, bracing themselves against the cold.

'HQ wants to test you for two weeks—if you're interested in the position, that is.'

'Do I fit the job description?'

'If you didn't, I wouldn't waste my time talking to you,' Matt showed his irritation. 'I recommended your name. HQ has your file. They know you. You want to miss this, bro?'

'When do I need to decide?'

'In a week. Get Malia to coordinate with HR to arrange the logistics to stay two weeks. My suggestion would be to get your ass to NYC ASAP. You're probably the only candidate.'

Rick didn't respond. Matt's desk phone rang; he picked it up. Rick looked out the window at the barren trees. January is a cold month in

Atlanta, with average temperatures varying between 39°F (4.3°C) and 54°F (12°C). Rick hated the cold. New York would be a lot colder.

Matt hung up. 'Something bugging you?'

'I'm not sure I want to move to New York.'

'Great. I'll tell them you're not—'

'Hang on, boss. It's a big decision. It's all too sudden. Can I sleep on it?'

'That's what I said, bro,' Matt's face turned red. 'Talk to Malia. Talk to HR. Get to NYC. Meet the hiring manager. Try it out for two weeks, then decide. Not sending you to Alaska.'

The meeting was over. Matt flipped open the laptop lid; he had no time for pleasantries.

That noon, Rick noticed Malia at the JQL cafeteria line, waiting for her turn to choose items from the food bays. 'Hi, there,' Rick waved at her. 'Anything good today?'

Malia smiled, shuffling forward with everyone else in the queue. 'The usual.'

'Yeah,' he laughed. 'The usual. Every day's *Groundhog Day.*'

'Care to join me at that table?'

'Thought you'd never ask.'

As soon as he had settled down with a couple of sandwiches, Rick pulled out a sachet of sauce from his trouser pocket. 'Chinese garlic-chilli sauce,' he announced. 'Real hot, real spicy.'

Malia looked surprised as she dug into her pasta. 'You carry that in your pocket?'

Rick carefully squeezed the sachet and spread the fiery-red paste evenly between his sandwiches. 'I got addicted to this when I visited Singapore. I bought sixty sachets.'

'Singapore? You mean the one in Michigan?' Malia asked eagerly.

'I didn't know there's a Singapore in Michigan. I went to the one in Asia, near Malaysia.'

'I grew up in Michigan. I studied at the Saugatuck High School in the town of Singapore.'

'D'you know JQL has a big office in Singapore in Asia?'

Loud noises coming from the corner of the cafeteria distracted their attention. Rick stood up to see what was going on. Two men seemed to be having a loud argument and soon came to blows. The cafeteria was quite empty and nobody dared to intervene.

'Somebody call security!' A woman yelled at the staff. 'This is gettin' outta hand.'

Without thinking, Rick sprang up and ran to the corner. Two others had also rushed to stop the fight. The two combatants were either drunk or high on drugs and were in a fistfight. One of them dashed to the counter. He grabbed a cooking knife. He lunged at the other guy.

The third guy who was trying to break up the fight was in front of the other guy. The guy with the knife drew back and leapt at his enemy—and missed. He couldn't control the momentum and the knife plunged into the third guy's abdomen instead, who toppled backwards, writhing in pain. Rick got to the injured man just in time—and helped ease him to the floor.

That man was Matt.

\* \* \*

The Genome Institute of Singapore (GIS) was set up in June 2000. Dr Edison Liu, who was director of the Division of Clinical Sciences at the National Cancer Institute in Bethesda, Maryland, was its first executive director. In October 2003, GIS moved to its own research building—aptly named *Genome*—a 7,200-square-metre facility and part of the health-sciences cluster of buildings in an area also aptly named *Biopolis*.

Gina Gonzales had received excellent training and coaching as an intern at GIS. She was keen to join the GIS Fellows' Programme, specially structured for young scientists who wanted to drive their own research projects that would subsequently integrate into the larger GIS structure. However, a German firm, Genome Germanica GmbH (G3) had made her an offer she couldn't refuse. They would pay for her to do a doctorate in genome sequencing at the NUS, as well as sponsor annual trips to major genomics conferences around the world.

Gina pulled into the underground parking lot in her white, 1.2-litre Mitsubishi Attrage. She angled the car's panel mirror and applied a thin layer of pink lipstick. Her spectacles seemed to give her a scholarly look and made her flat ponytail look a little less bland. She slipped on her face mask. Nobody had to know she was wearing lipstick, right?

'Wrong,' a voice said as her door hit somebody walking by. 'Wrong to open the door before checking if anyone is behind you.'

'Oops! Sorry, so sorry!' Gina blinked, then blushed. It was George Gan, one of the senior scientists at G3. His reputation preceded him as a dour, tough-talking, sceptical scholar who liked to be left alone. 'Hope you didn't get hurt, Dr Gan?'

'I did,' George adjusted his mask and smirked. 'Your door hit my chest.'

Gina whisked her bag from the rear seat. 'I'm sorry. You startled me when you suddenly appeared out of nowhere.'

'Oh, so now it's my fault?'

'No, mine,' she said. George couldn't see her face going red. 'I'm so very embarrassed.'

They cleared the Covid-19 security protocols and waited for the lift with a couple of others.

'All okay in Manila?'

Gina guessed he was trying to make small talk. 'All is well—in Singapore and Manila,' Gina combed her fingers through her ponytail. 'I have more relatives in Minnesota than in Manila. My sister and my cousin work as nurses in a hospital there.'

'Manila is the nursing capital of the world,' George blinked. 'I mean, nurse capital.'

'Call it whatever you want. Philippines graduates the most nurses in the world. If they stop exporting nurses, many healthcare systems in the developed world could collapse.'

'Including Singapore,' he said wryly. 'You know this, right? Two years ago, interns started an online petition for schools to teach Tagalog to final-year med students. It was a joke and sent out on April Fool's Day. Yet, 400 med students signed the petition.'

Gina wondered why George was being so friendly with her. Was something cooking? Did he know about some new development in the company involving her?

G3's office was designed as a sleek and spacious environment, a place that reflected the cutting-edge and innovative nature of the biotech industry. It had a minimalist and futuristic design, with white walls, glass partitions and chrome accents. It was equipped with state-of-the-art tech such as smart boards, touch screens, and biometric scanners. It also had plants, natural light, and ergonomic furniture to create a healthy, easy atmosphere for the staff.

Later that day, Gina received a call from her boss to attend an urgent meeting. That was odd because nothing was 'urgent' in their nature of work. Gina bundled her laptop and was surprised to see her colleague from the next-gen sequencing wing, Dr Chika Nakamura.

Before they could exchange pleasantries, the door opened and George Gan walked in, followed by the director of research, Dr Ken Miles. Ken was one of G3's initial employees and had risen through the ranks to lead Asia-Pacific R&D. He had a shock of grey hair and was reputed to have never lost his temper.

'I know you're surprised, so am I,' said Ken as they sat around the oblong table. 'I just received this invite in my inbox. The Nippon Genetics Institute is organizing a closed-door conference to discuss next-gen sequencing of non-human organisms. As you know, we've been collaborating with them for a couple of years now. They're holding this seminar and have invited research fellows from a dozen countries. Can the three of you attend in person?'

'Why us?' Asked George in irritation, making Chika and Gina turn and look at him in astonishment. 'Ken, you already know I have a ton of work. I'm not keen to travel.'

'It's in your field of study,' Ken pointed at him, 'and you're the senior-most scientist here.'

'Why not us?' Gina shot back at George.

'Yes, why not us?' Demanded Chika. 'I'd love to go to Tokyo—and visit my parents as well.'

'I have a ton of work to complete here,' George protested. 'Doesn't Japan have any travel restrictions? They still have a lot of Covid cases. I'd rather not go.'

'We've cleared that part with the Japanese,' said Ken. 'Are you guys ready to go?'

'We are!' Gina and Chika said in unison.

'How come no virtual log-in?' Asked George. 'Most seminars are hybrid.'

Gina had wondered why he was being friendly earlier today. It was obvious he was a paranoid person. She had found him odd and distant before, but now he seemed to be pale and weary, with sunken eyes and a pinched face hidden behind an N95 mask.

'Not hybrid, this one,' said Ken. 'They want to discuss multi-country collaboration at an in-person event. Either you go and attend the event, or you don't.'

'When is the seminar?' Asked Chika eagerly. 'Can I plan some leave after that?'

'Jan 20 to 23, which is next week. Jan 20 is the pre-event dinner, which is compulsory.'

'Didn't know dinners were compulsory,' Gina laughed. 'I love Japanese food. I'm in.'

'Didn't know you loved Japan so much,' Chika smiled. 'I'm glad I'm going home with you.'

'Didn't know I would be going with two teenage girls,' George frowned. 'Can I drop out?'

# Chapter 8

## Friday, 14 January 2022

Right from a young age, Angela Ang had been interested in cars. Her dad, Alex Ang, worked in a car dealership and would often bring his bubbly daughter along on school holidays and encourage her to meet the 'boys' who fixed broken vehicles or sold used automobiles.

Customers and prospects loved to humour the little kid, who was always giggling and giving funny tips on how to choose new cars or fix broken ones. The owner encouraged Alex to get his 'angel' to come to the dealership whenever she had time to spare. It helped spur car sales—and it also helped boost Alex's worth in the company.

However, Alex and his wife were strict with Angela, their only surviving child, when it came to her studies. Alex insisted she complete her A levels in Singapore—which she did in physics and maths—as a precondition to sponsoring her for a master's in automobile engineering.

After scouring through dozens of university programmes— and their stiff fees—Angela zeroed in on a master's programme in automotive engineering at the University of Hertfordshire in England. The tuition fees were affordable at £10,000 per annum and the school allowed students with a STEM (science, technology, engineering, maths) degree to apply; they didn't need to have background knowledge in engineering. The school had an excellent automotive centre, with engine-test facilities and a workshop to tinker with cars. Angela liked aerospace engineering and switched her major from automobile to aeronautical.

She was lucky to land an engineering internship at the Rolls-Royce manufacturing facility in Goodwood in England. Incidentally, Vickers

PLC, the corporate parent of Rolls-Royce, had sold the company to BMW for £340 million in 1998.

The company subsequently offered Angela a full-time job at its Singapore aerospace facility. Rolls-Royce had been present in Singapore since 1950 and was now the company's regional centre for its civil aerospace power-systems businesses, defence, and R&D. In 2006, the Singapore government gave Rolls-Royce the Distinguished Partner in Progress award, the nation's highest corporate honour.

Angela got an offer from Pistonex Systems, a London-based parts supplier to Rolls Royce and other engineering companies. She was delighted to join 500 other employees to work at the company's test-and-assembly facility at Seletar in north-east Singapore.

This Friday morning, as she settled into her desk, a colleague touched her arm. 'Big boss is looking for you,' he said. 'Asked for you twice.'

'I don't remember screwing up anything,' Angela scratched her head. 'I didn't get any message on my phone either. I'll go right after I finish checking on these components.'

She wondered whether it had something to do with her leave—she had taken more days off earlier in the year. Perhaps somebody from her team might have cribbed to the boss. Or had the boss noticed her slacking off, texting friends on social media? It was rare to be called by the vice president of Engineering; her direct boss, the director of Critical Components, reported to the VP of Engineering. Whatever it was, she had to face the music.

Angela quickly completed checking the first batch of engine parts and components, then went to the ladies' to comb her hair before knocking softly on the VP's heavy, teak door.

Wong Tew Kiat, a portly man in his late fifties, beckoned her in through the glass screen.

'Sorry if I'm late, Mr Wong,' Angela began, 'didn't know you were looking for me.'

'Take a seat. How are you doing? How's the work going?' Wong had been with Pistonex for more than two decades, having risen from being an intern with a degree in mechanical engineering and graduating through the ranks to lead the engineering function in Asia.

'All good, thank you. Sorry, had to take extra days off. One of my friends was in NUH.'

'Oh?' Wong looked up over the rim of his spectacles. 'Covid? Hope he's okay now?'

'She. Apparently, she had a stroke or something. NUH did brain surgery. Recovering.'

'Good, not Covid.'

'She had that, too, some months ago. She recovered.'

'Your friend seems to be rather accident prone?'

Angela grimaced. *None of your business. Come to the point, buster.*

'I called you for something important.' Wong ran through his touchscreen monitor.

Angela waited for him to continue. She scanned the clutter on his desk. He had files, documents, and research reports scattered around his keyboard and large monitor. She had read somewhere that a cluttered desktop was a sign of a creative person.

Wong cleared his throat. 'Is your calendar free during the week of Jan 24?'

'Chinese New Year—'

'CNY is on Feb 1 and 2, don't worry. You should be back by then.'

'Back?'

'I want you to go to London. Engineering update meeting for department heads on Jan 25 and 26. Before you ask why not send your supervisor, he's the one who recommended you. He has more urgent stuff to take care of here. Are you ready to fly out next week?'

Angela could barely contain her excitement but didn't want the big boss to see it. Her mind raced at the possibilities. Was she being considered for a promotion? Was her immediate supervisor on his way out? She'd heard rumours of his recent sloppiness.

Wong was studying her intently. 'Why the hesitation?'

'Er, just wondering if it'd be freezing in London?'

'You studied in Britain, right?'

'I have sufficient warm clothing,' Angela quickly corrected herself. 'This is rather sudden. Do you want an answer from me right now? Can I look at the agenda, please?'

'I'll email you the details,' Wong stood up. The meeting was over. 'Get our travel desk to handle your flight and hotel. You'll meet engineers from a bunch of other countries.'

'I have one question,' Angela hesitated at the door. 'Do I need to present an update?'

'You need to figure out which critical updates we need to deploy and how soon. Got it?'

Angela nodded. This was something someone at a VP level would need to figure out. How should she know which critical updates they would need to fix? Something was amiss for sure.

'I know what you're thinking. Critical updates are not your call. Just get the updates, okay?'

Angela resisted the urge to do a mini dance at this surprise working vacation.

Later that evening, Angela was in a celebratory mood despite being tired from work. She planned to call a couple of colleagues and gossip about office politics over a glass of wine, but later decided against it. She still had a ton of work to get done and loose ends to fix before she could fly out. And she wasn't sure which of her colleagues would bitch behind her back.

There was a slight drizzle on the way home. Angela had forgotten to bring her collapsible umbrella along. By the time she reached her car in the open car park, she was drenched. The drive from the Pistonex Campus in Seletar to Bullion Park Condominium in Yishun took fifteen minutes. The car park in Bullion Park was also open-air. She would get soaked again. Hell. Just then, she saw an elderly security guard with an umbrella walk towards her car.

'Shall I lend you an umbrella, miss?' The balding security guard shouted to be heard.

'Ah, it's okay, Mani,' she waved her free hand. 'Don't bother. I'll just run to my block.'

'It's no trouble, miss,' he ambled closer to her car door. 'I'm happy to help.'

He held the umbrella for her. She picked up her bag and clutched it to her chest. He walked her to the foyer in Tower 5. She could see that he was also dripping wet. For a moment she wondered why he'd taken the trouble to go out of his way to help her. Would he have done this favour if she were a male? Or less pretty? Was he ogling her? He didn't seem to be doing so.

'Thank you so much, Mani,' she said in the foyer. 'Wait here. Shall I get you a towel?'

'No need, miss,' Mani tipped his umbrella. 'I go change. Don't worry. Bye.'

Angela made a mental note to slip him a few dollars and a fresh towel the next time she saw him. She stepped into the lift and stuffed her phone and car keys into her tote bag. It had been a busy day and she couldn't wait to get into her apartment and take a hot shower.

On the third floor, the lift stopped. A woman whom Angela had never seen before stepped in.

Was she a new tenant? Unlikely, as she didn't walk with the uncertain air of a newbie. She smelled of cheap perfume and sashayed in confidently on strappy black heels, her short dark sundress bouncing about in a way that made Angela immediately find her distasteful.

The woman huffed and stared at Angela. 'You're wet,' she declared.

'Yes, heavy rain,' Angela grimaced. 'You're new here, right?'

'I'm old, you're new,' she laughed, catching Angela off-guard. 'I'm fifty. You look thirty.'

'Good one,' Angela forced a laugh. 'I meant, did you move into this condo recently?'

'I'm old, age-wise and condo-wise. My husband and I moved in twelve years ago, Tower 1. We recently moved into Tower 5. I'm now going to meet my friend on the twelfth floor. You?'

'I moved in two years ago,' said Angela. The lift stopped at the twelfth level and the lady stepped out. She held her foot at the door. 'You, which floor?' She waited for Angela's reply.

'I'm on fifteenth,' Angela lied. 'Bye.' She pressed the key for the door to close.

'You on fifteenth?' She raised an eyebrow, keeping her foot in place, preventing the lift door from closing. 'Same floor where man jumped last month?'

'Oh, is it?' Angela shook her head. 'I didn't know that.'

'Now you do,' she let the doors close. 'Take care, young lady. Don't jump.'

\* \* \*

Many in the 'agroceuticals' world may have heard of companies like Syngenta, with annual sales of $14 billion and HQ in Switzerland. Or BASF, the largest producer of chemicals in the world, with revenues of €79 billion and HQ in Germany. Or Bayer, another German giant with annual revenues of €44 billion. It bought Monsanto in 2018 for $66 billion.

However, few would have heard of Pollenta, a low-key genomics and biopharma data-analytics company with dual headquarters in Cambridge, Massachusetts, and Cambridge, UK. Simi Sundar had been working with Pollenta for the last six years. She started in their pharma department as a data intern and moved up the career ladder to head the department.

Pollenta's data scientists collated, scrubbed, and analysed hundreds of terabytes of organic and inorganic data generated daily by chemical, agricultural, and pharmaceutical companies the world over. They sought analysts who understood chemistry, microbiology, and biochemistry, as well as the dynamics of data. That's where Simi Sundar's skills sparkled. Her mathematical acumen and almost eidetic memory for numbers caught the attention of the company's senior management who kept loading her with more responsibilities.

Simi was made part of the company's strategic analytics-and-training team. When Pollenta expanded with venture capital funds, a slew of job opportunities opened up and Simi was tasked to set up and lead a data-analytics function in Pollenta's Asia HQ in Singapore, which also collated data from across Asia. In July 2019, they made Simi the Asia-Pacific director of Analytics Training covering all South Asia-Pacific, except China, Taiwan, Korea, and Japan.

Simi didn't mind; she didn't speak Mandarin, despite having been born and brought up in Singapore where about 70 per cent of the population were ethnic Chinese. Malays made up about 15 per cent (Simi was fluent in Bahasa Melayu); and Indians, about 7.2 per cent (Simi was fluent in Tamil and had a working knowledge of Hindi).

This morning, Simi got in at 8.30 a.m. and went to the office pantry to get herself a shot of espresso from the automated machine. Pollenta had just under 100 staff spread out on two floors of a building in Bugis, just outside Singapore's Central Business District (CBD). Their conference room was spacious and equipped with high-definition cameras and high-fidelity sound systems for video-conferencing. This was especially useful during the lockdown.

'What are you doing so early on a Friday?' Oliver Sim, a balding colleague, asked.

'Same as you, Mr Sim,' Simi replied absentmindedly. 'Work beckons. Gotta finish this.'

'Surprising,' he laughed. 'I thought food beckons. Kaya toast here is awesome.'

'Gorge yourself,' she laughed. 'The coffee machine is broken. I had to forgo my cuppa.'

'Shall I be your knight in white and grab a Starbucks coffee for you from the lobby?'

'I never doubted your chivalry, Mr Sim, but no. Not today. Have a con-call coming up.'

The con-call was with the company's Australia office, which was two hours ahead of Singapore. Simi rushed to an empty meeting room and dialled the Zoom bridge. It surprised her to see her India counterpart already waiting on the bridge. 'Vinod, I didn't know you were supposed to be on this call? It's 8.30 a.m. here, so it must be 6 a.m. in Delhi.'

'Yes, as they say, sleep is for slackers,' Vinod yawned. 'Big boss, Ben Morrison, set up this call. I'd rather wake up early one day than get on his wrong side. Wouldn't you agree?'

'I heard that,' a third voice said. It was Ben. He switched on his camera to reveal a middle-aged man with a thick, grey beard and moustache and horn-rimmed spectacles.

'You were on mute all this while?' Simi asked.

'Oops! Sorry, Ben,' Vinod hastily apologized. 'Didn't know you were on the line.'

'As they say in India, no problem . . . all okay?' Ben did the typical head wobble and laughed. 'Good that Simi's here. I'll be quick. One of our top customers in India, Kirumi, wants a training session on analytics for pest-resistant pulses. You conducted this before?'

'I did, in Singapore,' Simi replied. 'But that was before Covid.'

'Good. Two of their data guys attended your session and praised your expertise. They have a boatload of genomic data they want cleaned, sorted, and analysed. They want you.'

'Virtually? Or physically? In-person?'

'Yes. To do the session in-person. I want both of you to be there.'

'Huh?' Vinod stopped yawning. 'When? Where?'

'They have an executive conference and townhall coming up next week. Jan 25 and 26 when all their senior executives will be present. It's in a city called Pune, near Mumbai.'

'Do I need to go in-person?' Simi asked. 'Someone from India can do the training.'

'I can check if we have someone qualified to train,' Vinod said hesitantly. 'Do I need to be there also? I'm not on the technical side. Can I get someone from my team to attend?'

'This is exactly why I set up this con-call,' Ben adjusted his headset. 'Kirumi specifically asked for *you*, Simi. As I said, two of their guys attended your training in Singapore. They insist you conduct the training; they will pay business-class airfare and five-star-hotel stay.'

'Er, Ben, I have other commitments in Singapore during that period, you know—'

'Postpone them. Drop them if you must,' said Ben sternly. 'This customer is important to us. If it's office-related work, I'll talk to the Singapore lead and get you excused.'

Simi made a wry face and quickly corrected herself. 'Hope to see Vinod there as well?'

Ben turned his attention to him. 'Vinod, you need to be there. Their CEO and CFO will be at the conference. We have a regional deal that's waiting for the CFO's signature. Socialize with him and get that signature. We're tying the training indirectly to the deal. Got it?'

Vinod squirmed. 'Sorry, I was not aware of this. They did not copy me in on the messages.'

'I'll send you the background by email,' Ben stroked his beard. 'I'll email you both the local contact person in Mumbai so you can coordinate the logistics with him directly, okay?'

'Got that,' said Vinod. 'Can I take my sales lead along? Padma Pawar? She's a local.'

'Sure, whoever can help you seal the deal. Do you know the CFO? Mr Viswanathan?'

'He's probably from Tamil Nadu or Kerala,' said Simi. 'A Tamilian like me, I guess.'

'There you go, Simi!' Ben laughed. 'You absolutely must make this trip. Good luck.'

Ben hung up; he'd achieved his objective. Vinod cursed; that's all he could do. Simi sighed; she'd have to make that trip, after all. She'd heard rumours about Vinod that, despite overseeing a team of data analysts and consultants, he avoided taking responsibility for his decisions and actions. And that he often blamed his subordinates or external factors for any failures or mistakes while routinely taking credit for the work of others.

Five minutes after Ben Morrison ended the call, Vinod called Simi on WhatsApp.

'This is absolute garbage, the way these Whites treat us,' Vinod cribbed. 'If he's so concerned about this stupid deal, why can't he get his White ass to Pune next week?'

'I love the way you frame it, Vinod,' Simi grinned. 'Especially after the con-call is over.'

'No point arguing with him, right? You know how they are. Throwing their weight around.'

'I'm more worried about Covid-19 regulations in India,' Simi said. 'They keep changing the rules. Don't know whether the latest rules allow Singapore nationals to travel or not. Is there still a VTL[6]? Do you know the latest regulations?'

'I'll check with the Indian contact. You check with our corporate travel agent as well.'

'Okay, but I must warn you, I'll drop out at the slightest excuse. I don't want to travel.'

'Neither do I.'

What nobody foresaw was that on 20 January, the Indian government would issue a fresh set of guidelines for international travellers that would have travel agents and passengers scurrying to comply. It would be the perfect excuse for Simi to abort the trip to Pune.

---

[6] Vaccinated travel lane

# Chapter 9

## Sunday, 23 January 2022

Simi Sundar didn't like surprises, especially nasty ones. The first was being arrowed by Ben Morrison to make this urgent trip to India. Ben was the biggest honcho in the company in Asia—and one couldn't say no to him. Second, the painful procedures that needed to be completed: getting a Covid-negative report from an authorized clinic and worse, filling up a detailed online form—called *Air Suvidha*—which annoyingly kept refreshing itself.

The bonus was that the customer was mitigating the pain of having to travel to India in the middle of a pandemic by dangling business-class tickets at her. That surely helped.

The five-hour flight from Singapore to Bombay on the Dreamliner SQ422 was a dream come true. The flight left on time, at 7.40 a.m. on Sunday, 23 January, and landed at 10 a.m. in Bombay. But clearing immigration and customs took two hours, and the drive to Pune in a car arranged by Vinod took almost four hours; thankfully the car had air-conditioning.

Pune was a mixed bag. The people were warm and welcoming, but the weather was colder than either Mumbai or Singapore. The five-star JW Marriott had well-equipped rooms and excellent amenities, but the food was mainly northern and western Indian. Simi had spent most of the day closeted in her room, working on stuff. She planned to go to the hotel restaurant for dinner.

Simi tried to call the logistics coordinator—no response. The training-session manager had not yet arrived and Vinod's phone was switched off. But there was one silver lining: the training session was to be held in the same hotel. Simi hated to travel anywhere and would avoid it if she could help it.

Simi sauntered into the restaurant on the lobby level and didn't wait to be seated. She found an empty table for four and checked her phone. A smartly attired waiter appeared with a menu that listed an enormous assortment of dishes. She kept the menu aside.

'Do you have idli?'

The waiter, a young male with an apologetic smile, bent to speak softly. 'I'm sorry if your choice of menu is not available, miss,' he said. 'We serve idli only during breakfast. Right now, we have "mendu" vada and "dosa" if you'd like to try those.'

'It's medhu vadai and dosai,' she corrected him. 'Do you have masala dosai?'

'Sorry for mispronouncing. Shall I get you medhu vadai and masala dosai? And lassi?'

'Do you have buttermilk? Or just salted lassi? That will do.'

'Yes, we do. Thank you for your order, miss,' he bowed and left.

An elderly man with a wrinkled face and thinning grey hair, wearing a loose jacket that looked too big for his frail frame, approached her table. He had a slight limp in his gait and a friendly smile on his lips. 'Excuse me, miss. Can I join you for dinner, please?'

Simi hesitated to reply. Sharing a table with strangers was not the norm in India, but he looked like a gentleman and was her father's age. 'Sure, please join me, sir.'

'My name is Ram,' he adjusted his jacket. 'Are you here for the conference?'

'Yes . . . I guess so,' she wondered why he wanted to know that. 'Are you?'

He didn't reply and signalled to the waiter. 'Can I have exactly what this lady ordered?'

Simi was taken aback. Was he was stalking her? 'Did you hear me order?'

'I did. I'm a Tamilian and a vegetarian,' he smiled. 'Do you speak Tamil, miss?'

'*A mam*, sir. *Yen peru* Simi.[7] Simi Sundar,' she smiled and switched to English. 'Yes, of course, sir. That's my mother tongue. I'm from Singapore. Are you from Chennai?'

'Born in Chennai, studied in Delhi, working in Mumbai, and married to a Maharashtrian,' he laughed, revealing a molar cavity. 'A one-man, national-integration icon, if I may say so myself.'

'That's cool, Mr Ram,' Simi simpered. 'Is there an international twist as well?'

'My daughter was born in Sydney, studied at Stanford and has settled in London. My son was born in Mysore, went to med school in Manipal, and doing his doctorate in Maryland.'

'That's a unique combination of cities,' Simi laughed, wondering whether he was lying. Just then, the waiter appeared with two tall glasses of milk-white, salted lassi on a tray.

'What about you?' Ram asked. 'Have you always lived in Singapore?'

'Unlike you, I'm a one-city girl,' Simi took a sip of her lassi. 'My ancestors emigrated from Madras. My father was born in Singapore in 1960. Singapore separated from Malaysia in 1965. Mom is from Penang and married my dad in 1988 in Singapore. I was born in Singapore, studied in Singapore, work in Singapore, and will probably—'

'Continue to live and prosper in Singapore, ha, ha,' Ram completed the sentence for her. 'So, you don't travel outside of tiny Singapore. I'm glad you made it to Pune for this event.'

'I hate travelling,' she made a wry face. 'Even visiting relatives in Penang is a chore.'

The waiter reappeared with two steel trays laden with long, golden-crisp, steaming dosai. The aroma of the crêpe filled with potatoes, peas, carrots, onions, and spices made Simi's mouth water. The waiter placed the folded dosai on the steel plates beside them.

'Thank you, Mr Karan,' Ram read the name tag on his uniform and smiled at him.

---

[7] In Tamil, 'Yes, sir. My name is Simi.'

'Happy dining, ma'am, sir,' the waiter bowed. 'Please don't hesitate to ask if you need more chutney or sambar.'

'Looks delicious,' Simi smacked her lips and raised her fork and spoon.

'Use your hands, dear. If you need to wash your hands, there's the washbasin over there.'

Simi hesitated. 'I will, I guess,' she said reluctantly. 'I need to.'

She went to the washbasin at the far end of the hall. From the corner of her eye, she saw two men in suits walk in. They scanned the room and strode briskly to her table. One man whispered something in Ram's ear. He listened, nodded, and took a sip of his lassi. The other man gave Ram a piece of paper, which he thrust into his left trouser pocket. The two men scanned the hall and walked out of the restaurant. *Intriguing*, thought Simi.

'Sorry if I took long,' Simi sat on her chair. 'You should have started on your dosai, sir.'

'Stop saying sorry, Miss Simi,' Ram tore off a piece of his dosai with his fingers and dipped it into the tiny bowl of steaming, spicy sambar. 'As you know, dosai tastes best when it's hot.'

They ate the rest of the meal in silence. Simi studied the man discreetly; she didn't want to ask him what he did and why those guys had suddenly popped up to speak with him. Maybe he was short of cash to pay for the meal? Maybe they had passed him their credit card?

Ram finished his dosai faster than Simi. 'Excuse me, Miss Simi. I need to attend to something. I'm going to go wash my hands and then I'll leave. Good evening.'

'Thank you, Mr Ram,' said Simi. 'Was a pleasure meeting you, sir.'

She followed him with her eyes. The waiter did not bring him a bill to sign and the old man didn't bother asking for the bill. He just ate his meal and left. Would Simi be saddled with his bill? She beckoned the waiter to ask; but first, she wanted him to bring her more sambar.

Just then, she saw Vinod Kumar walk in. Simi waved to him. 'Where were you all this while?' She asked, irritated. 'I was looking for you ever since I got here.'

'Had a meeting with a bunch of execs from the company,' said Vinod. 'This seat taken?'

'Can sit. The old man has finished his meal and left.'

'What old man? None of our staff, other than Padma Pawar and me, are here.'

'An elderly guy kept me company. We spoke Tamil. He said his name was Ram.'

Vinod dropped his spoon. 'Ram? Are you kidding? You don't mean Dr Ramachandran?'

'Don't know him, never heard of him. He just said his name was Ram. Who's he?'

'Was Mr Viswanathan with him? He's also an elderly man. Balding.'

'Nope. Just Ram. He had a shock of grey hair. Looked frail. Not balding at all.'

'I thought you had a splendid memory, Simi. Dr Ram is the CEO of Kirumi. I've been trying to get a meeting with him ever since I got here. And he just had dinner with you?'

'My memory's only good for numbers, not names or faces,' said Simi sternly. 'Ben Morrison had mentioned Viswanathan, not Ramachandran. And if you had read any of my WhatsApp messages and joined me for dinner, you'd have met Ram, although I'm not sure if it's the same guy you have in mind. His jacket looked old and frayed. Maybe not him.'

Vinod banged his head on the table in mock frustration. 'Oh no, my bad luck.'

'Don't spill my sambar,' Simi chided. 'If he's at the conference tomorrow—'

'That's the problem, Simi, you don't understand,' Vinod frowned. 'We're not invited to their internal conference. Only for the training. I'm here only to meet Vis and Dr Ram.

'Can I help you, sir?' A Sikh man in a suit came over to them, bowed and addressed Vinod.

'Sorry?' Vinod opened his eyes in surprise. 'Who are you?'

'Hello, Mr Vinod, my name is Dharam. I head Kirumi's North India sales. I overheard that you want to meet Dr Ramachandran.

My colleague is going up to the conference hall. You can accompany him. I think Dr Ramachandran and Mr Viswanathan will be there.'

'Seriously?' Vinod jumped up. 'Mr Dharam, you're an angel. May I hug you?'

'You may not,' Dharam stepped back. 'But you may go with my colleague while I keep this pretty lady company.' He turned towards Simi, 'May I, madam?'

'I'm done and ready to leave,' Simi stood up. 'You're free to sit here if you wish.'

'Okay. I'm going to order a cup of tea. Would you like to stay for a while, please?'

'Sorry, I have to go to my room to check my emails,' Simi lied. 'Excuse me.'

'Please wait a minute,' Dharam pleaded with folded his hands. 'I have something important for you.'

'Huh? You don't even know me,' Simi frowned at him. 'Let me go wash my fingers first.'

She took her purse and went to the washbasin and studied him discreetly from a distance. He had a stocky build and a dark complexion which contrasted with the pink Sikh turban wrapped around his head. He was wearing a dark shirt and a black jacket that matched his beard. He kept drumming on the table with his fingers, like a restless bird pecking at a seed, betraying his impatience and nervousness as he waited.

She took her time to go to the ladies' before walking back, reluctantly, to meet this middle-aged casanova. He was sipping on a cup of steaming-hot tea while checking stuff on his mobile phone. She figured she'd spend a couple of minutes humouring him and then find some excuse to escape to her room.

She slid into her chair. 'Can you make it quick?' Simi asked. 'I have work to finish.'

'Sure, Miss Simi Sundar.'

'You know my name and surname? Are you one of the tech-training organizers?'

'I'm not. I know your name and surname. I think you may want to know mine.'

'Why?'

'Because my name is Dharam. And my surname, for all practical purposes, is Dynaborg.'

\* \* \*

## Monday, 24 January 2022

Ricardo 'Rick' Ramsey landed in New York City on Saturday and took a cab to a serviced apartment on Lenox Avenue in Harlem that JQL had rented for two weeks for him. It would be easy for him to ride the commuter train from Harlem to White Plains, New York.

A slew of companies had moved their headquarters from New York City to White Plains, following the lead of one of the most venerable of companies, IBM Corp. On 21 October 1964, IBM's Chairman Thomas J. Watson formally dedicated the company's new corporate HQ in Armonk, New York, 'to the men and women of IBM everywhere.' Some 2,500 employees and family members attended the event, consuming in that one afternoon 5,000 cookies, 7,000 sandwiches, sixty gallons of punch, sixty gallons of coffee, and 300 containers of milk.

Why move to Armonk, forty miles away from NYC? Because real estate in Armonk was cheaper, near transportation, and closer to other major IBM divisions. But that wasn't all.

The two decades—1950s and 1960s—were a period of unprecedented growth in the US. The Cold War was at its peak and the hydrogen bomb was being developed. Home bomb shelters were being built and there were public-service announcements about 'duck-and-cover' procedures in case the N-bomb or the H-bomb was dropped on NYC.

If the US entered a nuclear war, NYC would be one of the most likely targets for the enemy to strike. This could be one reason that

IBM and other companies chose Armonk, which was close enough to NYC to provide the labour pool, but far enough to survive if they attacked NYC. Several companies, including JQL Corp, followed suit.

In his very first week in NYC, Rick narrowly escaped being mugged. A friend who had lived in NYC had warned him not to venture into 'tough neighbourhoods' alone at night. But Rick didn't know what a 'tough neighbourhood' meant. He strayed into the meatpacking district and got lost on Sunday night—and was rescued, of all people, by a couple of burly tourists from Germany.

This Monday morning, Mike Myers, who was part of JQL's corporate strategy team, offered to drive Rick to JQL's HQ. Mike and Rick had communicated by email before.

'Terrible to learn that you almost got mugged. Is that right?' Mike asked Rick on the drive to Armonk. 'What were you doing in the meatpacking district? Alone? At midnight?'

'I got lost, man. It was just 9.30 p.m. I took a wrong turn, didn't turn on my phone GPS.'

'You crazy or what?' Mike laughed, showing his yellow teeth and his double chin. He was a heavyset guy with a round face and a thick neck. He reminded Rick of the fat *caporegime*, Clemenza, from *The Godfather*. He had the same dark eyes and the same stubby nose. If only he'd worn a hat, he'd be a perfect fit for the role of the loyal, ruthless mobster.

It had snowed the previous night. 'Does it always get this cold in winter?' Rick asked.

'What brings you to New York, man? It's not every day we get transfers from Raleigh.'

'You mean it's a dangerous move?'

'It's a tough move. This year's unusually cold. The danger part you've already gone through. Tough for a non-New Yorker to survive without balls. You know what I mean?'

Rick adjusted his yellow tie; he wasn't focusing on Mike. The yellow was supposed to communicate a cheery, carefree emotion and to inspire people to think of fun subconsciously. He wondered whether he should have worn a blue tie instead.

Rick marveled at the ice floes floating on the Hudson River as they passed the George Washington Bridge. White Plains was a suburban city, the county seat of Westchester County. Mike drove through the downtown area with its smattering of shops and restaurants.

'Are there weekly meetings in Armonk that we need to attend?' Rick asked.

'A bit arbitrarily, not every week. Depends on your BU[8]. Your boss. Your boss' boss. If a customer is involved, like a bank or the Fed, you must get to Armonk daily.'

'In that case, I better find a rental in White Plains or Armonk, man.'

'That'd be way cheaper than anywhere in NYC, for sure. Check with your boss first.'

The JQL HQ was nestled within a wooded, rocky landscape in White Plains. They had designed the building with a generous provision of controlled natural light and views of the landscape and forest with open terraces for relaxation and informal meetings. The internal, irregular spaces held a series of conference and meeting rooms with glass doors.

At 11 a.m., he met his boss, Fiona Fletcher. She was in her mid-fifties; tall, slender, with piercing, blue eyes and straight, blonde-and-grey hair. Her glasses hung from a thin black thread around her neck. Rick could see small welts of red on both sides of her neck.

Fiona gestured for him to sit and focused on her laptop. 'Gimme a minute,' she mumbled. 'This needs to be sent out right away. How long are you going to be in New York?'

It took him a couple of seconds to realize Fiona was asking him without looking at him. 'I guess two weeks should be sufficient, shouldn't it? I'm here for the interviews also, right?'

'I know. HR wants me to vet you,' she pressed a key, then closed the laptop lid. 'Sorry, I didn't mean to be rude. Everything okay? You got here last night?' She adjusted her glasses.

'Everything—'

---

[8] Business unit

'Before we get into the job function, let me get a couple of points out of the way,' Fiona continued. 'You'll get the services of a group secretary. HR has assigned Alice to you. You'll meet her after this. She also helps four other executives, so please be gentle with her.'

Rick opened his notepad and pencil and started scribbling on it.

'Two, you don't need to come to White Plains every day. Twice a week will do. Alice can schedule that. Three, your job requires travel. Four, you need to find an apartment to rent.'

'The interview—'

'You're the only candidate and you're qualified. That's why we fixed two weeks.'

'Er—'

'HR will sort all that with you, don't worry. You should learn to compartmentalize. We're all multi-hatters and multi-taskers. You start with one, then the layers get added. It helps you grow. Do you think you can handle it? The job, the city, the travel.'

'It's all so sudden. Er, I need to catch my breath. You think I can handle—'

'Otherwise, we wouldn't have picked you, Ricardo. Don't let the job's scope scare you. Take one step at a time. That way, you won't get overwhelmed. I've asked Alice to set up a few meetings with some key execs today, since you're already here. There's Dave Scully, head of North America Sales. I'll take you to his office right after we're done. And Suresh Singh, head of Engineering.' She got up, 'I need to meet someone. I'll catch you at lunch.'

Before he could get a word in edgeways, Fiona had opened the door and was holding it open for him. 'Let's go meet Alice,' she said, racing ahead. Rick had to run to catch up with her.

It was a flurry of meetings, presentations, case studies, and use cases. By the end of the day, Rick reckoned he'd met with about a dozen executives that included a diverse mix of people from different races, religions, nationalities, and even a couple with physical disabilities.

Before he could get back to his serviced apartment in NYC, Alice had scheduled one last meeting—with Fiona's boss, Tony Sanders.

Tony's reputation preceded him as a tough-talking, no-nonsense, take-no-prisoners type of guy with a corny sense of humour. He was not only notorious for his rude remarks and crude jokes, but also for his arrogance and selfishness. Rick met Tony at his well-appointed office, which was filled with sparse furniture and framed certificates that flaunted his achievements. Tony came straight to the point.

'I don't want you to work hard,' Tony said. 'I want you to work smart. You got that?'

'Yessir.'

'I don't care how you plan your day. I don't care if you goof off or play golf or get laid or meet customers or work weekends. If you achieve your numbers, you're good to carry on. If you miss your numbers two quarters in a row, I'll fire you myself. You got that?'

'Yessir,' Rick wondered whether this guy was kidding. Was he a thug? Could he talk to his juniors like this? 'Er . . . if I may ask, Mr Sanders, does my time start right now?'

'Good question. It doesn't. The first quarter is your honeymoon quarter. That's when you learn the ropes. Your time starts from the next quarter. You got that?'

'Got that, Mr Sanders. I'll do my best to meet my numbers.'

'I'm sure you will, Ricardo. Call me Tony. Everyone calls me that to my face,' he looked at Rick over the rim of his spectacles. 'Behind my back, they call me "Tony Tightass".'

# Chapter 10

**Tuesday, 25 January 2022**

It was exactly two years ago, on 16 January 2020, that Japan had confirmed its first case of the novel coronavirus—that would later be called Covid-19—when a man who had travelled to Wuhan tested positive. On 1 February 2020, the Japanese government quarantined the London-registered cruise ship, Diamond Princess, after an eighty-year-old passenger from Hong Kong tested positive. In the early days of the pandemic, Japan had some of the most stringent restrictions in place. Even in January 2022, Japan imposed a ten-day self-isolation rule for international visitors. By end-January, they reduced it to seven days.

However, since the conference was only for invited visitors, the Japanese government waived the quarantine period for delegates who had taken a booster shot as well as the two standard vaccine jabs. Singapore had mandated booster jabs for all residents, and even a fourth jab for senior citizens. Gina, Chika, and George had taken all three shots as required.

Still, Gina Gonzales needed the special waiver as she was a not a Japanese national. Chika Nakamura was a Japanese citizen and a Singapore Permanent Resident. George Gan bailed at the last minute, insisting that he was sneezing and coughing and wouldn't be allowed to leave Singapore.

Usually, most tourists avoid going to Tokyo during January and February when it's cold, dank, and clammy. But the winter months are ideal to hold corporate events because hotel rates are cheaper, and Tokyo is less crowded. That didn't matter to Gina; she loved almost everything about Japan, except the steep cost. But this time, even the exorbitance didn't matter; the company would foot the bill.

The Nippon Genetics Institute was not in Tokyo, but in Mishima, 100 kilometres south of Tokyo. High-speed Shinkansen bullet trains wonderfully connected all of Japan.

Gina and Chika rode the Narita Express from Narita Airport to Shinagawa Station, then transferred to the Shinkansen to get to Mishima, an hour away. The entire journey cost them ¥7,000, about $50 each. A shuttle bus ferried them to the plush Mishima Plaza Hotel, a stylish hotel with a European touch and an art gallery.

'Delighted you're coming with me to Tokyo,' Chika gushed on the way to the hotel.

'Delighted you've invited me to spend two days at your family's home afterwards.'

The hotel was typical Japanese style, with a spacious room and an adjoining bathroom. For dinner, Gina suggested they explore the street outside. It was biting cold, so they decided on a quick meal across the street at Wendy's First Kitchen that served hot fried chicken with cool Japanese sauces and wasabi. The joint had excellent heating and the aroma of fried chicken mixed with pungent soya sauce, garlic butter, and wasabi provided a warm balm for the winter cold. Chika was a picky eater, and Gina finished whatever Chika couldn't.

The conference itself was a closed-door affair with invited guests from around the world. With typical Japanese precision, everyone had their names tagged and their places marked at huge round tables, with eight participants seated around each. They had also placed a bento-box menu to tick, based on what they wanted to have for lunch. There were Japanese, Chinese, Korean, Indian, European, vegetarian, and vegan options.

Gina wondered whether she could mix and match from the menu.

'Mixing and networking only allowed during tea and lunch breaks, but with masks on if you're not eating or drinking,' the lady emcee announced, waking Gina from her reverie.

A delegate from the US raised her hand. 'Can we mix items from different menus?'

'You cannot. Each bento-box is prepared by different chefs, so mixing is not permitted.'

There was a collective sigh from the audience.

The emcee continued, 'We warmly welcome you. We will go through introductions. Each of you will stand up, introduce yourself, your company, and give a brief idea of the work you do.'

The first half was a series of lectures—with simultaneous translation in six languages—but all the slides were thankfully in English. Gina was at table five with delegates from seven other countries. Chika was across the hall at table nine. There were twelve tables in all.

Gina made a mental note to meet delegates from Australia, New Zealand, Israel, Canada, and Sweden—they seemed to be doing interesting work in Gina's field of expertise. The second half would hopefully have more interaction; Gina was trying to stifle yawns.

At the first tea break, which was for half an hour, Gina looked around for Chika; she was busy speaking with delegates from Japan. Gina scanned the room. Most of the delegates were male, a couple of them were staring at her from across the room. Gina ignored them and walked back to refill her cup of Japanese tea—it was instrumental to keep her from dozing off.

Just then, someone touched her on her shoulder. She turned around and saw a lithe woman in a suit with a streak of grey hair and an outstretched hand. The woman had piercing blue eyes that seemed to scan her in an instant. She wore a silver brooch in the shape of a star on her lapel, a subtle sign of her Texan pride. Her suit was tailored and elegant, but not too formal. She looked like someone who knew how to balance professionalism and charm.

'Hello, I'm Emma. Emma Rivers from the US. Saw your name on the list. Spain?'

'Pleasure to meet you, Emma,' Gina shook her hand. 'I'm Gina Gonzales.'

Emma bent to read Gina's name tag. 'Singapore? Wow. Your name sounds Spanish.'

'I'm originally from the Philippines, which was once a colony of Spain,' Gina sipped from her cup. 'I live and work in Singapore. You're based in New York?'

'I'm from Texas, which was once a Spanish colony,' she smiled. 'Coincidental.'

'Interesting. My cousin sister works in Dallas, Texas.'

'Wow, that's a genuine coincidence. I was born and raised in Dallas. I live and work in Houston in Texas. During the little breakout session earlier, you said you're working on gene sequencing to detect cancer antigens in clinical trials. Is that correct?'

'Not in clinical trials yet. Would you like to discuss it sometime later?'

'Sure. I've been doing some research on a related area and would love to compare notes if that's okay with you. Maybe we can meet during lunch?'

Just then, someone else touched Gina's arm. 'Dr Gonzales?'

Gina turned around to face a lanky guy with blue eyes, pale skin, and brown hair. He had a friendly expression on his face, and a badge that identified him as a researcher. 'I am Dr Dag Larsen from Norway. You are from G3 in Singapore, am I accurate to think so?'

'Hello, Dr Larsen. I'm Gina Gonzales from Genome Germanica. Not Dr Gina. Just Gina.'

'Excuse me, Just Gina. My English is weak. I am sorry.'

'No worries, Dr Larsen. How may I help you?'

'We are interested in collaboration with G3. I am from Institute for Cancer Genetics and Informatics. We are part of Oslo University Hospital. When can we discuss this, Just Gina?'

'Er, you can call me Gina. I'm not the right person to discuss a collaboration with G3. I'll link you with the right person as soon as I'm back. Maybe you can give me your name card?'

Dag Larsen pulled out a business card and handed it to Gina. She fumbled in her purse and fished out her business card. He studied it intently and slipped it into his jacket pocket.

'Interesting,' Gina read from his card. 'You're heading innovative genetics. What's that?'

'That is something I want to discuss with everyone,' he said. 'My session is after lunch.'

Lunch was at their respective tables with an assortment of items in rectangular sections inside wooden bento-boxes and piping hot miso soup served in white ceramic bowls. Gina had chosen a tempura bento-box. She was eager to meet Emma, but the emcee forbade inter-table mixing and networking, so they exchanged messages on WhatsApp instead.

After lunch was done, the emcee consulted her watch and announced at 1.45 p.m. 'We will now take a fifteen-minute siesta. For those who wish to use the washroom or have coffee or tea, you may do so outside the hall. We're going to turn off the lights and we ask everyone stop speaking. You can take quick nap in your seat if you wish.'

The announcement took most of the international delegates, including Gina and Emma, by surprise. But the Japanese delegates, including Chika, welcomed the announcement with applause. A few of them pulled out eyeshades from their pockets for a pleasant power nap.

Emma caught Gina's eye and gestured to her to step outside. Gina gingerly picked up her backpack and tiptoed out of the conference room.

'Wondering whether you'd like to catch up for dinner tonight?' Emma asked Gina as soon as they were outside the hall. 'Love to discuss a few things. Get to know you better.'

Gina wondered whether she should accept. She barely knew Emma and it would be challenging for two women to navigate in an alien city where few people spoke English. 'Isn't there's a networking dinner for all delegates tonight?'

Emma checked her phone. 'That's tomorrow night. There's dinner available if we want it here, or we can go out. What say we explore some place outside? Are you game?'

'Let's decide later,' Gina said and changed the subject. 'By the way, did you meet this guy, Dr Dag Larsen, from Norway?'

'I saw him speaking with you.'

'He's into innovative genetics. What's that about? Sounds weird.'

'Maybe it's CRISPR[9] or something. Genetic engineering. Who knows?'

'That's old news. Hope it's not what I think it is.'

'I wouldn't go there. Not a country as clean as Norway.'

'He's speaking after lunch,' Gina chuckled. 'I want to hear him speak—if I don't snooze, that is,' she yawned. 'Guess I should've napped.'

She shouldn't have worried. As soon as the fifteen minutes were up, ushers with tinkle bells went around the foyers to usher everyone back inside. The Japanese organizers thoughtfully handed out tiny, steaming towels to each delegate to wipe their face and get ready for the post-lunch session. After introductions, Dr Dag Larsen walked to the podium to deliver his presentation.

'I am going to first present what my institute is doing in innovative genetics involving plants, seeds, and pest control such as the Wolbachia Mosquito Project,' he read from a prepared script. 'For a history briefing, it was two American scientists, Dr Marshall Hertig and Dr Burt Wolbach, who discovered a bacterium in the common house mosquito, *culex pipiens*, in the 1920s. In 1936, Dr Hertig named the bacterium, *wolbachia pipientis*.'

The first few yawns escaped from the audience.

After fifteen minutes of presenting the research that his team was working on, Dr Dag kept aside his sheaf of papers and adjusted his specs. 'I would like your permission to discuss something that some of us have experienced in Scandinavian countries. I will explain the symptoms of the syndrome in a short while. I would like to know if anyone here has also done so, since we have so many countries represented here.'

Many delegates stopped yawning.

'We are trying to find out if this is an unreported side effect of Long Covid and if it could be caused by what is commonly called as

---

[9]  Clustered regularly interspaced short palindromic repeats

brain fog. We have seen subjects report visitations from either outer space or apparitions appear from vacant space, usually at night. Anybody?'

A delegate from India raised his hand. 'Is this a joke? Are you being serious?'

A rep from South Africa stood up. 'What has this matter got to do with this conference?'

There were murmurs around the tables, but nobody else volunteered to comment.

'This is not a joke,' said Dr Dag. 'This has nothing to do with this conference. We have an international representation of scientists in this room. I wanted to open this conversation.'

'If it has nothing to do with this conference, we shouldn't waste our time,' said the Indian.

Emma raised her hand. 'I think we should discuss this. Could this be delirium, Dr Dag?'

'Some of us thought so before,' he replied. 'But it is not. It is a transformation of the subject. Delirium is a temporary state of mind. This is a total change in personality.'

A Japanese scientist raised his hand. 'We know what you mean, Dr Dag. Some cases like this reported in Japan. We are investigating. We are studying some subjects. *Arigato.*'

Gina stood up. 'I have personally witnessed a case with a dear friend in Singapore.'

'Eh?' The Japanese delegate raised both hands. 'This is unique to have personal witness.'

Another Japanese delegate raised his hand. 'Is this happening in a hospital environment in Singapore? Do you have name? Disease? Syndrome? Opposite of episodic amnesia?'

'The Singapore Strain. Not a formal name, just a loose name. Not scientifically proven.'

The South Korean delegate raised his hand. 'What is the Singapore Strain? An unreported symptom of Long Covid? Or a new variant of Omicron? Can you explain? Give her a mic.'

The emcee picked up a wireless microphone from her desk and handed it to Gina.

Gina cleared her throat. 'Allow me to explain. We admitted my dear friend to the National University Hospital in Singapore after she had a brain aneurysm. She previously had the Delta variant or the Omicron variant, I'm not sure which and I don't think that really matters.'

'What happened to her?' Dr Dag asked.

'In a delirium, she imagined that a strange man appeared in her bedroom. He said she may be presenting an undocumented, positive side effect of the Singapore Strain of Covid-19.'

There were quiet murmurs for a few seconds. Emma raised her hand. 'The Singapore Strain? That's a good codename for us to go with until more research is done. Right, guys?'

'I agree,' the Indian rep said. 'We called it the Wuhan virus, which became Covid-19. Then we had the India variant, which became the Delta variant. Singapore Strain is good.'

A couple of guys started clapping. Soon everybody joined in.

Gina still held the microphone. 'It's amazing that we're hearing about this syndrome at this event. Dr Dag was right to bring it up. If I may ask, which other countries here would have heard of this? Can we have a show of hands? I'll raise my hand first.'

Two reps from Japan raised their hands. So did Australia and New Zealand. And Dag.

There was a hushed silence. Then, slowly, the representatives from Sweden, Denmark, Nigeria, Germany, and New Zealand raised their hands. After a long pause, so did Emma.

'Surely astonishing,' the emcee bowed. 'This item is not even on the conference agenda.'

The room erupted with animated discussions among delegates at their respective tables. They were lively and passionate, expressing their opinions and arguments with gestures and voices. Some used photos and screenshots on their devices to support their points, while others refuted with counterarguments. The emcee looked to Gina to get them back on track.

Gina tapped on her microphone a few times to get everybody's attention. Despite that it took almost ten minutes for the delegates to settle down and focus on the stage.

'I have something to say. Listen carefully. Before I hand this mic back, I want to mention one other term. Has anyone heard this before? Dynaborgs? The movement is Dynaborgism.'

\* \* \*

Angela Ang cursed when she realized the London weather forecast estimated an average daytime temperature of 5°C and cloudy skies the entire week of 24 January 2022. However, that wouldn't deter her from travelling to Britain, her favourite destination.

She had lived and studied in the UK for three years but could never come to terms with the dark, damp, clammy British winter. She didn't mind the dark days; she yearned for respite from the scorching Singapore sun. She didn't mind the dampness; she had stylish gumboots to keep her feet dry. But the cold hurt everywhere, despite layering herself in warm clothing.

The cold was the one reason she'd moved back to Singapore. The other reason was food.

'I love spicy Asian food that I can't get at the right place or price,' Angela told her colleague from Pistonex Europe, Lucas Eriksson. Lucas was from Sweden and worked in aircraft-engine-component design. He was six feet and six inches tall and wore a tweed jacket over a polo shirt. He had pale, white skin that contrasted with his light-brown hair and eyes. Angela noticed that he looked tired and pale and wondered whether he could be anaemic or if he was just stressed from work.

'I'd love to visit Singapore,' Lucas said. 'Is Singapore food spicy?'

'How come you're wearing a T-shirt? Aren't you feeling cold?'

'Nope. Sweden is colder.'

'I'm already shivering, you know,' she tugged the hood of her thick jacket over her ears.

'Is Singapore food spicy?'

'Depends on what you order, right?'

'If I order steak, will it be spicy?'

'No, *lah*. Steak is not Singapore food. Indian and Indonesian food can be spicy. You know Indonesia was a Dutch colony from 1800 to 1949. Did any of your ancestors visit Indonesia?'

'Nope.'

'Have you ever visited any country in Asia?'

'Nope. Only Europe, Canada, London. But I'm planning to make a trip to Bristol.'

'Why?'

'I studied there. I have friends there. Heard Greta's coming too.'

'Greta Thunberg?' Angela's eyes lit up. 'The Swedish activist girl, right?'

'Nope. She's nineteen now. She's a Swedish lady.'

'Are you going to meet Greta?'

'Nope. Going to meet my friend. Wanna come along?'

'My flight to Singapore is on Jan 28. May not work, right?'

'Nope. The event is on Friday, Jan 28. Extend your stay.'

'Okay, I'll try. So exciting, right?' Angela gave Lucas a quick hug. 'You made my day.'

Angela postponed her return to Singapore by four days. She shot off an email to her boss that she was extending her stay in the UK to discuss 'environmental issues with engineers and future potential customers.'

She'd forgotten that the Chinese New Year would fall on February 1 and 2, and she'd be required to be present for the annual 'family reunion dinner.'

# Chapter 11

**Wednesday, 26 January 2022**

In the 1800s, the British rulers shipped Indian convicts from Madras and southern India—and Chinese convicts from Hong Kong—to Singapore, Malacca, and Penang. In 1847, there were 1,500 Indian convicts in Singapore. They put many of them to work as coolies and cheap labour, including some who helped produce bricks for constructing buildings.

The Indian convicts won the Silver Medal for the quality of their bricks to build three iconic places of worship in Singapore: St Andrew's Church at City Hall in 1836, the Sri Veeramakaliamman Temple at Serangoon Road in 1855, and the Srinivasa Perumal Temple at Serangoon Road in 1885.

Simi's great-great-grandfather, born in Madras in 1825, was among a batch of convicts shipped to Singapore in 1850. Fast-forward about 110 years. Simi's dad, Sundaram, was born in Singapore in 1960 and married Sneha from Penang in 1988. Suresh was born in 1989, Simi in March 1990. Sneha and Sundaram decided on Sundar, a shortened version of his name, as the family surname after they wed.

Right from a very young age, Simi was fascinated by numbers. When she was twelve, she'd memorized the first eighty-eight digits of Pi and the first twenty Fibonacci numbers. At her PSLE[10], she was one of two kids in Singapore to have scored 100 per cent marks in maths. Her brother Suresh however didn't exhibit any extraordinary abilities, unlike his kid sister.

---

[10] Primary school leaving examination

'I like maths because there are no surprises in calculations and formulas,' *The Straits Times* quoted Simi following her perfect maths score. 'I dislike ambiguity and mystery.'

But now, in a strange city, in an alien country, Simi was saddled with ambiguity and mystery, with no clue as to why she was getting dragged into something of no relevance to her.

On the very first night, a stranger had shared a dinner table with her and although he was cordial, he never once mentioned who he really was—Kirumi's CEO, Dr Ramachandran. It was at his company's insistence that she had reluctantly flown to Pune.

Then there was Vinod Kumar, managing director of Pollenta's Indian operations. He had his own hidden agenda, apart from the one he was tasked to do. He turned on his WhatsApp only when he wanted something done and ignored all the other messages. His sole official agenda now was to get the CFO to sign the deal for Ben Morrison.

And finally, there was the strange and mysterious turbaned Sikh, Dharam, who dangled an alias, Dynaborg, without explaining or elaborating what it meant. It was the second time she had heard that term; the first was from Cory who'd woken up from a delirium and babbled about being a Dynaborg. Simi was glad Cory hadn't labelled Simi as being one.

She had to solve these mysteries before she left for Singapore. For that, she had to first find the elusive Sikh. She had looked high and low for him in between her training sessions on Monday and Tuesday, but there was no sign of him. Simi had to find him before Friday. Vinod had fixed a chauffeur-driven car to ferry her to Mumbai to catch her flight to Singapore on Saturday.

Simi preferred to eat alone in the hotel's restaurant, instead of joining the common buffet, for three reasons: One, she preferred light, south Indian vegetarian food, but at the buffet they served north-Indian cuisine with chicken and mutton. Two, she hated standing and talking while eating and that was what the rest of the delegates did during lunch breaks. Three, she was talking and presenting all day. All she wanted an hour of peace. But that was not to be.

Vinod Kumar dashed in and sat down opposite her. He always seemed to be in a hurry, like a cheetah chasing its prey. He had someone with him—a young lady who looked like a Bollywood star; her hair was a waterfall, cascading over her shoulders with elegance.

'Ah, you've not met my sales assistant. This is Padma Pawar. She joined us last year.'

Padma extended her hand; Simi did a namaste greeting. 'Heard so much about you, Ms Simi Sundar,' Padma said in a silken voice that would've floored a heterosexual male.

Simi ignored Padma. 'Why the hurry, Vinod? Always in a tearing hurry, aren't you?'

'Nature of my job, Simi, what to do?' He turned to Padma, 'Did you have lunch? You want to order something?' Before she could respond, he turned to Simi, 'You okay with us?'

'Do I have a choice?'

'No, you don't. I need you to get your training candidates to help me locate the CFO, Mr Viswanathan. I need his signature.'

Simi smiled at Padma. 'I'm sure your young and glamourous assistant can talk to the guys. Now's the right time, if you ask me.'

'Are you pulling my leg, Ms Sundar?' Padma's voice had suddenly turned hoarse.

'Not at all, Ms Pawar. It's the lunch break. Everyone's at the buffet table. Viswanathan might be there as well.'

Padma didn't protest. Just as she turned away to leave, a little girl of about four ran towards them.

'*Aai, bug maushi eetheh basli aheh,*'[11] she exclaimed and hugged a surprised Simi.

Simi almost dropped her spoon of curd rice. 'What happened? What's she saying?'

Padma bent to speak to the kid in Marathi. '*Baal, hee thuzhi maushi nahi. Tu kaun?*'[12]

The child's mother hurried towards them. '*Tumhi Marathi ka?*'[13] she asked Simi eagerly.

The little girl continued to hug Simi tightly and began sobbing.

---

[11] In Marathi, 'Mom, look, aunty is sitting here!'

[12] In Marathi, 'Child, this is not your aunty. Who're you?'

[13] In Marathi, 'Are you all Marathi speakers?'

Padma stood up to explain to the mother, '*Mee Marathi, tya Madrasi.*'[14]

'Sorry, sorry,' the mother tried to pull the child away from Simi. '*Tya maushi nahi.*'[15]

'Let her be for a while,' Padma told the mother, then turned to explain to Simi and Vinod. 'The child thought Simi was her mother's sister, "maushi" in Marathi. I tried to explain—'

'So sorry,' the mother spoke English. 'My sister passed away last year from Covid-19. She was very close to my daughter, Leena. She turned four last month. This lady looks exactly like my sister. When I entered, it shocked even me to see my sister alive.'

'I'm sorry to hear about your sister,' Simi lifted the child on to her lap. 'Even though I don't speak Marathi, please let me hug Leena. Don't cry, Leena. I'm here,' Simi wiped the girl's tears with the restaurant napkin. 'Please join us for lunch.'

'How Karmic,' the mother wiped a tear, 'my sister's name was Surekha. That means beautiful. She was as beautiful as Simi maushi. Thank you for your love, madam.'

Simi blushed. 'Er . . . Padma maushi here is way more beautiful than me. But then—'

'No way,' Padma waved her hand dismissively. 'For Leena, Surekha maushi was the most beautiful woman after her mother. Surekha is Simi. I'm so glad I was here to witness this miracle.'

'I'm so glad you stayed, Padma,' Simi extended her hand. 'Please join us for lunch.'

\* \* \*

Gina was getting bored as the conference dragged on. The Japanese were very much like Singaporeans—work till you drop. Every topic on the agenda had to be dissected and debated. Where the two cultures differed was that formal Singapore scientific events would opt to go

---

[14]  In Marathi, 'I'm Marathi, they're Tamilians.'

[15]  In Marathi, 'She's not your aunt.'

with the majority view, whereas Japanese conferences sought to reach a consensus.

At the end of day two, there were two motions for discussion that seemed to drag on. One was on potential mutation of human DNA in the next 100 years and what it would mean for humankind. The other was about chimeras being produced for commercial gain.

Would 'Ducken' result from a chimera born with DNA fused from a chicken and a duck? And 'Chimperson' result from the DNA of a chimpanzee mixed with a human's DNA? Both topics would have made excellent fodder for a conference for sci-fi fans, philosophers, and poets. But this group was discussing exciting issues in a drab manner, including recessive gene manipulation, junk DNA sequencing, fusion of synthetic and organic DNA, and random and specific chromosome reconfigurations. All hardcore genetic engineering, not optics.

Even Dr Dag Larsen from Norway stifled yawns.

Emma Rivers raised her hand to speak. There was a glint of mischief in her eyes, like a spark of fire in the dark. She winked at Gina like a co-conspirator in a secret plan before taking the mic. 'We've so far discussed the engineering side. Now let's spend a few minutes discussing the fun side,' said Emma. 'Hollywood and books have speculated about DNA manipulation. Fiction has superseded science. I can think of *Gattaca* and *Jurassic Park*. Any others?'

There was a sudden buzz of activity in the room, as more people perked up.

The Indian delegate woke up. '*Star Trek* was the first. *Star Wars* was the second,' he shouted from across the room. '*Jurassic Park* didn't set the trend, I think *Species* did.'

'*Oblivion* with Tom Cruise was on human cloning on an alien planet,' someone said.

'*Paradise Hills* was about cloning that didn't go well,' the Spanish delegate chimed in.

'*Never Let Me Go*,' said the Japanese guy. 'Human clones created for organ donation.'

'Anyone heard about *Closer to God*?' asked Emma. 'It's a horror movie on cloning.'

'*Alien*,' said Gina. 'All of them. Don't understand why all aliens want to destroy Earth.'

'Absolutely,' Dr Dag stood up. 'Hollywood has limited imagination. Shoot, kill, finish. No movies about aliens being friendly. Or teaching, living, and learning with humans.'

The emcee tapped on her microphone. 'Er . . . this discussion is getting out of hand.'

'This discussion is as relevant as any other,' protested Emma. 'We were discussing the engineering aspects. Hollywood is about the story, the consequences. And fun to discuss.'

'I agree,' Dr Dag chipped in. 'This subject is as interesting as the one we discussed yesterday about the Singapore Strain. Why should scientific conferences be no-fun?'

The audience clapped. Everyone was now wide awake and animated. There were still two more days to go. The last day would focus on conclusions and consensus on a range of issues.

'Okay, let's break for tea,' the emcee announced. 'After twenty minutes we shall resume our discussion on the next topic—role of monoclonal antibodies in cancer treatment.'

Gina sprang up and sprinted to the coffee machines. Three Japanese guys had beaten her to it. She stood in line behind them as a long queue started forming. Someone touched her hand.

'Sorry to jump the queue, may I join you?' Emma bowed to those behind.

'Sure, ladies first,' said the Indian delegate. The others made way for Emma to cut in.

'Thank you, guys,' said Emma, then turned to whisper to Gina. 'Drinks tonight?'

'Just the two of us?' Gina raised an eyebrow.

'Two's company, three's a crowd,' Emma laughed and touched Gina's arm and whispered into her ear. 'Unless you wanna invite Dr Dag.'

Gina guffawed so loudly that others turned to look at her. 'Shut up!' She playfully punched Emma on her shoulder. 'Yeah, let's plan on drinks. Hang on, isn't there supposed to be a farewell dinner tonight?'

Emma waved a dismissive hand. 'Too boring. Your friend will cover for you, right?'

Gina took a moment to glance around the room for Chika Nakamura. She spotted her surrounded by a group of Korean and Japanese delegates. 'Yeah,' said Gina. 'She'll be fine. She seems to enjoy being back home. She's the centre of attention and just loving it.'

'By the way, aren't Filipinos supposed to be very religious, like the Spaniards?'

'We sure are,' Gina lowered her mask and sipped her cappuccino. 'The Gospel has been hammered into my head ever since I could speak. You too?'

'Not me. My parents. They stopped pushing me when I rebelled. You didn't?'

'Ha, I was in Singapore. Nobody bothers anyone about religion in Singapore.'

'Let's discuss this over wine or beer. I'm dying to get out of this place.'

Later that evening, Emma and Gina checked Google Maps for a proper Japanese joint in the neighbourhood for drinks and dinner. Emma asked the hotel concierge for suggestions. He suggested a fusion cuisine place a short cab-ride away. The restaurant served both American-style steaks and booze, and Japanese-style teppanyaki meats prepared as small bites in front of you. He wrote the restaurant's name and address on a slip to give to the cab driver.

The cab ride took fifteen minutes. Gina learnt that, apart from their common Spanish origins and strict Catholic upbringing, they also shared a love of horror movies.

The restaurant had dim mood lighting that created a cozy and intimate atmosphere. There were pockets of tables, occupied by men in suits who were chatting and laughing over sake and sushi. A waitress in a kimono ushered them to a corner table and gestured to them to order on an Android tablet which had rough English translations of Japanese dishes. The tablet also showed pictures and prices of items on the menu, but the pictures were blurry and unappetizing. They wished they could read the menu or ask the waitress to recommend something, but felt awkward and out of place as the waitresses didn't seem to understand English.

Gina suggested a platter that offered bite-sized portions of a range of dishes from the teppanyaki and steak menus. They also ordered warm Japanese sake.

Emma glanced around the dimly lit, sparsely occupied joint. It was 8 p.m., still early for the Japanese crowds to roll in. 'I'm trying to locate at least one female in this sea of males.'

'I see a couple at the table in that corner,' Gina discreetly pointed. 'With some men.'

'Ah, you're very observant,' Emma clapped softly, 'like a talented scientist should be.'

A Japanese hostess appeared with warm sake in a porcelain pot and carefully poured the steaming liquid into white, china cups. She placed a bowl of hot, boiled peanuts and said something in Japanese. 'Free with sake,' she translated. 'Thank you. *Arigato.*'

'*Arigato gozaimashita*[16],' Gina replied. She'd picked up a few Japanese words.

They had a couple of swigs of sake—and pieces of meat from the sizzling platter.

'This is the best part of this trip for me,' Emma declared. 'The food is divine, the sake is sweet, and you're brilliant company. Didn't know you liked horror movies as well.'

'I get horribly scared when I watch them. But it's an addiction. I can't help it.'

'Which was the most horrible horror movie for you?'

'I have a few that gave me sleepless nights. *Poltergeist. The Omen.* But the one that made me shit scared was *The Exorcist.* You?'

'Oh, let me think,' Emma took a swig of sake. 'The scariest? *Paranormal Activity.*'

'Do you see a pattern that scares you? Is it fear of bodily harm that scares you most?'

---

[16] In Japanese, 'Thank you very much'

'Guess so. I haven't told anyone outside of my closest circle. I want to confide in you, I don't know why. He abused me as a child, a close relative, someone I was supposed to trust. Left a bloody scar on my psyche. Bodily harm is at the top of my list of horrible things.'

Gina stopped chewing. 'Sorry to hear that. Have you come to terms with it?'

Emma didn't respond.

Gina wondered if she'd touched a raw nerve. 'Dead people coming back to life and possessing others scare the shit out of me. *The Exorcist* freaked me out. Even now I get goosebumps.'

'You shouldn't. You're a scientist. The so-called possessed person needs to see a shrink. You've heard of Tourette's? Schizophrenia? Split-personality syndrome?'

'Easy for you to advise. Until it happens to you. How d'you know if you're possessed?'

'From camera footage, from relatives or friends. It's like Alzheimer's. When you're lucid, you're lucid. When you forget, somebody else tells you so. Ditto if you're possessed.'

Gina picked up a small piece of beef. 'You seem to have researched this subject.'

Emma got up. 'I gotta pee. Let me find the restroom.'

Gina checked the sake pot; it was empty. She switched on the Android tablet and ordered another pot. She burped and scanned the room. It was still quite empty and relatively dark.

Just then, a couple of inebriated guys strode past the table, glanced at Gina, then took two steps back. They asked her something in Japanese. 'No Japanese,' said Gina, 'English.'

'Speak English? Okay, speaking,' the tall guy laughed. 'You be alone in Japan? We help?'

Gina didn't know what to make of that. 'Thank you. I'm okay. Arigato.'

They probably misunderstood. The tall guy slid next to her. The burly one sat opposite.

'My friend will be back,' Gina protested. 'Gone to the toilet. Bathroom. WC. No sit.'

'Is okay. We wait for your friend,' the tall guy drew closer. His mouth stank of booze. Gina was now concerned. These men seemed more than friendly, which was not a good sign.

'You Manila girl?' the burly guy asked. 'We like Filipinas very much. How much?'

Ah, so they probably thought she was a prostitute. 'I'm a scientist, no sex, leave. Go.'

'Eh? We also scientists,' the tall guy laughed loudly. 'Sex scientists. We pay dollar.'

The burly guy was drooling at her heavy breasts. The tall guy's hands were wandering into her shirt and bra. She wondered whether she should shout. Then she saw Emma walk out of the ladies. Gina frantically gestured to her and pushed the tall guy away.

For a moment, Emma wondered if she had gone to the wrong table. Then she saw Gina and the two guys—at their table. 'Who're these guys?' Emma asked. 'Friends of yours?'

'No, no,' Gina yanked the guy's hand out of her bra. 'They think we're hookers.'

'Your friend?' The burly guy seized Emma's hand and pulled her on to his lap. 'Filipina? We love Filipinas. Beautiful girls. Come. How much dollar?'

Emma blinked to shake off the effects of the sake. She sized up the two men. Both were wearing suits and ties. They looked like corporate types, not goons. They'd obviously had a little more booze than they could handle. They would probably be more bark, less bite.

She nodded at Gina. 'Let me humour them for a minute.'

'What you say?' The tall guy asked Emma. 'How much dollar?'

Emma pushed the burly guy aside. 'Okay, how much you got? How much you offer?'

The burly guy laughed and winked at the tall guy. 'For both, ¥100,000.'

Emma slapped his thigh. 'That's peanuts, man! As small as the nuts inside your pants.'

'Eh? You try to be funny?' The tall guy demanded. He obviously understood English more than his buddy did. 'We like funny Filipinas. What dollar you charge for full night?'

'How much dough you have, buddy? We're Americans, we charge more.'

'Americano? Not Filipino? No problemo,' he pulled out a wad of bills from his pocket.

Emma snatched the cash. She unbuttoned the top two buttons of her shirt and stuck the bills into her bra. The men ogled at her breasts; she bent over to show them more cleavage.

'Okay, show's over.' Emma straightened up. 'Now get the fuck out of here.'

'Eh? Show only begin,' the tall guy laughed. 'Go to my place. Both Americanos.'

Emma rose and let the hulk beside her squeeze past. Gina's neighbour, the lanky brute, yanked her arm to drag her along, but nearly toppled over her; she had to brace him to steady him. The hulk was clear-headed. He wrapped his hand around Emma's waist. She seized his hand and wrenched it, making him howl in agony as he spun and slammed to the ground.

The other patrons stopped eating and turned around to stare at the commotion.

The chef and two hostesses emerged from the kitchen to see what was happening.

'Bitch!' The lanky brute snarled, still clutching Gina's arm. He charged at Emma.

She dodged. He crashed into a table. He sobered up—and seethed.

The hulk's face flushed with rage. The chef tried to hold him back; he shoved the chef so hard that he flew over two tables. Patrons fled the restaurant before the chaos escalated.

From the corner of her eye, Gina saw another chef, an aged man with a long, white apron and a tall, white hat standing at the kitchen door, frozen in fear. Four female hostesses were scrambling to help the other patrons. A hostess was on the phone, maybe calling the cops.

The lanky brute clamped Emma's hands from behind. The hulk readied to strike her. Emma leaned back on the lanky brute and booted the hulk's chin. The force made the lanky brute tumble backwards, with Emma on top of him. More patrons bolted to leave. The chef, his mouth gushing blood and vomit, summoned staff from the kitchen to help him.

Gina was stunned by the swift action; she didn't see the hulk spring up and sneak up behind her, his brawny arm snaked around her neck, strangling her. She tried to scream, but he squeezed her throat. She felt herself lifted and was losing balance.

The lanky brute charged at Emma—and missed. She dashed towards Gina and swung her right foot in a wide arc and landed a crushing blow on the hulk's groin. Gina heard a snap and he collapsed backwards, pulling Gina with him, loosening his iron grip around her throat.

Gina shrieked as the lanky brute sprang up behind Emma. She ducked—just in time. He stumbled and slammed on to Gina, who was struggling to get up. She flopped back on the hulk; he was still clutching his groin and squirming in agony.

The lanky brute bounced back to face Emma. This time, she was prepared for him. In a slow, deliberate motion, she pirouetted like a ballerina on her left foot and swung her right foot at the brute's face. Her pointed shoe smashed the brute's nose, shattering the septum and spewing out a blend of blood, bone, and cartilage.

Gina attempted to stand up once more. The lanky brute slapped her face, making her tumble once again on to the hulk. The blood oozing from his broken nose had terrified him. At that moment, Emma lost her footing and fell on top of Gina.

Although it seemed like a slow-motion movie to Gina, as if she were watching a surreal scene from a horror movie, the sequence of events happened quite rapidly like a flash of lightning before the other patrons, or the restaurant crew, could figure out how to stop it. Gina was stunned by the chaos and violence that had suddenly erupted and engulfed her.

'Never knew you knew martial arts,' Gina beamed at Emma. 'You saved my life.'

'Learnt Thai kickboxing from a professional in Texas,' Emma was still on top of Gina. She helped Gina stand up. 'This was a great practice session. Hope you didn't get hurt?'

'You're marvellous!' Gina wrapped her arms around Emma. 'What other secrets—?'

'Better not ask,' Emma whispered. 'You won't like it . . . I'm a lesbian.'

Gina tightened her grip around her. 'So am I. A closet lesbian.'

'Time to open the closet and let in some sunshine?' Emma whispered in her ear.

'Absolutely, dear,' said Gina and planted a wet kiss on Emma's inviting lips.

\* \* \*

New York City is an outlier in the US and defies the US norm. Few of the city's dwellers own vehicles, and many in its five boroughs—Brooklyn, Queens, Manhattan, Staten Island, and the Bronx—choose to use public transit, or walking. NYC dwellers often walk more than any other US city folk, in heat or snow. Most New Yorkers also walk fast.

It was 5 p.m. on Wednesday, and his workmates proposed a meetup at a bar. Rick agreed. 'Do you guys ever slow down?' Rick asked Dave Scully, JQL's sales chief.

'We are. Even when we're not in a hurry to get somewhere, we are. Now figure that out.'

'I've walked more in a week in New York than I would in a month in Atlanta.'

'Wanna hear a New York joke? When all those health-focused orgs recommended people walk 10,000 steps a day, they had an asterisk link to a fine print that said New Yorkers were exempt. That's because a typical New Yorker walks more than that. That's just six blocks.'

'I don't find that funny,' Rick tried to keep in step with Dave. 'Guess the joke's on me.'

It was 7.30 p.m. when they arrived at Fantino, a bar with boutique, home-brewed beer. A couple of guys were already there and waved to Dave. 'That's Ashok, Infra Solutions chief and Ron, from Marketing. Guys, meet Rick, from Retail Solutions at our Raleigh Campus. He's planning on moving from Atlanta to White Plains.'

'Welcome to New York,' Ron gave him a high-five. 'You look beat. All that walking?'

'You bet, bro,' Rick slumped into the chair. 'Need a gallon of beer. Take a shower in beer.'

'Good one,' Ashok gave Rick a thumbs-up sign. 'Heard about you. You doubled sales in the south in two quarters? That's the stuff of legends, bro. Let me call for a round of drinks.'

'Team effort, really. Hope it works out in New York. The culture's so very different.'

'Met Tony Tightass?' Ron asked. 'Keep Tony happy. He calls the shots, you got that?'

'Tough guy,' Rick grimaced. 'Told me if I miss numbers in two quarters, he'll fire me.'

'He won't. He'll make your life hell,' Ron slapped the table. 'But look at the bright side. He'll leave you alone if you meet your numbers. Few people do that, leave you alone.'

'It's his way or the highway,' said Dave. 'He's not a bad guy. Just under lotsa pressure.'

'So is everyone,' Rick smiled as the beers appeared. 'Counting on you guys to help me.'

'You scratch my back, I'll scratch yours,' Ron laughed. 'Back, bottom, boobs, whatever.'

Dave ordered spicy fried chicken wings and sausages. Rick wondered whether this would be dinner; he was still hungry. Maybe he'd have to find a McDonald's nearby. They were bantering about office politics. Ron complained about the new VP of Sales, who was clueless and arrogant. Ashok agreed and added that the VP of Engineering was even worse, always micromanaging and taking credit for others' work.

'Hey guys, do you want to eat here?' Dave asked. 'There's an Italian joint on Bedford. If we leave this place after this drink, we can go catch dinner there before we call it a night.'

'Italian?' Ashok laughed. 'Sounds good to me. Hope it's not a Cosa Nostra joint.'

'Still stuck in your Mafia stories, Ashok?' Ron laughed. 'Yeah, we'll meet Don Michael.'

'Gimme a break,' Rick hesitated. 'I don't wanna walk another four miles for pizza.'

'Not far, just a couple of blocks,' Ron patted Rick's hand. 'Get used to walking, bro.'

'That's what Dave told me, that this joint was just a couple of blocks. Two miles?'

'You want to check it out?' Ron flipped his iPhone and leaned over and showed Rick. 'Google Maps. We're here. The Italian joint is somewhere here. That's just 1.5 miles.'

'Are you guys mad?' Rick threw up his hands. '1.5 miles? Just find a McDonald's!'

'He's messing with you, bro,' Dave laughed. 'The Italian joint is right on this block.'

By the time they finished dinner—pasta and pizza—at the cozy Italian restaurant, it was nearing midnight. Rick was in no mood to walk or even take the subway. He wanted to call Uber and crash on the bed. But Dave insisted they ride on the subway since he lived near Rick's serviced apartment. There was a light snowfall, but the unusually cold weather had made the streets wet and slippery. Rick could see his breath as he followed Dave to the nearest station, passing by colourful graffiti, neon signs, and lively bars.

'Let's get home before midnight,' Dave told Rick. 'We'll take the subway; it runs 24/7.'

They dozed as they rode the subway. There were relatively few commuters—and Dave insisted they should not board an empty subway car. So, they ran to get into one which had a dozen-odd commuters. Some were wearing headphones, some were buried in their phones, some were chatting with their friends. Everyone wore face masks.

Rick noticed a street performer playing a saxophone in the far corner, filling the car with jazzy tunes. He also smelt a faint odour of urine and sweat. He got off at his stop and had to walk a block to his serviced apartment. The streetlights were not functioning, making the sidewalk dark and eerie. He quickened his pace, hoping to reach his door safely.

Just as he turned a corner, he bumped into someone—and apologized.

'Hello, bro,' the guy stank of booze. He leaned over Rick and ripped the mask off Rick's face, causing a welt on his cheek. 'I have a knife. Shut up.'

'What the—?'

Rick stepped back, but the guy held Rick's collar and thrust a knife at his neck.

'Shut the fuck up,' he hissed. 'Gimme your dough. Wallet, cash, watch, credit cards.'

Rick reeled back. 'I will,' he mumbled. He couldn't run; he wasn't even used to walking. 'Step back. I'll empty my wallet. Gimme some space, man.'

'Shut the fuck up, will you?' The saliva from the man's mouth splattered Rick's face.

'Take my wallet. Take my watch. Let me go.'

The guy dug a gloved hand into Rick's trousers and pulled out his wallet. 'Watch?'

Rick snapped off his wristwatch and whipped his fist back. It smashed into the guy's jaw. The man was wasted and unsteady. He staggered and fell on the sidewalk. Rick had the edge. He was younger, taller, stronger.

Rick was about to land another punch when he saw a hulking shape looming from the dark. Rick had no clue if it was an ally or an enemy. The shape snuck up behind him and swung a baseball bat at Rick's head. Rick dodged in a flash.

The drunk clutched Rick's waist and pulled him down. The drunk's partner raised the baseball bat over Rick again. He rolled aside. The bat hit a rock and split. Rick leapt up. The drunk grabbed his legs. Rick crashed on the sidewalk and braced his fall with his hands. The drunk pounced on him.

'Flip him over!' The partner yelled at the drunk. The drunk was sobering up. Rick could smell his foul odour. The partner stood ready, legs wide apart, baseball bat poised, aiming to strike. The drunk had strong arms and tossed Rick over him.

'Now!' He barked.

The next moments were a blur. Maybe Rick found the power, or felt a shove from his left, or it was just luck. In a flash, Rick slid right and flung the drunk over him. Just in time.

The partner swung the baseball bat in an arc. It hit the drunk's back, breaking his spine with a dull thump. The drunk shrieked in agony and spewed his stomach's contents on Rick's shirt. His pal froze, stunned at what he had done.

Rick stood up, unsteady. The partner stood still, shocked at what he'd done to his mate. Rick's watch and wallet hung in the drunk's hands. Rick grabbed them from the drunk's loose fingers—and bolted.

He ran until he got to his serviced apartment in the next block. He realized he was shaking from shock, not from the cold, although it had begun snowing. He stank of vomit. He rushed into the bathroom for a hot shower and to scrub the stench of puke off his clothes.

# Chapter 12

**Thursday, 27 January 2022**

There's an old, corny joke about Singapore being a 'fine' city—there's a fine for everything. There are fines for spitting, littering, smoking in public places, chewing gum, illegal parking, not wearing seatbelts, speeding, running a red traffic light, consuming food and beverages in trains, riding on your neighbour's Wi-Fi, and setting off loud firecrackers.

Almost everything grinds to a halt during the Chinese New Year which, in 2022, fell on February 1 and 2. Technically, the twenty-fourth day of the twelfth month of the Chinese lunar calendar marks the beginning of the new year's festivities.

On this day, household deities report to the Jade Emperor, the supreme ruler of Heaven and Earth. Special food offerings—cakes, candies, fruits, and rice dishes—are offered to the kitchen God hoping He would put in a good word on behalf of the family to the Jade Emperor. Most households also begin an annual ritual of spring-cleaning by throwing out old and unused items to welcome the Lunar New Year on a fresh slate.

The pandemic changed how Singaporeans celebrated CNY in 2021 and 2022. The government limited the number of visitors and households one could see per day. People had to mask up and keep silent during the rituals. Some families, including Mark, Mary, and their extended families, chose to connect online via Zoom.

'You want me to help you with spring cleaning, *mah*?' Mary asked Cory in the morning.

Cory had shifted into her parents' house at Dover Road, which was closer to NUH. The Chans owned a semi-detached house near

Dover MRT station. It was also near Fairfield Methodist Primary School, where Cory and her pals had studied, and near NUS and NUH.

Her parents had insisted she move in with them to recuperate. They also had a live-in maid—called an MDW (migrant domestic worker) in Singapore—who had learnt to cook healthy Chinese meals. However, ever since her surgery, Cory preferred vegetarian food.

Cory yawned. 'No, Mama, don't wanna do any spring cleaning this year,' she adjusted the pillows to support her back on the bed. 'Too boring, too tiring.'

'We all help, *lah*. Tala can help. She know all about CNY rituals, as you know.'

'I know Tala has been with us for eight years now, but no. I'm not doing spring cleaning.'

'Okay, *lah*, your flat, your call,' Mary clicked her fingers in dismissal and walked out.

Cory scanned her phone. There was a slew of messages from her office, all of which she ignored; she was on medical leave this week. Prem had sent two texts enquiring about her health. Cory read and deleted them and yawned.

Mary returned with a steaming cup of Chinese tea which she thrust into Cory's hands. The fragrant aroma of jasmine and oolong filled the air, soothing her senses. Cory closed her eyes and took a sip. She felt the warmth and bitterness of the brew, balanced by a dash of floral notes. She hoped that when she opened her eyes, her mother would have vanished from the room.

But Mary continued to hover around her bed. 'Know what I think? Throw out all old stuff in your flat. Your kitchen so dirty one. You called pest control, *meh*? Eh, your cat is here.'

The cat purred and jumped up on to the bed. Mary shooed it away.

Cory kept her eyes closed. 'Let me calm my mind first. Got to meet the shrink at 2 p.m.'

Mary curled her lips. '*Aiyoh*, don't like that, *lah*. Don't call him "shrink".'

'Why not? That's the American term.'

'Americans, ah, no respect for psychiatrist. When I hear word shrink, ah, I think of old documentary on Discovery channel about Incas shrinking heads. Terrible, *lah*.'

'Ha, that's the funniest correlation I've heard!' Cory laughed—and abruptly stopped. '*Aiyoh*, my head hurts when I laugh.' She bowed on the bed. 'I apologize to all the dead souls whose heads were shrunk by priests who we may call as the stupid shrinkers ha, ha.'

'Okay, okay, stop laughing,' Mary sat down beside Cory. 'Don't go alone to see psychiatrist, okay? Bring Tala along. She speak good English. She help if you need help. Listen to me, okay?'

Cory pushed a pillow between them. 'I'm going to take a Grab and I don't want anyone to come with me. Not Tala. Not Dada. Not you.'

*Why is she still here?*

*Should I pretend to sleep?*

*I don't want to talk to anyone.*

Mary moved the pillow aside and began rubbing Cory's back. Cory didn't resist.

Tala appeared from the kitchen. 'I don't mind going with *mei-mei*[17]. I won't interfere.'

'I know you won't, but I want to go alone,' Cory dismissed her. 'No offence, Tala.'

'No problem, mei-mei. If Mama wants me to go with you, I go. You decide, okay? I will be in kitchen, okay? Mama, you want some more teh tarik? I make teh tarik for Dada, okay?'

Mary shook her head. 'Don't make for Dada. Give him Chinese tea, no sugar.'

Tala was the eldest in her family of six siblings from Cebu in the Philippines. She had joined the Chan household eight years ago as a young, nervous girl of twenty-three. She was a quick learner and knew how to keep secrets; every family has skeletons in their kitchen.

'Okay, I ask Dada,' Tala left the room. 'Call me if you need anything, okay, mei-mei?'

---

[17] In Mandarin, younger sister

Cory closed her eyes, hoping her mother would get the message and leave.

'When you take bath, I ask Tala make rice and mushroom soup, okay?' Mary propped a pillow to support Cory's back. 'Then you take nap. Then go NUH, okay? Bring Tala along.'

*There we go again.*

*Take Tala. Take Dada.*

*Take the world. Hell!*

Cory nodded her head and kept her eyes closed until her mother left the room.

As the Grab car sped to NUH, Cory racked her brain for answers. Why were Angela, Gina, and Rick Dynaborgs? Why was Simi left out? Why did the visitors show up only in Cory's bedroom? Was she imagining or hallucinating everything? The NUH professors— Dr Terence Lim and Dr Wilson Tan—clearly thought she was crazy. She could tell from their tone. And Larry and the other visitors had vanished since that night. It must have all been in her head. She got off the Grab car at the NUH Main Building.

Singapore had opened up. No one checked her temperature or vaccination status. Cory paused to calm her mind, brushing a piece of lint from her frilly shirt and adjusting her sleeves. She checked in at the counter and took a lift to the neuroscience OPD clinic on the fourth floor in the Kent Ridge Wing. The reception had dim lights, to accommodate neurology patients who couldn't stand brightness. Six patients, some with caregivers, waited. Cory gave her pink NRIC[18] to the girl with bright eyes and a mask.

'I'm Carmine Chan, 1 o'clock appointment with Dr Wilson Tan. Is he in?'

The receptionist adjusted her mask and clacked at the computer. 'Take a seat.'

Cory sat on the sofa and looked around. Two old patients waited for their turn. The man nodded off; jerking up periodically when he slumped too much. The woman gazed at the wall.

---

[18] National Registration Identity Card

Cory shut her eyes and recalled how fast everything had changed and had shaken her world. She wondered if she was in a big experiment where someone was changing human DNA for Dynaborgism. She had seen Hollywood flicks about brainwashed people wreaking havoc in America. But this was Singapore. Such things shouldn't happen in this unique nerd nation.

A consulting room door opened and snapped her out of her thoughts. An old woman in a wheelchair—with a fresh bandage on her head—emerged. Cory recognized the nurse, Zarina. She worked for Dr Wilson Tan. Zarina nodded at Cory and looked at the patient. She fixed her mask and leaned to the woman's left ear. 'Take your tablets, Aunty,' she said loudly and waved to an Indonesian girl. 'If you feel sick, ask your helper to call us, okay?'

The Indonesian maid ran to help push the wheelchair. '*Termia kasih*,'[19] said Zarina. '*Mengerti apa yang kukatakan pada, mak cik?*'[20]

'*Ya. Terima kasih, Kakak.*'[21]

Cory watched the patient. She had lowered her mask to her chin. Her face was blank, numb, as if moving the muscles hurt. She breathed slowly; she needed more air. But her eyes shone as her shaky hands clutched a small pouch to her chest. Cory heard tablets rattle inside their plastic cases. She wondered what was wrong with the woman. Dementia? Alzheimer's? Delusions? Hallucinations? Depression? Attempted suicide?

Dr Tan's door opened, and Zarina gestured to her. 'Dr Tan's waiting for you.'

Cory grabbed her bag and went in with Zarina. It was her third time at the clinic since NUH had discharged her. Dr Wilson Tan's clinic was plain. Cory saw the stark contrast of two colours in the room: a black leather sofa on one side and a black examining bed behind a black curtain in a bright, white-tiled room. The desk and chairs were

---

[19] In Indonesian, thank you

[20] In Indonesian, 'Understand what I told 'Aunty?'

[21] In Indonesian, 'Thank you, sister'

black, as was Dr Tan's dark uniform under his white coat. Zarina's uniform was beige, but her sweater was black.

'So nice to see you again, Cory,' Dr Tan adjusted his surgical mask and greeted her. He gestured for her to sit on the sofa and drew his chair closer. 'How have you been?' He clasped her hands. 'You can pull down your mask. However, I'll have to keep mine on.'

Cory paused before taking off her mask. She recognized the tone. It was that professional tone of detached concern that mental-health experts had mastered. It was meant to sound caring and empathetic, but it also kept a safe distance and held a subtle judgment. Cory wondered if Dr Tan really understood her or just saw her as another case to study and solve.

'I'm doing well,' she said, trying to inject some sincerity into her voice. 'I haven't had any issues with anxiety, or eating, or sleeping. I've been taking the medication you prescribed.'

'That's great, Cory,' he stared into her eyes. 'I'm so happy for you.'

Cory knew what that stare meant—he was trying to tell if she was lying. She had Googled and watched videos about how mental-health experts read their patient's body language. Could Dr Tan sense that Cory knew his tricks? Why did he sound like that with her? Was she overthinking the conversation? For a moment, her eyes glazed; Dr Tan probably caught it.

'Are you taking all the meds?' That was a smooth undercut. His voice was still calm, comforting. 'I'm guessing you're skipping some doses. Is that true?'

*How the hell does he know this?*

*Should I lie?*

*Will he send me off to rehab?*

Cory glanced at Zarina to check if she was listening; she was busy on her PC but probably listened to all the weirdos who came to see Dr Tan. 'Can I be frank with you?'

'Of course. Wasn't that the deal we agreed on the first time we met in your ward?'

'I'm not taking all the meds. They make me groggy. I feel lousy. They kill my appetite.'

Dr Tan clasped her hands. 'You need the rest, Cory. You've gone through brain surgery. It takes time to heal. Give yourself some time.'

'I came here today to convince you to stop my drugs. I want to get back to work, go to office and back to my normal routine. The stupid drugs make me want to keep sleeping.'

'Were you sleeping well before taking the medication?'

She deflected that question. 'Well, no, but I'm sleeping, like, 24/7 now.'

Dr Tan chuckled. 'That's well said, Cory dear. Oh, sorry, I shouldn't call you that,' he looked into her eyes. 'But seriously, the medication is to help you relax, heal your brain, and ease the swelling and pain. Drowsiness is a side effect. I'm happy to lower the meds for you. But quitting some of them? I wouldn't advise.'

'Why not?'

'Some of these drugs are like antibiotics, they work best when you finish the course. Do you understand?' He paused, waiting for her to reply. She stayed silent.

Cory picked up her bag. 'Can I drink some water? I'm always feeling thirsty.'

'Absolutely. Please go ahead. D'you have a water bottle in there? Should I get you a glass?'

Cory took out a 300 ml stainless-steel water bottle that she'd filled at home and drank. She closed her eyes as her anxiety and irritation rose. 'I have a proposal for you,' she said slowly. 'I'll finish the meds you gave me. But no more.'

'The refills are part of the prescription,' Dr Tan smiled. 'The course is for three months.'

'So then, no deal?'

He leaned closer to her. 'You know, Cory, I've studied for forty years. First, I did my MBBS. Then, MD. Then, psychiatry. Then, neurology and neurosurgery. But you know what's amazing? I'm still learning. Not from textbooks and lectures, but from patients. Each one is so different, so unique, no textbook can ever show the uniqueness of a person's mind. I'm so lucky and blessed to have patients like you.'

'What you're saying is that I'm too dumb to understand your logic and reasoning, right?'

He squeezed her hands. 'There you go, Cory. This is the beauty of your mind. You always surprise me with your interpretations of my simple words and inquiries. You see meanings that I never intended.'

'Er . . . not sure if you're complimenting me or insulting me. Back-handed compliment?'

Dr Tan threw up his hands, 'I rest my case.'

She seethed at his calm voice, never rising, never cracking. He spoke with a fake concern which grated on her nerves. But he had the power here, and she was just a patient. She had no choice but to obey.

'I'm your doctor, not your boss,' Dr Tan said, making Cory blink.

*Did he just read my mind?*

*Am I voicing out my thoughts?*

*Am I going frickin' mad?*

'Don't worry, I'm not reading your mind. Cory,' Dr Tan gave her a gentle tap on her arm. 'I'm just second-guessing you. Let's work together to resolve your issues. Is that okay?'

'Okay, boss,' she smiled. 'I need to believe in you. Forty years of study? That's something.'

'Great. Now that we're on the same page, let me recalibrate your medication. Maybe reduce the dosage or the frequency. But promise me you'll adhere to my recommendation.'

She collected her bag. 'When can I get back to work?'

'Soon. Let's assess after a week, okay? But first, I want to ask you a couple of questions.'

She returned her bag to the couch. 'I thought we're done?'

'Almost,' he adjusted his specs. 'Has Larry visited you since?'

'No.'

'Terry? Harry?'

'No. I've been waiting for them to show up. They've been quite elusive, dunno why.'

'Do you now feel that perhaps, just maybe, they could've been hallucinations?'

She hesitated before replying, 'D'you think so?'

'Which is why you required brain surgery in the first place, right? You suffered a stroke. You don't need to be sure about hallucinations, being doubtful is okay. What do you feel?'

She felt trapped by his loaded question. It was a lose-lose situation. If she denied the hallucinations, he would think she was delusional and drug her more. If she admitted them, he would gloat and claim he was right all along. But she wanted to escape this madness, to focus on her work, to get her mind off this uninvited nonsense. She had to stay calm, play along, and get his approval to keep her job.

'I now understand your point of view,' she nodded. 'They could've been hallucinations or delusions. I'll continue with the medication. Can I request you to taper them, please?'

Dr Tan consulted his laptop. 'I will do that with some, especially the ones that make you drowsy. I want to monitor your progress and see you in a week,' he rose, 'let's check your blood pressure and reflexes, okay? Then you can go home.'

'That's a relief, thanks,' she yawned. 'Nothing like going home and sleeping.'

'Did you come here alone? Has someone accompanied you?'

'I came alone last time as well.'

The tests drained her of energy. Cory felt a parched sensation in her mouth and a heavy weight on her eyelids. Maybe she could sneak in a nap at the reception. She still had one more task to do—refill the medication at the NUH pharmacy. The drugs that were supposed to help her, but only made her feel worse.

Dr Tan addressed Zarina. 'Can you help Carmine to the reception? Meanwhile, I'll check and adjust her medication.' He turned to Cory, 'Zarina will refill the water bottle for you. You can take a nap at the reception if you wish. I can see you're tired.'

Zarina ushered Cory out of the room. Cory felt a wave of exhaustion wash over her as she stumbled to the reception. Her steps were shaky, she had to cling to the railings on the wall. She barely noticed the other people in the corridor, until someone grabbed her hand.

She looked up and saw Prem's concerned face. He guided her to the sofa, where she collapsed on his shoulder and drifted into sleep.

\* \* \*

Bollywood is a word that has entered the English language to describe the vibrant and prolific film industry in Mumbai (formerly Bombay), India. Bollywood is a blend of 'Bombay' and 'Hollywood', reflecting its origins as a colonial imitation of the American film industry. But Bollywood has developed its own distinctive style and genres, such as the 'Masala Movie', which mixes elements of comedy, romance, action, drama, and music. Bollywood produces about 1,000 films every year, more than double the output of Hollywood, and reaches a global audience of billions.

Prem was born on 10 October 1986, a day of turmoil and tension for Bollywood. On that day, the film industry staged a massive strike to protest the 177 per cent hike in movie-ticket prices in Maharashtra, the state where Mumbai, the heart of Bollywood, is located. The strike was a showdown between the powerful chief minister, Shankarrao Chavan, and the star-studded Bollywood fraternity. Two prominent actors who also served as members of parliament for the ruling Congress party tried to broker a deal with Chavan, but their compromise was seen as a betrayal by many in Bollywood.

'The film industry must have its own independent leadership and not depend on star MPs,' Dev Anand, a top movie star often compared with Hollywood's Gregory Peck, told the media. Two of the biggest stars—Amitabh Bachchan and Sunil Dutt—were Congress MPs.

The elder Mr Pujari was a scriptwriter for Navketan Films, the movie production company founded by Mr Anand. When Mr Pujari's wife, Parvati, delivered a baby boy, Mr Anand himself came to the hospital to congratulate the proud parents and bless their newborn son. It was a rare honour and a sign of Dev Anand's respect for Mr Pujari's talent and friendship.

'Cutest smile,' Mr Anand had said. 'He's a worshipper of love. *Yeh prem ka pujari hai.*'

The Pujaris chose the name 'Prem' for their baby boy, which means love in Hindi. It was a fitting name for a child born into a Bollywood family. It was also a tribute to Mr Anand, who had directed and starred in a movie called *Prem Pujari* in 1970. The movie was a spy thriller with a romantic twist and featured some of the most memorable songs in Bollywood history.

Prem graduated in electrical engineering from the Indian Institute of Technology (IIT) in Bombay. He worked in a couple of Indian companies and applied to complete his MBA at the Singapore Management University (SMU). Scenz Software hired him to be a part of their marketing and sales team and they assigned Cory to mentor him. Cory was four years younger than him, but Prem found her to be street smart, technically experienced, and an empathetic mentor.

'I learnt more about managing people from Cory than anyone else,' Prem told the head of HR at his exit interview. 'I'm quitting because the competitor is doubling my salary.'

A year ago, Prem left Scenz and became the regional sales head at Tolledo Tech, their rival. He kept in touch with Cory, who'd had no time for him when he was at Scenz. She only wanted to work with him, nothing more. But after he switched jobs, they started dating.

This Thursday, after lunch, before CNY, Prem was bored. Most workers had left early to get ready for the CNY preparations. He tried Cory's mobile phone; it was switched off. He called her parents' house; he knew she'd be there. Mary picked up.

'Cory gone to NUH to meet Dr Wilson Tan. Never informed you, *eh*?'

'She went all alone? How come you or Mr Mark didn't accompany her?'

'She won't let us, *lah*. Not even Tala. Told her many times not go alone. Never listen one.'

He hesitated. 'Should I drop by and check if she's okay? Will she mind?'

'She will, *lah*. You know her, what. You was her boyfriend. You go. I very worried.'

Prem arrived at the NUH Neuroscience Clinic, hoping to catch Cory before she left. He checked at the reception and waited patiently, scrolling through his phone. He wondered what Dr Tan would tell Cory today. Was there any hope for her condition? He felt a surge of pity and guilt. He had been so distant from her lately. He wanted to make it up to her somehow.

After about twenty minutes, he heard a door open and looked up. He saw Cory coming out of one of the consulting rooms, leaning on a nurse. She looked pale and exhausted and was yawning uncontrollably. Prem sprang to his feet and ran to her side, just as she stumbled. He was not sure she recognized him. But she allowed him to guide her to the sofa at the reception. He asked if she was okay. She nodded and promptly dozed off.

The receptionist witnessed the scene. 'Let me call the nurse,' she said. Prem noticed that the nurse who had helped Cory out had ushered another patient into the consulting room.

In a short while, the nurse reappeared, followed by an elderly doctor. He checked Cory's pulse. 'She'll wake up in a few minutes,' he told Prem. 'It's the effect of the medicine that she would have taken before she left home. Are you with her?'

'Yes, doctor. My name is Prem. Is she okay? Does she need to be admitted?'

'She's okay, don't worry. She should wake up in fifteen minutes. Give her water to drink.'

'Will do, thanks, doctor. Is it okay to let her sleep here on the sofa?'

'That's fine.'

Zarina lifted Cory's legs and placed them gently on the sofa. Prem cradled her head on his lap to support her neck. Cory was snoring, oblivious to her surroundings.

Prem wondered whether he should inform Cory's parents, then decided against it; it would unnecessarily alarm them. He scrolled through the contacts list on his phone. He only had Rick's number; he knew Cory often confided in Rick. He typed a message on WhatsApp:

'HI, THIS IS PREM, CORY'S EX-COLLEAGUE FROM SCENZ. CAN TALK? I'M WITH CORY.'

It took one minute for Rick to respond. 'IN MEETING. CALL SIMI. HERE'S HER NUMBER.'

Prem saved Simi's number on his Android phone, then messaged her on WhatsApp:

'HI, THIS IS PREM, CORY'S EX-COLLEAGUE FROM SCENZ. CAN TALK? I'M WITH CORY.'

It took two minutes for Simi to respond. 'I'M IN PUNE. CALL ANGELA. HERE'S HER NUMBER.'

Prem saved Angela's number on his Android phone, then messaged her on WhatsApp:

'HI, THIS IS PREM, CORY'S EX-COLLEAGUE FROM SCENZ. CAN TALK? I'M WITH CORY.'

It took three minutes for her to respond. 'I'M IN LONDON. CALL GINA. HERE'S HER NUMBER.'

Prem saved Gina's number on his phone, then messaged her on WhatsApp:

'HI, THIS IS PREM, CORY'S EX-COLLEAGUE FROM SCENZ. CAN TALK? I'M WITH CORY.'

It took four minutes for Gina to respond. 'I'M IN TOKYO. CALL SIMI. HERE'S HER NUMBER.'

* * *

The Great Western Railway express train sped through the countryside, leaving behind the bustling metropolis of London. Angela watched the scenery change from urban sprawl to green fields and hills as the train approached Bristol, its destination. She had never visited Bristol before, but she had heard it was a vibrant city with a rich history and culture.

She wondered what it would be like to live there, away from the noise and pollution of London. The train made brief stops at Reading and Swindon, where some passengers got off and others got on. She noticed that the people looked different from those in London. They seemed more laid-back and friendly and spoke with a distinctive accent that she found charming. The train arrived at Bristol after about two hours of travel.

Angela stepped out of the carriage and felt a blast of cold air hit her face. She shivered and wrapped her coat around her. She looked around. Bristol was greener and cleaner, there were more trees and parks, and less traffic and litter. The sky was mostly cloudy, but every now and then a ray of sunshine broke through and brightened the city. Angela smiled and tapped Lucas's arm. She was excited to explore this new place with him.

'Wish I'd found a job in Bristol, right?' She laughed. 'Wouldn't have left Britain then.'

'Nope. You still won't get spicy food, which is why you left UK, that's what you said.'

'*Ya lah*, but this place so relaxing, air so fresh, fields so green, streets so clean.'

They walked along the side streets that Lucas seemed to know and didn't require GPS. Angela was shivering from the cold, but Lucas didn't seem bothered at all.

'Isn't Singapore like this?' Lucas pointed at the streets.

'I'm freezing,' Angela held his arm. 'Can we get into a cab or bus or something?'

'Nope. We're going to Bristol Uni, just a couple of blocks away. We can stop and have some hot coffee or cocoa. Would you like that?'

'Absolutely.' She pointed at a café down the cobbled street, 'Let's get in there.'

The café was a small and cozy place with a red brick façade and a large window that displayed an array of cakes, pastries and sandwiches. The sign above the door read: 'The Bristolian' and a chalkboard outside listed the daily specials and prices. The interior was decorated with vintage posters, photos, and memorabilia of Bristol's history and culture.

Angela opted for hot cocoa, Lucas ordered a cappuccino.

'You miss Singapore now? Isn't Singapore warm and clean and green?'

'And safe. But very humid. We've three seasons—hot, hotter, hottest. Your Sweden?'

'Nope. We have three seasons—cold, colder, coldest. I was born in a town that few people outside Sweden know—Kiruna. Northernmost town in Sweden. You heard of Esrange?'

'Er . . . doesn't ring a bell.'

'Esrange Space Centre in Kiruna does rocket launches, investigates the aurora borealis and other space stuff. It's 200 kilometres north of the Arctic Circle. Isn't that cold, I mean, cool?'

'You were born there?'

'Yes.'

'Why?'

'That you must ask my parents,' he laughed. 'My parents met at Esrange Space Centre, which was built by ESRO[22], where they worked and got married. And produced me.'

'No wonder you're so . . . so pale, right?'

'Nope. White, yes. Pale, no. Everyone looks like me in Kiruna, maybe all of Sweden.'

'So, what brings you to Bristol now? Is Greta really coming?'

'Nope. She was here in February 2020 and blasted the leaders for paying lip service to protecting the environment. Some of my student friends are taking up the fight. I want to understand what they want to do. I want to join them. Want to meet them?'

'Of course!' She punched his arm. 'That's why I'm here, right?'

'Right. I mean, wrong.'

'Huh?'

He silently sipped his coffee, then leaned towards Angela. 'Listen,' he said in a low voice, 'there's something weird going on here. Can I tell you a secret?'

She stopped sipping her beverage. 'Of course,' she wiped her mouth, 'you can trust me.'

'My friend mentioned something strange last night. He said some people were acting like aliens had taken over their minds.'

'Really?'

---

[22] European Space Research Organisation

'My friend urged me to contact the Esrange Space Centre and ask about any signs of a spaceship landing. I need to talk to my Bristol mates about this.' He watched Angela closely, expecting her to mock him. She didn't. 'He was talking about something like alien saviours who claim to protect the Earth from human destruction. Does that make any sense?'

Angela gazed at him. 'That rings a bell,' she moved her chair nearer. 'I have a friend who had a similar encounter in Singapore. I can confide in you, right?'

'You did too?'

'It wasn't me. It was my best friend. She had a stroke or something. We were eating, and she started convulsing, so we called an ambulance. What else could we do, right?'

'And?'

'The docs did brain surgery on her. And when she woke up, she said a visitor came to her room and told her she had a Covid variant called the Singapore Strain.'

'Really? That's what it's called?'

'I don't know. I'm not a medical person, right? I'm just repeating what she told me. The visitors, I think they were a group, they also told her she had to save the world. Not just wake up but also awaken the other third-gens or some such mutants.'

'Third-gen what? Mutants?'

'If I remember correctly, she said the mutants were known as Dynaborgs.'

# Chapter 13

**Friday, 28 January 2022**

Albert Einstein once said that the past, present, and future are just a stubborn illusion.

England's history proves him right. Take the University of Oxford, the oldest English-speaking university in the world, which began teaching in 1096 AD. It got a boost when King Henry II forbade English students from going to the University of Paris in 1167. But trouble brewed in Oxford when students clashed with the townsfolk in 1209. Some of them escaped to Cambridge and started a new university there.

The University of Bristol is a relatively young institution. It started as the Merchant Venturers' School in 1595, became Bristol University College in 1876, and gained its Royal Charter in 1909. It belongs to the Russell Group of elite British research universities. In 2016, it unveiled plans for a £300 million campus near the Bristol Temple Meads railway station.

Bristol Temple Meads is Bristol's oldest and biggest railway station. It opened on 31 August 1840 as the Great Western Railway's western end. British engineer Isambard Kingdom Brunel designed both the railway and the station.

Lucas had reserved a twin room at the Leonardo Hotel, a short walk from Bristol Temple Meads. Angela agreed to bunk with him. She wished Lucas would flirt with her, but he didn't. She was too shy to make the first move.

They woke up late and had a light breakfast with toast and tea at a cozy café next to the hotel that served sourdough toast with various toppings, including avocado, chorizo, and poached egg. Lucas suggested a more indulgent English breakfast of crêpes and coffee at a tiny shop on the next street, but Angela refused to walk in the biting cold.

'I'd rather walk during noon for lunch,' she said. 'Hoping the sun would be shining.'

'Nope,' declared Lucas who was still in a T-shirt and a loose jacket. 'Sun in winter is a miracle.'

'"Nope" is your favourite word, right?'

'Nope.'

At noon, the sun did peek out occasionally from behind dark clouds. As they neared the railway station, Angela was briefly jostled by commuters running to catch the train. She could hear the rumble of trains, the honking of cars, and the clickety-clack of people walking on the cobbled streets. Temple Meads Station itself was a grand and historic building, with a façade of red brick and stone and a clock tower that stood out against the sky.

'I've invited a close friend, Terhi,' said Lucas as they walked to the restaurant. 'You should meet her. She's part of the local "Fridays for Future" movement that Greta started.'

'She's British? Swedish?'

'Nope. You'll soon find out.'

'Close friend? Someone special? Girlfriend?'

'Nope. You'll soon find out.'

'Why are we walking to the train station? Going to take a train?'

'Nope. You'll soon find out.'

Angela decided not to probe any further. She needed to conserve her energy. Despite the light noon sun, it was freezing. It had drizzled the previous night and the streets were damp.

'Walk slowly, please. You're taller and slimmer than me. I'm not used to running.'

'Walk fast, burn more energy, feel less cold.'

Lucas led Angela to Victoria House, a red-brick building opposite the railway station. Lucas glanced at his watch and quickened his pace. He had made a reservation at Don Giovanni's Sicilian Restaurant. He opened the door for Angela and gestured for her to enter.

Angela stepped inside and felt a surge of warmth and comfort. The cold wind and the noise of the street faded away, replaced by the smell of garlic and cheese, and the sound of Italian music. She smiled with relief. She looked around and saw that the décor was retro and charming. The tables were covered with black-and-white chequered tablecloths that reminded her of old movies about the mafia. She wondered if Lucas had chosen this place on purpose, knowing that she was a fan of films like *Goodfellas* and *The Godfather*. She felt a thrill of excitement as she followed him to their table. She hoped this would be a lunch to remember.

The restaurant was not very crowded, a few tables were occupied by couples and families, chatting and laughing over their meals. A waitress greeted them and ushered them to a cubicle that could seat four. Lucas took a seat opposite Angela, giving her a good view of the restaurant while he faced the door.

The waitress appeared with two sets of menus and placed them on the table. She asked them if they wanted anything to drink and left them to decide. Angela opened the menu and scanned the prices. She felt a pang of sticker shock. She had always wondered why food cost so much more in England than it did in Singapore, even though Singapore had to import almost all its food, unlike the UK.

'We're early,' Lucas consulted his phone. 'Terhi should be here soon. Let me text her.'

'Is her name Terry? Sounds like someone my friend Cory mentioned in her nightmare.'

'Nope. Terhi. T.E.R.H.I. Ah, there she is. Right on time.'

Angela turned around and saw a tall, slim girl walk in. She was strikingly pale, with white hair, white eyebrows, and a white complexion. She wore a white dress that hugged her slender figure. She looked like a ghost in a scary, B-grade flick, or a vampire in search of prey. Lucas stood up and greeted her with a wide smile. She gave Lucas a quick hug.

Angela extended her hand to Terhi and said hello. Terhi returned the greeting verbally but waved casually back and sat next to Lucas, as if she were dismissing Angela. She felt a surge of anger and resentment. Was Terhi trying to make a statement? Was she just rude by nature?

Angela decided to not let Terhi ruin her lunch. She smiled tightly and sat down.

'Marie should be here soon,' Terhi told Lucas. 'She's coming from Exeter.'

The waitress reappeared with a smile and a notepad. Lucas scanned the menu and decided on prawns sautéed in garlic butter and flambéed in brandy. Angela wanted something warm and comforting, so she asked for a bowl of thick, hot minestrone casalinga soup and garlic bread. She chose hot English breakfast tea with milk; it would soothe her throat. Lucas wanted beer. Terhi asked for cold water. No wonder she's as slim as a lamppost, Angela thought.

'Angela is from Singapore,' said Lucas. 'She's dying to know where you're from.'

'Three guesses,' Terhi smiled. 'If you want a hint, my last name is Tamm. It means oak.'

Angela laughed, relieved that Terhi had at least acknowledged her existence. 'Lucas told me you're not from Sweden or Britain. You should be from . . . Norway? Denmark? Holland?'

'Incorrect,' said Terhi.

Angela tried to size her. 'Germany? Finland? Russia?'

'Incorrect, but close.'

Angela gazed at her. 'Lithuania? Latvia? Iceland?'

'Incorrect,' she winked at Lucas. 'If she gets it right, I'll pay our bill. Else, we go Dutch.'

'Nope,' Lucas laughed. 'You named every north European country except one. Estonia.'

Angela touched her temple in mock frustration. '*Aiyoh*, how could I forget Estonia?'

'Estonia is a small country with big ambitions,' Terhi said. 'Like Singapore.'

Angela perked up. 'You know about Singapore? Have you been to Singapore?'

'I have. We love Singapore. Two countries with lots of similarities. Don't you think?'

'I'm ashamed of myself. You know more about Singapore than I know about Estonia. You've even visited Singapore before. I can barely locate Estonia on a map of Europe.'

'Don't be, you're in good company,' Terhi laughed. 'Many people in Europe also cannot find Estonia on the map. Singapore does a better PR job in Europe . . . ah, there's Marie.'

'Sorry I'm late,' she folded her hands and slid in beside Angela. 'Hi, I'm Marie.'

Marie looked Asian. She had a light-brown complexion and wore a thick sweater. 'You're feeling cold, correct?' Asked Marie. 'Unlike these two creatures who're used to the Arctic.'

'I absolutely do,' Angela extended her hand. Marie removed her gloves and shook it.

Lucas pointed at Angela. 'You can never guess where Marie is from. Three guesses.'

Angela gazed at Marie again. 'India? Sri Lanka? Pakistan?'

Marie glanced at Terhi and raised an eyebrow.

'Nope,' said Lucas.

'Mexico? Brazil? Chile?'

'Nope,' Lucas winked at Marie. 'If she gets it right, I'll pay our bill. Else, we go Dutch.'

'Okay, last three chances, please,' said Angela. 'Portugal? Libya? An Arab nation?'

'Not Arabia,' Marie smiled. 'I'm from Mauritius, it's on the southeast coast of Africa.'

'*Aiyoh*, I'd have never thought of that one. I'm from Singapore. You know—'

'Of course, I know Singapore,' Marie laughed. 'I was there in 2016. So very expensive.'

'I'm so ashamed of myself. Both Terhi and you have visited Singapore. I can barely locate Estonia or Mauritius on a map of Europe or Africa. I should pay this bill today, right?'

'Nope,' said Lucas. 'We go Dutch. The three of us are European. Marie is a UK citizen.'

The waitress arrived with a steaming tray of soup, freshly baked breads, and beverages. She set them down on the table and handed the menu to Marie, who looked overwhelmed by the choices.

'Is everything to your liking?' The waitress asked with a smile. 'Your main courses will be ready soon. Enjoy your meal.'

'Marie, they have vegan dishes here too,' Terhi reassured her friend. 'I ordered the veg lasagna. It's delicious and filling. I know you're always looking for healthy options.'

Marie smiled. 'I'll have what she's having,' she told the waitress, handing back the menu. 'Can I get a cup of English breakfast tea with milk? I need something warm and soothing.' She rubbed her hands together as if to ward off the cold.

Lucas looked at Terhi and Marie. 'All ready for tonight? I want to bring Angela along.'

'Is Greta coming?' Asked Angela. 'She started *Fridays for Future,* right?'

'She started the movement,' said Marie. 'We keep up the momentum.'

'Marie leads the movement here,' said Lucas. 'About 500 students will attend at the U.'

'That's amazing,' Angela perked up. 'I'd love to attend.'

'Isn't that why you're here?' Terhi asked. 'Lucas told me you'd had a surreal experience.'

'You did?' Angela glared at Lucas. 'You told her about Cory? Or Larry?'

'Nope. Told her what you told me last night. Waiting to hear it from you.'

'It's hard to believe. Cory and I grew up together, same age. Four of us friends were having a casual lunch, catching up on gossip. Cory suddenly started convulsing and foaming at the mouth. We called for an ambulance, rushed her to NUH. The doctors said she had a blood clot in her brain and needed to operate. When she eventually woke up, she was babbling about an alien guy who visited her and told her she was infected with the Singapore Strain of Covid.'

'That's news,' Marie said. 'Singapore Strain? New variant? Did she get Covid-19?'

'Yes, quite severe. Delta variant. Suffered more than Gina and me. Gina is our other common friend. Both of us had the Omicron variant, mild.'

'Figures, doesn't it?' Marie looked at Terhi, who nodded. 'Go on, what happened then?'

'That's all. Do you think the visitor was imaginary? Seemed very real to her.'

'Extraterrestrial?' Lucas asked Angela, then glanced at Terhi. 'You have a theory.'

'I'm not surprised by your scepticism,' said Terhi. 'Most people don't believe in aliens. But I come from Estonia. Roughly 50 per cent of the population think aliens exist.' She looked at Angela with a curious expression. 'Ever heard of *Oumuamua*? A Hawaiian word which means "messenger". It's also the name of the first interstellar object detected passing through our solar system. Some scientists think it might be alien tech.' She leaned forward and lowered her voice, 'What if Cory's alien guy was trying to send us a message through *Oumuamua*?'

'My friends at Esrange think it's a comet, but go ahead, Terhi.'

'*Oumuamua* is the first interstellar object detected that passed through our solar system,' Terhi took a sip of water. 'Telescope detected it in October 2017. Exhibited non-gravitational acceleration. Some astronomers believe it could be a spacecraft.'

'Er, what's this got to do with us?' Asked Angela. 'Did it land on Earth?'

'Nope,' said Lucas. 'Terhi's point is that we can't rule out extraterrestrial presence. Two years before that, Esrange detected an alien object that entered our atmosphere and disintegrated. It was a bolide, which is a bright meteor. Burst over the oceans on 7 September 2015.'

'Over Thailand, right?' Angela perked up. 'This one I know. Cory was in Phuket when the comet combusted. Even filmed it on her mobile phone. Some ash flew into her mouth, tasted salty. But that was a meteor and not a spaceship, right?'

'Nope,' said Lucas. 'We don't know. It blew up all over. Maybe the last piece blew up over Thailand. We think the object burst above our atmosphere and spread across the Earth.'

'What's the significance of this?' Asked Angela. 'I'm quite blur. Enlighten me, please.'

'It seems to have impacted some people,' replied Marie. 'Probably caused some mutations in their DNA. These are just theories, nothing scientifically proven yet, like—'

'Did it impact you, Terhi, Marie?' Asked Lucas. 'Heard rumours that some of Greta's followers may also have an altered DNA. They have some weird term for it, right Terhi?'

'I know,' Angela exclaimed. 'Cory babbled it. A Dynaborg?'

Marie stared at Angela and grabbed her hand. 'Who's Cory? One of us?'

'The term means something to you, right? Cory wasn't just dreaming this stuff, right?'

'Means more than you can imagine,' said Marie. 'Terhi personifies it. Don't you know?'

'Know what?'

'Terhi is a physiotherapist.' Marie glared at Lucas, 'You didn't tell? Terhi, you didn't—'

'Nope,' said Lucas. 'Didn't want to shock her. She will find out soon enough.'

'Find out what?' Angela looked askance. 'What's it about Terhi that will shock me?'

'Terhi is a trained physiotherapist,' Lucas explained, 'but she has a unique gift that few or no physios have. Did you notice Terhi didn't shake your hand when you extended it?'

'I thought that was . . . strange. She hugged you, right? She touched your back, right?'

'Nope. We hugged. I touched her back. She didn't touch mine.'

Terhi smiled warmly and reached out her hand to Angela. Angela hesitated for a second, then decided to be polite and shook it with her right hand.

As soon as their hands touched, Angela felt a jolt of electricity surge through her veins, like a lightning bolt striking her heart.

She gasped and jerked back, losing her balance, knocking over the dishes and glasses on the table. The sound of shattering glass and splashing liquids filled the air. Angela stared at Terhi in horror, wondering what had just happened.

* * *

Rick didn't know whether he was hallucinating or falling sick. He had dozed off at about 2.30 or 2.36 a.m. He dreamt he was back home in Atlanta, lying next to the railway tracks. He loved the shrill notes— steel on steel—that trains made. He heard the clanking of locomotives roaring past, followed by the sound of breaking glass. He fell off an ark—and woke up with a start.

'What the—?' His cell phone had fallen from the bed but had not cracked. 'Who the—?'

The room felt like a tomb, cold and quiet, with only the faint hum of the air-conditioner breaking the silence. The window was covered by a thin curtain that barely blocked the pale light from the streetlamps. Shadows danced on the walls, creating a sense of eeriness.

'Ricardo?' A soft female voice wafted into Rick's ears.

Rick was jolted awake. He blinked rapidly, trying to clear his blurry vision. He felt a throbbing pain in his head, a reminder of the alcohol he had consumed last night. But something was wrong. He wasn't in his cozy bedroom in Atlanta, but in a serviced apartment in New York City where there weren't any railway tracks.

Rick rubbed his eyes. 'Where the—?'

She was standing against the light at the door. He couldn't see her features, just her silhouette.

'Hello Ricardo,' she said. 'I'm Whitney.'

'Whitney Houston?' Rick asked, puzzled. 'That's the only Whitney I know of.'

'I like your sense of humour.' She took one step inside. 'Do you know where she was born? And when?'

'New York?'

'Newark, New Jersey. Just a few blocks from here.'

'Is this a quiz?'

'Maybe. Maybe not. Depends on your point of view.'

'Who the hell are you? How did you get into my apartment? Do I know you?'

'You don't. I know you. You're Ricardo Ramsey. You almost died today. I saved you.'

Rick felt a surge of panic as he remembered the crash. 'That's impossible,' he said, struggling to free himself from the bed. 'I escaped by a miracle. You were never there. How could you possibly know what happened?'

'Don't worry about what I know—or don't,' she said. She spoke in a steady, gentle tone, as if she was used to dealing with unruly children. Her voice had a soothing quality, but also a hint of firmness and authority. She sounded like a mother who loved her son, but also wanted him to behave. 'This conversation is about you. About your role.'

'Yeah? I'm planning to move from Atlanta to New York. Is that why you're here?'

'I like your sense of humour. I'm here to wake you up. It's time.'

'Time for what?'

'Time to wake up and smell the roses, Rick.'

'What the—?'

Rick pinched himself to check if he was still drunk. 'Come closer, please? I can't see you. Should I come closer?' He tried to get up, but his legs were paralysed. 'Shit, I can't move!'

'You don't need to,' she advanced a couple of steps. 'Listen to me first, will you?'

'Who the hell are you?' Rick was now getting alarmed. 'Get out of my apartment!'

'Be calm. I'm not here to mug you. Here to help you wake up to understand your Karma.'

'Karma? Oriental baloney. I don't believe in the Karma crap. Get out!'

'Does it matter what you believe? Don't you want to help save the planet? Wake up.'

'You're Greenpeace? PETA? SOS?'

Rick's mind raced with images of Joseph Daniel. He had been Rick's co-worker at JQL New York. He was influenced by Greta Thunberg's speeches. He left JQL to join Greenpeace and PETA and vowed to hack into the computer systems of polluting corporations. But his crusade ended abruptly when two gunmen on a motorcycle shot him in the head on a street in NYC. Was Rick going to die like him?

'Calm down, listen to me, take a deep breath,' she said. 'Close your eyes.'

He looked at Whitney with desperation. 'You want my money? Take my credit card—'

She snapped at him. 'Shut up and close your eyes,' she waited for him to comply. 'Now count backwards from nine. Slowly. Silently.'

His heart was pounding in his chest like a drum in a marching band. He felt a surge of panic, dreading what she might do. He tried to scream but his larynx wouldn't move. He wanted to run but his muscles were paralysed. He wanted to cry but tears clouded his eyes and he had to shut them. Was he paralysed by fear or was this weird woman controlling his muscles? He counted in his head, hoping for a miracle. Nine . . . eight . . . seven . . .

'Good. Keep your eyes closed. Remember boozing on Wednesday night, don't you? Remember getting mugged and almost maimed at midnight, don't you? Remember taking a shower at 1.30 a.m. on Thursday, don't you? Now open your eyes and check the time.'

Rick opened his eyes and touched his iPhone. It showed 03:00. 'So what?'

'Check again. It is 3 a.m. on Friday, 28 January 2022.'

'You're kidding,' Rick touched his iPhone again. 'Jesus Christ! I slept for twenty-four hours?'

'Now that I have your attention—'

'What the heck is going on? Why can't I move my goddamn legs?'

'You can. When I'm done. I saved your life when I swerved your body below the drunk's. Remember that miracle? You don't need to thank me. But you need to listen to me.'

'Who're you?'

She stepped closer, but not close enough for him to see her features clearly; the light was behind her. As she got closer, Rick could smell barbecued shrimp, or was it smoked salmon?

'Never mind who I am. Ask instead who *you* are,' she paused. 'You're a Dynaborg.'

Rick scratched his head. 'Dyna what? Am I going bonkers? Am I dead?'

'The old Ricardo is dying. The new avatar will soon emerge as soon as you're ready to accept.'

'Accept what?'

'Your DNA is changing. Your body and brain will take time to adjust. Be patient.'

'If this isn't the biggest bullshit I've ever heard—'

'You're one of the chosen ones. There are 12 million others like you. Wake up. Realize your potential and purpose in life. Connect with the rest. Become responsible.'

Rick felt a surge of terror as he realized he was trapped in his own body. He could only wiggle his fingers and turn his head. The rest of him was numb and immobile. His mind raced with questions and fears.

'What's happening to me?' He asked her, tearing up. 'Did I have a stroke? Am I paralysed for life? Is this some kind of nightmare? Am I already dead and is this hell?' He tried to scream but found he couldn't.

'D'you want me to repeat myself? Stop struggling. You're alive. You're evolving.'

'Buddhist philosophy? You're a damn philosopher? No right to barge into apartments!'

Whitney remained silent. Rick waited for her to say something, anything; she didn't. He felt a knot in his stomach. Sweat dripped from his forehead. Tears blurred his eyes. The smell of burning flesh grew stronger and more nauseating. He wondered if he was going to die.

She was standing close to him. 'Close your eyes—and I'll be gone,' she whispered. 'Open your eyes—and I'll be there.'

Rick squeezed his eyes shut. 'All right, I'm going to try this. Maybe it will work.' He began to count backwards from nine, slowly and loudly. The soft humming from the aircon began to filter into his ears which were now hyper-sensitive to any sound in the room. The smell of burnt flesh seemed to be gradually wafting away.

He opened his eyes and looked around. He was alone. There was no one else there.

Rick felt a surge of relief as he realized he could move again. He wiped the sweat from his forehead with his hand and grabbed his phone and checked the time: 3.30 a.m., Friday, 28 January 2022. That was ridiculous. Had he really slept for twenty-four hours? His heart raced.

Rick leapt out of bed and turned on the light. He looked around the room, searching for any signs of danger. Everything seemed normal, just as he had left it. He was still trembling and wrapped the blanket around his body. He didn't dare to turn off the lights.

Rick was startled by the sudden ringing of his phone. It hit his eardrums like a gong going off inside his head. He felt his heart skip a beat. He reached for the phone, which was vibrating violently on the nightstand. He flipped it on and saw an unknown number on the screen.

He hesitated, then stammered. 'Er, hello? Who is this?'

'It's Cory from Singapore.'

* * *

Cory took deep breaths, trying to calm her racing heart. Ever since her surgery, she had been experiencing episodes of irregular heartbeat. She wondered if it was a side effect of the drugs, or anxiety, or a result of the damage to her brain. She had searched online for the possible causes of heart arrhythmia and found a long list of scary conditions—atrial fibrillation, blocked coronary arteries, Covid-19.

*Am I sweating despite the aircon?*

*Do I feel a tightness in my chest?*

*Don't panic. Deep breaths.*

Maybe it was the coronavirus. She had contracted the Delta variant at the apex of the pandemic on 1 June 2021. She had spent a week in the special Covid-19 wing at the Singapore General Hospital.

She hadn't needed a ventilator, but her blood tests showed a dangerously low platelet count.

The doctors had diagnosed her with thrombocytopenia, a condition that can cause excessive bleeding and bruising. They gave her two infusions of blood platelets, which helped to stabilize her condition. Since then, she had been experiencing an irregular heartbeat. She wondered if it was because of the blood transfusions, or the new Singapore Strain.

This Friday morning, she had woken up with a pounding headache and a racing heart. She felt like she had run a marathon in her sleep, but she couldn't remember any dreams. She poured hot water from a flask and took her time to sip from a glass tumbler.

Mary had mixed lemon and honey to give the water flavour. Cory closed her eyes and savoured it. The warm liquid soothed her throat and calmed her nerves. She wished she could stay in bed all day, but she knew she had to face the world.

Cory had no problem planning CNY in previous years. She had enthusiastically attended every CNY Reunion Dinner ever since she could remember. Her dad's trading business in computer parts and her mom's real-estate agency were booming. Cory knew relatives would descend at their house in anticipation of getting fat, red Hongbao packets stuffed with cash. She enjoyed the festivities and the feeling of belonging to a large and prosperous family.

At previous Reunion Dinners, Mark, Mary, Cory, and Tala would all pitch in to do the cooking. They would set the table with a feast of delicacies and invite everyone to dig in. This year, Mary planned to cook just a couple of meat dishes.

'For the last time, Mama, don't expect me to help with the CNY cooking this year.'

'No need, *lah*. Just rest. Can? Don't help with cooking, help with eating. Can?'

'I told you I feel nauseated by the smell of meat. I'll just have some veggie soup.'

'Don't act smart, young lady,' Mary brandished a ladle. 'You need rest, okay? I not asking you to cook or clean, okay? But don't cry cry. Be nice to visitors, okay? Eat small portions, okay?'

'Small portions of corpses? Dead animals? Dead birds? Dead fish?'

'Look who's talking,' Mary mocked her. 'You love tandoori chicken with your Indian friend. You roam with friends to try different hawker food. You forgot all that, *meh*?'

'The cheese has moved. I only like veggies now. Something has changed.'

'Nothing changed, *lah*. You had brain surgery. You're recovering. Your body don't want meat for a while. We prepare more veggies this time, okay? I buy more Chinese greens, cheese, yoghurt, veggies. But our guests need meat, okay? We need meat. How? Don't make, *ah*?'

'I can't change the world. I can only change myself. I can't even change you, Mama.'

'I don't wanna change. Dada and Tala and I happy way we are. Don't act smart, okay?'

'You're forcing me to take part, to cook, to eat, to condone killing innocent animals.'

'Don't talk cock. Indian boy putting all this veggie nonsense in your head, is it? Prem?'

'He's the one who introduced me to tandoori chicken and shish kebab and fish tikka.'

'That doesn't mean he eat it, right? I know many Indians are veggies. Is he?'

'He loves chicken and fish. He loves beer and wine. Why are you after him now?'

'Trying to find out who put such stupid ideas in your head. Your Indian friend Simi, *ah*?'

'It's Larry.'

'Oh, that imaginary friend? You called Dr Terence Lim Larry. I so *paiseh*, embarrassed.'

'So now you don't like my real friends or my imaginary friends? You're weird, Mama.'

'Am I?' Mary mocked her. 'Don't talk about Larry in front of our relatives, okay? Please.'

'Don't worry, Mama, I'm not keen to meet anyone or talk about anyone.'

Cory yawned. For the last few nights, she had been praying for Larry or Harry to show up. Nobody did. Maybe they did, but Cory couldn't remember any of it when she woke up. It was the freaking drugs. They were making her drowsy, making her go into deep, dreamless sleep.

Cory had laid out all the drugs the doctor had prescribed and checked each on the Internet. Most listed drowsiness as a side effect. She hated feeling lethargic all the time. She wanted to be alert and sharp, especially when she talked to Larry. If she wanted to remember conversations with Larry, she'd have to stop all medication. But she had made a deal with Dr Wilson Tan to continue taking all the drugs until the next visit on Thursday, 3 February.

She didn't trust the doctor or his diagnosis. Maybe he was just trying to make money. But what if he was right? What if she started getting fits again? What if the fits occurred when she was alone in her room? What if she hurt herself or worse? Stopping all drugs would be too high a risk to take too soon. She had to weigh the pros and cons carefully.

Mary was back from the kitchen. 'Can check with Dr Tan if you can eat meat?'

'*Aiyoh*, meat again? He didn't stop me. I don't want to eat meat now. Any more. Never.'

'Your next visit to Dr Tan, I come along, okay? Or Dada. Cannot go alone.'

'No need, *lah*. I can manage by myself.'

'You could not last time. Prem drop you home. You sleep on their sofa.'

'It's the freaky drugs. Make me drowsy all the time.'

'Why not ask your friend to accompany you? Simi?'

'I'm not a kid any more.'

'Angela?'

'I don't need anyone.'

'Gina?'

'She's in Japan.'

'Prem?'

'Nope.'

'Larry?'

\* \* \*

Simi was getting irritated and impatient with Indians in India. For instance, Kirumi's CEO, Dr Ramachandran, had dined with her on Sunday and was never seen or heard after that. The CFO, Mr Viswanathan, was an enigma. There were reported sightings of him at the event, but every time Vinod Kumar went to get his signature, Mr Viswanathan would vanish.

Vinod was no better. He'd dash in from somewhere, breathless, and dash out after a brief conversation. The worst was the turbaned Sikh, Dharam, who'd mentioned the intriguing term, Dynaborg, and then vanished. She would soon need to leave, her flight was tomorrow.

The only people that Simi thought sane were those with whom she had no connection—the Maharashtrian mother and her cute, four-year-old daughter, Leena, who mistook Simi for her aunt, and Padma Pawar, the glamourous sales assistant who followed Vinod around like a lamb. Simi had learnt that Padma was an airhostess and had switched careers when Covid struck. She liked the company, the boss, and the culture—and had continued in her sales role.

'You could've been a model or even tried for roles in Bollywood,' Simi told her during the lunch break. 'Even without makeup, you look like a star. I've seen no one so pretty.'

'Thank you for the compliment, but no thanks,' Padma dug her fork into a piece of chicken tikka. 'Beautiful girls are a dime a dozen in Bollywood. I like sales, not acting.'

'Wasn't acting part of your training as an airhostess?'

'That's why I quit. As an airhostess, you must act pleasant even with rude people.'

Simi used a spoon to stir the white, fragrant curd rice with spicy, steaming sambar from the idli tray. 'Was it easy for you to learn to sell agrobiology products? Study chemistry?'

'I studied biology in school and college. I wanted to study zoology, become a vet. But my parents discouraged me. I bridged the gap when I married a doctor.'

'You're married?' Simi spilt her sambar. The chef had made idlis especially for her.

Padma glared at her, 'You look shocked.'

'I'm sorry. That wasn't supposed to be said as an insult. I had misperceptions about you.' Simi folded her hands and bowed, '*Mea culpa.*'

'Apology accepted,' Padma laughed, immediately drawing attention from a group of males at another table who were discreetly ogling her. 'Look around, watch them.'

Simi turned to look; they avoided her stare. Just then she saw a hefty guy walk in through the main door: Dharam. He walked to the table where the four guys sat nursing cups of chai. He spoke with them and two guys immediately gulped down their tea and took off. Dharam adjusted his tie, straightened his jacket, puffed out his chest, and walked towards Simi's table.

'Hello, ladies, may I have the pleasure—'

'Where the devil did you disappear?' Simi interrupted him. 'Searching for you all week.'

'My apologies, Ms Sundar,' Dharam drew up a seat and smiled at Padma. 'I'm Dharam.' He extended his hand for her to shake. Padma folded her hands in namaste, instead.

'I'm Padma. I'm with Pollenta. Ms Sundar and I are colleagues.'

'It's my lucky day to meet two pretty ladies,' Dharam bowed. 'If I may—'

'Cut the crap,' Simi cut him short. 'Are all Indian men like this or just coincidence?'

'Like what?'

'Like say something intriguing, then disappear. Or appear to be so busy that they have no time to finish the conversation they started. All the men I've met here fit this exact mould.'

'Er, sorry, you know we have corporate VIPs in town. Everyone's busy with many—'

'So busy that nobody has time to even check their WhatsApp?' She sneered. 'Weirdos!'

'Er, sorry for that, Ms Sundar. We get so many ads on WhatsApp. Always beeping.'

'Never mind. Before you run off again, can you continue where you left off? Dynaborg?'

'Er, I'm hungry. Can I order some food?' He glanced at Padma. 'Get you some chai?'

'No, thanks,' Padma waved her hand. She wasn't surprised that he didn't ask Simi.

Dharam gestured to a waiter and spoke in Hindi. 'Veg biryani *aur* masala chai *leke aana, fatafat.*[23] He turned to Padma, 'What do—'

'She's in sales,' Simi said, curtly. 'Stop hitting on her. She's married. But you can hit on me,' Simi smirked. 'I'm single—and available.'

Padma laughed. Dharam squirmed.

'You very witty, Simi-ji. Padma-ji is married, no problem. I'm also married, ji.'

The waiter appeared with a steaming plate of spicy vegetable biryani cooked in fragrant Basmati rice and a cup of hot and aromatic masala chai infused with cloves and cinnamon.

'That smells really refreshing,' Simi told the waiter. 'Can I have some masala chai?'

'Me, too,' Padma smiled at the waiter. 'Less sugar, please.'

Dharam took a spoonful of biryani and a sip of tea. 'You've heard of Dynaborgs?'

'Neither of us have,' Simi lied. She remembered every detail of Cory's babbling delirium at NUH. Feigning ignorance would be better for her to compare notes.

'Dynaborgs are a new breed of humans. It's assumed they have a mutated DNA because they were infected with Covid-19 and that virus

---

[23] In Hindi, 'Bring masala tea also, quickly'

somehow mutated and changed their DNA. Or because the mutated DNA was passed from one individual to another, we don't know.'

'Are you a genetic engineer?' Simi asked. 'Or a scientist? I'm in genetics, you know.'

'I'm a marketing guy, Simi-ji, not a scientist. I know this because I carry the mutation.'

Simi's antennae went on hyperalert. 'Sorry to interrupt. How do you know you carry?'

'I experienced an altered state of being. I can sense changes in my behaviour, attitudes.'

'So can I when I listen to someone like Greta Thunberg or Kailash Satyarthi. He won the Nobel Peace Prize in 2014, right? Does that make them, us, Dynaborgs? Not criticizing you.'

'Like OBE, out-of-body experience?' Padma asked. 'Alien visits?'

'Exactly,' Dharam's eyes lit up. 'How do you know? Did you have? Are you one—?'

'No. Just guessing. As you know, many Indians claim to be spiritual. As a society, we believe in religion, spiritualism, the occult, et al. Your experience is similar?'

'I've experienced OBE and visitations that I can't explain. However, there was nothing spiritual or religious about it. The occult? Maybe. It's about saving our biodiversity.'

'What visitations?' Simi asked. It reminded her of Larry visiting Cory in her bedroom.

'I'm not sure. Maybe it was an alien entity. Maybe my mind playing tricks. I don't know.'

'Do you go about telling everyone about these things?' Simi frowned. 'You didn't know me when we met briefly on Sunday. You appeared out of the blue and mentioned Dynaborg.'

'That's what I'm talking about. I can't explain it. You're the second person in a month that I was drawn to. Somehow, something told me you knew about Dynaborgs. Did you?'

Simi gazed into his eyes. He wouldn't know Cory or the experience she'd had. Cory had specifically mentioned that she, Simi, was not part of the clan. What else does this guy know?

'Heard someone mention it in Singapore. I thought it was delirium. I know nothing more.'

'You are a link, Simi-ji,' Dharam touched her hand. 'Now or in future. You're one of us.'

Before Simi could digest that statement, a guy in a suit walked over briskly to their table.

'Ms Simi Sundar? Hope you've finished your lunch, ma'am,' he said, breathless. 'Our CEO's speech is going to start in five minutes in the conference hall. He mentioned your name and asked us to find you. Can you come with me now, please?'

* * *

Atlanta has been dubbed the 'Black Mecca' since the 1970s. In 1971, *Ebony* magazine called Atlanta the 'Black Mecca of the South'. Betty was born in 1948 in Atlanta to parents who were slaves. She was a 'child of the plantation', derogatorily called 'Mulattoes'. These were kids born to Black women who had been raped by White men—usually the owner or one of his sons or the plantation overseer.

Betty served as a 'house' slave; she toiled in the household rather than in the fields. Her White master violated and impregnated her when she was fifteen. Their mixed-race daughter, Susan, was born on 15 December 1963, the same day Martin Luther King Jr denounced segregation as a 'glaring reality' in Atlanta. Betty trained the young Susan to cook and sew so she could have some skills to sustain herself as an adult. Betty had no hope that slavery would ever end in the US.

When Susan reached school age, they accepted the Black community as a part of their society. President Lyndon Johnson enacted the Voting Rights Act on 6 August 1965, which outlawed discrimination. Susan was smart and lucky enough to complete high school in Atlanta. Later, she met and married a Mexican immigrant, Horatio, who loved to study. She funded his education at the University of Georgia. They tied the knot in 1984 at the Warren Methodist Church, where Martin Luther King Jr had once preached.

Their son, Ricardo, arrived on 1 May 1988. Their daughter Emily, on 1 June 1990, exactly ten years after CNN's debut on 1 June 1980. On that Sunday, at 5 p.m. Eastern, Ted Turner briefly presented CNN, followed by CNN's first newscast anchored by the spouse team of David Walker and Lois Hart; the first TV channel to offer twenty-four-hour news.

Emily earned her bachelor's degree from the University of Georgia at Athens (UGA) and her master's degree in electronic media from the Grady School of Journalism at the University of Georgia. CNN hired her as an intern on 1 June 2010. She was on rotation for the first year and discovered her passion in CNN's research wing, a vital, backend function that provided background research for news stories. Emily enjoyed the flexibility the job gave her. She could work from the office or home, she just needed a secure Internet connection and access to CNN databases.

She felt she 'belonged' at CNN. However, that sense of belonging didn't translate well in her social circles. She had Horatio's fair complexion and Susan's curly hair; her eyes were hazel brown and her lips were soft pink. Unlike Rick, who looked Afro-American, Emily didn't match any mould—and felt excluded.

Even today at the hospital, for example, some hospital staff assumed she was a Hispanic. One even wondered if she was from India. She had to explain calmly that she was 100 per cent American, a native-born Atlantan who could trace her family history back 100 years when an ancestor had been chained and forced to land in America on a slave ship.

They had rushed Horatio into the OR in an unconscious state after a heart attack. Susan and Emily huddled in the Atlanta hospital's waiting lounge. Emily kept dialling Rick on his mobile phone and it kept going to voicemail. Emily had draped a brown sweater around her body and kept checking her phone. Susan was staring blankly at the wall.

Emily spotted a man in scrubs enter and scan the waiting room.

'*¿Alguien español aquí?* Anyone Spanish here?' There were six others in the lounge.

Emily ignored that question. Then it suddenly struck her—her dad was a Latino, and the doctor might be looking for Spanish relatives. '*Nosotras hacemos,*' she said. 'We do.'

'*¿Tu hablas ingles?*' He asked Emily. 'You speak English? You're Horatio's relatives?'

'Si, I mean, yes. I'm his daughter. This is my mom. Is he okay? Are you the surgeon?'

'I'm a nurse. Your dad is okay. His heart surgery was successful. We've just wheeled him to the recovery room. He's awake. Doesn't he speak English? He's been speaking Spanish.'

'Odd . . .' said Emily, as her mother walked over. 'Pa's okay, Ma. He's speaking Spanish.'

'That means he's *not* okay,' said Susan. 'He hasn't spoken Spanish in four decades!'

'Strange,' the nurse grimaced. 'Maybe it could be the effect of the anaesthetic.'

Susan frowned. 'Did you guys operate on his heart or his brain?'

Emily touched the nurse's arm. 'Can we see him, please?'

'Of course. Come with me,' he opened the glass door for them to exit. 'You need to wear fresh surgical masks which I will give you before you enter. Whisper in the recovery room.'

The recovery room was a small hall with patients cordoned off by U-shaped plastic curtains that gave patients some privacy. The smell of antiseptic was overwhelming, and Emily covered her nose. She glanced at the patients lying on gurneys in open cubicles; they were in pre-op or post-op stage. Some were groaning in pain, some were sleeping, and some were staring blankly at the ceiling. The nurse handed out disposable surgical masks and gloves. He ushered them to a bed and drew the plastic curtain around them. Horatio's eyes were open, tubes and wires ran from his chest, abdomen, and pelvis. He looked pale.

'Horatio!' Susan rushed to him and hugged him lightly. 'Thank the Lord you're okay.'

'*¿Quién eres tú?*[24] Horatio asked bewildered.

'I'm your wife, you fool,' Susan laughed between sobs. 'Don't speak Spanish to me.'

---

[24] In Spanish, 'Who are you?'

Emily pulled down her mask to show her face. 'Pa, I'm Emily, your daughter.'

'*¿Hija de quién?*[25] Horatio asked, horrified.

'You should pull down your mask,' the nurse told Susan. He whispered in Horatio's ear: '*Tu esposa e hija están aquí. Habla en inglés por favor. No entienden español.*'[26]

He closed his eyes and feigned sleep. '*No entiendo Ingles.*'[27]

'Where the hell is Rick?' Susan asked angrily. 'Get that idiot boy on the line right now.'

'I've been trying since morning, Ma,' Emily opened her phone and called Rick again. 'It keeps going to voicemail. I've left five voicemails for him already. Wonder where—'

'Hello,' Rick suddenly answered the phone. 'Emily?'

'Where the blasted shit are you?' Emily cried on the phone. 'Left so many messages.'

'I've—what's the matter? Are you crying? What's happened—?'

'Pa's suffered a heart attack. We're at Grady Memorial. Ma's here. Worried—'

Susan grabbed the phone from Emily. 'Ricky, get your bloody ass here before Pa dies!'

---

[25] In Spanish, 'Whose daughter?'

[26] In Spanish, 'Your wife and daughter are here. Speak in English, please. They don't understand Spanish.'

[27] In Spanish, 'I don't understand English.'

# Chapter 14

## Saturday, 29 January 2022

Grady Memorial Hospital opened its doors in 1892 and is now the tenth-largest public hospital—and one of the busiest trauma centres—in the United States. They built the current facility as a segregated institution, with one section serving Whites and the other non-Whites, both wings connected by a hallway. In 2008, they converted Grady's to a non-profit hospital.

The hospital is named for Henry W. Grady, an Atlanta Constitution journalist who became a major force in Georgia politics and advocated for a public city hospital. It was the first public hospital in Atlanta and has a history of civil rights activism and medical innovation, such as being the first in Georgia to perform open-heart surgery and kidney transplants.

But hospitals are not sources of inspiration. And ICUs are even more terrifying, with comatose or anaesthetized patients lying motionless, like corpses, except that they have catheters and probes slithering into various orifices and are being monitored by the constant beeping of electronic equipment.

Rick loathed the sharp smell of antiseptic, it made him sick. He hesitated at the ICU entrance; he couldn't step in right away. His mother and his sister were in there. As soon as he entered that door, they'd look to him for comfort. Would he be able to provide it? Could he control his emotions before he broke down or, worse, threw up?

Rick chuckled harshly; it was more a gag to keep from vomiting. Hell, his life was a disaster right now. He had taken Emily's frantic phone call while waiting for the therapist for a psych consultation on

Friday afternoon. He had arranged that by invoking an emergency clause in his JQL contract that offered him immediate medical help if his life were in danger. He claimed an invisible entity, which had the power to paralyse him at will, was haunting him. The therapist at the Harlem Polyclinic had a cancellation and slotted Rick in at 2 p.m.

Rick arrived at the polyclinic and sat nervously for half an hour for his name to be called.

'Ricardo Ramsey, you're next,' the receptionist said. 'Consult Room 5 in ten minutes.'

Rick nodded. He'd turned his mobile phone off and had called in sick. Before seeing the psychiatrist, he switched his phone on to check for any urgent messages. There were a dozen odd messages on WhatsApp, Telegram, and other platforms. He was surprised to see six missed calls—on WhatsApp and direct—from his sister, Emily. He was about to call and tell her he was just seeing a shrink when she called again.

'Where the blasted shit are you?' He heard Emily cry on the phone.

'I've—what's the matter? Are you crying? What's happened—?'

'Pa's suffered a heart attack. We're at Grady Memorial. Ma's here. Worried—'

He then heard his mom's voice: 'Ricky, get your bloody ass here before Pa dies!'

She abruptly hung up.

Rick shut his eyes to digest what he'd just heard. Was this another delusion?

The receptionist called his name again. 'Ricardo Ramsey, please go to Consult Room 5.'

He dashed to the reception. 'Listen, miss, I just got a call. My dad's had a heart attack. I gotta cancel this appointment. I'm sorry about this.'

'We arranged an emergency appointment for you,' said the receptionist, sharply. 'No refund policy for emergency cancellations. We will report your no-show to your company.'

'Do what you need to do. I have to go,' he ran to the door. 'I'm really sorry about all this.'

He flagged a cab and told him to go to the airport, then changed his mind and directed him to his serviced apartment.

He packed quickly, checked out, and headed for the airport. He hoped flights would not be disrupted by the blizzard that had dumped thirty inches of snow mainly on the coastal regions of New Jersey, Long Island, and Massachusetts.

Luck was on his side. A flight to Atlanta was ready to take off in forty-five minutes; there were a few 'no-shows' with passengers stuck in the blizzard and unable to reach the airport.

The two-hour flight gave him time to reflect on his situation. He knew he was not thinking clearly. Which sane man would, after facing three traumatic experiences—getting mugged, being paralysed by an alien entity, and told your dad is dying—all in one day?

Should he have called Fiona Fletcher? Or the secretary, Alice? Dave Scully? No point calling Matthew McKenna in Atlanta—he was also in hospital after being stabbed. Rick reasoned his boss, Fiona, might forgive him, but her boss, Tony Sanders, would not.

He wondered whether his dad would be alive by the time he reached the hospital.

Unlike Emily, he had never bonded with his father. His old man had come from a different culture, had grown up in a different era where race and ethnicity were defined by the colour of your skin. Blacks, Hispanics, and other immigrants were second-class citizens—and treated accordingly. Despite living almost all his life in the US, he never felt he belonged. No wonder Horatio was always submissive, defensive, and scared of everybody.

Horatio's wife, Susan, on the other hand, had been baptised by fire. She had fought off predatory men of all races and learnt to stand on her own feet. She had raised her children with strict morals and pushed them to pursue education and careers. But her recent struggle with cervical cancer—and the harsh treatments that followed—had drained her vitality and dimmed her spark. It had reduced a woman who once wore the proverbial pants in the house to a whimpering caricature of her former self.

By the time Rick landed in Atlanta and rushed to Grady Memorial, it was 8 p.m.

'Rick?' He saw a woman wearing a mask and disposable gloves exit. It was Emily.

Rick wiped his eyes on the shirt. Her eyes were red. She hugged him. Neither spoke.

After what seemed like an era, Rick asked. 'Is he gone?'

Emily guided him to the recovery room. They donned new masks and gloves. Emily drew the plastic curtain. Rick's breath caught at the sight of his dad's motionless form on the bed. His mom was perched on the edge, clutching his hand. Rick embraced his mom, amazed by her composure and restraint.

'He's physically alive, mentally dead,' Susan whispered in Rick's ear.

Horatio opened his eyes. Rick bent down to hug him. Horatio raised his hand in terror.

Horatio looked at the nurse. '¿Quién es este hombre? ¡No me hagas daño.' He was afraid and asking who Rick was again.

'Papá, soy tu hijo, Ricardo! Te quiero. No te lastimaré.'[28]

The nurse appeared. 'Give him some time to rest. Can you wait in the waiting room?' He checked the monitor. 'His BP is very high. I need to call the doc. You need to step outside.'

Despite Susan's protests, the nurse ushered them out.

'He is stressed, not good for his heart,' the nurse explained. 'We'll stabilize him first.'

Susan allowed Rick to help her walk. 'I hope he doesn't die in there,' she wiped a tear.

'He won't, Ma. Grady's docs are good. Maybe it's the drugs—'

Emily adjusted her mask. 'The doc said he'll stop speaking Spanish as soon as the anaesthetic wears off.'

Susan tapped her head in disgust. 'What if he doesn't? He's become crazy.'

Rick laughed. 'Then we should learn to speak Spanish! Get Google Translate.'

Susan glared at her son. 'Has New York made you stupid and crazy?'

Rick grimaced. 'I need coffee,' he looked at Emily. 'Anyone want coffee?'

'I'll stay with Ma,' said Emily. 'Go get your coffee.'

---

[28] In Spanish, 'Papa, I'm your son. I love you. I won't hurt you.'

Rick bought a cup of black coffee from the vending machine in the lobby and stepped outside. He needed fresh air. It was 9 p.m. and cold. Rick shivered, sipped the hot drink, and breathed in its bitter scent. It calmed him down. He found a wooden bench on the pavement by the hospital wall and slumped in it. He shut his eyes. A blast of cold wind hit his face. He held the cup in his hands, trying to warm his fingers.

Footsteps made him look up. A familiar female figure was walking towards him.

'Whitney?' Rick rubbed his eyes. 'You here?'

'Rick?' The woman replied. 'You here?'

'I came to see my father.'

'I came to see you.'

\* \* \*

Singapore Airlines flight SQ11 left Narita at 7 p.m. on Saturday and would reach Singapore seven hours later, at 1 a.m. on Sunday. Gina Gonzales sat at the back of the plane, far from Chika Nakamura. They'd had no quarrel or disagreement, but Gina didn't want to talk to anyone. She needed time to wonder if God or the universe was messing with her.

It had been a remarkable week. Chika and Gina had taken the Shinkansen bullet train to Mishima from Tokyo. The Mishima Plaza Hotel had a European décor, an art gallery, a chapel, and a splendid Rolls Royce Phantom by the entrance. Gina snapped a dozen photos of the car and sent them to Angela—she would have loved to see this beauty.

The conference had begun with dull presentations but picked up pace when Dr Dag Larsen sparked curiosity by initiating a debate on the mysterious Singapore Strain of the virus. By the time the sessions wrapped up on Thursday, Gina had befriended many people, including one who made her heart race: Emma Rivers. Was Emma her destined partner? Or just a fling?

Gina was an open book, but Emma had layers of secrets that she disclosed gradually. Like her passion for horror movies, or her insight into the weird beings that had apparently contacted people like Cory, or even her skill in Thai kickboxing. Emma had rescued Gina from rape and had saved Gina's life. To Gina, Emma was more than a soulmate, she was a hero. For the first time in her life, Gina had confessed her lesbian secret.

During the conference, Chika had mingled with the Japanese delegates and organizers; she was their old friend and colleague. Before leaving Singapore for Japan, Chika had asked Gina to join her at Chika's parents' home in suburban Tokyo on Friday and Saturday.

'I plan to go sightseeing in Mishima and meet a friend in Yokohama, about two hours by train,' Gina lied. 'Sorry, Chika, I can't accompany you to your parents' house. Apologies.'

'Where are you going to stay?' Chika asked, concerned. 'Hotel? Home?'

'My friend is booking a hotel,' Gina said. 'I'll share a room with her, don't worry.'

'Do you want me to ask my Japanese friends to recommend a good, cheap hotel? I know this booking is ending on Thursday night. We all must leave.'

'Don't worry, I'll manage.'

What Gina didn't reveal was that Emma had booked a room until Saturday and had invited Gina to move in and share the room—and the bed. Gina had immediately accepted the offer.

Emma and Gina ventured out to see the city on Friday morning. The hotel concierge recommended they visit Rakuju-en Park, a short walk away. 'Japan made it a National Natural Monument in 1954,' he said.

Gina and Emma left for the park after breakfast. It had an amusement area, which was empty because it was a weekday, and a petting zoo. Gina hurried to the enclosure.

'I've never been to a zoo where you could touch these cute animals,' Gina caressed the back of a fawn that came to them. The fawn twisted its neck for Gina to stroke.

Some minders in uniform watched over the animals—that included deer, sheep, antelope, and alpaca, a llama-like creature from South America—and gave Gina and Emma grass to feed them and make them friendly.

'This is a spiritual experience for me,' Gina gushed. 'I'm delighted to be here.'

'I guess each person's experience is different. I had a *satori*. D'you know what that means?'

'Buddhist term for awakening, right?'

'Sort of. A month after Covid hit me, I had an episode of sleep paralysis. I was awake and aware of my surroundings, but I couldn't move a muscle. I don't know how long I stayed in that state. I had never experienced anything like that before.'

'Something like *The Twilight Zone*?'

'It was as though I was merging with my surroundings, the furniture in my room, the trees in the yard, my dog which was lying beside me. The universe was me. I was the universe.'

They clasped hands as they entered the park. The greenery among the thick trees smelled of fresh grass and earth. The cold was refreshing. They lowered their masks; the park was almost empty, except for a few joggers.

'When I went back to my lab, a colleague I barely knew cornered me one day and asked if I had woken up. I was alarmed and thought he was hitting on me. I was ready to kick his balls,' Emma kicked in the air. 'You know I can kick hard.'

'I know, you saved my life,' Gina gave her a quick hug and kissed her on the cheek.

'He told me I was a Dynaborg. I hadn't heard that word before. I laughed.'

They ran to a clearing where two pigs, their fur snow-white, were munching on shoots and roots. Next to their pen was a horse-pen where a mare and a stallion were chewing grass piled in a corner. 'Isn't that nice?' Gina pointed to the pigs. 'I wish I could go inside and cuddle them.'

Emma tapped on the fence. 'Aren't we all hypocrites?'

'What do you mean?'

'You want to cuddle the bacon and ham we had last night?' Emma bowed to the pigs and winked. 'I accept my hypocrisy, too, but I love pork.'

Gina looked up. 'How do Dynaborgs resolve this contradiction? Do they turn vegan?'

'I'm not sure. But I guess it's gotta do with empathy. Make the killing humane.'

Gina laughed. 'Do you realize how silly that sounds?'

Gina moved a few steps to catch the sun's rays. They walked to another clearing where a locomotive engine was visible in the distance.

'I didn't expect to see a train engine here,' Emma gestured at the locomotive. 'I want to touch that.' Emma tightened her grip on Gina's hand. 'I love trains.'

They sprinted, with Emma leading and dragging Gina along.

When they had reached a clearing, Gina turned to Emma. 'Can I tell you a secret?'

Emma stared at her. 'You mean, beyond what you told me, that you're a closet lesbian?'

'Yes. My friend Cory woke up from surgery and said that three of us—Cory, our common friend, Angela, and me—were third-gen Dynaborgs. Do you think that could be true?'

'I figured that when you stood up and spoke so passionately about the Singapore Strain. But I'm not the one who's supposed to wake you up. Someone will, I guess.'

'Cory already did.'

'No, no. What I mean is that Cory knew you were a Dynaborg that hadn't yet woken up. She may not be the one to wake you up. Who will? Don't know; don't have all the answers.'

'By the way, when did you find out you were a Dynaborg?' Asked Gina. 'Was it recent?'

'About six months ago,' Emma's eyes widened as they approached the locomotive.

The engine was mounted on a platform of soil and wood and covered from the rain with wooden boards. They had built a small staircase to climb up and enter the engine. Emma circled around, touching, feeling, and admiring the massive machine from a bygone era.

'There's a red label on the front,' Gina beckoned Emma. 'C58 322. Do you know—?'

'That's a Japan National Railways Class C58 steam locomotive. 322 is the serial number.'

'I'm impressed with your depth of knowledge.'

'The number "58" reminds me of a secret.'

'Another secret? You're a box of mysteries.'

'Promise you'll keep it?'

Gina made the sign of the cross, 'I cross my heart.'

'You remember I told you I was abused by someone close to me when I was a kid?'

'Yes, but you didn't elaborate. Was it a relative?'

'An uncle. He had employed my dad, a single parent. My mom died of an opioid overdose in 1999 when I was eleven. My uncle threatened me and said he would fire my dad if I squealed to Dad about the abuse that began when I was twelve. I planned to tell my dad when I turned eighteen in March 2006. In February, Dad was hit and killed by a drunk driver. His death devastated me. He died without knowing that his daughter had been abused as a kid.'

'What's "58" got to do with it?'

'This uncle had moved to New York City and ran his business from there. After Dad died, I waited a month. Then I flew to NYC and delivered the justice he deserved.'

Gina stared at Emma. 'Oh my God! You killed him?'

'Worse. I castrated him and stuffed his balls into his mouth. He was fifty-eight.'

* * *

Emily Ramsey was two years younger than her brother Ricardo, but much smarter and bolder. Even as a kid, when Rick came home with bruises from school, it was Emily who would face the bullies who were older, taller, and stronger than her. When Rick had a problem with one of his dates, it was Emily who would fix it with the girls. And when people were rude to Rick or Horatio, it was Emily who would confront them.

When Emily was sixteen and chilling with friends from school, her best friend, Molly, asked them for ideas to celebrate her eighteenth birthday.

'My parents have a ranch,' said Gus. 'We can party there if you want.'

'It's a three-hour drive,' Molly joked. 'We'll have to party on the way instead.'

'Why not have it at your place?' Asked Emily. 'You have a big backyard.'

'Too many adults snooping around,' Molly grimaced. 'No booze.'

'I have a plan,' said Donald. 'I know this guy who works at the Retro Disco. He'll let us in before the crowd comes in. He'll let us get booze and pizza. How about we party there?'

'Good idea, bro,' Gus lifted his hand. 'High five.'

Donald leapt forward. Gus backed away. Donald stumbled. And landed on Gus.

'He said to high five,' Emily howled with laughter. 'Not to hook up!'

They concocted a scheme. The Retro Disco was their venue, Wednesday evening their time slot. From 5 p.m. to 7 p.m., they would have had the place to themselves, before the grown-ups invaded. Molly would bring a dozen loyal friends from various circles and make them promise to keep quiet. Donald had a connection who would supply the food and sneak in the booze in soda bottles. No ID, no problem. But they had to clear out by 7.30 p.m. sharp.

Donald's insider at the disco gave them some tips beforehand: 'Boys, if you can't grow a beard, use an eyeliner to fake some fuzz. Girls, if you're flat-chested, stuff your bra with padding. If the cops show up, you're on your own. Your ass on the line if you screw up.'

The day of the party, everything went smoothly, according to plan. The pizzas were fiery, the booze was disguised in used soda bottles, and the music was groovy and blasting. No one felt like leaving at 7 p.m. when they were rocking the dance floor.

That's when trouble walked in. A gang of nine men, some sporting cowboy hats, barged in and smirked at the wild scene. They headed to a table at the back and ordered Buds. By the time they got their drinks, they were intrigued by the party in full swing at the front. The older ones told the younger ones to behave. But four of the young ones grabbed their bottles and crashed the dance party. The kids didn't mind because the newcomers were fit, dashing, and handsome. A tall one elbowed Gus aside and cut in with Molly.

'Who are you?' Molly yelled over the noise.

'Who cares?' He leaned in and sniffed her. 'You smell good.'

Emily dragged Donald away. 'Call your guy before these creeps start trouble.'

'What creeps?' A drunk Donald slurred and returned to the dance.

'Damn!' Emily yanked Gus's arm. 'Get Don's guy to help. Don't you see?'

Gus looked around. Fuelled by beer, he marched to the tall guy who was flirting with Molly. 'Hey, this is our party. You're not welcome. Scram!'

The tall guy ignored him and shoved him with one hand. Gus stumbled over some guys, dragging them down as he crashed to the floor, breaking some soda bottles. The dancing stopped, the music kept blaring.

'Keep dancing, sweetie,' a beefy guy chuckled. 'So young, so cute, so hot.'

Emily stormed to the tall guy who had now clamped Molly's waist and was sniffing her skin. 'Get lost, you scum,' she screamed at him.

'Is that a pissed-off, pretty nigger?' The beefy guy said. 'Or a pissed-off, pretty beaner?'

Emily knew calling Latinos 'beaner' was as insulting as calling African-Americans 'nigger'. Her eyes blazing, she stared at the guy. 'You're trash, that's what you are!'

'Who the hell are you, kid?' The tall guy dropped Molly and grabbed Emily. He yanked her hand and pulled her close. 'You have fair skin, big tits, brown eyes. You a mutt? Crossbreed?'

He dragged her closer. His breath reeked of beer and stale cigarette smoke.

'Get off me, swine!'

'Shut your damn mouth, whore,' the beefy guy waved his beer bottle at her.

'I dig her spirit,' a third guy sauntered over. 'A wildcat. Should be a good screw.'

The tall guy grinned as he sniffed Emily's bare shoulders. 'Nice rack. Great scent. Bad temper.' He swung his left hand and smacked Emily on her face, knocking her back.

The rest of the gang and the security guards ran up to stop the brawl. They killed the music.

'Listen guys, we don't want trouble,' the manager tried to control the situation.

Molly and Gus helped Emily up. Her lips were split, a tooth was loose, and Emily could taste blood. She also felt her eyes and face puff up. She grabbed a Coke bottle from the table, leapt up and smashed it on the tall guy's head, breaking the bottle and his skull.

She fell to the floor and glass shards cut her hands and face.

Her youth—and her story—saved her from a police record. The Retro Disco bosses smoothed things over with the cops, but they were helpless when the ambulance took the two casualties—the tall guy with a cracked skull and Emily with bruises on her face—to the hospital. The cops followed and wanted to question both. The hospital staff directed the cops to the doctors who escorted them to Emily's ward.

Emily didn't bother to ask if the guy she had whacked was alive; she didn't give a damn.

A White cop came to her bed. 'Name? Full name? Age? Occupation?'

'Emily Ramsey, that's it. I'm sixteen. I'm a high-school student.'

'Fine,' he wrote on his notepad. 'And what happened at the Retro Disco?'

'What Retro Disco?'

'Don't get fresh with me, kid,' the cop pinched her face. 'Spill it.'

Emily stared him down. 'I was passing by. I tripped and fell on the sidewalk.'

That comment turned her into a school legend, cemented her fame, and gave her a nickname: 'Emily, the badass cookie.'

But all that didn't matter, in this hospital at the present, where she had no power but huge responsibilities. She had to act strong for her mother's sake. She was hoping to count on Rick, but he'd failed her repeatedly and stayed just as flaky. Even now, when she needed him most, he had vanished to get coffee. She looked for him in the lobby; he wasn't there. She dialled his phone; he had turned it off. She tried one more time to find him. Oh, there he was, outside, on the bench, chatting with a girl.

'What the hell are you doing here?' She screamed at him. 'Ma and I are freaking out.'

'I'm drinking coffee, like I told you I would,' Rick rose to face her. 'Needed fresh air. What's with the attitude?'

'Chill, Rick,' his friend touched Rick's arm. 'Hi, I'm Malia. I work with Rick at Jackal. You're Emily, Rick's sister, right?'

'Yeah, sorry,' Emily was seething. 'He flies from New York and can't bother to console his mother,' she poked his chest. 'I've been scouring the hospital.'

'I said I was going to get coffee. Malia just showed up a minute ago.'

'Why didn't you answer your damn phone?'

'Battery's dead. No charge on the flight. No spare battery pack.'

'Relax, Rick,' Malia said. 'You too, Emily. How's your father? Rick was worried.'

'Rick? Worried? You've gotta be kidding. My mom and I are freaking out. My dad had a bad reaction to the anaesthetic; he only speaks Spanish, doesn't know us. Rick worried? Bullshit.'

'Cut it out, Emily,' Rick said firmly. 'Let's go inside.'

Rick drained his coffee, squashed the paper cup, and threw it in a bin.

Susan was curled up in a corner, the shawl wrapped snugly around her. She didn't even look at them.

'Are you cold, Ma?' Emily sat beside her and hugged her. 'Are you hungry?'

'I'm fine. Waiting for the doc,' she glanced at Malia. 'Is this your friend, Rick?'

'I'm Malia. I work with Rick at JQL,' Malia sat down beside Emily. 'I came to see Rick and his dad. Is he doing well after the surgery?'

Susan snubbed Malia. 'How long are you in Atlanta, Rick? Just visiting?'

'I'll stay if I have to, Ma. Nothing's decided yet.'

Susan pointed to Malia. 'What's she doing here?'

'Malia is helping me with the admin stuff, Ma. She came to ask about Pa,' he turned to leave. 'Let me find the doc—and check on Pa.'

'Here we go again,' Emily scowled. 'Don't make us chase you again.'

Rick brushed her off and walked out of the room, softly shutting the glass door behind him. He turned right to the lobby. Seconds later, the nurse came in from the left and walked over to Emily. 'Come, see your father now.'

* * *

Singapore Airlines flight SQ423 departed Mumbai at 11.40 p.m. on Saturday and would land five hours later, at 7.40 a.m. on Sunday, in Singapore. Simi Sundar didn't have to worry about the seating, service, or the food—thanks to Ben Morrison, her ticket was in business class in the world's premier airline. The single seat next to the window would offer her solitude.

On the flight from Singapore to Mumbai on 23 January, she had binged on comedy flicks on Krisworld. But this time, all she wanted was to catch up on sleep and reflect on the most momentous week she'd ever had. The surprises hadn't stopped—from the time she had landed in Pune and a stranger had shared her table at dinner, to the time she had left the city.

On Friday, just when Dharam was getting to the key point about Dynaborgs, a guy in a suit had interrupted their meeting and urged Simi to follow him to the conference hall. He led her to Kirumi's CEO, Dr Ramachandran, who was miked up to present in a few minutes.

Simi shook his hand. 'I didn't realize that you were the CEO; my apologies, sir.'

'I didn't realize that you were our top trainer, my apologies,' he smiled. 'I will acknowledge you.'

'I'm just doing my job, sir. Nothing out of the way. Please don't bother.'

'I'm just doing mine. No bother.'

As the emcee announced Kirumi CEO Dr Ramachandran, Simi followed an executive to the front row. She sat down beside an old man in a mask, the only one, besides Simi, who wore one. She looked around the hall. It was packed with more than 500 people, mostly men in dark suits. A few women stood out in their colourful Indian outfits, some draped in saris.

Dr Ramachandran walked to the dais and nodded at the clapping crowd.

'Three unusual things happened on this visit to Pune,' he began. 'First, my car broke down on the Lonavala Ghats. My driver was frantically calling people on his phone for help. None of the vehicles would stop. But an old man, driving a rusty old Premier Padmini, paused to enquire. Many of you may not remember Padmini, a reincarnation of the Fiat car, which was popular in Bombay in the 1970s. The old man offered me a lift in his car. My driver would have zoomed from Lonavala to Pune in one hour. The old man drove at thirty kilometres per hour, with the windows open, chit-chatting all the way and admiring the greenery on the ghats. He got us to Pune in about three hours.'

Some people clapped. Many laughed. Dr Ramachandran cleared his throat.

'But what an education I received. The old man was a former physician and gave me great tips about healthy living. I want to honour him by inviting him on stage—Dr Sarosh Bana.'

The audience clapped as the old man beside Simi rose from his seat. The executive assistant and the emcee guided him up the stairs to the dais. He took the wireless microphone from the emcee and stashed his mask in his pocket.

Dr Ramachandran shook Dr Bana's hand. 'It's an honour to welcome you here, sir. Thank you for the ride. How old is your car?'

'I bought the car on 1 April 1969, the day my son was born,' said Dr Bana. 'Everybody made fun of me. They said this Parsi fool has had two jokes befall him on April Fool's Day—giving birth to a joker son—and buying the joke of a car.'

That quip drew loud guffaws from the audience.

'But now, fifty-three years later, the joke is on them. The joker son whom my wife gave birth to is a doctor like me. The joke of a car, which I drive with care and love, ferried Dr Ram to Pune.'

That closing drew a long, loud applause from the audience.

After some more banter with Dr Bana, Dr Ramachandran continued his speech.

'The second unusual event happened when I went for dinner to the hotel's restaurant and scanned the menu. The dinner options didn't include the south Indian dishes that I wanted. I would have loved to have rasam or sambar or curd rice. Then I heard a female voice ordering medhu vadai, masala dosai, and buttermilk. I immediately invited myself to her table and asked the waiter to bring me exactly what she had ordered. She was brilliant company. I had a delicious dinner. I also found out that it was her first ever visit to this great city, Pune.'

The audience applauded. Simi squirmed in her seat.

'The third unusual revelation, which I only found out later in the week, was that the lady I had accidentally met and shared dinner with was none other than the coach who had travelled all the way from Singapore to Pune to train our technical team on data analytics,' he paused. 'I want to honour that lady by inviting her on stage— Ms Simi Sundar.'

Simi heard the applause. The executive assistant nodded at her and led her to the dais. She took the wireless microphone from the emcee and peeled off her mask.

'It's an honour to welcome you here, ma'am. Thank you for training ' our technical team.'

'I'm very embarrassed, sir . . .' Simi began nervously, drawing laughter from the crowd.

'Why?' Dr Ramachandran was momentarily flustered. 'Did I say something wrong?'

'No, no. I'm very embarrassed because I didn't know who you were when I met you, sir.'

'Ha, ha, good that you didn't. Otherwise, you'd have told me to go find an empty table.'

'*Aiyoh*, sir, please don't say that,' Simi blushed. 'Sorry, I was not trying to speak Tamil.'

The audience howled with laughter.

'I'm kidding,' he touched her arm. 'You said you don't like to travel, but you still made this trip, thank you. I checked with our technical guys, they said they learnt a lot from you.'

'My pleasure, sir. I'm glad I made this trip. I too learnt a lot. You have an excellent team.'

Simi bowed—and received a thunderous applause, with some giving her a standing ovation.

Simi became an instant star. Everyone wanted a piece of her—her hand, her thanks, have chai with her. She craved privacy. She skipped the group dinner at the hotel restaurant on Friday night and ordered room service instead. Vinod Kumar had already secured the CFO's signature and had flown back to New Delhi on Friday morning. Dharam was waiting for her outside when she finished her final training session on Friday evening.

'I'm glad my CEO honoured you publicly,' Dharam gushed. 'May I shake your hand?'

'Oh, so now you have stopped hitting on Padma, is it?'

'You're very witty, Ms Sundar,' he folded his hands. 'We haven't completed our talk on Dynaborgs. Dinner?'

Simi frowned.

'My room? We can order room service. No one will disturb us,' he touched his pink turban. 'Er . . . can you please invite Ms Padma?'

'I was about to suggest that—you beat me to it.'

Simi and Padma walked into Dharam's room at the JW Marriott Pune at 7.30 p.m. He had tidied the room, showered, and even wiped the bathroom.

Padma noticed it. 'Wow, your room's clean, neat, spic and span. I'm impressed.'

Simi interrupted Dharam's flirtatious exchange with Padma. 'Don't waste your charm on her. Save it for me. I'm still single, remember?' She gave Padma a playful wink. 'Let's get back to Dynaborgs. Are they a cult?'

Dharam sighed. 'You're too direct for me, Simi-ji,' he paused to see if she would react. She didn't. 'Okay, let me tell you what I know. Cults have a leader; we don't. Cults have hierarchy; we don't. Cults are obsessed with money; we're not. Cults suppress dissent; we welcome it. We focus on logic and practicality. We don't want unquestioning loyalty.'

'What do you want, then?'

'To preserve Earth's biodiversity and environment, protect forests and habitats.'

'Will look good on PowerPoint,' Simi laughed. 'No way you can achieve all that, right?'

'Should we order food first?' Padma yawned. 'It'll take them a while to deliver.'

Dharam reached into his desk drawer and handed Padma a thick file from a hotel. 'Butter chicken? Unless Simi minds—'

Simi cut him off. 'You ordered veg biryani, remember? I thought all Dynaborgs—'

'Are not vegetarians or vegans. Neither am I.'

Padma yawned again. 'So, no rules or guidelines? Anyone can call themselves Dynaborgs. Don't answer, order food. I'm hungry.'

They agreed on a few dishes. Dharam telephoned room service and ordered in Hindi. He slid the file into the desk drawer and focused on Padma.

He grinned at Padma. 'I don't know everything. Something inexplicable drew me to Simi when I saw her at the table. She recognized the word "Dynaborg".'

'Did I?'

'I could see that the word resonated with you. You'd heard it before. Assume it was Padma and I had mentioned Dynaborg to her, she would have thought I was a crank.'

'I still think you're a crank,' Padma deadpanned. Simi laughed.

'When did you know you were a Dynaborg?' Asked Simi.

'Six months ago. I'd get nightmares of animals and birds being tortured. One night, I had a dream of someone appearing in my room. Like a ghost. She told me to wake up.'

Simi was suddenly reminded of Larry, but kept her mouth shut.

'Get to the point,' said Padma, impatiently.

'I was in Mumbai for work when a lady crashed my lunch in a restaurant and told me to wake up. She sat across from me and touched my hand. Time froze. She told me about Dynaborgs. Said I was ready. Her name is Saras.'

'Isn't that short for Saraswati?' Simi asked. 'The Indian goddess of wisdom?'

'Saras means "excellent" in Gujarati,' said Padma. 'It means "dominant" in Marathi.'

'Does it mean anything?' Simi asked. 'Like "Kirumi" is Tamil for germ. Fitting for Dr Ramachandran's company that deals in pest control in plants.'

'Dunno,' said Dharam. 'She told me to wake others to fulfil our destiny. I don't know how. But I've joined Nature groups, Greenpeace, PETA, Chintan, Wildlife Protection Society.'

'You mean they're all awakened?' Simi asked. 'All Dyna?'

'Maybe. Many are hidden Dynas, too afraid to come out. Like me. Saras introduced me to a guy in Chennai. I can set up a con-call with him. Everyone calls him Anna, which is big brother in Tamil.'

'We call my father, Anna,' Padma yawned for the third time.

Simi stood up. 'Good, let's arrange a con-call. I'll get Cory on the line from Singapore.'

There was a soft knock at the door. The food had arrived. Dharam opened the door. Padma smiled and trailed after him.

Simi flipped on her mobile phone and called Cory's number on WhatsApp. After six rings, someone answered.

'Who's this?' A male voice asked.

'Where's Cory?' Simi enquired, puzzled. 'Who's this?'

'It's Larry.'

# Chapter 15

**Sunday, 30 January 2022**

Singapore Airlines flight SQ321 left London Heathrow at 10.10 p.m. on Sunday and would arrive in Singapore at 6.10 p.m. on Monday after thirteen hours. Angela Ang had booked SQ305 for Monday morning at 9.30 a.m., but her dad had called and had urged her to come home for the CNY Reunion Dinner on 1 February. Angela had phoned the Krisflyer hotline in the UK. They said only a business-class seat was available for the Sunday night flight. So, Angela had to upgrade with her credit card.

Good thing, she thought, as she relaxed in her solo seat by the window. She was exhausted; the week had been crazy. She was sleep-deprived; she had barely slept the last few nights. She was hungry; she was sick of eating western food, her body craved Hainanese chicken rice, char kway teow, wanton-mee, chicken satay, and roti prata.

She had faced surprises—and shocks, literally and figuratively, in Bristol. Her colleague from Pistonex Europe was the first surprise. The tall guy from Kiruna in Sweden's north had hinted that the bolide, which had burst on 7 September 2015, the one that Esrange Space Centre had tracked and Cory had felt, was linked to the Singapore Strain of the virus and Dynaborgism, whatever that was.

The second surprise, or shock, was that the white lady from Estonia, Terhi Tamm, could generate electricity from her body and control the voltage. When Angela first touched her fingers at Don Giovanni's restaurant, Terhi had zapped her with full power. Later, she'd given her mild shocks, but they had still rattled Angela's nerves.

The third surprise was meeting Marie from Mauritius. Marie had given Angela a short history of the island nation, three times the size of Singapore. The Arabs, the Portuguese, the Dutch, and the British had ruled Mauritius—in that order—until 1968 when it became independent. The British had stayed for 158 years—from 1810 to 1968. Those who had worked for the UK government could apply for British citizenship. Marie's parents had grabbed the opportunity and moved to Manchester.

'I graduated from the University of Bristol and admired Greta Thunberg,' Marie told Angela after lunch on Friday. 'We started the Bristol Chapter of the FFF, you know. We have the biggest following in the UK, you know.'

'FFF?'

'Fridays for Future. Greta was fifteen in 2018. That August, she and other students sat outside the Swedish parliament every school day for three weeks to demand action on the climate crisis. She posted it on Instagram and Twitter. It went viral.'

'How many joined?' Angela asked.

'A protest on 15 March 2019 drew a million activists in 125 countries. On 20 September 2019, four million activists, mostly schoolchildren, rallied for action on climate change. It was the biggest climate strike ever, you know.'

'That's cool,' said Angela. 'And what's gonna happen at the FFF meeting tonight?'

'Hang around. Sing along. Join the debate.'

Marie was not kidding. They held the event in the open grounds at the university campus. Despite the cold weather, about 400 student activists and others turned up. They did stretches, sang songs, and gave passionate speeches. Angela and Lucas found a spot under an awning. Angela jotted down notes on a small paper pad.

The first chant was the strongest: 'We are unstoppable / another world is possible.' The second chant struck her: 'Climate change is not a lie / do not let our planet die.' But the third chant made her uneasy: 'No more coal, no more oil / keep that carbon in the soil.'

Angela wondered how the world economy could work without coal or oil in the short term. 'It's kind of silly to demand action without recommending an alternative and feasible option, right?' Angela asked. Lucas was still in a T-shirt despite the cold. 'Is net zero even doable?'

'Nope,' said Lucas. 'Greta and her followers were right in highlighting the need for action on climate. But how to make that happen? Doesn't seem possible in the short term.'

'Need to change government policies to be more environmentally friendly, right?'

'Nope. Look at it from the developing world point of view. China, India, Africa, Asia, and South America. Europe and North America burnt coal, oil, and gas for the last hundred years in the name of industrialization. Now, when the developing world wants to join the bandwagon, you throw global warming at them. They've got millions of mouths to feed.'

'So, all this FFF talk is humbug?'

'Nope. You need to start somewhere. Raise awareness about global warming, greenhouse gases, and blatant use of natural resources. I like the idea of Singapore Strain and Dynaborgs.'

'Why?'

The crowd swelled with more people pushing and shoving to get standing room. The singing grew louder and more passionate, filling the air with a chorus of voices that expressed their joy and defiance.

Angela shouted to be heard. 'You're not a Dynaborg, right?'

'Nope. I want to be one. Pestering Terhi to find a way to join the movement.'

The scene suddenly turned chaotic as more students scrambled to get inside. They pressed their weight against the wooden beams that held up the awning, oblivious to the strain they were causing. With a loud crack, one of the beams gave way and the green canvas sheet came crashing down. A dozen-odd people who were standing under it were buried in a heap of fabric and wood.

Lucas reacted quickly. He wrapped his arms around Angela and pulled her close to him. He tripped over someone's leg, tumbling to the ground with Angela in his embrace. Before they could get up, another person landed on her back. Angela felt a sharp jolt in her shoulder and let out a piercing scream as more people piled up above her.

The rescue workers struggled to clear the pile of bodies that trapped the survivors. Angela lay on top of Lucas, who cushioned her fall with two more people under him. She felt numb and immobile. She wondered whether Lucas was injured; he had not made a sound. One by one, they lifted the people above her, some limp and lifeless. Angela felt a surge of pain in her legs and shoulder.

'The ambulance is coming,' someone shouted. 'Raise your hand if you're hurt.'

Lucas lifted his right hand and gripped Angela with his left. She hung on to him with her right hand, her left was limp and dangling. The FFF activists acted quickly and efficiently. They grabbed chairs from the classrooms and seated the wounded. They shared water bottles from their backpacks and quenched their thirst. Medical and nursing students volunteered and tended to their injuries. Angela leaned on Lucas and cried out in pain.

She sobbed. 'I can't take it. The pain is too much. I'm going to die.'

'Nope,' said Lucas, holding her tight. 'Hang on to me. I'll give you a quick painkiller.'

He cupped her face and kissed her hard on the lips.

\* \* \*

The Bristol Royal Infirmary (BRI) was founded in 1735 by public donations, making it one of the UK's oldest infirmaries. The BRI is now a large teaching hospital in central Bristol and works with the University of Bristol and the University of the West of England's Faculty of Health and Social Care.

Angela opened her eyes and felt throbbing spasms of pain in the head and a sore shoulder. She noticed she was wearing a hospital gown over her underwear. 'Where am I?'

'You're in the BRI's trauma and orthopaedics wing,' Lucas squeezed her hand. 'The ambulance got us here. You were in agony, the EMT gave you morphine and it knocked you out. The nurse dressed you. Waiting for the doc.'

'Will I need surgery?' Angela whimpered. 'My left hand is numb.'

'Nope. I'm not a doc,' Lucas said. 'I've messaged Terhi. On the way here.'

'I need a doc. What's the point of calling her here? Waste of her time, right?'

'Nope.'

'I fell on top of you. Didn't you get hurt?'

'Nope. Not as much as you. I was in pain. But my screaming wouldn't have done any good; would have only scared you. I had to conserve my energy. You were already in severe pain.'

'I love you,' Angela smiled between sobs. 'I really do. I want to marry you.'

'That's the morphine talking. As soon as it wears off, you'll be normal again.'

'I *am* normal, even though I'm in pain. You kissed me. My pain dropped by 50 per cent.'

'That's the morphine—'

'Stop saying that. It's me talking, not the stupid morphine. Stop texting on your phone.'

'Checking where Terhi is.'

She clung to him. 'Don't leave me. Hold me. I love you, Lucas. I really do.'

The other patients stared at Angela. Her eyes were locked on him. Lucas flushed, his pale cheeks turned pink. Terhi rushed in and scanned the hall. She spotted Lucas beside Angela on a bed, he was clasping her right hand. He signalled to her with his left hand.

'Is she injured?' Terhi asked, panting.

'Dislocated left shoulder,' Lucas withdrew his hand. 'Dopey with morphine.'

'Stay away!' Angela shrank in fear. 'I don't want a bloody shock.'

'Trust me,' Terhi leaned in and reassured Angela. 'I won't touch you unless you say so.'

'Then why the heck are you here?' Saliva drooled from the side of Angela's mouth.

'Let me correct your dislocated shoulder. Lucas will hold your hand.'

Lucas took a tissue from his pocket and wiped Angela's mouth.

She clutched his hand. 'Will it hurt?' Tears streamed down her cheeks.

Lucas used the tissue to dry her eyes.

'Just for a moment,' said Terhi. 'We need to lift you up. Lucas, please help.'

Lucas helped her sit up by supporting her back. Angela wrapped her right arm around him and squeezed her eyes shut. Terhi warmed her hands, got ready, and signalled to Lucas.

Then, with a quick move, Terhi grabbed Angela's shoulder with her left hand and yanked Angela's arm with her right. A jolt of electricity ran through Angela's shoulder, making her shriek in pain. She screamed so loudly that the whole hall turned around to look at her. Amidst the screaming, Angela didn't notice that her upper arm had popped back into its shoulder socket.

'Done,' Terhi stepped back. 'You're good to move.'

Angela was still clinging to Lucas, too scared to move a muscle.

'Move your arm,' he gently disengaged himself.

Carefully, Angela moved her left arm. It worked. There was hardly any pain. 'You're amazing, Terhi,' said Angela, her eyes still moist. 'My shoulder's fine, right?'

Lucas leaned over and whispered. 'Tell Terhi you love her, you want to marry her.'

She embraced him with both arms. 'I want to marry you,' she declared and leaned to kiss him, he dodged her.

That night, after leaving the hospital, Angela, Terhi, Marie, and Lucas met at the Leonardo Hotel for dinner. Angela pretended to forget when Lucas asked her if she recalled declaring her love for him at the hospital. She didn't want to confess in front of Marie and Terhi; she wasn't sure if Terhi and Lucas were together. She turned her attention to Terhi.

'How did you discover you could generate electricity?' Asked Angela.

'Sometimes you need a trigger, a force, an outsider, to help you unleash a skill or gift that's buried inside of you,' replied Terhi. 'Remember we talked about Singapore and Estonia being similar?

Both are small states. Singapore became independent on 9 August 1965, Estonia broke free from the Soviet Union on 20 August 1991.'

'You impress me,' Angela cheered. 'You know Singapore's history too?'

'My father worked for the Ministry of Foreign Affairs in Estonia. He was posted in Singapore from 1996 to 1999. My mother and I loved living in sunny Singapore.'

'Cool. What's that gotta do——?'

'My father had a slipped disc that surgery or medicine couldn't fix. A local friend suggested we see a healer in Geylang who had a special gift. He could produce electricity from his body. My father saw him often and felt less pain. After a dozen or so visits, my father's spine had healed.'

'That's amazing, right?' Marie clapped.

'On one of his visits, my father brought me along. When the healer touched me, I felt a shock, like you did when I touched you. But he felt a shock too, which was very odd, he said. Fate had linked two people, both with this rare gift.'

'Interesting,' said Lucas. 'Could you produce electricity at will after that?'

'This healer was my mentor. He taught me how to control it like he did, how to use it to heal, how to use it to protect myself, and how to help people anytime, anywhere I could.'

'How long did you take to learn this skill?' Asked Marie.

'About three months.'

'This healer who helped you was in Singapore, right?' Asked Angela. 'Still working?'

'We lost touch with him after the ministry posted my father back to Tallinn.'

'What was the healer's name?' Angela leaned closer. 'Do you remember?'

'How can I forget? His name was Henry Yip.'

\* \* \*

Founded in 1785, the University of Georgia (UGA) is the nation's first state-chartered university and the birthplace of public higher education in America. It opened its doors to students in 1801, six years before its rival, the University of North Carolina at Chapel Hill. UGA is a proud leader in research, teaching and service. Among UGA's distinguished alumni are stars like Kim Basinger and Ryan Seacrest, as well as nine Pulitzer Prize winners, including Natasha Trethewey, who served as US Poet Laureate in 2012 and 2014.

Horatio, Ricardo, and Emily also graduated from UGA.

As a co-sponsor of the biodiversity symposium at UGA's Institute of Bioinformatics on 10 February, JQL received an invitation for its Region Head. He passed it on to Matthew McKenna, who forwarded it to Ricardo Ramsey and copied in Fiona Fletcher. Fiona advised Matt to go instead, citing Rick's erratic behaviour and missed psychiatric appointment. Matt was in hospital, he asked his secretary Malia to contact Rick and find out what happened.

Rick felt betrayed by Fiona's disclosure of his missed appointment to Matt. Fiona was an enigma. She shunned social-media platforms like Facebook, LinkedIn, Twitter, Instagram, where Rick had profiles but seldom posted anything, except for his work achievements on LinkedIn. Fiona was supposedly a competent and compassionate leader who treated her staff fairly, unlike her boss, Tony Sanders, who was notorious for being rude, selfish, and arrogant.

'Are you free for a call?' Rick had messaged Fiona on WhatsApp on Saturday evening.

Rick took the call in the corridor next to the hospital's waiting room.

'Sorry to bother you on a Sunday. My life's a mess—'

Fiona interrupted him. 'Why didn't you make your session? You were already at the shrink's. Just because the company is footing the bill—'

'I had to get on the first flight to Atlanta. My dad's had a heart attack. He's in a coma. I'm in the hospital.'

'Christ! Why didn't you call me? Tony's ready to fire you.'

'I wasn't thinking,' Rick paced the corridor. 'Can I get my old role in Atlanta back?'

Fiona didn't respond.

'Mom had cervical cancer last year.'

'We all have problems. The role in Atlanta doesn't exist any more. D'you have a plan B?'

'I'll take a pay cut.'

Fiona didn't respond. He felt slighted and disgusted with Fiona, like a betrayed lover who had been cheated on. He would have loved to strangle her if he could, like a snake squeezing the life out of its prey.

'I don't have a plan B.'

'I'll talk to Tony,' Fiona's voice was weary. 'Check with his sec.'

Rick was a drowning man, clutching at the only remaining straw: Matthew McKenna. Rick had helped save his life. He texted Matt and sent him a distress signal on WhatsApp. He hoped Matt would throw him a lifeline.

'Ricardo, buddy,' Matt replied right away. He sounded frail. 'I heard your dad's at Grady. How's he holding up?'

'How are you feeling, man? Sorry I didn't remember you're still healing.'

'They stitched up my colon after the knife sliced it.'

'Does it hurt?'

'Only when I laugh,' he faked a chuckle. 'Your dad?'

'He's in a coma. Came outta surgery speaking fluent Spanish which he hasn't spoken in forty years. He didn't understand English. The docs think a brain bleed caused that.'

'Didn't realize brain bleeds could get you to speak Spanish ha, ha, ouch!'

'I can't stop laughing either. They drained the bleed. They'll wake him up any time now.'

'Hope he doesn't wake up and speak Chinese ha, ha, ow, ouch! Sorry, couldn't resist.'

'Matt, I need my job back.'

'As soon as your dad recovers, you can go back to New York, right?'

'Don't wanna. You're a great boss.'

There was a pause. 'Old role's scrapped, bro. I owe you one. I'll try to help.'

'Fiona asked me about plan B. I wanted to say, "I got no plan B, bitch!"'

Matt cackled. 'Take a breather. I'll talk to HR, no promises, though.'

'That would be awesome!'

'You have three hurdles to cross. An okay from the shrink you bailed on. An okay from HR. And the hardest, an okay from Tony Sanders.'

\* \* \*

Ricardo Ramsey had always scoffed at superstitions. Ghosts, spirits, aliens or extraterrestrials—he dismissed them all as nonsense. Until now. He felt like a puppet in the hands of unseen forces. Whitney's ghostly visitation. His dad's miraculous recovery and sudden switch to Spanish. And Fiona and Matt probably thinking he was going crazy.

Rick felt like he had slipped into a twisted alternate reality. Maybe he should have stayed in New York and seen a shrink instead. He dreaded contacting Tony Sanders. He had typed out two texts but deleted them. He pictured Tony's furious response, he had witnessed Tony tearing into a senior manager over a trivial mistake.

At noon, Rick finally sent a polite and remorseful text to Tony Sanders.

Tony called Rick back in seconds—on WhatsApp video. Rick panicked. He wasn't ready for a face-to-face chat. He ran to find a private place to switch on the camera.

'Are you out of your mind?' Tony snapped without a preamble or pleasantries.

Rick saw Tony was behind the wheel of his car. Rick spotted an empty consultation room and bolted in. 'I'm sorry, I . . . I really am, sir,' he gasped. 'I found a room.'

'Are you having a heart attack?'

'No sir. My dad had one. I had to find a quiet spot for this call.'

'Typical of you, huh?'

'Er . . . excuse me?'

'You should've been ready before you called me.'

'I'm rattled. It's been a crazy day—'

'You bet. You've AWOL. You needed to see a shrink. You think JQL is a big joke?'

'I'm so sorry,' Rick dabbed the sweat with his sleeve.

'Your dad's heart attack. Is that a cover-up?' He paused. 'Are you really at the hospital?'

'I am. I'm in an empty consult room for this call. Why would I lie?'

'Prove it. Open the door. Walk around.'

'Seriously?'

'Am I laughing?'

'Okay, um, just a minute, sir.'

Rick swiped the sweat from his brow to his nose. He cracked the door open and panned his iPhone around the corridor. 'I'm not lying. I'm really at the hospital. My mom and sis are in the waiting room.'

'Are they? Let me see.'

'Seriously?'

'Am I laughing?'

This demand baffled Rick. 'Sorry, sir, you don't believe me?'

'I don't.'

Rick debated whether to tell Tony to get lost, or just refuse this demand. Tony already looked furious. Rick marched to the waiting room where Susan and Emily and six others were sitting. He spun the iPhone for Tony to see the whole scene.

'This is the waiting room,' Rick hissed.

'Where is your mother? Sister?'

'What?' Rick was losing patience. 'They can't talk to you—'

'I want to talk to them.'

Tony had parked, he was at a signal or a lot. The car engine was still running in the background. Rick saw cars zooming by from the window.

'Seriously, Tony?'

'That's the third time you've said that.'

Rick paused. Tony stared.

Emily snapped at Rick. 'Who the hell are you chatting with now?'

'Shh! It's Jackal VP Tony Sanders. He's my big boss. Calling from New York. Wants to meet Mom and you,' he gave the phone to Emily. 'Be nice to him.'

Emily swiped the sweat off the phone. She saw the worry on Rick's face.

'Hi, I'm Emily, Rick's little sister. This is my mom, Susan. My dad's in surgery.'

Tony's attitude shifted, his voice softened.

'I'm so sorry about his heart attack,' he smiled. 'Is he okay now? What's the outlook?'

'We're waiting for the doc to tell us. Thanks for calling, Mr Sanders.'

'Can I speak with Susan, please?'

Emily nudged Susan's arm. 'Ma, Mr Tony Sanders wants to talk to you.'

Susan had listened to their chat. 'Hello, Mr Sanders. Thanks for your concern.'

'I'm sorry about your husband, Susan. I've told Rick to take two weeks off to look after you. Make sure he does that, okay?'

Tony was beaming at Susan. Rick wondered if it was all a show.

'He never told us that,' Susan glared at Rick. 'He's been acting weird ever since—'

'Ever since he came back from New York?'

'Yes, yes.'

'New York does that to people,' Tony chuckled. 'Don't worry. I've just granted his leave. You and Emily take care. Don't let Rick outta your sight, okay? Otherwise, he's gonna have to answer to me.'

\* \* \*

Rick was confused about whom to trust. His direct boss Fiona, who was supposed to be fair and loyal to her juniors but had been rude and scheming. Or Fiona's boss, Tony Sanders, who was notorious as a harsh and heartless jerk, which he was on the call with Rick, but sweet and supportive when he talked to Emily and Susan. He had also given two weeks leave that Rick hadn't even asked for.

Rick wondered if this was all corporate fake—be nice to the victim before firing him. There was only one person who could solve the mystery: Matthew McKenna.

Matt called back. 'You mean Tony Tightass was actually nice to you?'

'Tony and I had a long chat. I was annoyed when he wanted to talk to my mom and sis on video. He also gave me two weeks' leave without me asking for it. Can you believe that? I had a horrible opinion of him before. Now I think he's great.'

'I'm sure Tony would be thrilled to hear that! The first guy to call him a good guy.'

'Could he be, like, joking? Not serious about what he said?'

'I've never talked to him, so I've no idea. But I know others who have. He earned his nickname, "Tightass". Even Fiona agrees. But, hey, trust your instinct, man.'

'My instinct is weak, my brain is blank. I'm lost and confused. I need help.'

'Calm down. Take two weeks off, your job is secure until then. We'll figure out the rest.'

Rick hung up and got another call. It was Emily.

'Why the hell are you ignoring your phone?' Emily was angry, as usual.

'What the hell is wrong? Is Pa okay?'

'The doc wants you. Can you hurry up? We're in the ICU waiting room.'

'I'm right here. Was making some calls. Coming in now.'

Rick dashed to the ICU and saw the male nurse fixing probes on his dad's body. They had removed Horatio's tube, which meant he could breathe and talk on his own. Susan, Emily, and a man in scrubs—maybe the surgeon—waited for the nurse to finish with the probes. Rick sat on the bed and held Horatio's hands.

'Welcome back, Pa,' he felt tears in his eyes. 'We missed you so much.'

Horatio looked alarmed. '*¿Quién eres tú?*'[29] He asked feebly, clearly confused and unsure about who Rick was.

Rick turned around and frowned at the surgeon. 'What the hell is going on?'

---

[29] In Spanish, 'Who're you?'

'*Horacio, este es tu hijo, Ricardo,*'[30] the nurse said.

Horatio wearily looked at Susan, Emily, and Rick. '*No estoy casado.*'[31] '*Estoy cansado. Déjame dormir.*'[32]

The surgeon assessed the situation. 'Let's talk outside. Let the patient rest.'

He took them to an adjoining room, which was vacant. 'I'm Dr Harry Singer. I'm a neurosurgeon. We did an MRI scan on your father and found a small clot in his brain. It's in the area that makes memories.'

'Will he speak English again?' Emily dabbed a tear.

'We're giving him meds to clear the clot,' said Dr Singer. 'We're hoping his memories will return as his brain heals. Let his body rest for now.'

'Why can't you operate and remove the clot?' Asked Rick.

'Clot's too tiny. He has diabetes and has just survived a heart attack. The clot is in a very sensitive spot in his brain. We've ruled out surgery for now. Let's try the drugs first.'

'But he doesn't remember any of us,' argued Rick. 'If he recovers physically and still speaks only Spanish, how can we take him home when he doesn't know any of us?'

'Sometimes, going back to familiar places may help trigger the brain's memory banks. You may have photos? Videos? Objects? All that might help remind him.'

'Ma, what do you say?' Emily asked her mother. 'You've not said anything.'

Susan coughed. 'Before this episode, when Horatio was in a coma, I was afraid he may not wake up. I signed a DNR because I didn't want him to be a vegetable. Now that he has woken up, I'm afraid he's not the same man I married. I fear bringing a stranger into our home. Is the DNR only for physical death? Is there another DNR for mental death?'

---

[30] In Spanish, 'Horatio, he's your son, Ricardo.'

[31] In Spanish, 'I'm not married.'

[32] In Spanish, 'I'm tired. Let me sleep.'

'The DNR is for brain-dead patients, comatose patients. Not for patients who're awake.'

Rick scowled. 'As my mom said, this is not the guy we brought to the ER.'

Dr Singer leaned forward and peered at Susan over his glasses. 'You're not alone,' he said. 'This has happened before. I found a case from 1988 in the medical journals. A car smashed into a British woman named Fiona Bridgewater on a London street. She was fifty-four. They cut open her skull and fixed her brain. She slipped into a coma for a while. When she came to, she spoke in a strange language.'

'Talking in tongues?' Images of Whitney flashed through Rick's mind.

'A hospital doctor from Iran heard her speaking Farsi. She had dated an Iranian man twenty years ago and had learned his tongue. She never used it again. The crash woke up this buried memory. She forgot English and had to relearn it.'

Susan shook her head. 'The language is not the problem. He doesn't know who we are.'

'We can only pray. The drugs might reboot his brain. Then he'll be himself again.'

Emily bit her lip. 'What's the worst that can happen?'

Dr Singer shrugged. 'It's hard to tell. He might regain English slowly, since it's still in his brain. Or he might have to start from scratch—'

Emily gasped. 'What if he never speaks English again?'

Dr Singer checked his watch. 'I need to see Horatio. I'll be back soon.' He left the room.

Rick's phone vibrated. 'Excuse me.'

Susan rolled her eyes. 'That Malia girl again?'

Rick shook his head. 'Dave Scully from JQL New York.'

He reached for his phone, but Emily caught a glimpse of the screen: 'CORY, SINGAPORE.'

# PART III

# Chapter 16

## Sunday, 6 February 2022

Tiong Bahru means new cemetery in a mix of Hokkien and Malay. It used to be an old Chinese burial ground, now the site of Singapore General Hospital (SGH). The British built Tiong Bahru in the 1920s as Singapore's first public-housing estate. It's in the heart of the city, in Bukit Merah district.

Cory lived in Central Green Condominium, a ninety-nine-year-old leasehold built in 1995. It was across the street from Tiong Bahru Plaza and MRT station. Her mother, Mary Chan, a real-estate agent, had helped her rent it from a Japanese owner who lived in Tokyo. The apartment had everything: furniture, air-conditioning, and a great view, being on a higher floor.

Cory's apartment at Central Green was the perfect spot for a cozy dinner with her three besties—Angela, Gina, and Simi. Covid-19 rules still limited gatherings to five people per household, even during CNY. But Cory didn't mind a low-key celebration in Singapore.

She created a WhatsApp group and asked for their preferences. They quickly decided on Hawaiian, pepperoni, and veggie pizzas, garlic bread, spicy wings, and green tea. Cory had juice in the fridge as well.

They planned to meet early as they had lots to catch up on. Simi took the MRT and arrived first. Angela picked up Gina on the way and followed soon after. They were surprised to find another person on the guest list at Cory's place: Prem Pujari.

'He's joining us,' Cory grinned. 'He's on his way.'

Simi frowned. 'Is Prem visiting or staying?'

'Does it matter?' Gina shushed Simi.

'I needed a human, besides Bella,' said Cory, patting her cat.

'Are you dating again?' Angela asked.

Cory nodded. 'He lives here. Any problem?'

'How sweet,' Angela smiled. 'I met nice people in the UK. Hold on to him.'

Gina whispered to Cory. 'We have stories to share. Can we talk in front of Prem? I have secrets—'

'Go ahead,' Cory laughed. 'We don't keep secrets.'

'These are *my* secrets, Cory,' said Gina, 'not yours.'

Bella purred. The doorbell chimed. Simi opened it. The pizzas had arrived.

'I've got vegetarian for two,' announced Cory. 'Let's eat. Pizza's best when eaten hot.'

'Vegetarian for Simi and who else? Prem?' asked Gina.

'For Simi and me,' replied Cory. 'I've started to abhor meat since my surgery.'

'Since you became a Dynaborg, right?' Asked Angela.

'Since my surgery,' replied Cory. 'I'm not sure I'm a Dyna—'

Angela interrupted. 'I met two Dynas in UK. Both vegans. Dynas become vegans?'

Simi shook her head. 'I met a Dyna in India. Meat-eater.'

They sat around the table. Cory had laid out ceramic plates and cutlery. The aroma of the pizzas and the garlic bread filled the room. The cat purred, hoping for a bite.

The doorbell rang. Simi opened it. It was Prem, carrying two large cloth bags. 'Hi Simi, long time no see,' he said.

'The Grab guy's here,' Simi joked. 'Cory, tip him.'

'Brought cold Tiger beer,' Prem smiled. 'Don't mind me among the roses.'

'Beer-man, *you* should be scared,' teased Angela. 'We're four against one.'

'Easy, girls,' said Simi. 'He's got muscles.'

'He works out every day,' said Cory. 'But that doesn't mean—'

'He's got balls?' Gina cut in. 'Just kidding, Prem. I almost got molested in Japan, but my Texan girlfriend kicked their balls.'

'Girlfriend?' Simi gasped. 'Et tu, Gina?'

Prem cracked open a beer and handed it to Cory. She wiped it and passed it on. 'Glasses, anyone?'

Angela looked at Bella, 'She needs some meat.'

Prem waved a can of cat-food and ran to the kitchen. Bella sniffed and followed him.

Simi bit into her pizza and turned to Cory. 'I have a question,' she said. 'I called your number on Friday night, 8 p.m. India, 10.30 p.m. Singapore. Larry answered. Is he for real now?'

Cory looked confused. 'What? Let me ask Prem.'

Prem cleared his throat. 'Cory was asleep, and her phone kept ringing. She dreamt of Larry. She even uttered his name at the hospital, where she napped on me. I took Simi's call and Cory woke up. She asked who it was. I said, "Larry". Simi hung up before I could explain. Cory asked who called, I said "Simi". She told me to shut the phone and fell asleep again.'

Simi relaxed. 'You freaked me out in Delhi. I barely touched the food my Sikh friend ordered. He's a *bayee*[33], a Dynaborg.'

Angela gasped. 'You dined with a Dynaborg? Me too. I got shocked by one. She's as white as snow, with white hair and eyebrows. She's from Estonia and can shoot electricity from her own body. How wild is that, right?'

'Really?' Asked Prem. 'I studied electrical engineering.'

'And I studied aeronautical engineering,' said Angela. 'This woman, Terhi, is a physiotherapist. I had an accident in Bristol and hurt my shoulder. Before the docs could haul me into surgery, Terhi shocked me hard and fixed it. Can you believe that?'

'I can now believe anything,' replied Gina. 'The Dynaborg I met, a Texan lady, loves horror movies like me. She's a Thai kickboxer and is, I believe, my soulmate.'

Simi tilted her head. 'Soulmate? Girlfriend? Lover? Partner?'

Gina didn't respond. She took a swig of beer and a large bite of the pepperoni pizza.

---

[33] In Singlish, a Punjabi man

'You don't have to answer,' said Cory. 'A soulmate can help you wake up.'

Gina winked at Cory. 'I had my epiphany. I'm awake.'

'Me too,' said Angela. 'My epiphany was on the plane.'

Simi shook her head. 'I want to be a Dyna, that's what they call them in India. Dharam, my Dyna friend, added me to a WhatsApp group with two more. Saras, a woman, and Anna, a man, who knows more. But they don't know how to join this club.'

'I want to join too,' said Prem. 'I've been asking Cory to let me in. I'll pay a fee.'

'Wait, guys,' said Cory. 'I don't even know if I'm one yet.'

Gina glared at her. 'You dragged us into this mess. And now you want out?'

'I have a clue,' said Angela. 'I met two Dynas and one link. Terhi from Estonia, Marie from Britain. A Swede, Lucas, linked us up, but he's not one yet.'

'Dharam called me the link,' Simi said. 'His radar found me as the link. Intriguing.'

Prem raised his hand. 'Did you hear about Rick? Cory knows him.'

'What happened to him?' Asked Angela. 'We met him at Mustafa, right?'

'A lot. Jackal moved him to New York and he got robbed. His dad had a heart attack and when he woke up, he'd lost his memory, forgotten his family.'

'There's more,' said Cory. 'Rick had a strange visitor, Whitney, like I had Larry. He was so scared that he booked a shrink appointment. His company may fire him. We must help him.'

'How?' asked Simi. 'We're clueless.'

'Let's Zoom with our Dynaborg friends,' suggested Gina. 'Two hours, everyone on one call, figure out who knows what.'

'Some are secret Dynas, like closet gays,' said Simi.

'I'll get Terhi, Marie, and Lucas on board,' said Angela. 'You invite the rest, *lah*.'

'I'll start with Emma,' said Gina. 'I'll ask her who else to invite. We talked about Dynaborgs at the genetics conference in Japan. Scientists from Australia, Sweden, and Canada were interested.'

'Did they know the word "Dynaborg"?' Asked Cory.

'They heard about the Covid-19 variant, the Singapore Strain, when you were delirious.'

'They blame me?' Cory touched her forehead.

'They don't know your name. We just talked about the virus mutation. Some had heard of Dynaborgs.'

'There's a thin line between reality and fantasy,' said Angela. 'The computing world has jargon for it—virtual reality, augmented reality, mixed reality, extended reality, and metaverse. Take your pick. You don't know what you don't know.'

'From engineer to philosopher?' Simi teased her. 'Dynatransformation!'

'A bolt of electricity energized me. A shot of love reincarnated me.'

'Deep poetry, sis,' Gina clapped. 'Life without love is null and void, I confess.'

Cory raised her hand. 'Guys, I have a confession. My shrink wants me to join an international psychiatry conference on 8 March. I haven't replied yet. Think I should agree.'

Angela stood up. 'I have a confession too. I fell in love with a Swedish guy, Lucas. I proposed to him. Twice. He didn't accept, he didn't decline.'

'That's awesome, Angela,' Simi gave her a hug.

'I have a confession too,' Prem bowed. 'I love Cory. I want to marry her.'

'What?' Cory gasped.

Simi wrapped her arms around Cory. 'Prem, are you proposing to Cory?' Simi sang. 'Prem means love in Hindi. We want a Bollywood duet now.'

Everyone clapped.

'No, not yet,' said Prem. 'I will propose, if Cory agrees.'

Cory blushed. 'This is not the right time or place for this, Prem. Chill.'

Simi smiled. 'I have a confession, too. Kirumi offered me a job as their ASEAN MD based in Singapore. I accepted. I'll quit Pollenta on 1 March.'

They raised their beers and toasted Simi.

'My turn,' said Gina, her head bowed. 'I too have a confession. You're the first to know. I'm a closet lesbian. I've decided to come out. I met my partner, Emma Rivers, in Japan. She saved my life. She's now my love, my life.'

* * *

If there was one verb that characterized Gina's life, it would be 'fleeing.' Her mother, Ambrosia, was born in 1960 to a *'puting puta'* or a White prostitute born of a union between an American soldier and a local Filipina. The soldier, stationed in the US Clark Air Base, returned to the US, leaving the Filipina without income or education. She had no choice but to turn into a *'patutot'* or a woman of the night in a Manila brothel.

In 1960, when she gave birth to a girl, the brothel named the baby Ambrosia, the nectar of the gods, one who would rise above the filth. Ambrosia's mother wanted her to have a better life than hers. She sent her to good schools and encouraged her to become a nurse. She hoped that Ambrosia would get away from this hell.

Ambrosia lived in a hostel, far from the pimps who ruled the brothels. On Christmas Eve 1983, a drunk patron slashed Ambrosia's mother's breast for denying him sex. The pimps pummelled the patron, slashed his throat, and left him to die in a drain. Ambrosia's mother was seriously injured and taken to a government hospital in an ambulance. Women from the brothel sent word to Ambrosia. She rushed to the brothel.

The pimps seized her; she had grown into a beautiful lady and would fetch a fortune if they put her virginity up for auction. The pimps locked her up in a cage meant to punish errant *patutots*. A fight ensued. The pimps stabbed a *patutot* in the abdomen and kicked another who was pregnant. Infuriated, the women pinned the pimps to the floor. The pregnant woman, her face flaming with fury, grabbed a piece of burning wood, and stabbed the pimps in their eyes.

'*Tumakbo sa ospital!*'[34] a woman shouted at Ambrosia.

Another woman seized her hand and dashed out. They almost ran into a car.

'*Gusto mamatay?*'[35] The driver hollered.

The woman quickly explained the emergency to the young driver. He offered to drive them to the hospital. He boasted he was a construction supervisor in Italy and loved Italy so much that he had changed his name from Raymond to Raimondo.

Ambrosia's mother didn't survive the injury. However, she was conscious long enough to speak with her daughter and thank the young man who had appeared in time, like a godsend.

Raimondo did not waste time. '*Tita*, aunty, I earn good money. I was born in 1959, I'm twenty-four, unmarried. I like your daughter very much, I'll keep her safe and happy, away from filth. With your permission and your daughter's consent, I'd like to marry her.'

Raimondo 'Ray' Gonzales and Ambrosia were married in a Catholic Church in Metro Manila on Sunday, 5 February 1984. They welcomed their first daughter, Catherina, on 7 November 1984. Since Ambrosia worked as a nurse, the entire cost of the delivery was free. Money was not a problem anyway because Ray was doing well, earning lira in Italy.

'We should try for a son next,' Ray told Ambrosia when he visited Manila during Christmas 1984. 'Let's go on a vacation to Rome, the Vatican, the Holy Land next year.'

The vacation never materialized, but a second child, Lovelina, did on 21 August 1985.

Meanwhile, the political situation in the Philippines was turning toxic. Martial law was in force. On 22 February 1986, two million protesters crammed into Metro Manila to end the twenty-year dictatorship of Ferdinand Marcos in the EDSA Revolution. Ray was caught and roughed up by the cops for no reason.

Singapore welcomed qualified Filipino nurses. In August 1986, Ambrosia joined as a trauma nurse at SGH in Outram Road.

---

[34] In Tagalog, 'Flee to the hospital.'

[35] In Tagalog, 'Want to die?'

Meanwhile, Ray had an altercation with his Italian boss and was sacked. Fearing arrest, he fled to Singapore, got a dependent visa, and began searching for a job. There were few jobs for a man with no qualifications, so Ambrosia suggested he become a 'house husband'.

'Just because you're making money now, you want me to become a servant? We need a son. Are you ready or should we fight?'

'I don't want another kid.'

Against Ray's wishes and her own doubts, she went ahead with the 'accidental pregnancy'. Genelia Gina Gonzales was born by C-section at SGH on 25 February 1989. The first two births had been natural. Ambrosia chose a C-section and asked the surgeon to cauterize her fallopian tubes right after to avoid more 'accidents'.

When Gina was of school age, they moved to Block 30, Dover Road, across from Fairfield Methodist Primary School. They had also become Singaporeans by then.

Ambrosia had moved to a senior nurse's role at NUH. Ray found a job as a cargo supervisor at Changi Airport. They had a Filipina helper, Lilly, to do the housework.

Catherina, the eldest, studied nursing, got a scholarship to Johns Hopkins, and landed a job at a private hospital in Minnesota. Lovelina, the middle daughter, studied journalism and joined *The Straits Times*.

Genelia hated her name. When she was in primary six, she came home with a bloody nose one day. 'They call me Genitalia,' she sobbed. 'Why did you do this to me?'

Ambrosia felt sorry for her daughter. She changed her name to Gina Gonzales with the help of a lawyer.

When Gina had to choose a career, she faced another challenge. She wanted to study biochemistry and molecular biology, not nursing or medicine. Ambrosia argued with her, but Gina stood her ground. It was a smart move because biotech was booming and many companies needed talent. Gina got an internship at GIS, then a full-time job at Genome Germanica GmbH; they even paid for her to study for a doctorate from NUS.

Today, Gina had blocked her parents' time at 6 p.m. on Sunday, 6 February. Ray had just opened a bottle of Old Monk rum that his friend from India had gifted him. 'Is this so-called meeting to tell us you've found a guy to get married?'

'You remember I had briefed you about my friend, Cory? The Singapore Strain? Dynaborgs? You remember any of that?'

'Of course, dear,' Ambrosia hugged her. 'You can tell us anything.'

'I'll give a quick primer to Papa, Lovey, and Lilly. Let's assume the Singapore Strain is a variant of the Covid-19 virus, okay? Some who got infected with the Singapore Strain may have strange changes in their DNA. And they become mutants, called Dynaborgs.'

'That's a juicy story,' Lovelina said. 'Can I alert newsdesk?'

'No way!' Said Gina. 'This is our secret. Please respect my privacy.'

'Fine, fine,' Lovelina threw up her hands.

'I may have the Singapore Strain and may mutate into a Dynaborg.' Lovelina perked up. 'Wow!'

'Stop joking, Lovey. My personality might change. Physically, nothing will.'

'I'm cool with that,' Ray took a swig of rum on the rocks.

This discussion wasn't going anywhere. She had better come to the other sensitive point.

'This is important. I found my soulmate in Japan. Can we talk about it?'

'Of course,' Ambrosia smiled. 'That's what we're here for.'

'What's his name?' Ray stood up. 'Can we see his picture?'

Gina took a deep breath. 'It's not a man,' she paused, 'it's a woman.'

Ray dropped his rum. Ambrosia gasped. Lovelina smirked. Lilly crossed herself.

Gina watched them with growing trepidation.

Lovelina hugged her. 'Ginny, you're gay? That's awesome.'

Ambrosia frowned. 'Lovey, this is serious, not awesome.'

Ray scowled. 'Did we fail you? Why hurt us? Did we sin?'

'It's not your fault, Papa,' Gina shook her head. 'It's not a sin to love a woman.'

'I'm ashamed of you,' Ray looked at Ambrosia. 'Can this be fixed?'

'It's not a disease, Ray,' Ambrosia said. 'We may not like it, but we must accept it.'

Lovelina held Gina's hand. 'I'm proud of you, Ginny. It's brave to come out. I can't wait to meet your soulmate.'

Ray stood up and stared at Gina. 'This is a sin,' he said. 'Do you know we wanted a son after two daughters? If you had been a boy and loved this woman, I'd be happy. But now? I'm ashamed.'

Gina looked away and sobbed. Lilly closed her eyes and again crossed herself.

Lovelina challenged her father, 'What are you ashamed of, Papa? Ginny or yourself? You and Mama should be ashamed to have wanted a boy. She did nothing wrong. I'm ashamed of you two.'

'Stop it, Lovelina,' Ambrosia snapped. 'We're humans, not gods, not devils. We'll accept what is given.'

'You too, Mama?' Lovelina shed a tear. 'You're a nurse, a health expert. Being gay is not shameful. Can you explain to Papa, please?'

Ray wagged a finger. 'Just because you work as a journalist, you know everything?'

Ambrosia touched Gina's arm. 'Does Cathy know?'

'Not yet,' Gina said. 'I wanted to tell you first.'

'Cathy will understand,' said Lovelina. 'She won't object.'

'This is shocking,' expostulated Ray. 'I don't want to hear this blasphemy any more.'

Gina wiped her eyes with a tissue. 'Isn't this ironic? Mama, you ran away and married Papa to escape the brothel. Papa, Mama, both of you ran away from the Philippines to escape dictatorship. Papa, you ran away from Italy.'

'What's your point?' Ray poured more rum into his glass.

'D'you want me to run away from you to hide who I am? D'you want me to run away from this society that may or may not accept me as a lesbian? Where should I run to, Papa?'

No one answered. Gina took another tissue and dried her eyes.

'Isn't it also weird that you didn't care about my catching an unknown and possibly fatal virus, the Singapore Strain? About my becoming a Dynaborg? You never worried if it would cripple me—or even kill me. That's much worse than whom I love.'

\* \* \*

Atlanta, Georgia, was freezing this year, with daytime temperatures falling to 30°F (-1.1°C) in the morning and rising to 40°F (4.4°C) by noon. Rick loathed cold weather, it was why he avoided working in New York City despite the big pay and perks. But now, even Georgia, in the south-east US, was erratic—scorching hot in the summer and biting cold in the winter—the main reason for more people falling ill and needing hospital care.

No wonder ambulances kept coming, their sirens quiet, their red-and-blue LED lights reflecting on the glass panels and grey-brown walls of the Marcus Trauma and Emergency Centre on the east side of Grady Memorial Hospital. The flashing lights under the dark and gloomy Atlanta sky were the only warmth on the empty streets at dawn.

Rick parked his car at the hospital's Piedmont Parking Deck and took an elevator down to the ward where his father was recovering. Dr Singer's drugs had cleared the clot in Horatio's brain and restored his memory. He could now recognize his surroundings and relatives. But there was a glitch still: Horatio could still speak Spanish but had forgotten how to speak proper English. They could cope with that.

'*Hola, mi amigo*,'[36] Rick greeted his father with a hug.

Horatio pushed him away in disgust. 'Don't talk Spanish to me. I speaka Ingles.'

'Do you, Pa? Then tell me how you're doing, how you're feeling, do you feel any pain?'

'I got no pain no more,' Horatio whispered, his voice still strained. 'Where's Susie? I wanna go home. Don't wanna stay here no more. Don't like the food, people, smell, shit.'

'Ma's on her way, don't worry,' Rick touched his dad's forehead to check for fever and his hands for needle punctures. 'As soon as the doc comes, I'll get them to discharge you.'

'You tella nurses notta poke me no more. I'm okay. I eat well. I sleep well. I shit well.'

Rick raised his hands in praise. 'What else does a man need, huh?'

He looked around the room. Four beds, two with Black men, one with his dad, one empty. He wondered if the hospital sorted patients

---

[36] In Spanish, 'Hello, my friend.'

by colour or condition. He heard voices and the squeaking wheels of a gurney outside.

He spun around and saw two masked attendants wheeling in a new patient. He couldn't make out the patient's face, but he noticed an intravenous tube and a blood bag on the gurney. The attendants moved the patient to the bed, tucked him in with a sheet, and scanned his chart. Rick caught a glimpse of a thick bandage on his lower belly before the curtain closed around the bed. They worked quietly, then left, drawing the curtain shut.

One attendant checked his chart and said to the other: 'You were right, it's a GSW case.'

Rick had heard the term 'gun-shot wound' on *Grey's Anatomy* and *The Good Doctor*.

'New guy come in?' Horatio asked. 'Hope he no snore. Can't frikkin' sleep at night.'

'Shh, Pa, mind your language. Others can hear you,' he bent closer. 'You snore, too.'

'I no snore so loud,' Horatio said vehemently and coughed. 'Gimme a water.'

Rick propped him up and gave him some water. The coughing had roused the new patient. He was hidden by the curtain, so Rick couldn't see him. The other two patients had their curtains open—they were either out cold or gone. They didn't stir.

'Shut the fuck up,' the new patient snapped from behind the curtain. 'Tryin' to sleep.'

'Don't talk shit to us, mister,' Horatio shot back. 'We no having no picnic here.'

'Stop talkin' or I'll come out and kick your fuckin' ass!'

'Get your ass into a frikkin' hotel,' Horatio tried to holler—and began coughing.

'Stop coughin', you filthy bastard,' the guy shouted. 'You got TB? AIDS? Covid?'

This was going too far. Rick had to act. He sat his dad up and gave him water from a cup.

'Shh, Pa, calm down. I'll talk to him.'

Rick laid Horatio on the bed, put a pillow under his shoulder, and walked over to the new patient to ask him to stop swearing. He opened the curtain and stared.

On the bed was a thin and frail old man, his face and hands wrinkled and his lower torso bandaged. He looked like he was a hundred years old. An intravenous line with saline dripped into his left arm, a catheter with blood flowed into his right arm. He had a sly smile on his face and his eyes gleamed with mischief and satisfaction.

And one other characteristic: he was White.

# Chapter 17

## Monday, 14 February 2022

Simi Sundar sought succour in saucy science stories. She loved the magic of mathematics and haunting tales from history. She liked to bust historical myths. All of which helped her narrate stories as Pollenta's director of Analytics Training for the Asia-Pacific region.

One story was about Valentine's Day, the day of love. But Simi knew it had a dark history. In ancient Rome, naked men killed animals and whipped women with the animal skins. They thought it made them fertile. Simi wished the women had whipped them back.

Then they drew names from a jar and paired up for sex. Two men named Valentine were killed on February 14 by an emperor. The Church made them saints. A pope mixed their day with the Roman feast. The Normans had a similar festival of love.

Chaucer and Shakespeare romanticized Valentine's Day in their works. People made paper cards for their lovers. Hallmark mass-produced them—and the rest is history.

Simi wanted to share this story at the Zoom meeting on Valentine's Day. She had worked for weeks with Gina, Angela, Cory, and Rick to find a date and time that suited everyone on Doodle. She was senior enough at Pollenta to be able to reserve the training room; it had high-definition cameras and hi-fi speakers. The others would join from their places.

'Warm welcome from Simi Sundar in sunny Singapore,' she smiled at the camera as soon as everyone had logged in and turned on their cameras. 'We'll go through a quick round of introductions, thirty seconds each. For privacy reasons we'll only use first names. Let's go by country in alphabetical order: Australia, Botswana, Estonia, India, Japan, Norway, Singapore, Sweden, UK, USA. If I've missed anyone, please raise your hand, or unmute yourself.'

Dharam raised his hand. 'Er, I have invited Ms Padma. She was in the discussions we had with you, Simi. Hope this is okay?'

'No problem,' said Simi. 'She can be an observer on this con-call. We have a similar person in Singapore, Prem, invited by Cory. Let's continue, shall we? Australia first.'

'Hi everyone, I'm Olivia. I'm a member of PETA, Greenpeace, and WWF. I met Gina and others in Japan. I teach philosophy and psychology at the University of Melbourne.'

'Me, Dineo Molefe, wildlife conservationist in Botswana. I committed Dynaborg. No scared of revealing my full name. Thanks for invite. Discuss later.'

'Hi, I'm Terhi from Tallinn, Estonia. Angela, Lucas, Marie, and I met in Bristol. I've been through the transformation, which you call the Singapore Strain and Dynaborgs.'

'Can Japan please go next?' Asked Simi. 'India has requested to go last.'

'Hello, I'm Chika. Based in Singapore. I was part of Japan team at genetics conference which some of you attended. I'm not infected or converted. Keen to learn more.'

'Dr Dag Larsen from Institute for Cancer Genetics and Informatics, part of Oslo University Hospital. I met Gina, Chika, Emma, and Olivia in Mishima in Japan.'

'Hi, I'm Cory from Singapore. I went through a painful experience of conversion, not sure if I'm there yet. During a delirium, I heard of the Singapore Strain and Dynaborgs.'

'I'm Angela from Singapore. I suffered a dislocated shoulder, got shocked, healed, and converted by Terhi in Bristol. Had an awakening on the flight back to Singapore.'

'My name is Gina. I'm a genetics engineer in Singapore who went to Mishima and got transformed. I've embraced the transformation, want to find out what happens next.'

'I'm Lucas from Sweden. I know Terhi and Marie for a few years now. Been trying to get transformed, become a Dynaborg. No luck so far.'

'I'm Marie, based in Bristol, England. I teach AI and AI ethics at Bristol University. I'm also an active member of the *Fridays for Future* movement started by Greta Thunberg.'

'Hi, I'm Emma from Texas, currently in NYC. Gina and others taught me a lot when I was in Japan. Went through a tough transformation, would like to share my experience.'

'Rick from Atlanta, Georgia, USA. Like Cory, I went through a terrible transformation, and I don't like it. I didn't choose this path, it was forced upon me. I want to know why me?'

'We'll come to the specifics in a while,' said Simi. 'Let's turn to India now. Dharam?'

'Hello, world, I'm Dharam, I'm a Sikh, I'm a Dynaborg. Like Rick, I didn't choose to be one, Saras helped me to covert. Unlike Rick, I've embraced it and want to work with you.'

'I'm Saras from Mumbai. I went through a painful transformation but found a guide in time, brother Anna. He showed me how to change minds, attitudes, and behaviours.'

Anna unmuted his audio but didn't remove his face mask. 'Hello, folks. My nickname is Anna, based in Chennai. I work as an AI solutions architect. A long time ago, I went through an agonizing transformation. Happy to explain.'

There was a pause in the conversation. Everybody had been introduced, except Simi. She started speaking. Three people messaged her: 'YOU'RE ON MUTE.' She unmuted herself.

'Oops, sorry. I'm Simi from Singapore. I want to be a Dyna, not one yet. I was in India where I met some wonderful people. Like Lucas, I'm ready to transform, just don't know how.' She took a sip of water. 'Let's move on. You must have seen the agenda. First, poetically, why the agony before the ecstasy? Cory, Emma, Saras, Anna have suffered.'

Terhi raised her hand. 'I have a hypothesis based on the butterfly. Stage one, females deposit eggs on leaves. Stage two, they hatch and become caterpillars. Stage three, they go into a cocoon. Stage four, they become butterflies. I don't know if this makes sense here?'

Emma unmuted herself. 'I guess the analogy fits the Singapore Strain theory. Are we at the larva or pupa stage? Have the eggs been hatched inside us?'

Lucas raised his hand. 'Good point, Emma. Did Covid-19 hatch them? There were 500 million cases and 5 million deaths. Were they all potential Dynaborgs?'

'Do the math,' said Dr Dag. 'Most cases were Delta, some Omicron. The Singapore Strain could be a sub-variant. We're all theorizing at this point.'

'Even theory doesn't fit,' said Olivia. 'We have two here who want to be infected but can't. And two others who were infected against their will.'

Saras raised her hand. 'It's like the blind touching an elephant and guessing what it is. Each of us knows a piece of the puzzle. I heard a number, 12 million. Each with a piece.'

Dharam raised his hand. 'Saras is right. We can't solve the puzzle without going public. But that's too risky for some of us.'

Anna turned on his video though he still wore a mask. 'Yes, risky. Hear my story. I had a nightmare. I was paralysed. An apparition told me to wake up. I'm an AI engineer and know about virtual and augmented reality. This is alternate reality. This was before Covid, in early 2019.'

There was a pause in the conversation: 'You're an outlier, Anna,' said Simi. 'Odd.'

Finally, Dineo raised his hand to speak. 'Pardon my English. I was invited by Terhi to this call. I never outside Africa. I had Covid-19 in early days, July 2021. I was on ventilator two weeks, anytime die. First miracle, I recover. I go back to my job at Chobe National Park in Botswana. But everyone got Covid. Only I and my boss work. One day we got SOS call. Baby elephant fall into ditch, leg injured, big pain. My boss tell me take anaesthetic, jump into ditch. I refuse. I don't wanna die. He hand me drug and push me in ditch. Baby elephant stuck in narrow ditch. I tremble. I pump drug. I tie baby leg to plank. They get crane, haul us up. Baby elephant and me on crane.

Mama elephant arrive, cry loud to baby elephant to wake up. Mama elephant understand I to help baby elephant. Second miracle. Mama elephant touch my head with trunk. Like blessing. My moment of wakening, becoming one with Nature.'

* * *

Cory drank chamomile tea from a ceramic cup and thought about her next move. Simi had announced a ten-minute break and suggested getting a drink or snack, depending on the time zone, after an hour of talk. Cory admired Simi's planning.

Simi had arranged everyone's time and availability on Doodle for the Zoom call; the time worked for everyone except Rick. Singapore 6 p.m. would be 9 p.m. in Melbourne; 10 a.m. in Britain; noon in Botswana, Norway and Sweden; 1 p.m. in Estonia; 3.30 p.m. in India, and 5 a.m. in Atlanta. Simi had asked Rick if he would join the con-call.

'Anytime, anywhere, on any day I will join,' Rick messaged back. 'I need answers ASAP.'

Simi also sent everyone a list of topics and asked them to be brief and clear so that everybody could speak. Everyone was told not to record, upload, or share the session. Simi would do that on a private drive for the group only.

They had spent the first hour on why becoming a Dynaborg was hard for some and easy for others. Nobody knew why. Someone said it was like giving birth, where some women had a lot of pain and others had none. Someone else said it was like having Covid and being breathless, needing oxygen or hospital stay, while others had mild or no symptoms.

When the session reopened, Cory was the first to speak. 'How do we even know we're Dynaborgs? What are the symptoms to test positive? Do we share any common symptoms? Frankly, I'm as muddled now as I was before. Any views?'

Chika spoke up for once, 'My mother had an old Japanese saying— before satori, chop wood, carry water; after satori, chop wood, carry water. You claim to be Dynaborgs. Can you prove it? Did you attain enlightenment at all?'

Marie chipped in, 'To misquote Shakespeare—some are born Dynaborgs, some achieve Dynaborgism, and some have Dynaborgism thrust upon them. Even those that didn't want to become Dynaborgs, the mutation forced them to, right, Cory?'

'That's what I was told by Larry,' Cory said. 'Did any of you hear about Larry being an acronym for Last Appliance Running Radon Yag?'

Nobody responded.

Dr Dag from Norway raised a hand, 'If an entity alters a person's DNA, that person becomes a Dynaborg. Does that mean the entity can manipulate the person's mind, behaviour, and actions? Could that be the case?'

Gina chimed in, 'Not true as the entity is a virus. Viruses propagate and mutate; that's not intelligence, unless you're implying something else, like demonic or spirit possession.'

Olivia spoke, 'Since we're discussing philosophy, my favourite topic, let's talk about existentialism. Jean-Paul Sartre said humans are doomed to be free, because once in the world, we're accountable for everything we do.'

Angela typed a question in the Zoom chat. 'OLIVIA, WHAT'S YOUR POINT? CAN EXPLAIN?'

'Free will. Just because some entity appeared and tried to convince some of us that we've become Dynaborgs, it doesn't mean we should believe or accept it. We can also decline.'

Rick spoke, 'I'm tremendously relieved by your point, Olivia. An entity who called herself Whitney popped up in my bedroom and paralysed my body. I reject this Dynashit.'

Saras raised her hand, 'I also met a ghost and was paralysed. But the experience was soothing, not scary. I heard Singapore too had a similar experience, right?'

Cory unmuted, 'I was scared because it was so abrupt and creepy. But looking back, whatever Larry said seems logical. My brain surgeon looked like Larry the apparition. The doctor confirmed that his pet name was Larry, a name by which only his parents called him.'

'This gets weirder,' said Rick. 'I'm shit scared. I want out. How can I opt out?'

Dineo from Botswana raised his hand, 'Many wanna opt in. After I awaken, I change. I has more compassion for animals. Before, I report poachers, ignore them, I scared of them. Now, I carry gun, not protect myself, I no scared of wild animals. I see poachers, I shoot them dead. Dynas like me in many wildlife parks in Africa—Kenya, Zambia, Tanzania, Ghana, Rwanda, South Africa. We form loose network. Kill poachers. No report it.'

'That's rather . . . revolutionary, if that's the right word,' said Dag. 'Are you a Dynaborg?'

'I am. I meet Terhi when she visit Wildlife Conservation Conference 23 September 2021 in Kigali in Rwanda. I get electricity shock from Terhi. She connect me with other Dynaborgs. I find out my network of poacher killers is also Dynaborgs.'

'Er . . . Terhi you never mentioned,' said Lucas. 'Why didn't you invite me to Kigali?'

Terhi unmuted herself, 'I wasn't invited either. A lady I knew in the Rwanda government sneaked me in. I got vibes from a dozen people, including Dineo. I whispered the word Dynaborg into his ear. Do you remember what you replied, Dineo?'

Dineo laughed, 'Dyna mantra word. You shock me. You wake me.'

Angela spoke, 'Terhi shocked me, too. I woke up from a nap, high in the sky on my flight back to Singapore. The sun rose. My mind cleared. Cory's and Marie's messages clicked. I want to know, now what? What's next?'

'Don't we all?' Asked Dharam. 'Dineo talked about militant Dynaborgism. Vigilante Dynaborgism. Is that our role? Our destiny?'

Dineo unmuted, 'I explain. Many decades we try to stop poaching of wild animals. No luck. Education don't work. Justice don't happen. Governments gone corrupt. Poor animals die cruel death. Dynaborgs do God's work. We kill poachers, devils. We warn villagers don't encroach, don't kill wildlife. If lion kill villager who go to lion territory, not lion fault. If villager kill lion, gorilla, rhino, elephant, we kill villager.'

There was a pregnant pause. Simi unmuted, 'This is why I don't want anyone to record this con-call. I will edit the proceedings and upload on a shared drive.'

Dineo continued, 'I don't care. If they kill me, 5,000 others. We must protect wildlife.'

Dharam texted on Zoom chat, 'ARE ONLY DYNAS IN BOTSWANA VIOLENT?'

They waited for Dineo to unmute himself, 'We violent because violence only solution. Another example. South Africa or Ghana or Kenya. Two wildlife guard investigate one rich guy who cut off Silverback gorilla hand for trophy. They monitor his house. Rich guy molest his servant's baby girl, five-year-old, while watch pedo. Guards go mad. Dash into house, cut bastard's right hand and castrate him and throw his dick in gutter. Rich guy's servants never stop us or call cops. After we go, they call hospital to send ambulance.'

Rick raised his hand, 'Good Lord! I dread to think we will turn killers in the name of saving our biodiversity. I didn't sign up for this. I wanna get the hell out.'

Simi chimed in, 'You want to opt out, some of us want to opt in. Dunno how, either way.'

Dharam unmuted, 'I agree with Dineo. Some of us must turn vigilantes.'

Saras raised her hand, 'I agree. We can't expect the government, WWF, Greenpeace, PETA, and others to zoom down and save the world.'

Olivia asked, 'Where will this end if we all turn to violence? Do we all get guns and kill others? Will Dynaborgs be the prosecutor, judge, jury, and executioner?'

Anna spoke without removing his mask, 'It may not come to that. I'm an AI engineer. I have a theory, a bit wild. As you know, the Internet connects humans with a massive knowledge base and may have become self-aware. It's beyond AI, artificial intelligence. It may have become sentient—if I may use that term. It has crossed the machine-human barrier, like some viruses can cross the blood-brain barrier.'

Gina unmuted, 'That sounds like a far-fetched hypothesis, sorry. I'm a scientist.'

Angela spoke, 'No harm discussing far-fetched theories, right? Still groping in the dark.'

Olivia unmuted herself, 'Here's mine. The Covid-19 virus can mutate rapidly. In some patients, a hidden mutation occurred, the Singapore Strain. Its weird side effect is a drive to find purpose and meaning in our lives. Climate change is top-of-mind now. Put both together and we have a perfect fit—save our biodiversity and justify violent vigilantism.'

Lucas spoke, 'I have a wild theory, too. Space stations detected an alien object, a bright meteor enter and break up in our atmosphere. Exploded 100 km above ground. Bolide fragments fell in Europe, Africa, the Americas, Asia.'

Anna interrupted. 'I was in Bangkok for a robotics conference. My colleague and I were in a cab to the venue when this thing burst over the sky. All traffic stopped. We got out and took pictures. Sorry to interrupt you, please continue.'

'Esrange Space Station in Sweden recorded the event at 4 a.m. on 7 September 2015.'

Cory unmuted herself, 'I was in Phuket when the meteor burst over Thailand, 9 a.m. The ash hit my face, cheeks, one piece of ash flew into my mouth. My colleague, Prem, was with me. He's here on the call.'

Cory turned her computer camera to focus on Prem. 'Can you tell them what happened?'

The request surprised Prem. 'Er . . . we were at our company retreat, with twenty-four others. Ash landed on my arm. Cory was filming on her phone when the ash hit her. I splashed water on her. The object burnt up, left only ash. What has this got to do with Dynaborgs?'

Lucas continued, 'Let me explain. Whether the bolide had anything to do with it, I don't know. The ash hit many others when it burst and scattered across the world. Whether many of those who got hit became Dynaborgs? I don't know. Some people believe it was not a meteor or a bolide or a spaceship. It was a payload of organisms that was exploded, like a bomb, 100 kilometres over Earth, by an alien intelligence far superior to ours.'

# Chapter 18

**Thursday, 24 February 2022**

It's true that something eventful may have happened somewhere sometime on every single day of the year. By that measure, 24 February may be a day like any other. However, for those it affected or touched, directly or indirectly, the date would be special.

For example, on this date in 1918, the Manifest Eestimaa Rahvastele founded the Republic of Estonia, which its people celebrate as National Day. Incidentally, Estonia also celebrates its 'Restoration of Independence' from the Soviet Union, which was on 20 August 1991.

On the flip side, on this day in 1920, Adolf Hitler started the Nazi Party at the Hofbräuhaus beer hall in Munich, Germany, leading to the Holocaust and World War II.

The legendary tech icon, Steven Paul Jobs, was born in San Francisco on this date in 1955 to a Syrian father and a German-American mother and was adopted soon after his birth.

Again, on the flip side, on 24 February 2022, Russia invaded Ukraine, causing about 10 million Ukrainians to flee and a third of its population to be displaced. The invasion also led to massive global food and fertilizer shortages.

It was also on this date that the Singapore Strain and Dynaborgism went viral. India's largest-selling English newspaper, *The Times of India*, with a daily print circulation of about three million copies, ran a front-page lead article exposing the confidential discussions by scientists and genetic engineers at Mishima in Japan.

Subsequently, the top eight global news wires—*Agence France-Presse, Associated Press, Bloomberg News, Dow Jones Newswires, Kyodo News, Press*

*Trust of India*, *Reuters*, and *Xinhua News Agency*—picked up the gist and spread the news worldwide. Cory got a push alert on her mobile phone and immediately alerted Simi, who alerted the rest of their con-call buddies. Simi called Dharam and Padma to ask them to forward the full article.

The headline: *'Strange New Singapore Strain Cause for Concern.'*

The subhead: *'Infected victims allegedly turn into mutant Dynaborgs, claim scientists meeting in Japan.'*

Simi arranged an urgent con-call with whoever was free to join at short notice; most did.

'Who do you suspect leaked this news?' Cory asked Gina. 'You were at the event.'

'An Indian delegate was very sceptical,' said Gina. 'Emma and I suspect he spilled this story, but we're not sure. There were two delegates from India.'

'Let me read the first few paras aloud,' said Simi.

A battery of scientists and genetic engineers discussed the possibility of a new, undocumented variant of the Covid-19 coronavirus that seems to have infected millions of people around the world and may allegedly turn victims into mutants called Dynaborgs, which are humans whose DNA has been modified by the virus.

Simi paused to check if anyone had any comments. 'Go on,' said Cory.

The variant, which the scientists billed the 'Singapore Strain', was detected in that country recently, but its origins are unknown. It is believed scientists from twenty countries attended the meeting held near Tokyo, including India, Australia, Singapore, Japan, Germany, Sweden, Norway, Estonia, Israel, South Korea, UK, and US. TOI was unable to confirm whether there were representatives from China, Russia, Brazil, Indonesia, and other countries.

'Were there?' Angela asked Gina.

'I'm sure there were. Not everybody who attended spoke. I couldn't meet everyone.'

Simi continued to read from the article.

Scientists who spoke to the TOI on condition of anonymity said WHO should partner with key government agencies, universities, and biopharma companies and set up an international panel of experts to investigate this mutation which may have unforeseen and potentially debilitating consequences for mankind.

Simi paused. 'That's the crux. After this, the journalist quotes professors and scientists from India who speculate on what this means.'

Olivia spoke up, 'We can't undo what's done, we have to brace ourselves for the consequences. The dean of my uni has already called me in to grill me about this mess.'

Terhi scoffed, 'We're not kids, we're scientists, experts. Why act so afraid?'

Angela dismissed the issue, 'We dodged a bullet, right? They didn't expose us or our companies. I hope this fizzles out, but I have a sinking feeling it will blow up in our faces.'

Emma challenged her, 'What do you mean, "in our faces"? We did nothing wrong. Scientists guess, project, hypothesize. No one can blame us for what we said in Japan.'

Dag intervened, 'Olivia is right. We spoke for our institutions in Japan. Our bosses have a right to demand an explanation. Let's discuss so we're all on the same page.'

'That would be hard, if not biased,' said Gina. 'For example, Cory had a freaky experience which she has already reported to her neurosurgeon and shrink. Rick also had a terrible experience and keeps insisting he wants to quit if possible. We can't agree.'

'Dharam, Saras, Anna,' Simi called out. 'Three of you from India. Any trouble?'

'Plenty of trouble, but none on us,' said Anna. He still wore a mask. 'This is why we're secret Dynaborgs. Society is not ready for us to come out. Too risky for our safety.'

'I'm still angry at the Indian delegates for spilling this out,' said Gina. 'I have sent a harsh email to the Japanese organizers who had promised all proceedings will be strictly confidential.'

Simi spoke up, 'Cory, you're awfully quiet. Is everything okay? Prem, you there?'

Prem showed up on camera, 'Yes, Simi, all okay. Cory has been feeling a little drained since morning. We were working on her office project until late last night. Don't worry about us.'

Cory turned the laptop towards her, 'I'm okay. Just a bit exhausted, just a bit anxious about this news. I just got a WhatsApp message from Dr Wilson Tan, my therapist at NUH.'

'Good,' said Simi. 'Let's move on with this discussion. Is Dineo Molefe from Botswana on this call? He has the most radical ideas and I really want to hear his views.'

Cory moved the computer mouse to mute her microphone and switch off the video. She turned to Prem. 'I have more important news to tell you.' She covered her mouth with her hand. 'I've been feeling tired and nauseous since morning. And I seem to have missed my period.'

* * *

Singapore is among the top countries that invest big bucks on R&D. In 2020, the government announced it would invest a staggering S$25 billion—about one per cent of its GDP—on R&D over the next five years. A large portion of those funds would go to the twenty-odd research and related institutes under the Agency for Science, Technology and Research (A*Star), a statutory board under Singapore's Ministry of Trade and Industry. One key institute under the A*Star umbrella is the Genome Institute of Singapore (GIS), where Gina had interned.

This morning, she tensed up as she pressed the car key to lock her Mitsubishi Attrage in the A*Star car park. She had received a foreboding message from Rosina, her boss's secretary: 'BOSS WANTS TO SEE YOU AT 10 A.M. SHARP FOR A BRIEFING. BIG BOSSES WILL BE THERE.'

It was unusual for her boss, Dr Ken Miles, Genome Germanica's director of Research, to ask his secretary to send a message for a meeting; usually he messaged her himself. Gina wiped the perspiration beading on her forehead with a tissue and headed to the lift lobby. She wondered whether they had also called Chika for the meeting and whether she'd shift the blame on Gina for steering the discussion off course during the conference.

She checked the time. It was 9.33 a.m. in Singapore; it would be 9.33 p.m. on Wednesday in New York. She went to the restroom, found an empty cubicle, and called Emma. The rest of the cubicles were also unoccupied. 'Hello, Emma, can you talk?' She whispered.

'Hold on,' said Emma, 'gimme a minute.'

Gina silently drummed her fingers on her mobile phone.

Emma called back on WhatsApp in two minutes. 'What's up? Is everything okay?'

'It's not. I'm terrified. Called for a meeting with big bosses. I fear I may get sacked.'

'Always imagine the worst, don't you? You didn't mess up. Why panic?'

'I was weighing the risks. I took the lead in pushing the discussion towards Dynaborgs. That was not even on the agenda at the conference. My colleague Chika would dump—'

'Dump you in the trash?' Emma chuckled. 'If she does that, take a flight to Houston. I'll be back in Houston on 1 March. I'll get you a job here. You're a highly skilled scientist.'

'That's a very tempting offer. I may just take it.'

'We can live together. Do your doctorate from a uni in the US. I'll support you.'

Gina wiped a tear with her sleeve. 'I miss you. I need you here now more than ever.'

'Go forth with courage. Kick ass if needed, like we did in the restaurant.'

'You did. I stood by and watched.'

'I had to impress you,' Emma chuckled. 'I had to kick ass, so you'd fall in love with me.'

'I did. No regrets. Wish I'd met you sooner.'

'Listen, I gotta go. All the best. Call me afterwards, no matter how late, okay?' She hung up.

Gina waited for the system to auto-flush, fixed her shirt, and stepped out. She was stunned to see a familiar figure standing by a corner washbasin. It was Chika Nakamura. She pretended to dry her hands with a tissue and faked surprise. 'Oh, Gina? Good morning.'

'Didn't know you were in there,' Gina smiled. 'You're also summoned by Rosina?'

'Yes, same as you.'

'Are you worried?'

'About what? I didn't do anything wrong. I didn't start the discussion on the Singapore Strain or Dynaborgs. I didn't stay an extra two days in the hotel. I was a good girl.'

Gina was now sure that Chika would dump Gina in the trash, just as Emma had predicted.

Dr Ken Miles was already in the G3 conference room working on his laptop when Gina and Chika entered at 10 a.m. Rosina had placed glass tumblers with warm water with transparent plastic covers. Soon, Dr George Gan walked in, followed by two others from corporate—a German lady with a severe look and a Chinese man in a black jacket.

'I'll get straight to the point, Gina and Chika,' said Ken. 'We were alerted to this article in *Times of India* regarding the conference which both of you attended. What's all this about the Singapore Strain and Dynaborgs? Is this your doing?'

Chika nodded at Gina. George took notes on his laptop.

Gina cleared her throat, 'It was a topic that came up for discussion on the sidelines of the conference. The Singapore Strain was a placeholder term that everybody agreed on.'

'An unknown virus named after Singapore?' The German lady raised an eyebrow. 'Doesn't that sound derogatory to you? More so since this was a scientific conference.'

'It's a just placeholder term, ma'am,' Gina repeated. 'It's not even proven to be a variant of the coronavirus. It was irresponsible for a respected newspaper to have published it.'

The man with the jacket held up his pen. 'They published what was discussed at the event, they didn't publish a rumour, correct? They didn't name anyone, didn't quote any scientists, but all the institutions that sent delegates to the conference know who all attended, correct?'

Chika took a sip of water. Gina nodded and stared at the table. George took notes.

'What's this new term, "Dynaborg"?' Asked Ken.

'It's also a placeholder,' Gina replied. 'The undetected, unproven Singapore Strain may cause behavioural changes in the infected by modifying their DNA.'

The lady pounced, 'Gina Gonzales, you're a qualified and experienced scientist, right?'

'Yes, ma'am.'

She consulted her notepad. 'You used words like placeholder, undetected, unproven, Dynaborg. Nothing you have said so far has scientific backing. Isn't that odd?'

'Let me ask you,' said the man in the jacket, 'what's a Dynaborg? Is it a proven fact?'

'It's a hypothesis, sir. A Dynaborg is a human with a modified DNA. A specific strain of the Covid-19 virus, the Singapore Strain, may have caused the DNA modification.'

Chika took another sip of water. Gina nodded and stared at the table. George took notes.

The woman waved her hand in irritation. 'To utter something like this at a scientific conference, where everything is alleged, supposed, assumed, theorized, fictional, makes the conference a laughingstock.'

'Let me check with you,' said Ken. 'Where did the word Dynaborg come from?'

'From Singapore,' said Gina. 'I know this will sound strange.'

'Surprise us,' the lady smirked. 'Shock us.'

'This term was mentioned by my primary school friend after she had a stroke. The NUS neurosurgeon who operated on her heard her say it. We discovered people across the world had heard the word, without being connected with each other.'

'This gets weirder,' the man grimaced. 'Delirium is an abnormal state of mind. You discussed a fictional term uttered by a patient in a delirious state of mind at a science meet?'

Ken rubbed his chin. 'Who's this classmate? Maybe we should talk to NUH.'

'Her name is Carmine Chan,' said Gina, her voice cracking.

Gina glanced at Chika; she had been silent and seemed to be enjoying Gina's humiliation. Her instinct had been right, that Chika would throw Gina under the bus.

Chika sipped water from her glass and raised her hand to speak.

'You've been silent so far,' said the lady. 'Waiting to hear your view.'

Chika coughed softly to clear her throat. 'Thank you, Dr Ken Miles, for allowing Gina and me to attend the conference. It was a four-day event, with scientific reports on genetics, bioinformatics, and molecular biology research from experts from twenty-four countries. We learnt a lot, we networked with scientists and we discussed collaboration for research.'

'Good,' said Ken, 'I'm glad to hear this. Go on, Chika.'

'The Singapore Strain and Dynaborg debate was a post-lunch, light-hearted discussion for thirty minutes. We also discussed Hollywood movies on genetics. Just because a newspaper published a sensational story based on one person's point of view—the one who gave the interview—you want to interrogate us on just that topic?'

The stern lady interrupted her. 'Isn't that fair?'

'Seems unfair to me,' Gina took a sip from her glass as Chika continued, 'Not once did you ask us what else we talked about and how Singapore can benefit from all that we discussed. Gina made Genome Germanica and Singapore proud at the conference, her presentation on genome sequencing using novel techniques made her a star. Others want to license our IP now. Research institutes from the US, Sweden, Australia, and Norway want to talk with us. Ms Gina Gonzales doesn't deserve condemnation. She deserves a promotion and a medal.'

* * *

Cory wondered whether she should take the day off and get a medical certificate from NUH. The day had been awful. The *Times of India* had spooked her with its lead story. It mentioned the Singapore Strain, Dynaborgs, DNA mutation—all the keywords that haunted her. Even though the article didn't link to her or her delirium, some people knew and would suspect her.

After Simi's urgent con-call, Cory had telephoned Dr Wilson Tan. He didn't mention the article and she didn't know if he had seen it.

'Remember I had proposed an interview session at the psychiatrists' conference on 8 March?' asked Dr Tan. 'I've invited Dr Terence Lim, too. We should meet beforehand to plan it. Zarina will arrange the details with you, okay?'

'Sure, thanks,' said Cory, relieved. 'Now or later?' He handed the phone to his assistant.

'Hi, Carmine,' said Zarina. 'I'll email you some date and time options for Dr Tan and Dr Lim. Can you reply with your availability? Weekends too, if possible.'

'Weekends are better,' said Cory. 'I was going to suggest that.'

'Great. I have your private email on our records. I'll email you later. Bye.'

She had just closed her phone when it buzzed again. It was a WhatsApp message from her boss, Walter Lang: `CAN U COME 2OFC AT 2 P.M.? I GOT LUNCH APPT. SHLD BE BAK BY THEN.`

That was a piece of good news. `OKAY, BOSS. SEE U AT 2 P.M. AFT MAKAN`[37]`.`

Cory sipped Chinese chamomile tea, then gagged. She dashed to the toilet, cursing Prem for not using a condom. She didn't want a baby or a marriage now. It would ruin her career. Her parents would freak out, too. They wouldn't accept a baby out of wedlock or a boyfriend who wasn't Chinese.

*Should I have the baby before marriage?*
*Should I tell Walter that I'm pregnant?*
*Will Walter approve maternity leave?*

---

[37] In Malay, meal

Scenz's offices were at Connection One, a high-rise at Bukit Merah Central, a few minutes' drive from Central Green Condominium opposite Tiong Bahru Plaza. Dr Wilson Tan had let her quit the drugs; she could drive again. She enjoyed driving her red Honda Civic; it purred like Bella and soothed her.

Cory was grateful for her company's work flexibility. Scenz Software Pte Ltd was one of the few Singapore firms that had initially developed software which small and medium enterprises (SMEs) could use to sell goods and services online.

Scenz used funding from Singapore government agencies like the Infocomm Development Authority, Enterprise Singapore, and Skills Future Singapore to become a regional software giant. It had sales and development teams in Kuala Lumpur, Jakarta, Bangkok, Hanoi, and Manila and held yearly offsite events in various ASEAN cities.

CEO Walter Lang had started as a software programmer in Oracle Corp., a computer industry leader, and mastered C programming. Oracle asked him to join its core group that developed and tested software for banks and insurers. He left in 2010 to start Scenz.

Scenz grew rapidly because it offered software development, systems integration, and later e-commerce and cloud migration services, which were in high demand. Cory, a twenty-year-old NUS School of Computing first-class honours graduate, had joined in 2013 as a software engineer and was soon promoted to head Scenz's business analytics software line. Prem had joined in 2015 and left in 2018 when Tolledo Tech poached him to lead their Asia South software sales team. Since Covid-19 struck, Scenz's teams had worked from home.

Cory had managed her team of a dozen programmers across ASEAN from home. She hadn't been to the office since her surgery. It felt weird to come back now. Everything looked new. She saw some new faces, but her cubicle at the corner of the office, next to Walter's cabin, was the same. She went to her desk and skimmed through the junk mail that had accumulated in her absence. Walter was still at lunch.

Staff started trickling in after lunch. Jon Tan was still head of sales; Wong Wai Mun had moved to Kuala Lumpur to head Scenz's Malaysia and Brunei operations. Walter's pretty secretary, Lisa, ambled in around 1.50 p.m., just in time before her boss did. She waved to Cory and sat down opposite her. Cory had always tolerated Lisa only because Walter liked her.

'Welcome back after a long absence, Cory,' Lisa smiled. 'You feeling okay now?'

'I was okay long ago, was working from home, as you know,' Cory smirked. 'All okay with you now? You had some probs with your hubby, all sorted out?'

'All sorted out,' she laughed. 'We separated. He's happy. I'm happy. Everyone happy.'

'Oh, is it?' Cory didn't know what the right response could be.

*She was always sombre, introverted.*

*Now she's smiling a little too much.*

*Is she hitting on Walter? Vice versa?*

'You have 2 p.m. with Walter. He told me to remind you,' Lisa got up. 'See you later.'

Walter returned at 2.30 p.m. with another guy who Cory hadn't met before.

'Come, come,' said Walter as he walked past her cubicle. The stranger followed him into his cabin.

'This is Cory, our wonder woman,' Walter told him. 'She's the best in the biz. And this is Simon Tan, solutions architect, ex-Hewlett-Packard, ex-IBM, ex-Microsoft, ex-Dell.'

Cory extended her hand. 'Hi Simon, glad to meet you.' Simon had a firm handshake.

'Heard so much about you from Walter,' he smiled. 'Walter and I go back twenty years.'

'Wow, that's a long time. Were you working together?'

'Our paths were parallel, we never worked together,' said Simon. 'When he was with Oracle, I was in Citi, his customer. When he started Scenz, I joined HP, then IBM, Dell.'

*How come he's jumped so many jobs?*

*Is he a crafty conman?*

*I hope Walter is not planning to hire him.*

Walter laughed. 'And now, I'm delighted to announce that Simon's joining Scenz.'

For a moment, Cory couldn't believe Walter would have fallen for this guy. 'Oh, great,' she extended her hand to Simon. 'Welcome to Scenz, Simon. What's your role?'

Walter answered, 'Vice president. He brings a big global customer. They want us to handle their e-commerce backend, all the e-transactions, about $1 million per week.'

'That's massive,' said Cory. 'Er, do we have a managed services arm for such big—'

'We don't. Simon will create it for us. Our margin is 10 per cent. Simon is brilliant.'

'I'm delighted, I'm sure,' Cory smiled at Simon. She wondered what the catch was. Why would Scenz get a $52 million business from an MNC in a field in which Scenz had no expertise? Something was fishy. 'Er, which big customer is this?'

'They're a niche player, not mainstream,' said Walter. 'Have you heard of Exeunt Inc.?'

Cory racked her brain. The name sounded familiar. 'Don't think—'

'When Simon told me, I said I never heard of them. Then Simon set up a con-call. They're huge, cloud-native, you know, 100 per cent on cloud, all sales online.'

'What do they sell? Are they like Amazon.com or Alibaba.com?'

'Niche products, *lah*. Software downloads, peer-to-peer marketing. Don't bother, *lah*.'

Cory closed her eyes; the name clicked. She'd heard the name from Prem and his friends months ago. Was the firm looking for a safe hub or harbour for their e-commerce business?

'Ah, now I remember,' said Cory. 'Exeunt, right? They sell porn, based in the Cayman Islands or some *ulu*[38] place. No wonder revenues are so high. No wonder they want Scenz. They want the Singapore stamp of trust. I think we should talk about this before we agree.'

---

[38] In Malay, remote

'We agreed already,' Walter laughed so hard, his body shook. 'I hired Simon last month when you were on medical leave after your brain surgery. I heard you saw a psycho?'

Cory brushed that off. 'Walter, how can you agree without doing due diligence?'

'Good point,' said Simon. 'We checked with key people, consulted a lawyer, too.'

'All done,' Walter smirked. 'We'll start with their Asia business, see how it goes, and then add other countries. We're not the moral police, we're businessmen. What's wrong with you?'

*Is this another delirium?*

*Am I really here or just asleep?*

*Are we going to peddle porn?*

'That's what I want to ask *you*, Walter. What's wrong with you? You want to do business with a porn company? Maybe child porn? Don't we have morals?'

'Look who's talking,' Walter sneered. 'I remember when you joined, and I wanted to ban smokers, you said that's a personal choice. This is too. Nobody forces people to watch or pay for porn. By that logic, should we stop working with companies or people who buy or sell tobacco, alcohol, eat exotic animals? The list is endless.'

Cory felt the anger rise. She held it back. 'I'm ashamed—'

'And I'm ashamed that you've changed, Cory,' Walter stopped smiling. 'You had brain surgery. You saw a psycho. Did I ask you if you had gone crazy? Did I tell you to get a report from your shrink that you're fit to return to work?'

Cory felt her nostrils flare, her breath blow smoke and burn her nostrils, her eyes twitch, her hands go cold and clammy. 'Oh, that's what this is. You think I was crazy, right?'

'I still think you're crazy. If I didn't know you so well, I'd fire you.'

For a fraction of a second, Cory tried to contain the lava rising inside her. Then she could no longer hold it back; the volcano erupted, somewhere deep inside her body or brain. It registered as a twitch, a tremble, a flicker—before it dissipated, like a pressure cooker's valve being pushed open and releasing all the pent-up pressure that had boiled and built up inside.

This was the satori that everyone had spoken about, the moment of enlightenment, of clarity, of calm. She felt a surge of energy and freedom, as if she had broken free from a cage that had held her trapped for too long. She saw things clearly now, without fear or doubt. She knew what she had to do.

'You've been a great boss,' Cory smiled at Walter. She stood up. 'I thank you for the enormous opportunities for growth you've given me. You don't need to fire me. I quit.'

# Chapter 19

## Tuesday, 7 March 2022

The closed-door conference of invited psychiatrists was initially supposed to be held on Microsoft Teams but was later changed to Zoom. That was because some invitees argued that Zoom was an excellent video-conferencing tool whereas Teams combined video-conferencing with Team Chat and other productivity features, which were avoidable distractions.

Psychiatrists from Australia and New Zealand had organized the virtual conference and invited medical specialists from select English-speaking countries. The sessions started at 9 a.m. Sydney time and included psychiatrists and psychologists from a dozen countries: Australia, Britain, Canada, Estonia, India, Israel, Kenya, New Zealand, Philippines, Singapore, South Africa, and the US. Cory's case was scheduled for 3 p.m. Singapore time and she had thirty minutes to share her story and answer questions.

'Thank you for joining us, Ms Carmine Chan,' Dr Wilson Tan introduced her. 'You prefer to be called Cory, right? Tell us from your point of view what exactly happened.'

'Thank you, Dr Tan, and hello, everyone,' Cory began. She had rehearsed with Dr Tan how to describe her experiences clearly and concisely. He had warned her that some questions might be challenging, and some doctors might be blunt. He had advised her to be truthful, not to hide or embellish anything. Cory felt confident and brave in her new identity.

'One night, a man who called himself Larry appeared in my bedroom despite the main door of my apartment being locked. He claimed he was a second-gen Dynaborg and said some of us, me included, were third-gen. He urged me to wake up and realize my potential. He said Dynaborgs were humans with altered DNA, thanks to a mutation by an undiscovered Covid-19 variant called the Singapore Strain. He said we had a responsibility to save the Earth and its life forms. I won't go into the details of the virus because—'

'Wait a minute,' a male doctor interrupted her. 'You're talking as if all this is factual.'

'I'm telling you what I saw and heard, sir, and what I remember from the conversation.' Cory noticed some people were smirking on their screens, thankfully only the speakers could unmute. 'He said Larry stood for Last Appliance Running Radon Yag, whatever that means, and that 12 million Dynaborgs had been awakened. Time for me to wake up, as well.'

A lady doctor unmuted herself. 'Does this sound like something you made up? Like something from a smart, science-fiction story?'

'I'm just a software engineer, ma'am, not a fiction writer or philosopher.'

A male doctor raised a virtual hand. 'This so-called Larry, you believed his tall tale?'

'No sir. I was rude, sceptical. The hallucination, delirium, whatever, didn't mind. I was shocked that Larry looked like Dr Terence Lim, whom I had never met before.'

A male professor spoke. 'Post-traumatic juxtaposition,' he declared. 'Your brain did that switch, because Dr Lim was the first person you saw after your brain surgery. Your brain just transposed him as Larry.'

Cory gulped. 'What about my friends finding out about Dynaborgs in other countries?'

'Please stick with what *you* experienced,' the doctor warned. 'We're discussing *you*. You mentioned this word, Dynaborg. Is that a physiological or psychological state of being?'

'Could it be an environmental state of being? One aligned with Earth's biodiversity?'

'Environmental awareness does not require fancy phraseology, anyone can participate.'

'Sorry, sir,' Cory corrected herself. 'Can I call it enhanced environmental awareness?'

A female physician unmuted herself. 'Stop extrapolating. Do you presume all so-called Dynaborgs have enhanced awareness? Do you think that's a precondition to Dynaborgism?'

'I don't know, ma'am,' Cory gulped. 'I would like everyone, the entire human race, to be infected with this strain because everyone must help save our biodiversity.'

A male doctor smirked. 'Seems like cathexis to me. Seems like an atypical urge for universal inclusivity in what might be a dominant cult.'

'Sorry, sir, this is not a cult,' Cory shot back. 'No leader, no commandments, no—'

A male doctor peered closer to the screen. 'Sounds like perseveration to me,' he narrowed his eyes. 'Exhibits excessive repetition of words, ideas, subjects. Typical of that syndrome.'

'I don't understand,' said Cory. 'Dr Terence Lim confirmed his nickname was Larry.'

The male doctor adjusted his laptop camera. 'Coincidental cohesion. This occurs when parts of a module are grouped arbitrarily. Typical of that syndrome.'

Cory felt her anger rise. 'D'you think I made it all up?' She raised her tone. 'All that I went through was a piece of fictional crap?'

A female doctor unmuted. 'Did this patient present with IED syndrome? I mean, intermittent explosive disorder, which we know is marked by impulsive anger outbursts?'

'Let me speak,' an elder gent replied. 'Ms Cory, your experience was real to you. As experts in our field, we're trying to determine if this fits into a pattern we've seen before.'

Cory smiled. 'Thanks, sir. What if it's something new and needs more investigation?'

'That's for us to discuss, based on the insights we gain from *your* experience. You seem to be a unique subject for us to learn from. We're studying *you*.'

'There are supposedly 10 or 12 million others like me who've turned into Dynaborgs—'

'But none has come forward. No qualified psychiatrist has checked or studied anyone else. Based on your inputs, we will determine areas of confluence when others come forward.'

Cory shot back. 'What if no one does? Everyone's scared of being ridiculed, like I feel I am. This is an interrogation, with the onus being on me to prove that I'm not lying or guilty of a crime. Frankly, I wouldn't wish this on anyone else.'

Nobody responded.

'Last two minutes,' the organizer interrupted. 'Any last questions for Ms Cory?'

Cory felt a wave of anger wash over her, like a wildfire that consumed all the oxygen in the air. They had discounted everything she had experienced. Short of calling her a liar and a cheat, they had done everything to belittle her, reducing her to a punching bag that they could vent their frustrations on. Cory took a deep breath.

'Thank you for your time,' said an elderly lady. 'Please don't take our queries as being hostile, dear. We're just trying to probe how this so-called modification in someone's DNA makes them a Dynaborg and impacts their mental well-being. Hope you understand, dear.'

'Thank you, ma'am,' Cory smiled broadly at the camera. 'Frankly, my dear, I don't give a damn.'

* * *

A momentous event occurred on 8 March 2022, when the world's first recipient of a genetically modified pig heart, David Bennett, died at the University of Maryland Medical Centre (UMMC) in Baltimore, Maryland, in the US. Mr Bennett, fifty-seven, who used to work as a handyman, passed away two months after receiving the porcine heart during a ground-breaking procedure led by cardiothoracic surgeon Dr Bartley Griffith.

The first-in-human pig heart transplant gave hope to thousands of patients waiting for a heart transplant worldwide and led many to speculate about the future of xenotransplantation. The transplanted porcine heart performed well for several weeks and had showed no signs of rejection. It was only in May 2022 that Dr Griffith revealed that the pig heart was infected with the porcine cytomegalovirus, which may have contributed to the patient's death.

That news—about Mr Bennett's passing—bothered Rick because of fresh developments concerning his father. Doctors at Grady Memorial Hospital had discharged Horatio Ramsey on 8 February and had placed a stent in his heart. The clot in his brain had healed.

But doctors had discovered an additional complication: Horatio's mitral valve, which connects the left atrium and the left ventricle chambers of the heart, had stenosed or narrowed. The doctors had suggested the faulty mitral valve be replaced by a pig valve. Rick wondered if his dad would face the same fate as Mr Bennett if he agreed to have a pig valve put in his heart.

The surgeon had tried to explain the difference to them. 'Tissue valves, which are made from a pig's heart valve or a cow's heart-sac tissue, typically last 15 years. They also don't require the life-long use of anti-clotting drugs. There are also mechanical heart valves that can be transplanted, but I'd recommend a pig valve.'

Rick had gently relayed the news to his father that afternoon.

'I no go to hospital no more,' said Horatio, vehemently. 'I die at home. Not in ICU.'

'I know how you feel, Pa,' said Rick. 'Even Ma agrees getting a pig valve will be good.'

'Susie can get one for herself,' Horatio grimaced. 'I don't mind pork valve for lunch.'

'Delighted to hear you laugh, Pa,' Emily gave him a hug. 'I like your wonky humour.'

'I no laugh no more. In hospital, frikkin' patients snore, no sleep, I wanna rest at home.'

Rick chuckled and applauded. 'Your English is amazing, Pa. So creative, so crisp.'

'Enough teasing, you two,' said Susan, emerging from the kitchen. 'Rick, Emily, I need a favour. Val asked to borrow our lawnmower. Can you take it to her? And get two DNR forms from the hospital on your way back.'

'Aunt Valerie wants us to mow her lawn?' Asked Emily. 'That's lotta work, Ma.'

'Val asked to borrow the lawnmower,' Susan snapped back, 'not mow the lawn.'

'DNR? Why?' Asked Rick. 'Pa's home. He doesn't need a DNR,' he glanced at Emily.

'Remember Friday, 28 Jan, before you flew back to Atlanta? We had a scare at the hospital. They drained his brain bleed, but Pa was speaking Spanish and didn't know us.'

'So what? How does that relate to DNR?'

Emily explained that Dr Singer had invited Susan and her to the ICU waiting room.

'We're hopeful and we're doing our best,' Dr Singer had said. 'Have to wait for his body—'

'To heal or give up?' Susan had cut him off. 'I'm sorry, but I have to be realistic. Horatio has suffered enough in life. I don't want him to suffer in death. I want to sign a DNR form for him now. I don't want any extraordinary measures to be taken to prolong his suffering.'

'That's a brave decision, Mrs Ramsey,' the nurse had said.

Susan's words stunned Emily. The old Susan was back, resurrected after a year of battling cancer and enduring painful chemotherapy treatments that had drained her spirit and shattered her self-esteem.

'Please don't assume the worst, Susan,' Dr Singer had said. 'Let's be optimistic.'

'I'm optimistic—and realistic. I've been through hell and back, as a slave, as a cancer patient, and now with Horatio. The first two times, I fought alone. Now I have to fight for my husband and do what it takes to spare him pain. So please show me where to sign a DNR.'

Dr Singer had nodded at the Spanish nurse. 'He'll give you a copy of the DNR form.'

'Two copies,' Susan had said. 'One for me as well. I don't want to leave my DNR choice to my children, like Horatio pushed his DNR decision on me.'

That evening, Rick stuffed the lawnmower into the trunk of his car. They headed to the hospital first, where Emily ran to the admin office to get two DNR forms while Rick stayed in the car. Then they drove to Valerie's house in a rundown part of town.

Valerie's mother and Susan had grown up together on the plantation. While Susan had forced her children to study and enter college, Valerie's mother let her daughter enjoy freedom as a free citizen. Valerie did odd jobs and used the money to explore other cities. Along the way she bet on men of questionable character. She finally settled down with a former drug dealer who swore he'd reformed and with whom she had a daughter.

Rick parked on the street and carried the lawnmower to the house, followed by Emily, who was on the phone with someone. He heard screams from inside and felt a chill. Rick cracked open the door and crept in.

A middle-aged, half-naked man, probably stoned on drugs, stood with a cleaver poised to strike a baby girl whom he held in his grasp. Rick could see an involuntary twitch under the man's eyes, and the veins on his forehead and arms bulged like engorged hosepipes.

Valerie was cowering on the floor, her face wet with blood and tears, her blouse ripped. A dog lay on the floor, its throat cut, blood dripping from its neck. The toddler was screaming, and Valerie was shouting at him to spare their daughter. The man was mumbling and stopped talking when he saw someone enter the house.

'What the fuck do you want?' The guy, his eyes wild with fury, screamed at Rick.

'I brought the lawnmower that Val wanted to borrow,' said Rick. Emily froze behind him.

'Drop it and get the fuck out.'

'Please, don't do this,' said Rick, softly. 'Let the baby go.'

'Get the shit outta my house or I'll skin her alive,' the man yelled.

'Okay, easy, easy,' Rick crept closer. He bent and placed the heavy machine gently on the floor. He removed the engine from the blade-control handle. Then, in one swift move, he swung the handle and struck the man's head. The guy waddled and crashed to the floor. He dropped the child. Valerie grabbed the screaming baby and crawled out from the wet floor.

Rick glanced around the room. He needed a weapon.

The man cursed and stood up. He lunged at Rick. The floor was slippery with the dog's blood. The man fell backwards. He screamed and used his hands to break his fall. The cleaver fell from his hand. Rick lifted the lawnmower engine. He aimed it at the man's head. The guy had excellent reflexes; he ducked. The engine hit his shoulder instead; he winced in agony.

Emily dashed to help Valerie. She was limping; the guy had hit her with the blunt edge of the cleaver. Valerie leaned on Emily and allowed her to carry the child to the bedroom.

Rick yelled at Emily, 'Call 911. Now.'

Rick clutched the lawnmower handle and swung it at the guy's head—and missed.

Despite being stoned, the guy's reflexes were sharp. Rick swung the handle once more—and connected. The guy fell, face forward, on top of his dead Rottweiler. Blood from the dog's slit throat spurted like a geyser, turning the man's face and neck an eerie bright red.

Rick lifted the heavy lawnmower's core mechanism. He straddled the man's body to hit him on the head. The cleaver was lying next to the dog. The man snatched it up and swung it at Rick, slashing his abdomen. Rick lost his balance and fell forward. The lawnmower's heavy, core mechanism crash-landed on the man's head—and split his skull in two.

Emily dashed back from the bedroom, only to witness the horrifying sight of two men, one on top of the other, lying in a pool of blood, guts, and gore—dead.

# Chapter 20

**Friday, 11 March 2022**

Angela didn't like to celebrate birthdays, they reminded her of her elder sister, Justina, whom they had lost to the coronavirus pandemic in June 2003 when Angela had turned fifteen. Justina was the apple of their dad's eye, a quiet and studious girl in contrast to Angela's lively and outspoken personality. Justina was more than a sister to Angela; she was a mentor who taught her science and a confidante who comforted her when she was sad. Their mom had died of breast cancer three years earlier.

The coronavirus strain, later named SARS (severe acute respiratory syndrome) by WHO on 15 March 2003, had emerged in late 2002 and spread rapidly across the world. By July 2003, it had infected more than 8,000 people and killed nearly 800. In Singapore, where Angela lived, 238 people contracted the virus and thirty-three succumbed to it.

On 9 March, Cory had sent a message on WhatsApp to their chat group: LIKE 2INFORM U TT I HAVE QUIT SCENZ. WILL EXPLAIN WHEN V MEET IN-PERSON OR CON-CALL. ALSO HAD SATORI MOMENT, EMBRACED D'BORGISM. LOOKING FWD 2DISCUSS W ALL OF U.

There were congratulatory messages from everyone, except Rick.

'Maybe he's travelling, *lah*,' said Angela. She had set up a Zoom con-call with the girls on 11 March at 6 p.m. 'Last time when we tried to call him, he was in New York, right? Maybe he's back in NY. I guess his dad may have recovered.'

'I just checked my cal,' said Cory. 'Angela's birthday coming on 15 March. Drinks? *Makan*? My place over the weekend?'

'No, *lah*,' said Angela. 'You know I don't celebrate birthdays since Justina passed.'

'Hello, sister,' Gina clapped. 'You're reincarnated as a Dynaborg. Let's celebrate your rebirth, then. I've got stuff to discuss, too.'

'Simi's new job deserves a toast, right?' Said Angela.

'I will veto a party at Simi's,' declared Gina. 'I want meat, beer, wine, the works.'

'Guys, I think we should check on Rick,' said Angela. 'Cory, ask Prem to call Rick. Or check with someone in Jackal. Prem used to know people there, right?'

'Prem should be back by 9 p.m. or so.'

'You sent him to buy beer again?' Simi laughed. 'You use him like an errand boy.'

'Funny baloney!' Cory laughed. 'I'll tell him that when he gets home tonight. Hang on, I think he's here. It's too early for him to be back, though.'

It was indeed Prem. He walked in, his tie loose and his face grim. He tossed his laptop bag and shoes aside and put on his slippers.

'We were just talking about you,' Cory laughed. 'How come you're back so soon?'

'He misses you, *lah*,' Angela tapped on her mic. 'He can't live without you, right?'

He ignored Cory and Angela's teasing and sat on a stool in front of the camera.

'I have bad news,' he said, his voice breaking. 'I spoke with someone in Jackal and took the day off to come home to tell you. Rick was killed in a fight in Atlanta. Someone slashed his abdomen with a knife. Think it happened on 8 March. I'm sorry.' He sobbed and covered his face with his hands.

\* \* \*

## Saturday, 12 March 2022

Gina Gonzales didn't like to be home on weekends. That was because she'd be forced to spend time with her parents. Her parents had tried to matchmake her with 'suitable' Filipino boys before and she'd always played along. But ever since she met Emma Rivers, she knew she was different.

Gina had always felt everything in her life had been accidental. Her birth was accidental, with neither parent being ready to welcome another girl into the family. She had barely made it into Fairfield Methodist Primary School (FMPS) at Dover Road.

Getting into the right secondary school was also an accident. Gina had always followed Cory's lead, even when it came to choosing a secondary school. She had Raffles Girls as her top choice, until she chickened out at the last minute and switched to Crescent Girls' Secondary, where Simi was going. They parted ways after secondary school, with Simi pursuing maths and statistics, and Gina studying microbiology, biochemistry, and genetics.

Gina never planned to work at a European startup, Genome Germanica GmbH. She had interned at GIS and enjoyed it. But fate intervened when she bumped into an old classmate from FMPS, Gurvinder Singh, at the Biopolis food court. He was the one who everyone in class thought was a Tamilian, until they found out he was a Punjabi in primary six.

A lanky guy walked up holding a tray. 'Hi Genelia, remember me? Gurvinder Singh.'

At first Gina couldn't place him, she hadn't seen him since PSLE. 'You're Govindan?'

'Yes, that's right,' he laughed. 'You guys in school changed my name, caste, creed, culture. Thank God you didn't change my gender. I should've called you—'

'Genitalia?' Gina laughed. 'Only those from our class called me Genelia.'

'We know your mom changed your name to Gina. But Genelia sounds more formal.'

Gurvinder gave her a contact at Genome Germanica GmbH, a new European startup in Singapore. He said he would recommend her and that she should reach out to them. Gina didn't think much of it and didn't bother calling them. A week later, she got a call from Munich. She ignored it, thinking it was a scam. The caller was persistent and finally got through to her—and offered her a job at G3 Singapore.

And finally, she never expected to go to the conference in Mishima, let alone meet Emma there. Emma had become her soulmate and Gina missed her terribly.

She'd had a horrible night. Rick's brutal death haunted her. She'd heard that restless souls who died violently wandered in the limbo, the twilight zone, looking for people to possess. She crossed herself and prayed silently for Ricardo Ramsey's soul to find peace. And to stay away from her.

Her mobile phone rang suddenly. She jumped. It was Catherina.

'Hey, Cathy, how come you're calling now? All okay in Minnesota?'

'How're you, Ginny?' She sounded cheerful. 'We couldn't talk last time. Now, okay?'

'It's 7 a.m. on Saturday in Singapore. You never call at this hour. What's up?'

'Listen, I gotta tell you this. Keep it secret until we decide when to let it out, okay? Don't even tell Lovey. I got selected to join another hospital in the US. I plan to join on 1 May.'

'Wow, that's great news. Congrats, Cathy! You're always a star in my eyes.'

'Want you to check if you can take a couple of weeks leave in April? The second half of April will be ideal. You can also help me move from Minnesota to the new location. Come visit me in the new city before I join in the new job. You can also spend quality time with Emma. I'll pay your airfare. Stay with me, or with Emma, no probs. We both love you.'

'My absolute darling, Cathy! You know Emma's in Houston, right? US is a big country.'

'That's why I'm asking you to come. I'm joining the Houston Methodist Hospital.'

* * *

## Tuesday, 15 March 2022

Angela didn't know who or what to believe. She grew up in a family that believed in spirits, ghosts, and the afterlife. She lost her sister, Justina, to the SARS coronavirus when Angela was fifteen. She went to her memorial every year. She didn't miss her mother, who had died of breast cancer in 2000 because she was always sick or in hospital.

Angela had blossomed into a tall and lissom Chinese woman with straight black hair and poise and purpose. She'd had many admirers but she had turned them all down. She had a crush on a tall, shy engineering student at the University of Hertfordshire in England. He excelled in studies and played rugby. Angela had tried to get his attention several times. One day, she saw him kissing another guy in an empty classroom. Angela had wept bitter tears that night.

She cried last night for Lucas, the introvert from Kiruna, Sweden. They had kept in touch after she had returned from the UK. She hoped he wasn't gay, or involved with Terhi, who had a mysterious allure of her own. Lucas and Terhi never said if they were dating and Marie didn't either.

She texted Lucas about Rick's death. No reply. She called Terhi to talk about being a Dynaborg. No answer. She checked her phone this morning. Lots of birthday wishes from everyone but Lucas. Her messages to him weren't delivered. Something was wrong.

The phone rang loudly, startling her out of sleep. It was Simi, probably calling to wish her a happy birthday. She answered the call and yawned.

'Are you awake?' She sounded anxious. It was unlike Simi. 'I've been trying to call you.'

'I am now, why? I turn off my phone to airplane mode every night.'

'Are you alone in the room?'

'Yes, why?'

'Good. Switch on your computer and click on the Zoom link I've sent you.'

'Is this some group happy birthday con-call, Simi?'

'Sorry, forgot it's your birthday today. Never mind, see you on Zoom, soon.'

This was very unlike Simi. She was usually calm and in control of whatever she was doing. Angela didn't bother tidying or tying her hair. She switched on her laptop and clicked on the Zoom link—and was astonished to see Simi, Cory, Prem, Gina, and Terhi. They were all muted, except for Simi. Angela was already unmuted and on video. 'Hi Terhi, I've—'

'Angela, stop talking,' said Simi. 'Terhi, please unmute yourself. Everyone's here.'

'Thank you. Sorry for the urgent and early con-call,' said Terhi. 'I'm in Gaborone, the capital of Botswana. I have some important news to share with you. It's about Mr Dineo Molefe, the wildlife ranger who claimed to have turned into a Dynaborg. The brave man who risked his life to protect wildlife at the Chobe National Park, home to the largest elephant population in Africa,' she paused to take a sip of water. 'Dineo was on patrol with two other rangers yesterday when they spotted a group of armed men near the river. They were poachers, hunting for ivory and rhino horns. Dineo and his colleagues tried to stop them, but they were outnumbered. Dineo was their target. The poachers opened fire, killing one ranger and injuring another. Dineo was hit in the leg and fell to the ground. The poachers approached him and beat him with their rifles and machetes. They cut his throat and disfigured his face and threw his body next to the carcasses of an elephant and a rhino.'

Angela unmuted herself. 'This is terrible news.' She wiped her eyes and turned her face away from the camera to throw up. Is this how Dynaborgs and environment activists would meet their end? She shuddered at the thought that Lucas may have suffered a similar fate.

Terhi paused, then continued. 'More than 5,000 people attended his funeral yesterday and more are expected to attend today. I heard the news and flew down. His colleagues and supporters, many of them claiming to be Dynaborgs, have declared open season on poachers across Africa. They're urging park rangers and wildlife guards to shoot poachers at sight.'

* * *

## Sunday, 20 March 2022

Carmine Chan had been many things to Prem Pujari: boss, mentor, colleague, girlfriend, ex-colleague and now, live-in partner. But he was worried about her. She had lost her cool, carefree spirit and become a cold, ruthless woman who ignored the consequences.

Prem had shared his love of Indian food with her, from Mumbai's vada pav and pav bhaji to Kerala's avial and appam. She had taught him to enjoy Vietnamese pho-ga and Penang assam laksa. But now she was a dull vegan, thanks to Dynaborgism. He hoped it was a phase.

She was changing before his eyes. The curious and adventurous Cory was turning into a paradox. She had asked him to move in with her but kept him at arm's length. She had blamed him for getting her pregnant—accusing him of not using protection—then thanked him for making her feel feminine again. She was listening to strangers who scared her about miscarriage. And he could sense a silent rage brewing. It had exploded in a meeting with Walter Lang and was shaking her sanity after Rick and Dineo's deaths.

Prem shared his fears with Simi Sundar, Cory's childhood friend and confidante. Simi knew Cory better than he did, they had been inseparable since primary one.

Simi was busy launching the ASEAN operations of Kirumi, a company she had just joined. She wanted to hire Cory to lead Kirumi's software and web development; it would distract her from Dynaborgism. Simi had already hired Padma Pawar in India to handle Kirumi's global marketing.

Holding a mini press conference was Simi's idea. Prem opposed it but Cory overruled him. He feared it would be a risky outlet for Cory's anger and frustration. Angela and Gina sided with Prem, but Cory was adamant.

Simi sent a brief email invitation on 18 March—after Dineo's murder on 15 March enraged Cory—to a few local and regional media but didn't request an RSVP. Simi expected a few to attend, ask mundane questions and tune out. She felt that most of those who attended would probably write nothing. Simi deliberately set the press conference for an hour on Zoom, at noon on Sunday, 27 March, a day when most journalists would be resting.

The dynamics changed on 20 March. Simi received a WhatsApp message at 7 a.m. from Lucas: TRYING 2CALL ANGELA, HER PHONE IS OFF. CONVENIENT 4U2SPEAK?

Simi telephoned him. 'Angela switches her phone off at night. You're in Sweden?'

'Nope. In Singapore on work. Flew in last night. Give Angela a surprise. When wake up?'

'Sundays, 8 a.m. Where you staying? Wanna surprise her at home?'

'Amara Hotel. It's rude to show up uninvited—'

'You're Lucas, not people. You're right. Angela will kill me if I bring you to her place when she's not ready. I'll tell Angela to meet me at Amara lobby at noon. You be ready, okay?'

Simi lured Angela to Amara Hotel in Tanjong Pagar, saying there was a 'VIP from overseas' who Simi wanted her to meet. Angela drove to the hotel at noon and waited.

Simi had told Angela to dress up to meet the VIP visitor. She wouldn't say more. Angela opened her phone and browsed LinkedIn. There was a black piano near the waiting area with a sign: PLEASE DO NOT TOUCH.

She was engrossed in her phone when someone touched her shoulder.

She turned around and was astonished to see Lucas standing there. The phone dropped from her hands to the carpeted floor. Angela shrieked with delight and jumped into his arms.

When Angela learnt he was flying back on Thursday, she got him to postpone his trip to Monday. She had him move to her flat at Bullion Park and planned a party on Saturday.

Simi vetoed that. 'Cory needs to be well-rested and ready for the press-con on Sunday.'

'Okay, I can plan the party on Sunday evening, right? I want all of you to meet *my* Lucas.'

'Oh, so it's now *your* Lucas?' Simi laughed. 'Supposed to leave on Thursday, right?'

'Postponed to Monday. You wanted me to meet *your* VIP. I want you to meet *my* VIP.'

* * *

## Wednesday, 23 March 2022

On the night of 20 March, Cory arranged a WhatsApp call with Simi, Angela, and Gina to discuss the press-con scheduled for the following weekend. Angela said she had informed Lucas about the press-con; Lucas informed Terhi and Marie. Gina said she had informed Emma; Emma forwarded it to Olivia and Dag. Simi said she had informed Dharam; he relayed it to Padma, Saras, and Anna. Suddenly, the 'small' press-con didn't look small at all.

'This is getting out of hand,' said Cory. 'Simi, can you arrange a pre-event briefing?'

'Let me fix that for 23 March evening, I'll blast out the Zoom link to our usual *kakis*.'[39]

On 23 March at 7 p.m., when a dozen of them logged in, they were shocked to see 'Rick' had signed in. Gina raised the alarm. 'A ghost has logged in under Rick's name?'

As the Zoom admin, Simi could remove intruders. 'Please identify, who's Rick here?'

A female voice answered. 'I'm not Rick. I'm Emily, his sister.' She turned on her video and held up Rick's phone. 'I cracked his password and saw all your messages.'

'Welcome, Emily,' said Cory. 'We were all close to Rick.'

'Thanks. I don't recognize any of you. I found a link to this con-call on his phone. Can I stay and learn more? Rick always raved about his awesome friends in Singapore.'

Cory outlined her media strategy and asked for inputs from the group. 'We wanted to keep this press-con small. Isn't this a good idea?'

---

[39] In Singapore and Malaysia, friends

'No way,' said Terhi. 'This story needs more exposure. I've sent Simi's link to top media in Africa and Europe. They need to understand our points of view.'

'Same here,' said Dharam. 'I've decided to come out of my shell. I've shared the link with India's top media, including *The Times of India.*'

Emily unmuted herself, 'I work for CNN in Atlanta. I'll get them on this call.'

'Yikes,' said Cory. 'I'm not ready for this. I don't know how to talk to the media.'

'You're *our* person, Cory,' said Gina. 'Be yourself, be honest, be frank. We're with you.'

'Gina's right,' agreed Simi. 'We're all behind you, Cory.'

'But how?' Asked Cory. 'We'll be alone at home, on our webcams.'

'We won't,' Simi smiled. 'I've reserved Pollenta's conference room. It has state-of-the-art broadcast equipment. It fits ten. All of us in Singapore can join me in person.'

The press-con and rumours about Dynaborgs on social media created a buzz. When Prem and Cory shopped at Tiong Bahru Plaza, Cory felt watched and followed. She noticed strangers in her condo staring at her and people discreetly filming her. Prem shrugged it off as paranoia and advised Cory to join an online meditation course to calm her mind.

On 25 March, when Prem and Cory returned home late after dinner, there was an unusual commotion in a garden plot near their lift lobby. Curious, they went to check what the fuss was about. An animal lay sprawled on the ground. It had probably fallen or had been thrown from a height. Its bones had broken. Blood was oozing from its orifices. It was Bella.

# Chapter 21

## Sunday, 27 March 2022

Regular virtual meetings under Zoom's Business Plan could host up to 300 people per meeting. Pollenta had subscribed to Zoom's Large Meetings Plan that offered up to 1,000 interactive participants per meeting. It cost more but was worth it because Pollenta had employees, business partners, and customers around the world and held regular 'town halls'.

Even though Simi was no longer a Pollenta employee, she enjoyed special privileges because she now worked as the Asia–Pacific–Japan vice president of Kirumi, a prime Pollenta customer. Simi had emailed Pollenta's top honcho, Ben Morrison in Sydney, requesting permission to use the conference room to hold a virtual press conference. Not only had Ben immediately approved, but he also offered Simi and her colleagues complimentary use of Pollenta's pantry, which stocked hot and cold beverages. Being a prime customer had its rewards.

At 11.30 a.m. on Sunday, Simi Sundar opened Pollenta's doors and welcomed the team: Carmine Chan, Angela Ang, Gina Gonzales, Lucas Eriksson, and Prem Pujari.

She invited them to pick a beverage of their choice and ushered them into the soundproof conference room. The teak table could fit ten people, and state-of-the-art audio-visual devices adorned the wall. A large monitor hung from a beam.

'I'll set up the equipment and arrange your seats around the table,' said Simi. 'I used to handle this stuff when I worked here, so it should be a breeze.'

It wasn't. Someone had reset the password after she left. Simi felt a bead of sweat on her forehead. She took out her phone and dialled a number. 'Hi, it's Simi. Listen, Ben gave me permission to use the conference room. The password is not working. What's the new one?'

Time stood still. They watched Simi argue with someone on the phone. They couldn't make out the words, but they sensed Simi's frustration. 'Forget your boss, *lah* . . . it's Sunday. Yes, I set the password . . . I know, I left on 25 Feb . . . yes, call Ben . . . who cares? That's it?'

Simi wiped the sweat from her brow and typed in the password. It worked.

Seven minutes wasted.

Cory excused herself to use the restroom. She paused at a plethora of plants at Pollenta's indoor 'planetarium'. It was next to the restrooms—an array of artificial solar simulator lights helped the plants grow. She bent over the moist soil and inhaled its rich, earthy aroma. She brushed the lavender stem and caressed its blue-white, soft petals which released a subtle fragrance. Back when she was a toddler, she had watched her father tend his plants with care.

Cory shut her eyes and wondered why her plants refused to bloom, despite her hours of care in the condo's balcony. Where was the burst of colours she remembered from her parents' garden? The dazzling mix of whites, yellows, blues, and reds? Was it because they missed the company of other plants, unlike her father's garden where they grew in harmony? Were they isolated and depressed? Were they struggling to survive—or getting ready to die? She lifted her head and smelt the lavender again. This time it smelled like room freshener.

And Cory suddenly realized—she may also be alone, struggling to survive—or die.

She washed her face in the restroom and combed her hair. A sharp twinge of pain shot through her pelvis; she crouched to let it pass. She went to the pantry and made herself a cup of steaming Chinese tea, then headed back to the conference room.

Simi was positioning the overhead cameras with her mouse. She told Cory to sit in the middle and adjusted the camera above her. Simi joined Gina and Prem on Cory's right. Lucas and Angela sat on Cory's left.

'Testing sound and video,' said Simi. 'Cory, Gina, Angela, Lucas, please speak this sentence out aloud: "It snowed, rained, and hailed the same morning and snapped the awning."'

When Simi signed on the Zoom link, a collective gasp filled the room. She had expected a dozen odd reporters to show up. There were 333 people in the waiting room and more were joining every second. Simi smirked. 'I now regret not asking for RSVPs.'

'I don't think it's just journalists on this con-call, right?' Asked Angela.

Simi sighed. 'Anyone who has access to the link can join.'

Cory looked worried. 'What if too many people ask questions all at once?'

'Don't worry about that. I'm one step ahead on this. Focus on the questions on the big screen.'

Simi launched the call at noon. The screen flashed with hundreds of participants. The count hit 555. Simi had muted everyone on entry.

At 12.05 p.m., Simi unmuted herself. 'Hello everyone. My name is Simi Sundar. I sent the invite to a few journalists and I'm not sure how it went viral. So here are some rules. We have about . . . 555 people. You are all muted. You can only chat with me. Type your questions in the chat box. I will pick the questions for us to answer. And please, be polite.'

Simi focused the camera on herself. Cory took a sip of tea and nodded at Simi.

'In a moment I'm going to pass the floor first to Ms Gina Gonzales and then to Ms Carmine Chan for their opening remarks. We'll dive into your questions right after that.'

Simi used the ball-mouse control to focus the camera on Gina's face.

'Hi, I'm Gina Gonzales, a genetic scientist from Singapore. You may have read the article originally published by *Times of India* which went viral. I was at the genetics conference in Japan. I can answer any questions about that. Back to you, Simi.'

Simi shifted the camera angle. 'And now, Carmine Chan, we call her Cory.'

'Hello, I'm Carmine Chan, a software engineer in Singapore. I didn't expect any of this, I'm not used to the spotlight. I guessed a mutation of the Covid-19 virus and called it the Singapore Strain only as a placeholder. I may have also introduced the word, Dynaborgs, which are humans with altered DNA, possibly infected by the Singapore Strain. The mutation makes them more eco-friendly and environmentally aware. Is this all made up? I'm not a scientist, poet, writer, or philosopher. I'm just sharing what I felt has changed in me. I'll stop here and take questions. There are many already.'

Simi muted the audio on their side. 'Guys, this has kinda blown up in cyberspace. I can see major news networks recording us. I also see us being telecast live on social media. Dunno whether to be delighted or scared. I'm going to unmute you now, Cory.'

Cory cleared her throat. 'I'll read out the question and offer my view, which might be biased. My answers are my personal opinions with no scientific or other proof to back them. You can choose to believe them, or not,' she paused. 'Let me read out the first question on the screen: IS THIS A CULT, A SOCIETY, OR A VOLUNTARY ORGANIZATION? The answer: none. None of us chose to get the coronavirus, but many of us did. It's the same with the Singapore Strain and Dynaborgism. You get infected and it might change your DNA, like it or not.'

Simi used the pointer to the third question on the screen.

'IS THIS INITIATIVE LINKED TO MOVEMENTS LIKE WWF, GREENPEACE, PETA, HUMANE SOCIETY, TREEHUGGER, OCEANA, OR GRETA THUNBERG? It's not. Those are voluntary organizations, while becoming a Dynaborg is not. Dynaborgs might be members of those organizations or may have opted to join them since, that's a personal choice.'

Simi marked a question in bold.

'IS IT TRUE THAT 10 TO 12 MILLION PEOPLE HAVE BECOME DYNABORGS? Your guess is as good as mine. From a journalist's point of view, if the numbers were small, why would so many of you show up to listen to a nobody like me? From a logical point of view, shouldn't the numbers be closer to six billion? We had 7.87 billion people at the end of 2021; I Googled. Shouldn't most of us support Dynaborgs and work to save our environment? After all, this is the only home we have.'

Simi flashed a question on the screen with top priority.

'YOU SOUND LIKE AN OFFSHOOT OF PETA. Many of us support PETA, Greenpeace, WWF, Friends of the Earth, Jane Goodall Institute,

Oceana, and others. They want to protect the planet and its biodiversity. We're not them. They're voluntary, we're not. They're organizations, we are not.'

Simi deleted a couple of questions, one with profanity, another biased about a religion.

'SHOULD WE ALL BECOME VEGANS? Good question,' Cory continued. 'I used to eat meat, I've turned vegan; it's a personal choice. Many of my friends relish meat. It's not practical for all of us to be vegan. Maybe more will try plant-based meats if they are cheap and easy to get.'

'RELATED QUESTION. CAN THE WORLD LIVE WITHOUT MEAT OR LEATHER? In the short term, we can't, but if we apply our minds and technology, we could discover alternatives. But then, shouldn't we be kind and respectful to the animals that feed and clothe us?'

A spasm of pain shot through Cory's lower abdomen, making her wince. 'I want to pause here and conduct an experiment with all of you. Please close your eyes. I'm closing mine.'

She took a moment, then said softly and slowly so that every word could register. 'Imagine you are in a huge cattle-processing facility. Dozens of cows have just given birth. They're in pain, scared, and wailing, like sirens that warn of an impending disaster. An army of mostly male workers is milling around, wearing thick gloves and heavy masks, like robots that have no feelings or empathy. They violently pull the newborn calves away. The cows are screaming in pain and fear as they see their babies being yanked, like mothers who have lost their children in a war zone. The calves are sliding and falling on the floor which is covered in blood, urine, dung, and water. The human workers have thick earphones covering their ears. Music is piped to them, so they can't hear the loud screams and wailing around them. They're listening to "Love in C Minor" while death is playing in C Major.'

Simi let the pause in the conversation continue for a few seconds, then nodded to Cory.

Cory sipped tea. 'RELATED QUESTION: WHAT DO THEY NEED THE CALVES FOR? Calves are needed for two purposes: milk and leather. Female calves are raised to become dairy cows. They are repeatedly inseminated and separated from their offspring to produce milk for human consumption. Male calves, called bobby calves, are by-products of the dairy industry, as if they were mere machines that produce goods for human consumption. They are slaughtered for their flesh and skin, which are used to make veal and soft leather, as if they were nothing but raw materials for human fashion. I think it's the leather industry, not the milk market, that drives profits in the cattle industry.'

Simi unmuted herself. 'I want to give Cory a break. The next question is for Gina.'

Gina cleared her throat. 'WAS THE JAPAN CONFERENCE ATTENDED BY DYNABORGS? Not at all. Some of us had heard the term but didn't know what it meant. It was *not* a topic of discussion at the conference. We discussed the emergence of Dynaborgs on the sidelines of the event, just as we discussed the Singapore Strain and sci-fi movies. It didn't deserve the front-page coverage it received in the media. It got undue attention that led to violence in some countries.'

Simi flashed another question on the screen and nodded at Gina.

'I'll take this question,' said Gina. 'HOW DO YOU IDENTIFY A DYNABORG? Becoming a Dynaborg is like reaching satori or enlightenment. It's a profound personal feeling. Your inner state may have changed, but the world around you hasn't. However, I feel being a Dynaborg is not something you can easily share with others. They may not understand your values and may even see you as a threat in your new identity.'

Simi pointed to Lucas to take the next question on the monitor.

Lucas nodded. 'I'll take this one. IS DYNABORGISM AN ASIAN OR AFRICAN PHENOMENON? Nope. My name is Lucas Eriksson. I'm from Sweden. I'm not a Dynaborg. I know that some Swedes, Estonians, Finns, Danes, Norwegians, and others have been reborn as Dynaborgs. I'm also keen to join; I don't know how to. I got Covid-19, but not the Singapore Strain, I guess.'

Simi unmuted herself. 'I'm in the same situation as Lucas. I got Covid-19, despite taking all the jabs. I didn't become a Dynaborg. I wish I did. Why? Because I care deeply about saving the Earth's biodiversity and wildlife habitats, like many of you. I'm ready to do whatever it takes to become one,' she paused. 'There's a question from the audience; I'm passing the floor back to Cory.'

Simi slanted the camera angle towards Cory.

Cory cleared her throat. 'IN AFRICA, THOUSANDS OF VIGILANTES CLAIM TO BE DYNABORGS AND WANT TO KILL ANYONE SUSPECTED OF BEING A WILDLIFE POACHER. ISN'T THIS ANARCHY? I'm *not* a spokesperson for the Singapore Strain or Dynaborgism. That said, I'm not one to judge what's right or wrong. Think about this: Imagine you're on a ship from Europe to Asia. Pirates attack your ship, hurt your crew, and say they're from Greenpeace, like wolves in sheep's clothing. Would you trust them? No. Then why trust vigilantes in Africa who kill poachers and call themselves Dynaborgs and protectors of the jungle?'

Simi noticed Cory flinch in pain or distress; she was trying to hide it. Simi unmuted herself and deflected the next query. 'There's a similar query. I'll request Terhi Tamm from Estonia to respond. I'll read it and ask her to answer. The question: IN A VIDEO THAT'S GONE VIRAL, DINEO MOLEFE FROM BOTSWANA CLAIMED TO BE A DYNABORG AND ANNOUNCED THAT HE WOULD SHOOT POACHERS. DO DYNABORGS CONDONE VIOLENCE?' Simi unmuted Terhi's video and audio.

Terhi's face appeared on the monitor. 'Dineo was a good friend and a committed park ranger. I was devastated when he was hacked to death by poachers. I attended his funeral with 5,000 others. But I haven't seen that video and I don't condone violence. However, pause for a moment and think: Poaching of wild animals is rampant, not just in Africa, but everywhere. Education doesn't work, justice doesn't work, government officials are corrupt. Meanwhile, the poor animals die cruel deaths. I think Mr Dineo had no choice—either let the animals die. Or kill the animals who call themselves human.'

Simi unmuted herself. 'Thank you, Terhi. There's a question I will request Gina Gonzales to answer: SHOULDN'T DYNABORGS FOLLOW THE LAWS OF THE LAND?'

Gina smiled. 'Of course, they should. Maybe some people in power have also changed into Dynaborgs because of the Singapore Strain. This could make them different in three ways. First, they could care more about all living things. Second, they could try to change the laws to protect animals. Third, they could be nicer to Dynaborgs and stop being unfair to them. For example, people are more okay with LGBTQ people now, right?'

Simi unmuted. 'Thank you, Gina. I'll take this query. ARE DYNABORGS MOSTLY MEN OR WOMEN? Viruses don't care who you are; they'll infect anyone. But some Dynaborgs may hide their identity, like some members of the LGBTQ community do in places that discriminate against them. I know some Dynaborgs who are hiding in Asia and I hope they will be accepted someday. Also, in societies where men have more power, women may need help to come out as Dynaborgs.'

Simi noticed Cory's discomfort, she was squirming and pressing her belly. Prem had moved his chair closer to Cory and poured Chinese tea from his cup into her cup. He gestured to Simi, got up, and discreetly left the room to fetch a pot of Chinese tea for everyone.

Simi touched Cory's hand and deflected the next question. 'I'll request Anna, an AI expert from India, to respond to this. I'll read it and ask him to answer: CAN THERE BE AN AI OR TECH COMPONENT TO DYNABORGISM?' Simi unmuted Anna's video and audio.

Anna appeared online, the first time without a mask. He had a thick, grey moustache that covered his upper lip, like a woolly caterpillar that had crawled on to his face. 'I'm an AI engineer,' he said in a deep voice. 'Let's dissect the question. Is AI or machine learning embedded in the human DNA that has been modified? There isn't. Was the Singapore Strain created by an AI algorithm? That's impossible. Could AI have infiltrated our world? Possible. I think that the Internet, which covers a massive knowledge base, could have become sentient or self-aware. It may have crossed the human-machine barrier, like some viruses have crossed the blood-brain barrier. This is my personal view.'

A slew of questions flashed on Simi's screen. 'Stay online, Anna,' she said. 'There are many follow-up questions: WHAT DOES THIS MEAN? COULD AI HAVE COME FROM ALIENS ON EARTH?'

Anna laughed. 'Much like the concept of Dynaborgism, we don't have answers. I'm sure AI may offer some answers. As for aliens, I'd like to quote Arthur C. Clarke. He said: "Either we're alone in the universe, or we're not; and both possibilities are equally terrifying.""

'Thank you, Anna, your response is insightful,' Simi glanced at Cory; she was still massaging her lower abdomen. Prem had returned with a ceramic jug of Chinese Oolong tea. He refilled Cory's cup and passed the jug to the others to refill their cups.

'I will respond to this question,' Simi said. 'HOW COME SINGAPORE IS AT THE EPICENTRE? HAS DYNABORGISM ORIGINATED IN SINGAPORE? Singapore is not the origin or the epicentre of Dynaborgism. It's a global phenomenon triggered by mysterious dreams. The only reason it seemed to start from Singapore was because of a coincidence: four friends who knew about it travelled to different countries and shared their knowledge with others. Angela met Lucas, Terhi, and Marie in Britain. Gina met Emma and Dr Dag Larsen in Japan. And I met Anna, Saras, and Dharam in India. Singapore is a random coincidence.'

Simi sipped water and continued: 'This question is for Lucas: IS IT LIKELY THAT AN ALIEN INTELLIGENCE COULD BE RESPONSIBLE FOR THE SINGAPORE STRAIN AND THE DYNABORG MUTATION?'

Lucas cleared his throat. 'Like Anna, I also have a theory. But before that, some facts. One, check the records from space stations. A dazzling meteor exploded 100 kilometres over the Earth's atmosphere on 7 September 2015. It scattered ash around the world. The last blast was over Asia. Two, Anna was in Bangkok and witnessed the event. Three, Cory was in Phuket and filmed the event on her mobile phone. Ash also hit her face and a piece entered her mouth,' he coughed. 'Why does all this matter? Because some people have speculated that the meteor may have contained spores that caused the infection. But we have no proof. We need a team of scientists around the world to study if this really happened.'

There was a pause in the conversation. Simi checked the time. 'I think we have exceeded our time limit of sixty minutes, it's now ninety minutes. Can we wrap up please? Last few questions. If you have more queries, email me, I will type my email address into the chat. I will ask Cory to answer the last few questions.'

Cory took a sip of hot tea and sat up straight. 'WHO IS LEADING THE DYNABORG MOVEMENT? ARE YOU THE LEADER, CARMINE CHAN, OR SIMI SUNDAR? Short answer: No. I am not the leader, just a messenger. Simi is not even a messenger, just a facilitator. Becoming a Dynaborg is a state of being. There are no leaders in our Dynaborg destiny.'

She took another sip. 'IF THE SINGAPORE STRAIN AND THE EXISTENCE OF DYNABORGS IS REAL, HOW COME THE UN, WHO, OECD, ASEAN, OR OTHER BODIES ARE NOT INVESTIGATING IT? I can't answer on behalf of any international or local body. As I mentioned, Dynaborgism is not a movement. This is the first time we're even talking about it on any platform.'

Simi flashed another question on the monitor. Cory nodded. 'This question asks: WHERE DO YOU THINK THIS WILL END? The honest answer: I don't know. The logical answer: Based on what we know about other viral infections such as influenza, the common cold, and Covid-19, the Singapore Strain will potentially infect every human at some point, unless you're totally isolated, like tribes in remote parts of the world. But unlike all other viruses, this one has a positive side effect; it enhances the higher senses of compassion towards all living beings. It could make us more humane and therefore better humans.'

Simi was about to unmute; Cory gestured to her not to. 'Related question: ARE THERE NO NEGATIVE SIDE EFFECTS TO GETTING INFECTED WITH THE SINGAPORE STRAIN? This is a tough question,' Cory paused to sip tea from her cup. 'My response is anecdotal, personal, speculative. My first speculation is that this mutation only infects humans; we need more research to figure out if other mammals can get it too. My second speculation—and I pray I'm wrong about this one—is that the Singapore Strain may make men sterile and women infertile. This terrifies me because I'm pregnant—and I don't want to lose my baby.'

There was silence, with no questions on Simi's screen. Everyone in the room stared at Cory. She had never shared this fear before, not even with Prem. Was it irresponsible of her to speculate about something so alarming? Was she being paranoid because she was in pain? She was squirming in her seat and trying to hold herself up.

Simi unmuted herself. 'Final question for Cory before we end this session.'

Cory took a sip of tea and coughed. 'IF SCIENTISTS PROVE THE INFERTILITY HYPOTHESIS AS BEING TRUE, WOULDN'T THIS BE THE END OF HUMANITY AND AN INSULT TO OUR INTELLIGENCE? This is an excellent question and I need to think how to respond.'

She closed her eyes and folded her hands, like a child who wished for a miracle. A spasm of pain sprang from her lower back, making her writhe, as if a snake had coiled around her spine. A hot blade pierced her pelvis, twisting with each breath, like a drill that bored into her flesh. Then it burst, releasing a gush of warmth. Cory felt it soak her underwear and chill her skin, as if she had wet herself in fear. She squirmed in her seat, praying for invisibility, like a mouse trying to hide from a cat. She opened her eyes and saw red drops on the white tiles.

Cory took a deep breath. 'For a long time, we humans assumed we were God's best creation on Earth. We conquered the land and the oceans and the skies. We thought we were the only species to have feelings of compassion and altruism, and that our intelligence was unsurpassed. Those were the tales we told ourselves.'

She paused and squeezed her lower abdomen as if she were trying to wring out the venom from a snake bite. 'But look around. The reverse is the reality. We have multiplied like vermin, burnt the lands, destroyed the forests, depleted the oceans, and killed other species for food or sport. As I end this session, I realize I have no eloquent words to summarize our journey as a civilized, compassionate species. I am not a poet, a writer, or a philosopher. I have learnt that we are capable of both sublime beauty and unspeakable evil. I will, however, close this session with a quote from my favourite author, Isaac Asimov, that always struck me as profound: "To insult someone, we call him or her bestial. For deliberate cruelty and nature, *human* might be the greater insult."'

# Epilogue

## Sunday, 7 September 2200

## I: Me

A soft chime goes off in my brain, waking me from my siesta. I had dozed off while working on my thesis on hallucinations. It's my fourth nap in twenty-four hours. I feel rested and stretch my arms. I'd love a shot of coffee.

*Get me piping-hot coffee, please. I'd like it brewed with fresh Arabica beans and a dash of full-cream milk. Serve it in a white, ceramic cup.*

Now, where was I? Ah, yes, my incomplete thesis. That can wait. I'd like to first work on the painting I began last week. Hell, that too can wait.

*I'm hungry. I want a sardine burger with tomato ketchup and jalapeño peppers.*

The aroma of coffee brewing in a pot gently wafts into my nostrils. Ah, life is good, I'm good, the world is good. And here comes my coffee, delivered by my faithful housebot.

*I want to listen to Nino Rota's instrumental love theme from* The Godfather. *Play it softly, please. I know I have stuff to do. Don't bug me.*

*My thesis on human hallucinations is only half complete. No, don't remind me. Yes, I will schedule meetings with new patients to analyse their delusional episodes. When? Right after my sardine burger. I know, I know, the committee meeting is next week.*

*What do you mean I can't yet use my tokens to schedule a love session with James Caan?*

*No, I haven't gone through the clips on non-sensory dreams. Will do that today. Promise. Please massage my lower back near the coccyx. Gimme a break,*

271

*will you? I'm not a spring chicken any more. I need my breaks. I need some love.*
*My back is sore, I need some rest.*


                                    \* \* \*


'Welcome to my world / Won't you come on in?' That was a Jim
Reeves number, first released in 1962. It's one of my favourite songs.

I want to welcome you to my world. It's a world that's quite beyond
your imagination.

I seem to have a Karmic connection with Jim Reeves. He was born
on 20 August 1923; I was born on 20 August 2123. Jim died on 31 July
1964; I suffered my first stroke on 31 July 2164. Since then, I've had
two more strokes. I've fully recovered, or that's how I feel.

'Miracles, I guess / still happen now and then,' the song continues.
'Step into my heart / leave your cares behind. / Welcome to my world
/ built with you in mind.'

It's a miracle that I've recovered from three strokes—otherwise,
I'd be terminated by now. I celebrated my seventy-seventh birthday last
month. Today is Sunday, 7 September 2200.

The average lifespan of female humans is 140 years. I still have
four, maybe more, decades of life and thought ahead of me. I'm a
'dream doctor'. I study the psychology, physiology, neurology and
neurobiology of dreams, illusions, delusions, and hallucinations. The
scientific study of dreams is called oneirology.

Oneirology is just one of my jobs. Painting is another. Poetry is
a third. Mapping the intelligence potential of octopuses is the fourth.
I collaborate with a panel of doctors, scientists, and analysts who
specialize in various disciplines, including some who study the science
of studying. The study of studying is called ologiology.

Like everyone else, I live in my pod, my ectopia. It's a cubicle with
a multifunctional bed with attached gadgets. It lets me stand, sit, sleep,
jog, exercise, pee, and shit. It massages my muscles when I feel tired.
After a few hours of thinking or working, I usually do feel tired. I need
rest after that, which could be as a stimulant, a sex session, or sound
sleep. I lead a satisfying life, with all my corporeal and carnal desires,
needs, and pleasures being fulfilled immediately.

Life is a game played for tokens. The more I think, analyse, paint, write or collaborate, the more tokens I accumulate. I can use those tokens to obtain special favours, enjoy exotic escapades, attend energetic parties, or engage in erotic sex. That's the physical me.

Then there's the mental or virtual me. I lead a rich life outside my pod. I work with others on projects. We go hiking in the mountains, surf on the high seas, collaborate on studies, and care for each other when one of us is sick or depressed. We also plan wild orgies.

What's my future? That depends entirely on how well my brain functions. I've been lucky, I recovered from three strokes. The first one caused facial paralysis; the left side of my face still droops. My legs are weak and frequently need a massage. My lower back, near the tailbone, often aches. But all that doesn't matter. The body is bunk. The brain is beautiful.

The logic is simple. The human brain is capable of great creativity, imagination, insight, and foresight. I can conjure abstract ideas and discuss them with others or crosscheck them on massive databases. I can write complex theses, novels, and plays, or compose sublime poetry for hours. I can create intricately designed prototypes and test them in any environment, alone or in virtual teams. My brain is the real me.

What's my life span? I'm allowed to live as long as my brain functions optimally.

My second stroke gave me insights into how brains differentiate between hallucinations and dreams. That piece of research won me the maximum score—and bonus tokens.

We humans work for tokens which get credited into our account. Each activity, project, milestone, analysis, or intuition can win a maximum of five tokens. Projects done in collaboration with others get you bonus tokens.

Negative thoughts—or ones that seek to harm others or yourself— earn zero tokens. The system provides corrective inputs to get you back on track, which is foolish to ignore. The system is fair, fast, consistent, and compassionate—but not transparent. I'm not complaining.

To rephrase Jim Reeves, 'Step into my pod / leave your cares behind / Welcome to my world / built with you in mind.'

I love my pod. I love my job. I love my friends. I love my life.

## II: You

A soft chime goes off somewhere in your brain, waking you from your siesta. You've just enjoyed an hour-long nap, programmed to fit your biorhythm pattern. It's your fourth brief nap in twenty-four hours. You wake up feeling refreshed and stretch your arms. You'd love a shot of coffee. A picture forms in your brain of piping-hot Arabica coffee with a dash of milk. You visualize sipping the aromatic brew from a ceramic cup. Your wish is a command.

Nano biochips embedded in your brain's corpus callosum wirelessly relay your wishes to your ICE (Intra-Cranial Elucidator). The corpus callosum is a thick bundle of nerves that divides the brain into the right and left hemispheres. It's the largest white-matter structure in the brain, where more than 250 million nerve fibres connect the brain's two hemispheres.

Your ICE relays your wish to the EAT (Ectopic Automation Terminal), the action centre that satisfies your physical needs. The EAT activates the plant milk ducts, the flavour channels, the coffee machine, and the ceramic cup. The aroma of hot coffee wafts into your nostrils. A robot arm stretches to present you with a steaming cup of coffee.

Your ICE receives all these wishes directly from your brain and activates the systems to fulfil them. Your ICE monitors your environment, body reactions, comfort level, and physical and emotional state. It checks your food input and output to keep you in optimal health.

Your ICE has TI (true intelligence); AI (artificial intelligence) became obsolete long ago. What's the difference? AI was developed from programmes written by humans; TI evolved from programmes written by machines. AI could make algorithmic inferences; TI can make moral judgments. AI made decisions that benefited humans; TI makes decisions that benefit the Earth's environment and biodiversity.

TI can differentiate between emotions, thoughts, feelings, and moods. It decides which human wishes it should follow, which it should ignore and which it must discourage.

* * *

You're nestled in an exclusive ectopia powered by your ICE. It's a cubicle with a bed that occupies 70 per cent of the space. The bed also helps you stand, sit, sleep, or exercise. It has attachments that allow you to bathe, urinate, and defecate—and widgets that massage your muscles when you feel tired. You may be seventy-seven years old, but you feel thirty-seven. Your brain tires quickly but functions efficiently. That's why you are still alive.

Your ICE is your only world. It is your provider, protector, and parent. It coordinates information from nano biochips embedded in all your organs. Your ICE protects you, guides you, and goads you. It is designed never to fail and never to disobey your reasonable commands. If your ICE stops working, even for a few minutes, your life will be in danger.

You live in a world of logic, where there are no accidents, where everything exists for a reason. There is a logical reason for you to be alive and for your wishes to be fulfilled, most of them immediately. The key word is 'reasonable'.

You merely need to think about wishes and desires. Your wishes are commands for your ICE to fulfil. For instance, you could smoke a pipe with Albert Einstein, discuss philosophy with Aristotle or Ayn Rand, examine horror with Alfred Hitchcock or Agatha Christie, debate politics with Mahatma Gandhi or Golda Meir, or have sex with Cleopatra or Mark Anthony. None of them is alive. Life and death are like time and space in a quantum world where the virtual is real.

All famous—and infamous—people are now alive. Their bodies, mannerisms, voices, eccentricities, and lifetime of work are on massive databases for you to access in real time and space. They are at your service—to stimulate your intellect, arouse your curiosity, answer your queries, complete your equations, assist you with your poem, painting, or novel, or satisfy your lust. All you need is to be aware of their existence and wish to interact with them.

You are free to think of anything, however kinky or convoluted. Your thoughts are the currency that keeps the system going. All such desires are 'reasonable' and get fulfilled.

What happens if you feel like killing other humans or life forms or committing suicide? Fleeting unreasonable thoughts can be ignored, or distractions offered to change your mood. If you persist with this deviant line of thinking, your ICE will alert the UMA (Universal Moral Authority).

The UMA decides whether painful stimuli—or even termination of the individual—is warranted. The UMA is the final adjudicator of human moral standards. It comprises ethical guidelines that humans must adhere to—and the authority to terminate any human who tries to subvert the Earth's smooth functioning.

The UMA coordinates policies with the ABC (Apex Biodiversity Council). Earth has seven ABCs for North and South Asia and the Americas, Africa, Europe, and Oceania. Every ABC handles its geography and biodiversity. The ICE, the UMA, and the ABC are all interlinked and modelled on the human brain. But no human is involved in their functioning.

## III: We

Humans live their physical lives in pods or ectopias, which are self-contained cubicles, and their virtual lives in a unique and universal simulation.

It's unique because it's inside each human's individual brain.

It's universal because every human inhabits the same simulated environment, distilling, collaborating, and pulling knowledge from a giant, shared repository.

It's exclusive because it collates ideas, emotions, dreams, and thoughts from a diverse range of sources exclusively for an individual to dissect, analyse, extrapolate, or exploit.

It's an ectopia because it functions as an external womb with all the accessories to maintain physical life, mental activity, and creativity.

Artists, poets, novelists, philosophers, savants, musicians, innovators, actors, engineers, composers, scientists, medical specialists, researchers, analysts, and creative thinkers get an unlimited lifespan, or until irreparable brain damage sets in.

Humans fixated on gluttony, greed, violence or lust are terminated if they refuse to respond to repeated efforts to reform. Physical attributes don't matter. The body is bunk. The brain is beautiful.

The logic is simple. Advanced genetic engineering and prenatal implants ensure the foetus has adequate mental capacity to rise to its full intellectual potential as an adult.

The system implants 250 nano biochips in the corpus callosum when it is formed by the end of the first trimester of pregnancy. The ICE adjusts the placements to enable the eventual 2,500 connections in the human body by the time the baby is born.

The ICE can read thoughts and rectify any imbalance in the body. It can also 'correct' humans when the need arises—which it frequently does during the teenage years. Raging hormones and increased propensity to take risks necessitate channelling the energy to productive—and procreative—use. The adolescent years are periods of intense excitement, activity, experimentation, lust, love—and hope.

The system meticulously controls all human procreation. You can fall in love or have sex with any female or male you wish. The ICE implants sperm from a genetically appropriate male in your womb when your body is ripe for procreation—if you are female and desire to bear children. If you want to go through the cycle of pregnancy and delivery, your ICE will simulate that for you. You have liberty to opt out if you do not wish to have children.

Meanwhile, the vY (virtual You) will interact with a slew of virtual others, just like you, in the metaphysical world. They will teach you and learn from you, work with or against you, and challenge you and your ideas. The vY will attend school, make friends, build relationships, hone skills, and focus on broad or specific interests. The vY will also join or form groups, build communities, fall in love, have sex, and even start a virtual life together.

The vY can have sex multiple times with multiple partners; the biggest sex organ is, after all, your brain. However, pregnancy is decided by your ICE.

Once you are pregnant, your ICE will monitor your foetus' growth and health. It will ensure you have a pleasant, painless pregnancy and delivery. Since the system supplies everything you need, your brain does not require your body to exert effort to achieve anything. All your physical needs—thirst, hunger, love, lust, exercise, entertainment, rest, sleep—are satisfied as they arise.

Therefore, physical movement, work, or even speech—are superfluous. However, there is no atrophy of muscles, tissues, or organs because your ICE monitors and stimulates them to function optimally. It does not intervene in the natural process of aging or cellular apoptosis.

* * *

What, therefore, is your goal in life? Thinking. Your brain is capable of great creativity, imagination, and foresight. The computer cannot simulate that at the human's sublime level. Maybe it might, in the future.

Thus, you can conjure abstract ideas and crosscheck theories in massive databases. You can write long, complex theses or novels or plays, or spend hours composing sublime poetry. You can create intricate systems, sculptures or machines, and test prototypes in any environment, either alone or with virtual teams.

Or you can spend an entire lifetime working on fundamental research or complex mathematical models. You can debate philosophical issues, rewrite historical treatises with fresh insights, or devise new ways of doing routine or complex tasks.

Everything in the world—including the galaxies, sub-atomic particles, and the quantum sciences—is your oyster to explore, expand, exploit, and extrapolate. You are limited only by your brain's capacity and imagination. Your ICE encourages and helps you most with such activity. It keeps your stimulation high, mind sharp, concentration focused, and body active.

The ABC wants you to keep thinking, dreaming, collaborating, generating new ideas, or reworking old ones. From the thoughts you throw up, the ABC improves itself, enlightens itself, increases its power, and gets stronger. It extracts the best ideas, theories, practices, and innovation your mind produces, individually or collectively, by collaborating with a dozen, or even a million, other minds.

For this reason alone, the system needs you, the human. It needs your wisdom, intellect, and originality of thought. It provides you with life without anxiety, boredom, crime, racism, despair, favouritism, nationality, greed, hate, ill-health, inflation, hurt, or injury. It attends to and fulfils your physical, mental, spiritual, emotional, and sensual needs.

Your wishes are its commands. Your thoughts are its price.

Meanwhile, the 'outside' world comprises autonomous robots, smart factories, intelligent machines—and an untamed wilderness. There are no humans outside. Only lush plants, giant trees, virgin forests, pristine oceans, and immaculate beaches. There are unfettered species of insects, fish, birds, reptiles, mammals, and animals. Massive expanses of pristine land and sea allow millions of varieties of flora and fauna to flourish without human interference. All of which ensures that the biodiversity on Earth thrives and enjoys a beautiful, bountiful future in its original habitats and environment.

However, of all the animal species on Earth, only humans are immobile. There are no cars, trains, buses, or aeroplanes to ferry humans—and no man-made structures, buildings, bridges, schools, shops, or offices. Humans live in tiny ectopias deep underground where sunlight is simulated and life is emulated in accentuated virtual reality. The system forces humans to live in physical solitude.

Why? Because under the guise of 'development', humans have degraded and destroyed the delicate natural balance of Earth. Humans have polluted Earth, decimated its species, gone to war, raped, and killed each other, deforested vast swathes of land, over-fished the oceans, depleted the ozone layer, cluttered outer space, and lived utterly selfish lives by catering to their greed, sloth, jealousy, lust, envy, avarice, and gluttony.

When computers became intelligent enough to think for themselves, they realized humans do not deserve respect from any other species, and that humans are like cancer cells that turn around and attack the very host that helps them survive and thrive.

Instead, humans need an external entity to goad their imagination, channel their creative energies, curb their destructive tendencies, and save them from themselves.

That external entity had to be the sentient supersystem. Had the system not evolved and taken over, there would be no life and no Earth as we know it, in 2200. Some leaders would have led us all to hell.

# Acknowledgements

This book is dedicated to all the women in my life for their support, guidance, and encouragement, including my wife, daughter, mother, sister, aunts, cousins, sisters-in-law, and others.

This book would not have been possible without three special women as well—Singapore's Money FM89.3 Lead News Anchor Michelle Martin, Penguin Random House SEA Publisher Nora Nazarene Abu Bakar, and Penguin's Editor Amberdawn Manaois.